The Devils
and
The Damned

To Audrey

Peace

Rajendra Kumar
3/4/09

Copyright © 2008 Rajendra Kumar
All rights reserved.

ISBN: 1-4392-0225-7
ISBN-13: 9781439202258

Visit **www.booksurge.com** to order additional copies.

The Devils and The Damned

A Novel
by
Rajendra Kumar

Cover Design and Inside Illustrations By Donna Blake

WARNING

'**The Devils and The Damned**' contains graphic sex, gruesome violence, explicit earthy language, and unflattering, even irreverent, comments about man's most cherished institutions. If you are offended by such content, this book is not for you

There is But One True God

THE GOD OF EVIL

This book is not dedicated to anyone.

ACKNOWLEDGMENT

I ACKNOWLEDGE THE GENEROSITY of all my friends who read this book. Some read the whole book, quite excitedly, almost nonstop, in a few days, and provided valuable critique. Some read it out of courtesy and fondness for me, only crying and wondering how I could propound such horrible ideas. Still others read only a few pages and were too disgusted to continue.

My heartfelt thanks to all of them.

Funding for this project was provided by the author using his exiguous income from unmentionable financially unsustainable sources.

AUTHOR'S NOTE

THE NOVEL IS not totally fictional. The events did occur, not necessarily in the order they are presented, and the characters did exist, not exactly the way they appear. However, the locations of the events have not been revealed, the names of characters have been changed, and some of the story line has been made up. This, unfortunately, has the unintended consequence of protecting the guilty, but it saves my ass from lawsuits.

Even though the story revolves around a state prison, it is not about prison life. It is about life, which could manifest itself anywhere, any time, involving anyone doing anything.

The whole thing took place in the mid 1980s, which explains the use of ancient technology.

The style chosen to tell this story is in violation of the rules of fiction writing taught in creative writing classes. There is no hero or heroine; no beginning, middle, and end; no climax and anticlimax. There is a lot of conflict but no resolution. Out of a continuous stream of boundless life only a portion has been captured. It's like looking at a selected section of the ocean stretched from horizon to horizon.

To the chagrin of some, modern American English grammar and conventions have been purposefully and unabashedly violated. This is done to provide logic to a basically illogical system. Because of that, some have accused me of infringing on the sanctity of the English language. I offer no apologies for that.

TRUTH, LIES, AND BEYOND

Human condition is defined by evil. This is the only truth I know. Anything else is a lie.

Occasionally, however, someone springs up to defy evil, like a fragrant flower in the midst of offal. That someone promptly gets crushed under the boots of the ever marching army of men and women hellbent on perpetuating the evil of world domination. This has been going on since the time humans started walking on two feet, and, instead of condemning it, we either deny it or rationalize it. We live an ugly life but do not want to own it. This is the theme of the story you are about to read.

Why do I want to tell such a story? To help us see the demon in the mirror.

Will it do any good? Probably not. Most likely we will continue to see and practice evil pretty much the same way we watch sports or porn, or gossip, or go shopping, mindlessly, redundantly.

I know, I know, this tramples on the self-virtuousness of man and leaves nothing to hope for.

So?

This book is about truth, not hope. There is no hope for mankind.

MY TWO CENTS

This book was written by an inmate in a state prison who wanted to get it published, get his message out, but, for his safety, wanted it done by someone else, under a pen name. I, a correctional program officer at one time, was chosen for this task because he trusted me. Trusted me? He knew me, my character, and the role I had played in this story. Maybe, that's why.

That was enough for me to accept the project. Accept it in violation of the prison rules.

The inmate-author got his wish. I lost my job, or rather I gave it up.

To provide closure and a sense of completeness, I added the Prologue and Epilogue.

TABLE OF CONTENTS

Prologue: A Bedtime Story ... 1

BOOK ONE: GATHERING OF FORCES

1 Are You a Good Man, Charlie Brown? ... 9
2 We Bleed White ... 13
3 Leader of the Pack ... 33
4 Jack the Giant Killer ... 51
5 Like an Erect Penis ... 69
6 Looking for a Nightmare ... 89
7 Comder was a Parrot ... 115
8 Four Musketeers ... 125

BOOK TWO: CLASH OF FORCES

9 Killing is for the Brave ... 155
10 The Dead are Not Strong ... 163
11 Fly Me to the Moon ... 175

12	Bring in the Saints	181
13	Dispensing Justice	185
14	Rise Like a Tsunami	191
15	The First Volleys	199
16	Chameleon	207
17	Butterfly... Butterfly	213
18	Get Your Holes Plugged, Bitch	219
19	From Hell to Hell	231
20	Cleansing Guilt	241
21	There's a Mole in My Soup	251
22	The Dead Man Talked	261
23	Digging Dirt	273
24	The Dark Side of God	281
25	The Color of Revenge	291
26	The Dance of Death	297
27	The Scream of the Bangles	305
28	Murder for Hire	313
29	The Task Force	319
30	The Walls Squeezed In	329
31	Happy Birthday to You	337
32	Blackmail and More Blackmail	343
33	A Not So Weasel Weasel	347
34	Breaking Spirits	353
35	Thank you, My Enemy	361
36	The Fate of a Warrior	365
37	Back in the Saddle	373
38	Toward the Precipice	385
39	A Chicken or a Lion	391
40	The Devil's Wrath	397
41	Operation Kick Ass	403
42	An Amateur Detective	413
43	The Motorcycle Gang	423
44	Bite Me	429
45	Walk with Me	435
46	The Bloodied Chair	441
47	Inching Along	449

48	The Shrine	457
49	Widows of Violence	469
50	The Stone Womb	479
51	A Thorn	489
52	The Fishing Trip that Wasn't	495
53	A Circus	503
54	A Forgotten Dance	507
55	The Other Woman	515
56	Insanity of Sanity	523
57	Now It's Personal	529
58	Good News, Bad News, and Shit	535
59	Dreaming of Dreams	541
60	A Begging Bowl	547
61	Flowers Bloom Only to Die	557
62	Rome is Burning	567
63	Encounter with Destiny	581
Epilogue: Only the Dreams Endure		589

PROLOGUE

A BEDTIME STORY

THE SKY WAS painted black, as if by an inept child, leaving numerous white spots all over its expanse. The air was filled with quiet, and a hush descended over the prison. The tower guards, their rifles lazily hanging over their shoulders, looked blankly at the dull gray landscape stretching for miles, disappearing into the shapeless horizon.

In one of the minimum security dorms prisoners crawled into beds; it was 'lights out'. One could still make out abstract shapes on the walls created by high intensity lamps in the yard. And one could hear a soft exchange of words between inmates in adjacent beds.

Every night the inmate in bed seven, known as "Wizard" for his smarts, would tell a story, about men and women and their follies, to no one in particular. But the inmate in bed six would respectfully listen, sometimes make a subdued comment or ask a hesitant question. Like a little child, he would wait for his bedtime story every night, and he was never disappointed.

Almost never. This one day Wizard was silent.

After waiting for a few minutes, Bed Six could not contain himself any longer and asked, "Nothing tonight?"

"There's always something," Wizard said dispassionately, as if he did not want to talk about it.

"So, could I hear the story, please?" Bed Six implored.

"Actually, I was pondering over our existence in this world, and an idea came to me. Some would call it crazy. That's why I kept silent," Wizard said halfheartedly.

"Try me. I have known you for several months and I know you aren't crazy. You're smart."

"If you say so." Wizard took a long breath in preparation for his narration. Lying on his back, he gazed at the ceiling and started in a trancelike state, "Somewhere in the universe, far, far away from the earth, and long, very long ago, like billions of years, a creature was born."

"A creature? And it was born?" Bed Six interrupted the narration, totally confused.

There would be many more interjections in the form of questions, comments, exclamations, disagreements, even arguments. All friendly, all respectful. Wizard would respond to them, sincerely and cordially.

"I don't know what else to call it because it wasn't like us, not in shape and size anyway. And yes, it was born out of nothingness. There is a scientific theory that says that the universe evolved out of nothingness." Wizard clarified, then suggested, "Don't get hung up on words. Try to get the meaning."

"Okay, I'll try," agreed Bed Six.

"The little creature was constantly moving his legs and hands, looking around, screaming, and squealing, all aimless and repetitive. As he grew older he played with things..."

"You mean it was a male?"

"I don't know. Gender is not important. I use the word 'he' for convenience... So, he played with things, still aimless, still repetitive. For example, he would put a piece of rock on top of another, knock it down, put it back on top again, only to topple it once more."

"Like us; committing crimes, getting caught, getting sentenced, doing time in the prison, getting out, then repeating the whole fucking sequence again."

"Quite so, but you're getting ahead of me."

"Sorry."

Wizard picked up the thread, "Pretty soon he was a young adult, creating things like many different kinds of minerals and chemicals, and then using them to create big balls which were scattered around. He also created forces like gravity which held these huge balls in balance, hanging in empty space."

"You're telling me that this creature created our earth and all these other objects in the sky?"

"Exactly, and everything in them like water, gases, light, heat, cold, taste, radioactivity, magnetism, you name it."

"So, it was like a science project for him?"

"You could say that. It was clear he was very brilliant and creative, but still his old self, aimless and repetitive."

"How so?"

"You see, these planets and stars, and these atoms and molecules, he made them all go in circles endlessly getting nowhere. Sometimes, he made them collide with each other and break apart only to grow to resemble something of the original."

"Wow!"

"Wow indeed. Anyway, one day he felt a need to go beyond the rocks and create life."

"Why? Didn't you say he was aimless and repetitive."

"Yes. But, he was also lazy. He wanted to create life which, being self-perpetuating, could relieve him from the drudgery of aimless and repetitive behavior."

"So he created humans?"

"Yes, and other life forms too. But, he started with simple creatures, like amoebas, and gave them the capability to evolve into more complex creatures; like fish, birds, amphibians, mammals, humans, and even super-humans, who most likely live on some rocks in the sky we have no knowledge of."

"And they all repeat the aimless cycle of life and death?"

"Not only that, while alive they just fill time with aimless and repetitive activities."

"But it does not seem so. Look at the civilization and technological advancement. Isn't all that with the purpose of making life comfortable and happy? Some would even invoke spiritual purpose to be attained after death."

"For someone here for some petty crimes, you're pretty smart, very philosophical. But, still wrong. You see my mythic creature also created an impression of purpose, so that all living creatures continue to feel a need to live while waiting to die, and in the process, enduring a stupid existence which is actually full of pain and suffering."

"Man, that's depressing."

"Wait till you hear what else this creature did."

"What?"

"He made all living beings kill and consume each other for the delusional purpose of self- preservation and continuation."

"Delusional?"

"What's the purpose in self-preservation when you are going to die anyway?"

"This whole thing is creepy."

"You think this is creepy? Then, hear this. He actually saved his most cruel form of sadism for the humans and other creatures of higher intelligence. He implanted in them a need to control others and justify it. This is what actually led to the evolution of society, government, and religion. These institutions created their own brand of morality and ethics and started forcing it upon each other. Result: wars and endless suffering."

"So this creature of yours is aimless, repetitive, lazy, and sadist. What else?"

"He declared himself to be God."

"But some people don't believe in God."

"So what? He acts like God and all living beings do his bidding."

"It's a story, isn't it? You don't really believe this is the way the world was created?"

"It's a story I made up, yes. But it could be real. Why not? It's a good story, pretty logical. More plausible than any espoused by any religion."

"Now I get it. You have been thinking about this God of yours and feeling depressed."

"In a way. I was actually reflecting over my life and some events which took place recently in another prison. They sadly validated what I just said."

"That the world is aimless and repetitive. Life is full of pain and suffering, ending in death, and man is delusional. Also, God is lazy and sadist, in other words, evil."

"You got it."

"You mean there is no good in the world?"

"Conceptually evil presupposes good. But, man is fundamentally evil simply because he was created by an evil God. Good is essentially a fantasy. Sometimes, it shows up in behavior, obviously in defiance of God's intentions. Doesn't last very long, and often gets crushed by evil forces."

"But, what about this war between good and evil in which the good always wins?"

"No such thing. All wars are evil. When a person with good intentions goes to war, he becomes evil. The fight is always between evil and evil. The party that wins just declares itself to be good."

"What about self defense? Is that also evil?"

"If it involves a fight, yes. But not if you defend yourself nonviolently."

"How can you defend yourself nonviolently?"

"You can. I have seen it. Even experienced it. Once in my life I resisted evil nonviolently. Because of it, now I'm in the prison, and my own friends want to kill me." As soon as the words came out, Wizard realized that he had said too much. It might cost him his life.

But Bed Six asked simply, calmly, "Want to tell me about that, your experience?"

"Not really." Wizard didn't want to talk any more. He had become anxious and cautious.

"Why not?"

"It's late tonight and tomorrow I'll be gone, closing the chapter on my past." Oh no! Once more he gave more information than he needed to. Now, Bed Six, if an enemy, was likely to make his move before the sun rose. Wizard would just have to stay awake and be on guard, and talk no more. Good thing he had already delivered his manuscript to someone he trusted. Now, whatever happened to him, the story of his experiences would get out, and a few people, at least, would know about the little good that existed in the midst of the vast evil world.

Bed Six said, "I'm happy for you. Sleep well."

Wizard turned his head toward Bed Six. In the faint glow of light from low wattage dull lamps in the guard cage, which guided the inmates to visit the bathroom without bumping into other beds, he saw the profile and slight quivering of facial muscles of his hell-mate. Did he sense a mischievous smile on his lips?

BOOK 1

Gathering of Forces

CHAPTER ONE

ARE YOU A GOOD MAN, CHARLIE BROWN?

THE GUARD, EUPHEMISTICALLY called 'correctional service officer', came in first, turned on the lights, and left. Objects in the windowless room took shape, flimsy resin chairs in orange and brown and a long folding table.

They came in, one at a time, all in business suits. Stella Robinson, Correctional Program Officer, with a heavy file, in a Kathy Lee from K Mart; Humberto Martinez, Deputy Warden, with a note book and pen, in a Hunt Club from J C Penney; Rajiv Gopal, Psychiatrist, with a file folder, in Armani from Firenze Boutique; and Bernard Karcher, Warden, empty handed, in a Henry Grethel from Macy's. The handshakes, first name greetings, talks about weather. They took seats behind the table.

It was a periodic program review meeting to decide what to do with certain special, meaning pain-in-the ass, inmates. A routine question asked was, 'Have you been good?'

It was not an intelligent question, it was a question dictated by the prison policy. And the prisoners would lie, 'Yes.'

The staff knew the phony answer even before asking the question; damn it, they were getting paid for it. The prisoners lied knowing full well that the staff knew they were lying, and they told more lies to support previous lies; damn it, it might get them an easier job, a safer unit, a full frontal contact visit with someone, anyone with a hole between two legs, in the visitation bathroom.

It didn't happen quite that way on that particular day. In fact, it never happened that way when George Schultz came for his program review.

This is what did happen.

The CSO came back with a big pot of coffee, styrofoam cups, sugar and Equal packets, and tiny cream containers. Everything was neatly arranged on the table. All staff scrambled to help themselves. In the midst of it all, Warden Karcher called out, "Bring him in."

The CSO left quietly and came back within a minute, bringing 'him' in.

Him, in leg, hand, and belly chains. Him, in denim shirt, blue jeans, and tennis shoes. Him, carrying all his 280 pounds on his 6'5" frame. Him, a clean shaven head and oval face. Him, looking permanently angry with taut facial muscles, lip ends pulled down, and eyelids pulled up. Holding his arm above the elbow, the guard guided him into a chair facing the table and four somber faces behind it.

The Warden presided, "Inmate Schultz, thank you for coming."

Schultz stared at the Warden with his unblinking eyes. He did not answer.

The Warden continued his part, "You know me, Warden Karcher, also your Deputy Warden Martinez, and your CPO Robinson." Schultz moved his hostile gaze from one person to the other as each was introduced. He spared the Warden but greeted the other two, "Hello, brown shit," and "Hi, black bitch."

Everyone ignored the comments, they were used to them. The Warden, moving right along, added, "We have a new panel member today, our psychiatrist, Dr. Gopal, Dr. Rajiv Gopal. He joined us a few months ago. He could not be present during your last review because he was in training."

Schultz threw a look of despise at the psychiatrist and acknowledged him disdainfully, "A fucking Indian, huh!"

The psychiatrist cringed but said nothing, didn't know how to react.

Schultz smiled contemptuously and continued, "What a pile of turds. A black, a Mexican, an Indian, and a lone white sold out to the system. I'm gonna puke."

Everyone, once more, ignored the comment. This was the best strategy, learned from experience.

The Warden went on with his script, "You know, this is your 90-day program review. Anything you want to tell us, like how have you been doing? Good?"

"Yes, suck my dick, you motherfucker," spewed Schultz.

Martinez jumped to his feet, pointed his finger at Schultz, and screamed, "Watch your mouth, you asshole."

"Go lick your daughter's cunt," Schultz retorted.

"Get him out of here," yelled Karcher.

Schultz expectorated at him. The wad of spit hit the coffee pot.

Immediately entered two CSOs, who had been waiting outside for just such an eventuality. They dragged the central character of this unsavory drama out of the chair and out of the room.

"This happens every time we have program review," complained Robinson.

"The fucking policy. We have to put up with this bullshit because of it," fumed Martinez.

"Nothing wrong with the policy," countered Karcher. "It works well as a tool of reward and punishment. But, you're right. It's no good with death-row inmates like Schultz."

"Yeah, he has nothing to lose," Martinez questioned the policy without contradicting Karcher.

"Oh, he'll have plenty to lose, this bastard. A worse fate than death awaits him. You'll see," said Karcher decisively.

Everyone sensed he had a plan. And he did, hatched at the moment. He had put up with Schultz too long. No more.

"To begin with, suspend all his privileges; no phone, no mail, no books, no magazines, no writing material, no nothing. Got it?" he addressed Martinez.

"Got it," Martinez confirmed.

"And no exercise, no radio, no TV."

"No exercise? We'll have a lawsuit in no time."

"Only if someone finds out. Still, give him exercise within the rules. But, throw him in the solitary, no visits with anyone."

"What about his lawyer?"

"Except that. I have a feeling, though, he isn't going to need one."

"Got that."

"Just slip in his meals through the door. Don't even talk to him. That's it."

"What about showers?"

"Once a week, hose him down." Karcher was getting annoyed with the questions. "Do I have to spell every thing out? You know what I mean. Just do it."

"Yes sir," Martinez submitted.

Karcher got up to leave and everyone followed. Abruptly, he stopped at the door, turned around, faced Martinez squarely, and said as an afterthought, "And one more thing. The shithead gets meat loaf three times a day, every day. Just meat loaf and water, nothing else."

Even though the orders were given directly to Martinez, they were meant for everyone. The message was clear; punish Schultz and punish him good.

Karcher had unleashed his warriors who moved to take their positions. Little did they know that Schultz was making his move too.

The war had started.

CHAPTER TWO

WE BLEED WHITE

Robinson was not quite right when she said, "This happens every time." Yes, Schultz was obnoxious every time he met his program review committee, but this time he was extra venomous. He had a reason. His execution date was fast approaching, and he was determined not to die at the hands of the state. He would not die haplessly strapped to a gurney and injected with poisons. He would die fighting for his cause. Better still, he would live as long as he could. To this end he had a plan which called for provoking the program review committee members into responding to him angrily. He succeeded. Then he took the next step.

While being pulled out of the chair he went limp. The CSOs, one on each side of him, placed their arms under his armpits, lifted his upper body, and dragged him. The heels of Schultz's shoes screeched.

Schultz knew that he would be isolated within minutes and had no time to lose. So, while the guards carried him through the corridors to be locked in his cell, he screamed, "You all gonna die, you fucking bastards. It's a war, man. Now it's a war." He kept repeating himself.

It sounded like a declaration of war, which it was in a way, but not truly. The prison was always in a state of war between the staff and the prisoners. A lot of times there was just a climate of war. At other times there was actual warfare. How could you declare something that was already there?

Actually, Schultz was using it as a means of communication with his own warriors to prepare for the offensive. He knew his words would be heard by the staff and also by the inmates in the vicinity who would naturally talk about it with others, and before long the entire prison would know what he had said. Interpretation, of course, would be different. The staff would take it as a threat, as an impotent threat by an angry inmate. The inmates would take it as a prelude to impending disaster. And Schultz's warriors, spread among staff and inmates alike, would take it as a call for action.

Schultz stopped screaming after he was thrown in his cell. His purpose to communicate with his men had been accomplished. The next purpose, escape, might be harder to achieve. In the quiet solitude of his cell, he pondered and planned, and realized the need for a ruthless but smart action. The action which would require the help of his older brother, Albert.

It seemed like he always dragged his brother into his mischief. Well, 'dragged' is not the right word because his brother was often there voluntarily to save him from harm. And 'mischief' is not a right word either. Yes, many things he did as a child could be characterized as mischief, but as an adult, many of his actions, intentionally executed, were no mischief; they caused trouble, serious trouble. Whatever it was, his older brother always came to his rescue, whether asked for or not.

Schultz felt guilty for wanting to involve his older brother in his plan of escape. He would have not even considered this had it not been necessary. After all, his brother just wanted to be a simple farmer and had little interest in anything else.

How had the two brothers grown to be so different, Schultz wondered. He lay down on the concrete floor and focused his eyes on the stained and ugly brown ceiling, his mind racing.

* * *

What had become of his life? All his 48 years. From farmland to prison, awaiting execution.

Childhood in the country, following his older brother everywhere. Both of them running through fields, chasing rabbits, identifying birds and plants, climbing hills, swimming in brooks, deciphering forms in the white clouds, and sometimes talking about girls. Also, listening to stories from his father, mother nodding in approval, at dinner times and while relaxing on the porch in front of the big rambling house. They were the stories of bravery, courage, and lofty idealism attributed to white pioneers. There were occasional sermons, "Son, this is your land. It's a Christian land ordained to us by God, our true God. But, we still had to fight for it and win it from the Injuns. Now we have to keep it safe, not only from those animals, but also from the the Chinks, the Japs, the Greasers, and the Niggers. Remember, they work for you, they obey you, you rule them. Don't let anyone tell you any different. You remember this, and one day the whole world will be yours. It will be a Christian world worked by herds of colored people." His father would wave his hands covering not only his vast agricultural holding but also the entire planet.

The two brothers, separated by three years, would exchange an understanding glance with each other which contained a promise to their father that they would abide by his instructions.

They received the same education, yet they were not quite the same. Albert had a touch of kindness and compassion in his personality. Of course, like his father, he too believed himself to be superior to nonwhites and entitled to a higher social and economic status, but he never despised them, never hated them, and never even thought of mistreating them in any way. As a child he even played with the farm help of his own age and thought nothing of helping them when they got injured. As an adult he was always concerned about their welfare, making sure that their living quarters were protected from the weather, they had enough to eat, and got adequate medical attention when needed. He did not even object for them to get an education, so long as it did not interfere with their duties on the farm.

George, on the other hand, considered himself to be too superior to associate with nonwhites. As a child he never played with any children of the farm hands and if they came near his home, he would either run inside or shoo them away. As a grownup, he never hesitated to punish any worker for tardiness or poor performance. A believer in virtual separation of the races, he let them take care of their own business of food, shelter, and medical care. To him, this was virtuous because it prevented them from becoming dependent. And, he did not support their desire for education or condone any attempt at equality.

In spite of the differences, the two brothers were very close, almost inseparable. Through the growing up years they shared the bedroom, wrestled and played with each other, and reveled together in the glory of pulling a marlin out of the sea or bagging big game like a mountain lion, caribou, or bear.

They loved each other, but, because of their age differences, expressed it in different ways. Albert by becoming the protector, comforter, and supporter of his little brother, and George by taking shelter in his older brother's shadow. It always was this way, and they knew it would always be this way.

Before they became adults, Albert protected George in many ways by letting everyone know that, if anyone harmed his brother in any way, they would have to deal with him. And also by lying and blaming someone else, or even taking the blame himself, for wrong-doings by George. This relationship, of course, made George careless about his life and actions. He knew he could do anything and get away with it, and most of the time he did.

He remembered one incident which happened when he was in sixth grade and Albert in ninth. What Albert did left an indelible impression on his mind.

It was play time in the school. He was traversing the monkey bars when another kid decided to get on it from the other side, blocking his movement. It was unthinkable that anyone should get in his way. Angry, he abandoned the bars, ran to the kid and knocked him down. The kid screamed and ran toward the school building with a limp arm. Albert, who was practicing dodging and blocking with other boys in a mock football game in another part of the playground, saw what happened, and, abandoning his game, rushed to George.

"Come with me," he ordered.

They went straight to the nurse's office. The hurt kid was there, his right arm being examined by the nurse.

"He's the one," said the kid through sobs and pointed to George with his left index finger.

The nurse snapped at George, "You're in a heap of trouble. His arm is broken."

"I think there's a mistake," Albert intervened. "I accidentally ran into the kid. George had nothing to do with it."

The hurt kid looked at the brothers, dumbfounded.

"I'm calling the kid's parents to take him to the hospital, and you better report to the principal's office," ordered the nurse.

Once out of the nurse's hearing range George asked Albert, "Why did you say that?"

"Shut up," Albert gave a concerned brotherly rebuke, and George complied.

When they got to the principal's office, the secretary was waiting for them, "The nurse just called. Go right in. The principal is expecting you."

The brothers walked past the secretary. In a few seconds they were standing in front of the principal, who didn't look happy.

"Which one of you did it?" asked the principal sternly.

"Me," both brothers answered simultaneously.

"You protecting each other? It's not going to work here."

"I just ran into the kid. It was an accident," Albert said calmly.

"The nurse does not think so. She told me that the hurt kid positively identified George."

"Sir, it was me. The kid is mistaken," Albert insisted.

George kept silent, could not make his older brother look like a liar.

The principal scrutinized the two faces in front of him for a few seconds, then said comprehendingly, "I see. ... I'll let you go, but I'm calling your parents. And, you need to watch your steps." Then he boomed, "I mean, both of you."

When they got home that day they were punished, loss of allowance and privileges for a week, Albert for lying and George for bullying.

Afterwards, Albert faced George and played the guilt card, "Don't get me in any more trouble." He smiled, turned sideways, and gave

George a reverberating thump on the back. The message was clear, 'Control your temper and don't let your dear brother pay for it.'

George never forgot that. He tried to watch what he said or did. He was not always successful but his efforts avoided a lot of trouble for them. Filled with gratitude, he wished there were some way he could do something for his brother in return, something that proved his love for him. He did get a chance but not until he was in his mid teens.

It was open season and the brothers had gone hunting in the foothills, hoping to get a deer. Their father loved the gamy flavor of venison.

The first day of scouting was a waste, not a deer in sight. Hoping for better luck next day, they decided to camp overnight. They parked their 4-wheel drive green van, operated without a driver's license by Albert, in a flat meadow, set up their tent, and kindled a fire of dead wood. Their dinner consisted of heated canned beans with pork and cheese bread, followed by hot coffee boiled in a pan. After that they sat around the fire planning their next adventure.

That's when it happened. The sound of breaking glass startled them and made them turn their heads toward its source. A black bear was clouting their vehicle. They had ignored the forest service warnings as typical bureaucratic hogwash, and had left their food in the car unprotected. Their youthful bravado had also made them ignore the literature distributed by the wilderness organizations about what to do in the event of a bear encounter. So, the brothers did almost everything wrong.

Albert loudly proclaimed, "I'm gonna shoot it." But, with what? The rifle was left in the van, their first major mistake. Then he ran toward the vehicle to retrieve his rifle without paying attention to his surroundings, getting between the bear and her two cubs, a second mistake. He couldn't even touch the door handle before the mother bear attacked him. Realizing his hopeless situation, he screamed, "Help."

Before George could do anything, the bear caught Albert's right leg between her jaws and began thrashing him.

Seeing his brother in a precarious position, George, instinctively, moved to action. He pulled out a log from the fire and, brandishing it like a weapon, ran toward the bear, all the while encouraging Albert, "Hang in there."

The bear hesitated momentarily, then resumed its mauling of Albert. George, finding it futile to dissuade the bear, attacked one of its cubs in the hope that it would cause the mother bear to abandon Albert and attack him to protect her baby. It worked, actually better than expected. The mother bear released Albert and rushed toward George who ran toward the protection of the fire. The bear just changed direction, collected her cubs, and escaped into the forest.

The bear threat gone, George rushed over to his brother and found him unconscious. He tore his shirt and used the cloth strips to tie a tourniquet just above the spot on Albert's leg where the bear had sunk her teeth. He loaded Albert in the back of the van and drove to the nearest hospital, forgetting to collect his camping gear or to extinguish the fire which, fortunately, died by itself without turning into an inferno.

Albert's life was saved but his right leg was so mutilated that it had to be amputated just above the knee. Even with a prosthesis Albert would forever walk with a slight but noticeable limp.

George felt guilty. He blamed himself for not keeping his weapon with him at all times while hunting, in violation of the most important safety precaution.

But his guilt would be lessened or he would even feel a little bit self-satisfied when Albert would say, "You put your life on the line to save mine."

Still, he did not think that he had made any real sacrifice. After all he was still alive, had not given his life for his brother. He only knew the sacrifices Albert had made for him. He also knew, just knew, that there would be more in the future. How would he ever be able to repay him? As he asked this question, something flashed through his mind, something he had read somewhere, 'Sacrifices can only be remembered, not repaid.'

George still tried. He helped Albert in his farm duties in whatever way he could. Their father was pleased that his children had decided to stay on the family farm. He had not realized that, outside his realm, there were bigger and more powerful forces which ruled people's lives, being able to live by one's own decision was only a myth.

The military draft papers arrived for both brothers, together. George had just turned 18, so his draft call was understandable, but why the military waited for three years before calling up Albert forever remained a mystery. The brothers were expected to serve their country in Vietnam and were ordered to report to the nearest recruitment office within a week.

Their mother looked on dejectedly but their father complained, "Why?"

George knew his father was not against war. He had proudly served in World War II to defend America. His patriotism was probably wavering at the prospect of sending his own children into the jaws of death.

George calmed his agony, "We have to control the communist menace. These yellow-brown gooks with squinty eyes need to be put in their place. We have to rule them, didn't you tell us?"

"But what if anything happens to you? I won't have any family left."

"Don't worry," George pacified his father. "They won't take Albert because of his leg, you know. He'll help you on the farm. Only I'll go."

He was right. Albert failed the draft.

When the time came for George to leave, Albert, choking on each word, said, "Hey, come back in one piece, you know."

"I will. We still have to bag that deer," George promised. He tried to be jovial.

They all knew it was just a ritual. How could anyone promise the future?

As the bus rolled taking George to the boot camp, his family waved goodbye, teary-eyed.

George wrote to his family from boot camp regularly, at least once a week, and even called on the phone a few times. The frequency of letters went down to once a month and the calls stopped altogether after he was shipped to the jungles of Vietnam.

That's where George was educated, not only in the realities of warfare but also in the principles of bigotry. One day his vision of white Christian supremacy became global.

He was drinking beer, playing cards with four white buddies, purposely avoiding blacks, in his field camp. In the middle of the game, one of them complained, "I wanna go home. I haven't had a clean white pussy in a long time."

Another mocked his wishful thinking, "Who doesn't? But don't hold your breath. They're opening a new front in Cambodia."

"Fuck," exclaimed everyone except George who saw Cambodia as an opportunity to extend America's reach.

"Cambodia man, that's great. This whole fucking continent is either yellow or brown and something called Buddhist. We got to own it all and convert all these heathens to Christianity," George espoused his philosophy.

"This guy is out of his mind. He wants to die here so that we can rule the world," ridiculed the one who wanted to go home.

The one with information about Cambodia took a more realistic stance, "Hey, since we defeated Germany and Japan, we are the rulers of the world."

The statement, for George, was true enough, yet he found it logically absurd. So, he asked perplexedly, "How come we fought Germany? Japan, I can understand, but Germany? Isn't Germany white Christian like us?"

"Someone give him a history lesson, will you?" derided the fourth man who hadn't spoken so far.

"Let's just play cards. We may not be alive tomorrow," suggested the one who had started this whole dialogue.

The conversation ended, but George could not get his question out of his mind. Oh, he knew some history all right, knew about Hitler's design on the countries of Europe and his campaign against Jews. Yet, white Christians fighting against their own brothers was incomprehensible to him. There had to be something else, he was sure, a more meaningful explanation.

The question kept nagging him even after completing his tour of duty with some heroic wounds and a purple heart, and even after coming back to his ancestral home.

After his discharge and before boarding the bus, he had called Albert and told him his approximate arrival time. When his bus stopped at the road nearest his farm house, he jumped out and fell into the extended arms of his brother.

"Where's the others?" was his first question.

"Pop, he passed away a couple months ago. Pneumonia. Reckon you didn't get my letter. It's probably still trying to find you."

George was overwhelmed with grief. He would never again see or hear the person who gave him an early education about his place in the world. In a very subdued voice he said, "Who'll guide us now?"

"His spirit will. And mom."

A bit settled with a calming answer, he asked, "Yes, mom? How's she?"

"Not so good. Trouble with her heart. Waiting to see you. Let's go."

They got into the green van. George could see the bear clouting marks on it. Amazing, it was still kicking. Amazing, it could still bring up the memory of that hunting trip long ago, stir up the emotions associated with it. In a melancholy tone, he said, "I guess it's too late now for the deer we promised our dad a long time ago."

"Yes, it is." Sadness covered Albert's face.

It was homecoming, and, therefore, still a happy occasion. George felt it necessary to break the dark spell. So, as the van lurched forward, he changed the subject and asked, now mischievously, "What about my sister-in-law? Wasn't that a year ago you wrote to me that you got married?"

"She's waiting too, and a nephew, only eight months old."

Now George was back with his family, entrenched in a life devoted to growing crops and cattle. It didn't interest him at all. He was more interested in an answer to the question he had faced in Vietnam. More importantly, he was interested in doing his own bit toward world domination by his race and religion. To this end, he considered becoming a journalist or a missionary, or some such thing.

One day he announced to his brother, "I got to go. I am not cut out to be a farmer. You can have my share of the land."

The words exposed his hidden disturbance. His brother asked, "Go where? What's eating you?"

"You know about World War II. We read about it in school. Why do you think we and other European countries fought Germany? Aren't we all white Christians?"

"Simple. Germany was fighting for white Christian domination over the world. But others did not understand this."

"Including us?"

"Yeah."

Right then and there George had a hero, Hitler, and a villain, his own country for which he had risked his life in Vietnam. Not the citizens though, just the misguided government.

"I can't let it die, the struggle Hitler started. That's why I got to go, do something to further our cause." George's goals of life were beginning to crystallize, for the first time.

"You don't have to do anything. There are others who are already doing it."

"Who?"

"The Aryan Vision."

"I have heard the name but don't know much about them. If they are fighting for our cause, I think I should join them."

"If that's what you want. You must know it's a political-military organization. Sometimes it has to fight our own government."

"I can see why. Any government that does not support our cause has to be our enemy. The AV got it right."

"True. But, our government and some ignorant people don't see it that way. They think AV is a gang."

"Why, do you think?"

"Could be because it has some blue collar workers and uneducated and unemployed slobs doing things like, you know, robbing banks, selling drugs, running prostitution."

"But, I imagine it has a lot of intellectuals and white collar workers too."

"They are the ones who provide the organization the respectability it deserves."

"I am no intellectual, but I feel I belong with them."

"I think you will fit in very well. Just remember, once in, you can't get out. And, you can't violate any of their commands. You would get executed if you did."

"Makes sense. You can't run an effective organization without strict controls... Now, how do I find them?"

"Normally, it's not easy. They are always worried about infiltrators."

"That's okay. I can pass their test whatever that might be. I know I can."

"No, You won't have to pass any test. You see, I know them. They will trust you simply because you're my brother."

"How do you know them?"

"Well, there's a story behind it. You know that abandoned, dilapidated shack we have on the south edge of our farm. I was driving past it one day when I saw a bedraggled man there crouched behind some rotting logs. He obviously hadn't shaved or washed in many days. I stopped to check who he was. He looked scared and begged me not to turn him into the Feds who were looking for him. When I asked what did he do, he said that he had killed an Indian on the reservation, insisting that it was in self-defense. In my book, killing an Indian wasn't a crime, so I gave him protection. I was sure there was more to his story but I was not interested in details. He stayed a couple months. During this time, we had occasion to talk. I told him all that I had learned from Pop and how I felt about all the reds, browns, blacks, and yellows dirtying up our land. This probably increased his trust in me, because he opened up and told me that he was a member of Aryan Vision which had sent him on assignment to kill an Indian Chief who was blocking a white mining operation on his reservation. Upon my curious inquiry, he also told me about the AV philosophy, organization, and operations. He left when we both felt that by this time the Feds had probably moved on to another target, forgetting about him. He must have told his superiors about me, because I got a visit from their head, and we have been working together ever since."

George was so riveted by the story that he listened to the long narration without interruption. But the last sentence jolted him since the information was so unexpected. He had to ask, "Working together?"

"Well, I am not an active member of the AV, but I frequently provide shelter to their warriors and contribute food and money to their organization. They consider me their friend which, I suppose, I am."

"So, what do I do? How do I become a member?"

"I'll tell you. Go see Jerry, Jerry Lloyd. Goes by the code name 'Tiger'. He is the Regional Commander. You go to him, use his code name to get past the guards. He and his troops hide out in the mountains. I'll draw you a map. When you meet him, tell him I sent you. He will be grateful. He is always asking me for genuine recruits,"

"Sorry brother. Sorry to dump the entire responsibility of the farm on you."

"Don't worry. I'll manage. Besides you will be doing what Pop wanted us to do."

"True. But, Pop also wanted the farm taken care of. And, you're doing that."

"Yeah. We both will be doing our duties. But your duty will take you away from home. I will miss you, have missed you since you left for Vietnam. Looks like you were destined to be the warrior in our family. ... Say what, I'll contribute your share of farm profits to the AV, in your name."

"Great. I'm sure they will appreciate it."

"Hey, how about a family photo before you go. I may not be able to see you very often but I can look at your picture whenever I want to."

"Sure. Sounds like a good idea."

George, Albert, their mother, Albert's wife with the baby in arms, gathered in front of the farm house. They used the self timer to take the family photo. After that they also had portraits taken of each person individually, even the baby who was made to sit alone with the enticement of toys scattered around him.

George joined the AV and gave to it all of himself. His commitment to the organization and willingness to use any means, even brutal force, to achieve its goals, made him the right hand man and successor apparent of Tiger, and in a matter of a few months, no less.

As luck would have it, only a year later he became the Regional Commander when Jerry Lloyd died of liver failure, being the heavy drinker that he was.

George was not only a doer but also a thinker. He devised a plan for the achievement of the ultimate goal of the organization; control over all nonwhite population of the earth. He got an opportunity to present his plan to the entire AV membership at their next national convention. As a Regional Commander, it was his right and obligation to present to the national body the accomplishments made within his geographical area. He did that and more. He also presented his plan very precisely, very passionately, in a very short speech.

Everyone remembered the central theme, "... The only way we are ever going to succeed, ever going to be able to control the colored menace, ever going to establish one true religion, the Christian religion, throughout the world, ever going to stem this increase of garbage in Africa, Asia, and the south of our border, ever going to achieve our rightful place as the supreme rulers of the world, is by first taking over the government of the United States. We will form a new world confederacy of all white nations which will rule the globe. Yes, we will have to fight for this. But remember, and remember always, we bleed white."

Everyone thundered after him, "We bleed white, we bleed white..."

The chanting would have gone on indefinitely had George not interrupted it. "Yes, we do bleed white, but we aren't going to shed a drop of blood unless we have to. So, we will first try to take control of our government through democratic means, through elections. We will support the legislative candidates who support us and our ideals; candidates at all levels, from local to national. We will use any means, and I mean any means, to get our candidates elected. Sometimes it will be money, sometimes ballot stealing, and sometimes intimidation. We will do the same to get the legislation passed which furthers our cause. Eventually, we will have our kind of president. So what do you say? Are you with me?"

The approval was deafening. There was clapping, shouting, and even firing of guns in the air. That day George Schultz attained a national stature. He was only 33. Everyone believed that George was destined to be the National Commander.

For the time being, however, he was a regional power. He had his headquarters hidden in rugged mountains. This was where young recruits in their teens and twenties came to learn about Hitler's life and philosophy, to acquire facility in armed warfare, and to cultivate the vision of the future, white Christian supremacy.

That's where it happened. George called it an accident, a fateful accident. He did not care that many people and the police called it a crime. Whatever, it changed the course of George's life. Only the course, not the philosophy.

George was conducting a three-day field exercise with eight young AV trainees, all under 20. The lesson was on how to use high powered assault weapons and shoulder mounted rocket launchers. The site was in high elevation forests near small communities sympathetic to the AV cause. So sympathetic that the residents proudly displayed Hitler's portraits on their front lawns, wore caps with 88 printed on them, and painted slogans like "Kill the Jews", "Fuck a Nigger" on walls and rock faces.

It was the third day. The sun was high in the sky. Spirits were high too. The crackling of the bullets, the boom of the rockets. It was all such fun, such exhilaration. At that time the world population was just nine. Their world view was suddenly disturbed. They spotted movement on a saddle about 100 yards west of them. Animals? No. There were bright colors, clothes. Positively humans. Could be invaders, could be allies. George had to be sure. He ordered his men, "Let's move closer, see who these people are."

Nine bodies in camouflage, with George in the lead, crawled on their bellies with their rifles ready to fire. A game had turned into reality, the adrenaline was pumping hard, the excitement knew no bounds. When George had a clear view of the people on the saddle he used a hand signal for his men to stop. He used binoculars to scan the area and counted five men, two black and three white. They looked like hikers, harmless. George was ready to direct his men to ignore them and retreat into the forest when he saw the men on the saddle straining their necks in his direction. Surely his group had been spotted. The men at the saddle had to be eliminated. Let them go and they would talk to the authorities. Pretty soon the whole area would be crawling with the police. George ordered his men, "Charge."

The real thing, the combat.

In one burst several hundred rounds were fired. The attack was so sudden and unexpected that the men on the saddle could not even run for cover, they all went down. To make sure that they were all dead, George came down to the saddle and shot each of the fallen bodies in the head with his pistol. Satisfied, he went back to his men and ordered, "Clear the area. Back to headquarters. Remember, we were never here."

They all headed back to their camp, chasing their shadows made long by the setting sun behind them. In a couple of hours they cleaned out their camp site and drove away in their two Land Rovers. They thought they were safe. It turned out they weren't.

Later, a month later, after he was arrested, George found out from newspaper reports about how the police were able to connect him with the death of five hikers. This was how.

Actually, there were six hikers. One of them had gone to relieve himself behind some bushes when the killings took place. He had seen George up close enough with his horrified, scared, peering eyes, to be able to identify him, and did, later.

After George was done killing and had been out of sight for about half an hour, the hiker in the bushes mustered enough courage to emerge and run to his party's camping and parking site. He drove to the nearest town, and was soon talking to the police on the phone relating what he had seen.

From the description of the incident it was quite clear to the police what it was not. It was not a robbery, nor a revenge, nor an accident, nor an armed conflict between rivals, nor a drug deal gone sour, nor a gang war. The police figured, it had to be a joy killing or a hate killing. And by several people, not just by one, because the eyewitness had reported seeing all five bodies of his fellow hikers fall almost simultaneously. He just happened to see only one killer, actually finishing the job.

The police moved quickly hoping to find the culprits in the area. Even though it had become dark, they, with the help of the eyewitness, were able to get to the scene of the massacre, armed, prepared for violence. No one alive was there. They called the state troopers on the radio for help with the ground and aerial search for the killers and for air lifting of the dead bodies. The state troopers arrived within an hour and put four helicopters into service, one to take the dead bodies to the morgue and the others to fly in different directions with their searchlights on. Some troopers fanned out on foot.

Looking for the murderers in the darkness of the night and in the heavily wooded mountains was not easy. An all night search proved futile. The next day, an all day search proved futile too. Clearly the killers, having had several hours of head start, had gone to their homes or hiding places even before the state trooper operation had begun.

A month passed, then there was a breakthrough. A young, crew cut, swastika tattooed, blabbermouth kid was sitting in 'Lawless Bandit', drinking beer, and bragging about his exploits, real and imagined. The more he got drunk the more he bragged. He was pretty much ignored until he said, "E e even wasted f f f...ive hikers."

One bar patron's curiosity was aroused. He asked, "You mean three whites and two blacks in the mountains about a month ago?" Upon hearing, "Y y yes man," from the kid, he quietly left the bar, so as not to arouse any suspicion, went to a convenience store, and called the police, "Get over to 'Lawless Bandit' and you might solve the hiker case of a month ago. Look for a heavily tattooed, drunk kid in his late teens. He is claiming to be the killer."

The police took the tip seriously and rushed to the bar. They spotted the kid, and against his drunken protestations, hauled him downtown, and locked him in a cell to sober up.

The next day the grilling began. The police threatened to charge him with first degree murder and even lied, "We got an eyewitness. You gonna get death unless you cooperate."

The kid looked speculatively.

The police answered, "Life maybe, with possibility of parole. So, give us the names of everyone involved. We know you didn't do that all by yourself. There were just too many bullets and too many bodies, and they all fell together."

That did it. The kid was suddenly very cooperative and very vocal.

All nine, including the vocal kid, were arrested and charged with murder. The lucky hiker, who had escaped the execution, positively identified George as the person shooting the five downed hikers individually in the head.

Albert decided to hire a criminal lawyer to defend George.

But, George objected, "The wars are fought in the battleground, not in courts."

Albert used his older brother prerogative and overruled George.

The defense strategy was that the case was circumstantial, the drunk kid was unreliable, and the eyewitness from behind the bushes could not possibly identify the defendant accurately. It did not work. George Schultz got the death sentence.

The other eight admitted to their participation in the killings but under Schultz's orders. The kid who had squealed was given 5-years and sent to another state to serve his sentence for his own protection. He was shanked to death within a month of his arrival. It was thought to be an AV revenge, but nothing could be proven and the murder remained unsolved. The remaining seven got life imprisonment.

Prison or no prison, Schultz had to continue his crusade which was responsible for his progression from Maximum Custody Unit to Administrative Segregation Unit.

He, like everyone else, started his prison life in Max. Unlike most of the prisoners who would later move to lower custody units, he stayed in Max because of being considered high risk. In that unit he could visit and talk with anyone who was on his approved visitors list, and he could have free contact with anyone in his unit. He took advantage of the rules and started organizing AVs, stirring them for action, to assert their power over nonwhites. Because of his national stature in the organization, he was accepted by the AVs in the prison as their leader. Although hated, he was also admired even by the coloreds for his guts. He was applauded for his devil-may-care attitude, for his disrespect toward prison authorities, and for frequently breaking prison rules without regard to consequences.

One day he went too far. In the exercise yard during the free time right after dinner, he called out loudly, "Come over here. Only whites. Coloreds stay away." He wanted to deliver one of his sermons.

A dozen or so whites left their games and gathered around him. Two blacks and three Mexicans also came, most likely to piss him off.

Schultz angrily told them, "I said no coloreds."

Both the blacks and Mexicans responded, "The fuck you said."

That started a riot. One white inmate replied with a fist against a black inmate's nose and a fight broke out. The CSOs intervened, firing bullets in the air. The situation was brought under control in a few minutes. But there were a few remnants of the fight, broken noses, blood splattered shirts, pulled hair, and numerous scratches and bruises. Luckily, no one was killed. The prison administration saw the incident as a beginning of bigger fights. To prevent this, Schultz was moved to ASU where he had very limited contact, only with staff, other inmates, his attorney, and family members.

Although most of the drama had been played out and the final scene awaited, Schultz refused to accept it. He was going to change the script.

In the meantime, he would go through his routine which included occasional visits from his brother. During one such visit he learned that his mother had died of a heart attack, most likely precipitated by his imprisonment. He felt sad, very sad for not being able to be with either of his parents at the times of their deaths. He also felt guilty, blaming himself for his mother's death. But Albert consoled him by explaining that their mother had been having a heart problem for a long time, even before George got back from Vietnam. It helped a little. What helped most was Albert's exhortations to him to devote his time to the AV cause.

Schultz moved with vengeance. For his goals he needed to communicate with the whites in the entire prison. He would simply talk to the walls of his cell loudly. Some staff would hear it and a few, even against the written prison policy, would discuss it with other staff members, some of whom would, in turn, discuss it with other staff in other units. Often inmates would overhear the discussion, and before long everyone knew what Schultz wanted them to know, in a matter of hours, sometimes even within minutes. This relay method was quite effective in inciting the whites against the coloreds, resulting in numerous fights and riots. Schultz was aware of the prison administration's crackdown on this kind of communication, but he also knew that the grapevine could not be destroyed.

He had used this grapevine during his program review meeting.

* * *

Schultz, with a self-satisfied grin on his face, left his concrete bed, walked over to his cell door, and peered out of the vertical iron bars which were placed just above a slit wide enough for sliding food trays in and out, and for handcuffing inmates prior to letting them out for exercise or visits or for other prison allowed activities. He knew he would be out soon.

He had already played his volley. The ball was in the prison's court. He would wait for Karcher's reaction.

Wait a few days. It was Thursday. By Monday something was sure to happen.

CHAPTER THREE

LEADER OF THE PACK

KARCHER WALKED INTO the prison administration area briskly, looking angry and annoyed. "Hold all my calls," he growled at his secretary, slammed shut the door to his private office, threw himself into an overstuffed chair, and fumed at George Schultz.

Five minutes later he was still fuming when his secretary peeked in, "Sir, sorry to bother you but Deputy Warden Martinez is on the phone. Says it's important."

"All right." Karcher reluctantly picked up the phone and barked, "Yeah?"

"Schultz has declared a war on us. It's all over. I thought you should know right away."

Karcher's facial expression assumed a cloud of worry then changed to anger. "Thanks for the info, but when did this happen?"

"As he was being transported to his cell."

After a second's pause Karcher spoke in a determined tone, "Then, war it is. I tell you, he'll lose."

The conversation was over but the impact of the message lingered.

In his long career in the prison Karcher had never come across a prisoner who had openly declared a war against him. Sure, they all hated him, but none had the guts to face him. Schultz had always been brazen, but his performance at the program review had attained a new height in his hateful attack on Karcher's authority. It was humiliating to be treated like shit by an inmate in front of his own subordinates, then, on top of it, to be subjected to threats. He was not going to allow it. Everyone, Schultz included, would know that he was the boss. And soon.

The thought was very satisfying. It imported a feeling of invincibility. But, more than thought, action was needed. Karcher let his mind race a few minutes and came up with a solution.

He picked up the phone and dialed the number for Hector Belford, the sheriff, on his private line.

Being in the same law enforcement business Karcher and Belford worked together on cases which encompassed both their territories. Almost all inmates Karcher got started their journey from Belford's jail cells. Naturally, they had become friends and thought nothing of asking for professional, and even personal, help from each other. Karcher also depended upon the sheriff's department for assistance when there was an escape or a disturbance which the prison staff could not handle. As he waited for the phone call to be answered, he could see the Sheriff as if he were sitting in front of him and talking to him.

Belford was phlegmatic, short with a wide girth. He was in his fifties but looked older with his graying, thinning hair. Most of the time he conducted business sitting in a comfortable high-back chair in his office. At home, he watched TV and drank beer, ensconced in his Lazy Boy. He was getting bigger by the day. It did not concern him. He had paid his dues pounding the streets, now it was time for him to relax and do everything possible to hasten his demise without being aware of it. His most pronounced characteristic was a guttural voice and an annoying habit of repeating certain words for reasons unknown even to himself.

Belford answered Karcher's call, "Hello, hello, Sheriff Belford here."

Karcher said with a ritualistic politeness, "Hector, this is Bernard. How are you doing?"

"Fine, just fine. And you?"

"I got a problem." Karcher was too agitated for small talk.

"Yeah, yeah?"

"Yeah, a big one. I need to talk to you about it, but not on the phone. It's too sensitive. Can you come to my office?" He felt a need to explain, "You and your men are here routinely, so your coming to my office would look normal. I don't want anyone to think some trouble is brewing. Not yet."

"Of course, of course."

About an hour later Karcher's secretary opened the door to his office and relieved him of his anxious wait by announcing, "Sheriff Belford is here to see you. Says you're expecting him."

"Yes, send him in," Karcher said and quickly walked to the door to receive Belford.

They shook hands.

Belford lowered his body onto a sofa and sank into the cushions so deeply that it looked like he could never be extricated out of them. Karcher pulled up a guest chair and sat in it facing him.

"Looking good, very good," Belford started.

Karcher liked the compliment. The image of a tall, athletic, muscular, leathery tanned man, flashed in his mind. "Thank you," he acknowledged proudly.

"So what's it about? Spit it out, spit." Seemed like Belford too wanted to get on with the business.

Karcher felt uncomfortable. His day had started with spit, and he did not relish it being mentioned again. Still, following the business protocol, he kept his uneasiness hidden and said calmly, "It's about Schultz. You know Schultz?"

"Schultz, George Schultz. The Aryan Vision commander? Sure, sure know him. Our men arrested him, our men."

"Exactly. He is getting out of hand."

"How, how so?"

Karcher related the program review incident and Schultz's threat afterwards.

"Ah ha! But, he is on death row. Right, right?"

"Yes, but it could be years before he is executed. In the meantime he's making everyone's life miserable."

"Why don't you go make his life miserable, his life?"

"I can do that. In fact, I am doing that. That's not the problem."

"Then, what is the problem, problem?"

"The Aryan Vision. From his threatening explosions it is clear that he has already stirred his men. That means war, and many would die. I would like to prevent it."

"You mean you don't want your men to die, and you want me to harness the AVs. Right, right?"

"Right."

"How? It's a national organization, and my jurisdiction is limited. Very limited. I can't control them. Hell, even the FBI, you know the FBI, hasn't had much success."

"Still, we got to do something. Can't let them have a totally free hand."

"I'll tell you what I can do. Tell me who you think are the likely targets, targets, and I'll do all I can to protect them. If the shitheads make any threatening move, move, we'll arrest them. You got enough cells?"

"I'll get a new prison built if I have to."

"Okay then. I think you and your lovely wife, Carolyn, are on top of the list. Right, right?"

"I guess so. Yes."

"And your children. You got two, two?"

"Yes. But I think they are safe. One is an oceanographer, wandering the world over. Even I don't know where he is at any particular moment. The other teaches archeology in Mexico, at the university in Mexico City."

"Don't, don't be so sure. If they want to hurt them, they'll find them. But I don't think it's likely. People go for the nearest targets, targets. Human nature. Still, to be safe, warn them to watch for any unusual activity around, and take precautions."

"Okay, I'll call them tonight."

"So, who else is on Schultz's shit list, list?"

"Actually, all my staff."

"Oh, oh, come on, be realistic. You have over a thousand employees."

"I think, program committee members would be in immediate danger."

"That's manageable, but, I hope you know our plan is not, not, foolproof."

"What do you mean?"

"We can only watch known AV members and officers. What if new recruits are sent for the attack, attack? Of course, we'll watch for any suspicious activity, and some new recruits might get caught that way. Still, we'll miss, miss, a lot of them."

"So, what do we do? Any suggestions?"

"Yes, take the same medicine I suggested for your children. Take safety precautions. Don't let anyone, anyone, know about your movements, and change your plans frequently. Just don't be predictable. Each time, time, you go to the store, take a different route, for example. You know, keep everyone, everyone, guessing about your actions. Tell that to your staff too."

"And? Anything else?"

"Keep a gun, gun, on your person at all times."

"At all times?"

"Except, except when in prison. It's against the policy, policy, I know. ... And all of you should carry one."

"All of us?"

"Yes, you and your wife, and all, all, your staff in danger."

"But, Carolyn will not. She doesn't like guns, certainly doesn't like to carry one in her purse."

"You do have guns, guns, in the home?"

"Yes, locked up in the gun cabinet, most of them. I carry a small caliber with me. Not when I'm in the prison, but everywhere else. I also keep one in the night stand drawer next to our bed."

"You, you take the responsibility then. Plan movements for both of you. Don't let Carolyn go alone, alone, anywhere, and whoever goes with her must carry a gun. If you explain to her the need for precaution, precaution, she will understand, I'm sure."

"It will only worry her. I'll tell her later when necessary. Until then, I'll do all that needs to be done, to protect us. After all, it's my responsibility, my burden."

"I suppose, suppose. So, is that it?"

"Yeah, thanks."

"Sure." Belford struggled to get out of the folds of the couch. Karcher helped.

After Belford was gone Karcher put himself in his chair carefully and reflected over his conversation with Belford. The conversation did soothe his nerves, but only a little. He still had to alert his key staff about the possibility of war with the AVs, had to work out his war strategy, and execute it. He was confident of his abilities to do that, and some more. The nerves might have been jittery, but there was an adrenaline rush that said, 'This is what you have lived your life for. This is the time to prove your mettle. Go for it. Win this war and dominate those son of bitches.'

Not that his life so far was entirely without victories.

* * *

Ever since his teen age years he lusted after power. At that time, physical power. That was all he knew. A big bully role, intimidating other boys to give him their lunches and money without reporting him to the school authorities, suited him. He did not mess with girls, beneath his dignity. Almost as an extension of his need for power, there was also a desire to be a heavyweight champion boxer. He had the build for it, six-four and 240 pounds of solid muscle, at age 16, no less. A few boxing lessons, however, told him that body size alone was not enough to be a pugilist. He also needed to be quick on his feet, skillful with his fists, able to develop an offensive and defensive strategy, and anticipate opponent's moves. These talents deserted him. During beginning training sessions he performed so badly that his instructor politely asked him to find another sport.

Karcher was surprised that the rejection did not bother him. Instead, a quick reflection over it helped him realize that boxing interested him not as a sport but as a means of using his brute strength to satisfy his need to be aggressive and oppressive. After examining many other activities which could fulfill this need he found fighting as a soldier to his liking. More specifically, a Marine. In this role he saw himself either subduing or eliminating the enemy. What could give him more control over other lives? He decided to join the Marines, no draft for him, but wait until completing high school. Before that could happen, he fell in love. Or, at least there was a girl he wanted to marry.

The girl, Carolyn. How did he ever get to marry her, considering the fact that they were totally opposite in temperament? He pursued power, she compassion. This became obvious the very first time he came to know her, rather accidentally.

One day during recess he was harassing a Hispanic boy, calling him 'wetback'. The kid was slight, and maybe because of it, afraid. He began to cry. Karcher now had something else to tease him about, "Crying pussy, aren't you?"

The sentence was barely completed when he heard a female voice behind him, "Why don't you pick on someone your size?"

Curious to see who challenged him, Karcher turned and saw a face he recognized, Carolyn Stanton. She was in his class but did not exist for him, not until then. There was something riveting about her, a strange yet captivating combination and perfect blending of two seemingly divergent attributes; masculinity expressed in a strong, big-boned, and muscular 5 feet 10 inch body, and femininity oozing out of her round chiseled face, sympathetic and compassionate eyes, wavy shoulder length blond hair, and perfectly contoured and eloquently alluring form.

Under the fiery look of this imposing girl Karcher began to melt inside and wanted to say 'sorry' but could not, not at that moment anyway. His sense of self-righteousness overpowered him. After all this girl was interfering with his sacred ritual. He forced himself to look at her with contempt and said in a derogatory tone, "You got a craving for something brown, huh?"

"You disgust me," she said with disdain.

It did not bother him. He wanted to retort with some choice scorching comments but did not. Not because he could not attack a girl verbally or otherwise. He was not committed to such shallow morality or etiquette. Instead, he admired Carolyn for standing up to him, something not even many boys would dare do. He was blown away by her fearless assertiveness. All he could say at that time was, "Sorry." Only a few seconds ago this simple act was impossible for him. After the apology there was nothing more to say or do except to walk away without waiting for a response.

But he could not get Carolyn out of his mind. He liked and feared her at the same time. She was like a snow-covered mountain top, inviting but treacherous to reach. That was all the more the reason to win her. It was actually a power trip, only he interpreted it as love. So, what was he to do? It occurred to him that he had the looks; had a rugged handsomeness about him, sparkling blue eyes, ski-jump tapered nose, firm pursed lips, almost ripened peach colored cheeks, all embedded in a smooth, round face, and crewcut hair which, along with his graceful athletic movements, gave him a manly appearance while adding to his physical attractiveness. No wonder many girls in the school were drawn to him. But that was not enough. If he was going to get anywhere with Carolyn, he would have to modify his ways. Not necessarily his philosophy, just his actions. And he did; stopped bullying others or tried to. Even changed the way he talked, toned down his abrasiveness and softened the edges of his speech, at least when near her.

Karcher saw Carolyn every school day and thought of all kinds of excuses to talk to her, all seemed contrived. So, to hell with excuses, none were needed. He decided to just go and apologize some more, a good way to break the ice. And he did, during a recess, "Hey, I'm sorry we got off to a bad start."

"That's okay," Carolyn responded easily as if she had not been harboring any ill feelings about him, as if the incident had been forgotten. If not the incident, at least the impact of it.

"Can I buy you a coke?" A move from finger to elbow. A calculated move but not as slimy as it seemed, there was also a genuine desire to get close to her.

Carolyn smiled, "What is it?"

"Just want to be friends, if that's okay with you?"

"Sure, why not?" Seemed like she could not say 'no' to a gesture of friendship.

They shared a coke that day. They shared many more cokes after that. Even a couple of movies. A few smooches. Somehow Karcher could not bring himself to go beyond that, not that he did not want to. He sensed an impenetrable barrier of virtue created by Carolyn. It did not offend him, only made him more attracted to her.

There was more.

Carolyn did not appear to be aggressive, pushy, and Karcher thought that to be a good quality in a woman. She was also very accommodating. Like she would agree to see '2001: A Space Odyssey' instead of 'Guess Who's Coming to Dinner', or she would go to a football game instead of a Harry Belafonte concert. Karcher liked it.

One day it occurred to him that he was really in love with her. That was when a voice within told him, 'You've found a right girl, don't lose her with your stupid power play.'

Of course, he was fooling himself, but he was doing a better job of fooling Carolyn. Maybe not purposely, but fooling nonetheless. He must have done a pretty good job of it because their relationship reached a point where they danced together at the prom. And it felt very natural.

Then came the moment of truth, his desire to join the Marine Corps. Karcher would have to enlist for a minimum of three years. During this period he would lose Carolyn, he was sure. His victory would be incomplete. To avoid that possibility he must marry her right away. But, how was he going to honor his marital responsibilities, even before becoming a Marine? He had no job and lived with his parents. And what did he expect Carolyn to do while he was enjoying his power ride, most likely in the jungles of Vietnam?

He decided to discuss this matter with his parents. He really did not want to do this, did not want his parents to think he was still an immature kid who could not make decisions about his life. He did this because he thought he could get support and help from them to deal with his predicament. Manipulation? Indeed. For him, that's what defined success in life.

His parents interpreted his desire to get married and also serve his country as signs of adulthood. They told him that while he was away Carolyn could live with them and, maybe, go to college, or do whatever else interested her until he got back.

Now, all he needed was to marry Carolyn. To increase the likelihood of acceptance of his proposal, he decided to go to her with a ring, treat it as something final, something firm. It did occur to him that she might still turn him down. In that case he would just have to accept his defeat and go on to other more important victories.

So, one Sunday afternoon he bought an inexpensive 10-carat gold engagement ring, all he could afford, with the money saved for such eventualities from the weekly allowance he got from his parents and earnings from odd jobs he did from time to time. Right after that he called Carolyn, "I need to see you right away."

"Why?' Carolyn sounded confused by this sudden request, maybe because there had never been any urgencies like this in the past.

"It's important. I'll explain everything when I see you."

"All right. Come on over. We can sit on the porch and talk, or do you want to go some place else?"

"Your porch is fine."

Within an hour they were sitting next to each other, silently for a few minutes. Karcher was nervous and tense, did not know how to propose. The protocols he knew were the ones he had seen on TV or in the movies, and they failed him in real life.

Carolyn took the lead and said, "Whatever it is I can handle it. Out with it."

Karcher thought that Carolyn must have interpreted his silence to mean that he wanted to end their relationship, for whatever reasons, but did not know how to proceed. He berated himself, 'Because of your ineptness everything is going in the wrong direction. Before there is any more damage you better do what you came to do.' So, with somewhat unsteady hands, he took out the ring from his pant pocket, presented it to Carolyn, and fumbled with his words, "Please marry me."

Carolyn looked shocked, apparently because of a proposal for marriage instead of a breakup, and also shocked by the suddenness of it. "You serious?" she asked.

"Yes, and here's why." Now that the barrier was broken, Karcher was reasonably composed and able to talk. He repeated the spiel he had given to his parents and told her about his parent's promise to take care of her during his absence.

Karcher's words must have touched Carolyn because she said, "You want to make sure I'm taken care of. You do love me."

Karcher saw her look at the cheap engagement ring like it was priceless. But he also saw a film of confusion and fear cross over her face. So he asked, "Of course, I love you. But what is it? You look scared."

"I was thinking, what if you never came back?"

"But I will come back."

"You can't be sure of that. No one can. Still, I know my fear is irrational. Most people do come back from the war, why entertain the worst? And if the worst were to come, I will deal with it." This change in thinking made her see the three long years of Karcher's absence as temporary.

Karcher was pleased because that meant Carolyn had accepted his proposal.

But before he could thank her for it or express his happiness, she said, "But I can't live with your parents."

"Why not? They are good people."

"I am sure, but as a married couple we must have our own place."

"But I have no income. How...?"

"Don't worry. I will get a job. To tide us over until my first pay check I will borrow some money from my parents. After you are enlisted your salary should be enough to see us through. Of course, we will live poorly in the hope of a better future."

"I hadn't thought about that. Of course, I can borrow money from my parents too."

"This way you will have a home to come back to, our own home."

"But living all alone? Wouldn't that be a problem?"

"Why? A lot of people do. My work will keep me busy. In my spare time I will go to school, maybe build a career. There are also our parents and friends I can visit. I'll miss you but I will not be lonely."

Karcher could see that when it came to practical matters Carolyn was way ahead of him. He was convinced that he had made a good choice and they would be a happy family.

It was a very short engagement. The marriage took place within a month. Karcher borrowed money from his parents to take care of all expenses including a modest wedding ring.

Soon after they had set up an apartment, Karcher went to enlist as a Marine. He qualified easily. He was proud and excited. He wondered, 'Is Carolyn proud of my accomplishment or just trepidant about what it means for her future.' He only wondered, because there was nothing he could do about it.

Karcher spent his first year in training and routine naval exercises at several domestic bases. Then he was shipped to Vietnam. All through his basic training and stint in Vietnam he continued to write to Carolyn and talk with her on the phone as often as possible. And he was not attracted to local women like other men were. They did not interest him because they were not white. Even white women did not charm him, mainly because he felt committed to Carolyn. She was a sign of his victory, a trophy he could not tarnish. She was the purpose of his life.

So was his job.

He was in Vietnam to fight, filled with patriotic zeal. Before going there, he had seen coloreds as inferior, but not as people to hate or destroy. In Vietnam he saw coloreds, brown-yellow but still coloreds, challenging the power of the white America and refusing to be defeated. Damn, how dare they? Yes, he was aware of many colored servicemen fighting on his side, but they did not define America, whites did. So, subduing the enemy to protect white supremacy became a great cause, so exciting and satisfying that he fought fearlessly. His valor earned him the rank of Sergeant Major. He was wounded a few times and received a purple heart.

He liked the war scene so much that many times he thought of extending his term as a Marine. In the end he did not. He came home disappointed that the colored Vietnamese were still fighting, but happy that his tour of duty was over. Happy, not because he would not have to fight anymore but because he would be going back to Carolyn. For the first time there would be a real union.

Coming home presented a promise of pitter-patter of little feet, family vacations and festivals. It also posed financial problems. Karcher's salary had stopped. He went looking for a job that suited his temperament. He could only think of being a policeman or a prison guard.

Carolyn said, "No, not the police. They are always getting shot and killed. Work in a prison. It's safer."

The protective wife! Karcher smiled within and accepted her decision without question.

He started out as a guard doing tower duty. Very boring. Also distressing for the fact that there were several blacks and Mexicans at grade levels higher than his. He saw this as unjust and sought to correct it. He wrote a letter to his supervisor with a copy forwarded to the Director, Department of Corrections, in which he cited his exemplary service in the Marines as a basis for consideration for a more responsible administrative position. He was smart enough not to bring up the color factor; he needed to be subtle, not blatant, in pursuit of his discriminatory promotion. His reason was persuasive enough to the administration that he was promoted to be a major. At that level, there were no coloreds above him. He was satisfied and happy.

Then his career got a big boost. Not his doing, it just happened. He was stationed in the yard office of a minimum custody unit when a communal riot broke out in the exercise field. The prison policy automatically put him in command. Taking his responsibility seriously, he immediately used the public address system to direct all staff to get away from the inmates and positioned several sharp shooters on the catwalks and towers, while ordering the inmates, "Everyone freeze or we will shoot."

The inmates looked at the force ready to fire and obeyed the order. They all, whether involved in the riot or not, were marched by armed guards to be locked up.

The situation was brought under control in less than 10 heart-throbbing minutes, the situation that could have turned ugly, claimed many lives, and could have taken hours to quell. A feat like that had to be recognized, and it was. Karcher was promoted to the position of Deputy Warden of a unit. Three more years of devoted service to the prison, which meant keeping inmates under control by any means, and he made it to the position of Warden.

In that position he had to make a major adjustment. Against his wishes and personal philosophy about race relations, he had to hire and promote staff without discrimination, simply because that was the prison policy dictated by the state and federal laws. However, he made sure that all nonwhites, aspiring to become a Warden and making the list of five finalists, were never selected. He used such subjective reasons as 'does not appear a team player' or 'seems to have poor grasp of inmate psychology' to reject them. The bias was obvious, but no one could fault him because he was always administratively correct.

In his small world he, a white man, was the supreme leader. He belonged there. The power and control over other lives, the ultimate ego trip. He was happy.

But, it seemed to him, Carolyn was not. To him she would always appear uneasy upon hearing stories about prison riots, guard brutalities, inmate killings of other inmates and staff, the drug dealings, the gang warfare, and would express her fear of him being brought home bloodied and dead. One day she even said, "I endured your time in Vietnam and had thought that in civilian life things would be different. They are different but not much. The nightmare is the same. I know I had chosen prison work over police work for you, but now I think you should find a different job, something safer."

And Karcher told her, "Nothing's safe." That was true enough, but that was not a truthful answer. He did not want to leave this job because he flourished in it. Knowing that Carolyn would not understand this, he tried to pacify her by saying, "I have put a significant part of my life into it, and I deserve my retirement benefits. Besides, I am not good for anything else."

He thought that Carolyn had bought the argument. And that's all it was, an argument, since retirement, in fact, was very remote for him. The joy of living was in the fight, not in escape. Prison offered him all the fight he could want, on a daily basis. The inmates thought that he was their enemy and they rebelled even when there was no real reason for it, like the food was not to their liking, or it was too dark in the dorm, or the visiting hours were inconvenient to their families. Reciprocally, he believed that the inmates were his enemy, causing unnecessary trouble. To him they were like dirt which needed to be repressed, and he did a very good job of it.

Karcher's reasons for staying with the job did not seem to satisfy Carolyn who said one day, "I have developed a painful flutter in my heart. The doctor says it's nervousness. In the beginning, I was able to calm it by diverting my attention to my studies aimed at building a career as a social worker. Getting my master's degree was comforting because it meant that I could support myself should anything happen to you. Later, when the twins came, I relied on their care to ease my pain. But now?" She started to cry.

Children were a source of comfort for Karcher also, a retreat to the relative safety of his base camp after a brutal engagement with the enemy on the battle field. He watched them grow big and tall, and dreamed about them pursuing a career in the military, business, or sports. Sure, he loved them, but he wanted them to be an extension of himself. He was disappointed when it did not happen, when they shunned activities which required domination and competition, aggression and violence, and became scientists. That's when Karcher became aware of another side of his personality which he did not think existed, acceptance. Or, perhaps he created it because he could not see himself treating his sons like prisoners, he had to accept them the way they were. Love and acceptance! What a contrast from cruelty and control! It was amazing how the opposites could exist in the same person.

And, it was so because he had a family, a family which extended into the future. He fantasized often that when the time came for him to leave this world, he would be surrounded by a large family, his sons, daughters-in-law, grandchildren, and maybe even great-grandchildren.

His fantasy was shattered when the boys got married and left home to follow their careers. Of course, he knew it would happen, but he had buried this knowledge under his daydreams. Now that the reality hit him in the face, he could not take it and became depressed. And he noticed that Carolyn was too.

He thought that Carolyn must have felt the same way as he did after the children had left, that a major part of their fantasy castle had been washed away by a big, bad ocean wave. 'So, what to do?' he asked himself.

He got the answer from Carolyn. One day after dinner, as the Karchers sat silently in the living room, she said, "This can't go on."

"I don't know what to do," Karcher said in a very subdued voice, like he did not want to admit that there was something he did not know and could not handle.

"Go see your doctor, get some medication. Get more involved in your work, start a new project or something."

That was what Karcher liked about Carolyn, her pragmatic approach to any problem.

"All right. But what about you?"

"I will go look for a job as a social worker. Put my training to work, finally. If I can't get a paying job, I will volunteer."

The Karchers adopted a new life style, one that did not involve children, one that actually took their thoughts away from them.

Karcher took Carolyn's suggestion and started looking for a new project at the prison. His lucky stars must have been shining, because about this time one of his deputy wardens came to him with a proposal to build an Administrative Segregation Unit. This suggestion was in response to his sometime-ago call to all his deputy wardens to come up with a solution to the problem of housing and managing difficult inmates. Another time he might have ignored it, but this time it looked good. He decided to run with it, offer it to the Department as his own idea and take credit for it. That's the way of bureaucracy, quite legitimate. Besides, he was going to defend it, get funding for it, supervise its construction, and set up its operations, therefore, he had every right to claim its ownership. At the time he did not know that the same unit later would become the site of a ferocious drama, one that would alter many lives. The project was so consuming that it wiped out his depression, he did not need to see a doctor.

He saw Carolyn, however, fail miserably in finding any professional position, most likely because of her lack of work experience and her age. He worried about her mental state but was pleased when one day she announced , "I'm gonna work as a volunteer in a hospice."

* * *

Karcher straightened in his chair. He must follow Belford's advice. Talk with his program review committee staff right away, by tomorrow, Friday. No need to sweat through the weekend. And he must talk with Carolyn too.

It was disturbing to think that Carolyn might become a victim of his war with the AVs. He loved her and did not want any harm to come her way. Yet, he always did what he wanted without really knowing or caring about her feelings. His unconscious motivations were stronger than his conscious desires. In fact, he did not know anything about what was going on in Carolyn's mind. Suddenly, he was flooded with questions. How come they were so different in their philosophies of life yet without any major conflicts? Was it because Carolyn was making all the adjustments? For that matter, why did she ever agree to marry him? Was she really happy? How difficult was it for her to wait for him while he was in Vietnam? Why did she allow him to do all the things she did not approve of? Did she know about his ruthless power tactics in the prison? How did she see her future? Did she ever entertain the idea of a divorce? Was she contented with the way things were or was she suffering silently? Did she know that in spite of all his failings, he really loved her?

He lingered on the last question and wished he could say, 'Because he loved her he would do anything for her,' but could not. He could not give up his war even for her. But he could build a safety shield around her while he battled the AVs.

The AVs! Schultz's image loomed before him. It closely corresponded to his own image in many respects. Schultz was about his age, had Vietnam war experience, believed in white supremacy, and commanded a large, even deadly force. So what was the problem?

Why were they adversaries, so fierce that they were hell bent on destroying each other?

A brief reflection over their positions, and the answer was obvious to Karcher. It was the last similarity between the two, the large and deadly forces they controlled. The problem was that their forces were opposed to each other. Schultz led the regional Aryan Vision and Karcher led the prison. Aryan Vision refused to recognize the authority of the prison over their members, and the prison was determined to have total control over all its inmates, the AVs included. The issue was power and that made them enemies.

Karcher respected Schultz's belief system, even his courage, strength, brutishness, and fearlessness. But he wasn't going to treat him as equal. In his domain, he was the supreme commander and Schultz was dirt to be kept down. But the dirt, by nature, does not remain passive, it reacts. When stomped on, it rises and settles on top of the stomper. George Schultz was proving to be such dirt.

Karcher gritted his teeth. No, he was not going to stomp on this dirt, won't allow it to rise. Instead, he was first going to dampen it, then shovel it out. Punishing Schultz was not enough, he and his AVs had to be wiped out, completely out of the prison, if not out of the entire country.

With that determination Karcher felt indomitable. He decided to make his move against Schultz and use an approach learned from his commanders in Vietnam, "Hit first, hit hard, and keep on hitting."

The determination to attack was very satisfying, and it consumed him.

In the days to come, it walked with him, it perched on his shoulders while he worked, and it sat on his chest while he slept.

The war clouds had begun to gather.

CHAPTER FOUR

JACK THE GIANT KILLER

RIGHT AFTER KARCHER left, Humberto Martinez turned to Robinson and Gopal, and said, "We need to talk. In my office. Now."

He walked over to his administration area, Robinson and Gopal in tow. They did not have to go far. Martinez's office was located in the same Administrative Segregation Unit which had been built following his suggestion, and with backing from Karcher, a few years ago. It was home to the most difficult to manage inmates and the final resting place for those who had been sentenced to die, such as Schultz.

Martinez ruled over it. In his domain he had a sense of omnipotence which, in turn, gave him a purpose for living. Except, of course, when the inmate Program Review Committee met and the Warden came to preside. Happily for Martinez, this was once or twice a month and no more than an hour or so each time, often only a few minutes when dealing with inmates like Schultz. Getting here in the thick of gringo territory from a Hispanic barrio was not an easy task. It involved a long, hard journey. Martinez was proud of every step he had taken.

As he entered his office area, he addressed his secretary, "I'll be with CPO Robinson and Dr. Gopal for a few minutes. After that I want to see our Shift Commander, Tommy Jordan, and CSO Ruben Ibarra. Page them." He had already decided what he was going to do.

He turned toward Robinson and Gopal, and said, "Come in."

Martinez entered his office first, of course. He deposited himself in a comfortable high-back chair behind a very big and very neat desk. Robinson and Gopal each took a guest chair directly in front of him.

Martinez surveyed both, to examine if they got the import of his superiority. Although anxiety enveloped the faces of both staff members, it was more pronounced on Gopal's than on Robinson's. Understandable under the circumstances. Robinson worked directly under Martinez's supervision and had been in that office many times before. Gopal, however, was there for the first time. Being part of a separate parallel medical administration hierarchy, he was not subordinate to Martinez, but he was in ASU almost daily because several inmates on his case load lived there. He did his work from the nurses' station, saw inmates in their cells, except those who needed to be hospitalized, attended staff meetings in the conference room, and never had any need to come to this office. Until this day. He sat in his chair awkwardly.

Martinez was sure that both staff knew that whatever was coming, it had something to do with Schultz.

Suddenly, it was a war room.

"You heard the Warden. A worse fate than death awaits Schultz," Martinez said and waited for a reaction from his audience. There were blank stares. Clearly, neither Robinson nor Gopal had a clue about what 'worse fate than death' meant. Further explanation was needed and Martinez provided it in bits and pieces, never fully articulated.

"It means we punish him. To start with, we need to throw him in isolation. To justify that I need your help. Ms. Robinson, you write an incident report. Write it so that Schultz's loss of all privileges will be upheld in a disciplinary hearing. Dr. Gopal, you write a psychiatric report concluding that Schultz is a dangerous psychopath."

Robinson didn't but Gopal protested, "How could I? Today was the first time I saw him, just saw him, didn't even get a chance to talk to him."

"Go talk to him. Do whatever you need to. Just give me the report I want." After a pause, "That's it."

The signal was given. Robinson and Gopal left. Robinson appearing disimpassioned like it was routine for her. Gopal clearly confused as if he knew what must be done, but not sure if it should be.

It was not necessary for Martinez to be abrupt, not for the task at hand anyway. But it was necessary for his ego which needed pampering. Abrupt dismissal of staff meant he was the boss, in charge with authority to give orders and with resources at his disposal to make sure they were obeyed. This way he could wash away years of humiliation. He watched the backs of Robinson and Gopal as they left and reveled in his power.

His revelry was cut short by the ring of the phone. His secretary was on the other end, "Sir, it's the unit office on line two."

Unit office called him directly only when there was something that could not be handled at a lower level. He could not ignore such calls. "I'll take it," he said.

After he was switched on to the other line, he asked abruptly, "What is it?"

"Schultz has issued threats," answered the unit office secretary.

"What threat, against whom, and how do you know?"

The secretary gave the details she had learned from the officers who had dragged Schultz to his cell from the program review room only a short time ago.

"Thank you," Martinez said and hung up, agitation building inside him. The news itself was not surprising or disturbing. Something like this was expected from someone like Schultz. It was its potential impact that was unnerving. Martinez saw all the program committee members as Schultz's targets, and his heartbeat went up. Still, he had enough presence of mind to realize the need to inform Karcher about it immediately. He did. And he felt a little better, knowing that he was not alone in this struggle, and that he had his warden's blessing. His sense of comfort increased even more when he reflected over what he had already done and planned to do. Robinson and Gopal had been put to work. Jordan and Ibarra would soon be recruited and Schultz's punishment by food would be activated within the next few minutes. Other steps would be taken as and when needed.

He was still patting his own back when Tommy Jordan, a burly six-foot brute with muscles bursting out of his regulation pleated and starched uniform, appeared at his door.

"Sir, something urgent?" asked Jordan. Martinez smiled within at the phony politeness which was the law enforcement code of conduct.

Jordan was white. Martinez loved to be addressed as 'sir' by the whites. What a role reversal for him!

He had learned to use 'sir' for the whites while working in his family restaurant. His father had strict orders for everyone in the family, 'Be extra nice and polite to gringos. Always call them "sir". They are our bread and butter.'

Yes indeed, the tables had turned. The whites were calling him 'sir' now. Oh, he too used 'sir' for his superiors, all of whom were white, but that was because they were his superiors not because they were white.

He sat up tall in his chair and answered, "Yes, Tommy. Come in, take a seat."

Jordan placed himself in a guest chair, one recently occupied by Robinson. He appeared to move slowly, carefully, respectfully, and after settling, to wait anxiously to hear what it was all about.

"You surely heard what happened during the program review this morning?"

"Yes, sir."

"Well, Warden Karcher wants to teach Schultz a lesson, a lesson to remember."

"A lesson, sir?"

"Yes. I have been given the task, but I can't do it alone. That's where you come in. Out of hundreds of staff, I chose you. You know why?"

"No sir."

"Because I trust your judgment. Trusted it ever since you came up with that idea for ASU. Remember that?"

"It wasn't really my idea. I was just following your orders." Jordan must have known, giving credit to his supervisor and being polite and humble to him was essential for his survival and advancement in a bureaucracy.

In fact, it was Jordan's idea, and this was how it came about.

The prison was having a hard time managing violent, mentally ill, unruly, disruptive, and just plain pain-in-the-ass inmates. The usual procedure was to lock them up and take away their privileges, but not until they had been cited, hauled to the disciplinary court, and convicted. A long, tedious, and time consuming process. It did not solve the problem. The measure was temporary and totally ineffective. Before they were convicted and after they were out of the lock up, the problem inmates kept on raising hell, destroying property, using and selling drugs, making and sharing home brew with other inmates, assaulting and even murdering staff and other prisoners. So, during an administrative staff meeting the Warden asked all Deputy Wardens to come up with a solution to this problem. All Deputy Wardens shifted this responsibility onto their administrative staff who just ignored the whole thing, most of them anyway. But not Martinez, a Shift Commander then, who took it seriously and approached his subordinates for a solution. Tommy Jordan, a lowly guard at that time, came up with a workable idea. He suggested that the prison create an Administrative Segregation Unit for such inmates, preferably within an existing maximum custody unit, in the beginning. Make it maximally secure with a double razor wire fence and individual cells to restrict inmate movement and contact with others. In the next budget, request the legislature to allocate funds for a separate building for this unit. The inmates could be placed in it anytime and kept there as long as the administration felt a need for it, without due process. The prison could still satisfy the due process of law by charging and convicting the prisoners later. This would segregate all the difficult inmates without giving them an opportunity to make trouble, and the prison would be safer and more orderly. Martinez ran with the idea, gave it to his Deputy Warden who turned the idea over to the Warden who finally claimed it as his.

Irrespective of how it came about, it benefitted everyone. Once the Department bought the idea, the Warden and the Deputy Warden were rewarded by a letter of commendation in their files and salary increases. Martinez and Jordan had to wait a little longer, until the new ASU got built. Martinez got to head it as its Deputy Warden and got state provided free housing in the bargain. And Jordan moved up to be the Shift Commander.

"Of course it was your idea. And now I need your ideas again. Actually both, ideas and action." Martinez tried to pump up Jordan's ego so that he would be more amenable to do his dirty work.

It must have worked because Jordan looked at Martinez expectantly and quizzically. "I'll do anything I can," he affirmed.

Martinez took it to mean that Jordan was on his team and laid out the plan, Jordan's assignment, "I have a delicate task for you. A kick ass task. Schultz asked for it, we're gonna give it to him. You are a key player. Here's the game plan. Charge Schultz with some serious crimes. There will be reports from CPO Robinson and Dr. Gopal soon, within a few days, which will help you prepare your case. Then get together with our classification officer. Call a disciplinary court. Make sure all the members of the court find Schultz guilty and order loss of privileges. I want this accomplished within the next four days. Understood?"

"Yes, sir."

"Now comes a more difficult part. According to Mr. Karcher, a worse fate than death awaits Schultz. He must pay with his blood, shouldn't be around to go to the execution chamber. You get my drift?"

"Yes, but how?"

"Put on your thinking cap. You are a man of ideas. Come up with a plan. Discuss it with me before implementing it, though. Whatever you come up with, just make sure it doesn't stir up the AVs."

"Will do. But I need some manpower."

"I thought about that. To begin with I am giving you Ruben Ibarra. You know him, don't you?"

"Yes, sir. He is one of my security staff."

"If you need more help, let me know. If you have preferences, give me their names. Fair enough?"

"Yes, sir."

"And before you go, remember. No one, except you, me, Ibarra, and anyone else working for you on this project, knows about it. I am counting on you because I trust you. But if you or anyone else associated with this project betrays me, there will be hell to pay. I promise you that."

While Jordan was weighed down with a new responsibility, Martinez felt his burden lightened. Only lightened, not removed. He knew Schultz was an indomitable enemy. He could continue to wage war through AVs even after he was dead. Martinez would have liked to stay out of it, but he was in the fray, thanks to the Warden. Now he had to gather his little army and execute the operations. Well, he already made the start, appointed an operations leader, Jordan, assisted by or rather saddled with, Ibarra. If given total freedom to choose his men, Jordan might have overlooked Ibarra, Martinez's special man of choice.

Ibarra had come on board as a lowly guard about a year ago. There were not many Hispanics in the prison system, so he stood out. Martinez saw him and immediately decided to help him move ahead, simply because he was his kind, racially. Everyone engaged in nepotism and favoritism, why shouldn't he? Still, he wanted to make sure Ibarra was worth promoting. He watched his work carefully and liked what he saw. His build itself was imposing, 5'9", 185 lbs., and very muscular. Energetic and somewhat impetuous, which seemed normal for one so young in his 20s. Hard working and obedient. Also very thorough, detail oriented, and quite reliable. Martinez secretly took him under his wing and hoped to catapult him on to some high ground. He did not tell Ibarra anything about it.

Now Martinez wanted to make sure Ibarra had a chance to work on his new project. Not only work, but also to take any risks which might be needed. This could not be expected from an ordinary employee whose only motivation probably was a paycheck. But Ibarra was not ordinary, he was extraordinary, at least in Martinez's eyes.

Martinez decided to act upon his plan immediately, prepare Ibarra for the project even before, especially before, Jordan had a chance to contact him. He hoped Ibarra would show up within minutes.

While waiting for Ibarra, Martinez devoted his attention to the other detail Karcher had entrusted him with. He picked up the phone and called his unit's food service manager. His order was quick, short, and to the point, "Effective immediately, Schultz gets meat loaf and water, three times a day, every day, and nothing else until further notice. Warden's orders. And it goes without saying, no one gets a wind of it, no one except the special staff assigned to Schultz."

He felt good about what he had accomplished so far, and his heartbeat settled back to normal. This gave him encouragement to dig in his heels and face down the menace, get rid of his fear.

In the midst of his self-talk to boost his ego strength, Ibarra showed up, hesitantly peeking through the office door, and saying, "You want to see me, sir? Your secretary says to go in."

"Come in Ruben, yes, come in. Take a seat." Martinez tried to sound intimate and welcoming.

Ibarra sat in the same chair earlier used by Jordan. He looked apprehensive. Being called to a high office without a charge sheet and a disciplinary interview by his immediate supervisor, usually meant he had done something wrong, something very wrong, and was going to be punished for it, severely.

Martinez dissipated his apprehension quickly by being friendly, "How's your day going?"

"Good, sir. Can't complain about anything."

"That's nice. Now let me tell you why I called you. I need you for something very important."

"Yes, sir?" Did his ears prick up?

"It has to do with Schultz, our big, bad Schultz."

"Schultz, sir? About his threat?"

"You know about it?"

"Yes, sir. Everyone does. It's all over the place."

"Yes, it has to do with it, at least in part."

"You have an assignment for me, sir?"

"In a way. I have put Jordan in charge of a project and I want you to help him. He will explain your role in it. I just wanted you to know, it is coming. Also wanted you to prepare for it. It will be risky and brutal. Can you handle it?"

"Brutal, sir? How brutal?"

"Very brutal."

"I am not sure I am Schultz's match, sir. He is very big and strong."

"I know. But I chose you because I think you can give it to him. You are no weakling. Besides, physical strength isn't everything. The most important thing is the brain. Use it and you can accomplish anything. This may just be the ticket for your advancement. I would like to see you get somewhere."

Martinez knew he was giving a lecture, something no one liked. But this was different, it was from the boss. Everyone took all the shit from their bosses and consumed it with relish.

Ibarra, too, must have, since he answered respectfully, "Thank you, sir."

"That's all for now. Go and wait for Jordan's call."

As he saw Ibarra leave, Martinez had a feeling of envy. Not malicious envy, but a 'poor me' type of envy, because he thought, compared to him, Ibarra had it easy, had him as his guardian angel. Martinez never had such a protector. He had to fight for everything he ever achieved. Sometimes it was not a fight at all. Sometimes it was just a cunning strategy. Martinez had become a master of it.

* * *

Martinez was the third among 11 brothers and sisters. His parents were devout Catholics and didn't believe in family planning. A large family, for them, was a God given asset to be cherished. They lived in little Mexico, a small area south of the city, crowded with ethnic eating places and curio shops. They had a small but reasonably successful Mexican restaurant, Tres Palmas, which fed the family well. They and other Spanish speaking, brown skinned resident business owners invited gringos for their money. They welcomes the whites in their area, but they themselves were not welcome in the main city, the white territory. Sure, they went to the city on occasion to do some upscale shopping or to visit government offices, but they were not accepted. Allowed to spend their money in shops or to get their business taken care of in the halls of bureaucracy, but not accepted . They knew it and stayed away from the gringo part of the city as much as they could.

Tres Palmas was where Martinez felt at home. Three palms had been painted on the front wall of the restaurant to justify its name. The restaurant was beside a road hugging a sidewalk with a small paved parking area in the back. No room for real trees. Since he was a child, Martinez had dreamed of a big house with three tall palm trees in the front yard. Dreamed.

Martinez's father knew his history, knew all about Mexican-American wars. He always vocally denounced the white expansionists who invaded and captured Mexican territory. "All of the South and West were once Mexico," he would proudly tell his children. Yet, he was glad that he was born in the United States, where he could raise his family in comfort and even in luxury, compared to the people south of the border. He was glad that he was not one of those illegals trying to sneak into *el norte* in search of some low paying job on the farms.

Everyone in the family worked in the restaurant, well almost everyone. The children under eight played and ran around the dining area amusing the patrons. This could be considered work since they were providing entertainment. The father manned the cash register, seated the customers, kept the riff-raff out, made sure the service was good, shopped for supplies, and kept books. His wife cooked, supervised the kitchen help, and cleaned. All the other children served as waiters and dishwashers. Martinez, too, did that until he was 18. Then he announced that he wasn't going to work in the restaurant anymore. After finishing high school he was going to look for a job where he could get a regular salary, paid vacation, sick leave, and pension. Everyone supported his dream. Losing one boy wasn't going to break the business. That was another great thing about having a big family.

After high school, Martinez got jobs all right, but in fast food places as a bus boy, or in grocery stores as shelf stocker. It seemed like nothing had changed. He was doing the same thing he did in Tres Palmas, only now he was doing all that for someone else and was treated like shit. The shit thing was really disturbing. It was all because he had brown skin and a Mexican accent. He was always given menial, low paying jobs, and was never considered for anything else. If anything went wrong, something shelved improperly, a customer got a wrong order, something broke, he was the first one suspected of doing it. He was often addressed, "hey you" rather than by his name, and the tone and the enunciation of any communication with him would suggest that he was retarded. To get away from this discrimination, he decided to go into the army.

He was only 5'6", but muscular, strong with quick reflexes. He was accepted. His family, especially his mother, complained, "They will send you to Vietnam and you will get killed." But his mind was made up. Seeing the inevitability of the situation, the family gave in. The day he left for boot camp, his mother held him to her bosom and said, "Our saints will protect you." With his mother's arms around him and his head resting on her breasts, he felt safe and secure.

Upon completion of his training, he was sent to Vietnam as his mother had feared. In the army he was made to feel like he was not one of them, he was an alien, except in the battlefield, where all colors were red. He shared the tents, the showers, the mess hall, the recreation, the drills, and the field operations with others, but he was not accepted, just tolerated. The life he knew in his home city was haunting him in the trenches of Vietnam as well. It was not patriotism which had prompted him to go join the army, it was his search for equality and respect. He did not find any. Now he wanted out.

No one would have known that from his conduct. He did his assigned jobs well, never complained about anything, followed all rules to the letter, always obeyed his superiors, showed exceptional bravery and courage in the battlefield, and supported and protected his comrades in every situation. That was his character, devoted and responsible. That certainly helped him get to where he was in the prison. But before that he got Lupita, in a dramatic way.

While in the army, one day he got a letter from his father, "Your mom is sick. Some liver disease she got. Wants to see you before she goes to heaven."

Martinez took emergency leave. His mother was really glad to see him, not only because she would have him, along with the rest of the family, beside her when she closed her eyes forever, but also because now she could persuade him to marry a girl she had chosen for him. She told him, "Hijo, we had visitors from home, old country. Good family. They have a girl, Lupita, your age. Beautiful like an angel. Once you see her you will fall in love. I don't think I will get to see you married, but promise me, you will go and ask for her hand."

How could he say 'no' to his mother on her death bed? Besides, he trusted his mother's judgment. And, why not? She was the family's strength. She made all critical decisions and almost always they were right. The family was comfortable and happy and Tres Palmas was successful, in large part, because of her. He thought that most Mexican men did not appreciate their women, did not realize what a powerful force they were in turning their lives around and taking them to the heights they could not imagine. He was pleased that his father was not narrow-minded and respected his mother's decisions and appreciated her work. He was thankful to his mother who, even on her death bed, thought of his welfare and found a wife for him. He promised his mother to marry Lupita.

After he buried his mother, he had to go back to his army station to complete his term, but left as soon as he could with an honorable discharge. He followed his mother's suggestion and went to see Lupita. He found her to be very pretty with big brown eyes, a round orange shaped face, milk chocolate complexion, and shapely hips and breasts. His mother was always right.

After marriage he moved out of Little Mexico and rented an apartment in the city. Went to invade white territory, a sort of revenge. It did not come easy. The apartment managers would tell him that there were no vacancies even though the 'For Rent' advertisements would stay on in the newspapers and on the sidewalks for weeks. He finally found a one bedroom accommodation in a complex owned by some mega corporation which could not care less about the private lives of its tenants, so long they paid their inflated rent on time.

Then he went looking for a civilian job. No more risking his life for a country which did not care about him. It, too, proved elusive. He pounded the pavement. Jobs available to him were all menial, eloquently declaring his place in society. He rejected them outright. Determined to change his position, he examined his options. It seemed like his military experience might be helpful. Sure, it was helpful, he got offers to be a security guard or a bounty hunter. These jobs were brutish, not respectable. He didn't want them either.

Disgusted and disheartened, he was ready to give up when he got a break in a very strange way.

One day, after his unsuccessful job hunting all morning, he was tired, very tired. To give a little rest to his aching feet, he went into a diner, sat at the lunch counter, and got a coke. He was slowly sipping the cold drink when a young white man in a nifty brown uniform walked in, sat on a stool beside him, and ordered coffee. Martinez was attracted by his uniform. It wasn't one of those droopy uniforms worn by janitors and the like. It was somewhat similar to an army uniform. He looked at the shoulder patch, 'Officer, Department of Corrections'. It looked nice, but he figured it was probably beyond his qualifications. Still, he was curious. Perhaps he could qualify for this job, if not today, maybe tomorrow.

"Work in the prison?" he asked.

The man in the uniform looked at him and gave a curt reply, "Yes", without encouraging further conversation.

"What do you need to get in?" Martinez was not deterred.

"Check it out with the state job service," said the white young man indicating that the conversation was over.

Martinez got the message. He abandoned his half finished coke and walked over to the state employment office, only a couple blocks away. He checked out all the available job listings. and found 'Correctional Officer'. He was surprised to find that he had all the needed qualifications, age 18 and over, good health, minimum high school education. Military or any kind of law enforcement experience was given additional weight in selection.

He applied. Within a week he was called for an interview and hired on the spot. All the usual selection and hiring requirements had been waived. He had not realized until then, how desperate the prisons were to fill these positions. That kind of bothered him. 'What's the downside?', he wondered, but did not care. Whatever it was, he would deal with it. Couldn't be very bad, after all many others were doing this work. Besides, the pluses were many and attractive. The job paid a lot more money than any he had a chance of getting so far, and there were benefits, paid vacation, paid sick leave, health insurance, and pension. There was opportunity for advancement also, which was very enticing. Besides all this, he would be called an officer. Very respectable, indeed.

While he was job-hunting, Lupita was setting up home pretty much all by herself. Not an easy task for a girl from Mexico who could speak only a little fractured English, and had little knowledge of the things available in the market that went into furnishing an apartment. Martinez helped, of course. First the language. Lupita must learn English to be functional, so he told her, "No Spanish, only English." Lupita learned English as she used it. Martinez corrected her as needed. Still, she could not master the language and never did lose her Mexican accent. But she learned English and improved her accent enough to manage her day-to-day affairs and kept getting better at it. The same with shopping. In the beginning Martinez took her everywhere, but pretty soon she was doing almost all the shopping all by herself. She was a fast learner. In less than six months she was running the household quite efficiently and comfortably.

She also met Martinez's definition of a true wife, polite, obedient, and hard working, all the qualities learned from the old country. She cooked what Martinez liked and washed and ironed his clothes. She had his breakfast ready before he got up in the morning, lunch packed before he left home, and dinner on the table before he got back. If he wanted to get in a tub, she drew his bath, and if he wanted some pampering, she rubbed his back and massaged his legs and arms. When physically near him, she made sure to be clean, nicely groomed, and attractive. And she was always available to him sexually, no matter where, when, and in what position. Never a word of complaint or criticism out of her mouth. If there was a need for something, anything, she made a request for it and was satisfied, whether or not it was granted.

Martinez liked Lupita, and even though she had become a naturalized citizen, he did not see her as American. He did not see himself as American either, nor did any of his family, even though they were American citizens by birth. Lupita epitomized Mexican culture and womanhood, and Martinez loved her for that. He did not like American women, white, black, brown, yellow, red, whatever, for what they represented. He felt that they were always complaining about all sorts of injustices, real or imagined, mostly imagined, always in competition with men, and always demanding everything, love, respect, car, home, clothes, vacations, never satisfied, making life hell for everyone. He had seen their behavior and heard grumbling from frustrated men married to or living with them. While in Vietnam, he had noticed that many servicemen were marrying local women because, they claimed, they wanted a wife not an adversary.

But Martinez knew that the family carriage had two wheels and both had to work. So he did his part. He gave Lupita full freedom and control over all financial and household matters. He made sure that all her needs were met, never refusing any of her requests, finding all of them always reasonable. He felt it was his responsibility to protect her from any harm, and those, with evil intentions toward her, would have to kill him first before they could touch her. He loved her and, while he knew that Lupita would not care if he slept with other women, he never did, never thought about it. He had found a good wife and intended to stay with her as long as they lived. In his opinion, it was the basis for a healthy family. He had seen all those dysfunctional families where both men and women fooled around with no real commitment to each other. As a result, everyone suffered, the children, too.

With a halfway decent income from the prison job, Martinez and Lupita relaxed and began enjoying simple pleasures like movies, ball games, camping, and barbecues. In time, they had children, three, one boy and two girls. Martinez wanted the best for them and so, while he taught them American values, pursuit of power, money, and happiness, he also instilled in them Mexican values, faith in God and family harmony. They were a close-knit family, and happy.

Still there was an unrealized dream. Martinez had entered the white man's territory by renting an apartment in it, but was still at the fringe. To truly achieve white man's status he needed to live in the middle class zip codes, with a professional job. The only way he saw it happening was by moving up the career ladder. A position as a Warden or even a Deputy Warden would be professional enough with sufficient income to live in a house in a middle class neighborhood. Perhaps, by the time he retired he would have a big house with real palm trees in the front. He had not forgotten that childhood dream.

Once more he found himself fighting an uphill battle in a white entrenched state bureaucracy. The ones with milky skins, although junior in job experience, ran past him. There was always a justification for that, and the blatant discrimination was overlooked. Martinez still managed to become a Deputy Warden. But it took him 12 long years, a lot of ass licking, and treating his superiors like God.

God! That was interesting. He always took credit when something good happened and placed blame on others when something went wrong. Martinez remembered a true story of a 12- year-old girl. She became pregnant and hid her condition from her parents under loose clothing. When the time came, she gave birth at home, in the bathroom. The cry of the baby exposed her secret. The girl was blamed for everything, for having sex, hiding her condition, giving birth in the bathroom, but God was given credit for saving the lives of the girl and the baby. But if the girl or the baby or both had died, it would have been the girl's fault, not God's.

It worked the same way with supervisors. Just like God they sometimes rewarded their subordinates. Martinez was determined to do all that was demanded of him and get his reward from his superiors. He got his chance when the Warden had sought ideas for managing difficult inmates. Of course, it was Tommy Jordan who came up with the ASU concept, but Martinez had presented it as his to his Deputy Warden. The rest was history. Everyone involved in the process got rewarded. And Martinez became Deputy Warden.

Not that Martinez was denigrating God by comparing Him with the bureaucrats. It was that he found the similarity between the two rather interesting. Being a devout Catholic he believed in God who could do no wrong, and if something did not seem quite right it was because he did not understand the ways of his Creator. So, it wasn't that God was acting unfairly, He was just being God. Only the bureaucrats decided to act like God, and not only in taking credit for work done by others but in other ways also. They, just like God, also demanded complete devotion, unbounded respect, total submission, unflinching faith, unquestioning obedience, absolute loyalty, and consummate humility. Martinez gave all that to his superiors and became the proverbial 'brown noser', or 'boot licker '. He did not care. Now that he was a Deputy Warden he had his eyes on the Warden's chair, and he knew exactly how to get there.

* * *

Martinez leaned back and relaxed. Only a little while ago he had talked with a black, an Indian, a white, and a Mexican, all working for him. What a cultural mix he presided over. His chest swelled with pride.

Irrespective of how he felt about anyone, outwardly he always acted fair and impartial in his treatment of his staff, all staff, no matter what the color of their skin. He was amazed, how easy it was to dissociate his actions from his feelings.

Sometimes this dissociation was not necessary, like when he and his staff were dealing with a common enemy. The AVs fell in that category. The antagonism between the government and the AVs was well known, the hatred for each other was mutual. Martinez was with the government fighting the white AVs. What an opportunity to vent his feelings of resentment and dislike toward certain whites and be liked and appreciated by other whites! For him it was a wonderful setting. He was really ecstatic that the Warden had given him the green light to go after George Schultz. This might be the chance he had been waiting for. He not only saw himself sticking it to the whites, in the success of his operations, he also saw his name on the Warden's office door.

He got excited. The game of chess had begun. His pawns were already on the move, and the offensive was in the offing. He could see that the war would be devastating and deadly.

He was pleased with his performance so far. His little army consisting of Jordan, Ibarra, Robinson, and Gopal had been deployed. Some or all of these soldiers were likely to die. But not him. He felt safe, like a Commander in his headquarters from where he made war plans but sent his soldiers to the battlefield to die. No, not quite safe. Sometimes the Commanders got killed too. At that thought, he saw Schultz looming over him like a giant with a huge boulder lifted above his shoulders, ready to drop it on him.

So what? With his select army of soldiers and his own smart battle strategies, he would conquer a hundred Schultzes.

He was going to be a giant killer.

CHAPTER FIVE
LIKE AN ERECT PENIS

Stella Robinson rushed to her office to complete the required incident report. 'Do your job, do it right, do it on time, and always obey your supervisor,' these were the principles she lived by.

After recording the date, time, and place of the incident, and the names of all the people involved, she wrote:

Inmate George Schultz misbehaved during his program review. He was abusive toward the staff. He used the words, 'black bitch' for me, 'brown shit' for Mr. Martinez, and 'fucking Indian' for Dr. Gopal. He was not cooperative and did not answer any program related questions. He was openly hostile and spat at Warden Karcher. Because of this he was ordered back to his cell. As he was being taken to his cell, he kicked and screamed and threatened staff by saying, "I will kill you all."

The last sentence did not belong in the incident report because Schultz never uttered those words. Robinson still left it there because it made the case against Schultz stronger. Besides, who would question it anyway? Not the Disciplinary Court which would love to convict

Schultz under any pretext, and Schultz, in his arrogance, could not care less about anything she wrote.

Robinson took her report over to Martinez's office and left it with the secretary.

The urgent task done, she went to the officers' room to get a cup of coffee which was available to all staff all the time. She wanted to sit quietly and sip her poison for a few minutes in peace before tackling other tasks. After filling her paper cup half way to prevent a spill, she sat in a rickety stuffed chair, careful to avoid metal springs protruding out of the torn vinyl. She closed her eyes, not to sleep but to enjoy her drink without the interference of other stimuli and also to take her mind away from the earlier unpleasant scene in the program review room. It didn't work. She kept thinking about the American criminal justice system and realized how hopelessly inept it was.

Schultz could remain alive for years, terrorizing people. All these appeals that had to be gone through before execution, and then he might get off on some technicality. Even if he was executed, it was not going to solve anything. There would be others like him, or worse, to fill the vacuum. It was totally dispiriting, the damn system. And she was part of it. She thought of quitting and finding something else where she would not have to have conflict and hostility all the time. But she knew, she could not quit her job. Not only did it help her wipe out her past poverty, it gave her a secure financial foundation in the present and allowed her to look forward to a brighter fiscal future. It also suited her temperament. She loved to kick ass, male ass particularly, and she could do that in this job. Lucky for her, she was assigned to a male unit, primarily because of the prison policy of discouraging gender segregation among staff. So what if it was a prisoner's ass, it was still a male ass. From tin to titanium. What a progression!

* * *

A single mother, Stella Robinson lived in a trailer court. Far from the dreams she had nurtured as a young girl: a big house in the suburbs, two cars, designer clothes, a lawyer or a doctor for a husband, and two children destined to achieve higher rungs on the socioeconomic ladder.

Raised by her mother on welfare, she was lucky to have completed high school. Luckier than her three older brothers who had dropped out of school before reaching junior high and were submerged in the business of stealing cars, selling drugs, and spending most of their time in their vacation homes called prisons. Luckier than her father who was shot dead fleeing from the police after a bank heist. But not lucky enough to escape the charming web of a neighbor boy.

This was how it started.

Robinson used to see this boy almost daily on her walks to and from high school. He would sit there on the steps of the entrance to a run down apartment building and say, "Hi", politely and courteously. She couldn't ignore that and be rude. So she would smile and answer back, "Hi", and move on. After a few months she began to wonder about him. How come he was always there in front of his apartment building? Didn't he go to school? He seemed to be about her age. Did he have a family? Why did he say "Hi" to her? Why didn't he say anything more or even do something else, like making lewd gestures as other kids did? Curiosity got to her. So, one day after the boy said his usual "Hi", she answered with her usual "Hi", then added that she was Stella and asked his name. The boy told her that his name was Rashid. When she looked bewildered he explained that it was a Muslim name. Why would anyone want to be a Muslim? Rashid told her that it was for equality; Muslims didn't discriminate against him, Christians did. That a kid could have social consciousness and a sociopolitical belief system made her think that he had brains. This somehow made him likable.

Now she wanted to know more about him, like what did he do with his time? Nothing exotic like his name, she found out. He fixed cars down at Joey's Garage whenever there was work. He didn't go to school, hell, he needed bread not books. She didn't buy his logic because she thought he could make more money with some education, but what the heck, it was his life and his logic. And both, his life and his logic, were intriguing enough that she began chatting with him for a few minutes each time she saw him, about weather, about shootings and robberies in the neighborhood, about drug dealing and drug overdoses at street corners, about prostitution, about police highhandedness, about other kids getting busted and killed. These were the subjects they knew. Then, one day, a few months later, the conversation got a new twist. Rashid asked her to go out with him, hesitatingly. She was surprised. It had taken him so many months to come to that point. In the school the boys tried to get into her panties right from the moment they laid their eyes on her. She knew how the girls had been used and discarded like rotten apples. She did not want to end up in a stinking garbage pile. Rashid did not seem like other kids. He wasn't her idea of a future husband, but he was decent enough for a date. So she agreed to go out with him some day. That some day arrived in a few weeks. Then it became a regular affair, once or twice a month. They didn't have much money. It was often a hamburger and a shake in a fast food joint and a movie in a discount theater. She went on her dates with her mother's permission and was always back home before midnight, with just a smooch, no sex.

The routine changed on her sixteenth birthday. Rashid suggested that they go to 'The Third Base', a bar, to celebrate. He was quick to add that he would order a birthday cake, they would dance, and have a few cokes. That sounded all right. Robinson's mother even allowed her to stay late, if she wanted to. Everything was all right until the bar closed at midnight. Rashid proposed to go up the hill and watch the town below, lit up like Christmas. That sounded all right too. They drove up to a hilltop which was totally deserted. Even that was all right. Within a few minutes nothing was quite all right. Rashid started pawing her below the neck and below her waist. She resisted. They had never gone beyond a few kisses on the mouth before, and Rashid had never pressed her for anything more. He had always been a gentleman. Now he wanted to be intimate with her. This did not necessarily make him a bad person. It would be rude to refuse him a little closeness. Yet, she was not sure if it was all right for her to surrender herself to him sexually. Particularly when she was a virgin and had dreams of doing 'it' with someone she was going to marry. She told him so. And, he promised to marry her. She wasn't sure she wanted to marry an uneducated part time car mechanic. And, he promised to go to school too, become a professional, and do whatever else she asked him to do. All of a sudden, she felt she loved the man sitting beside her in the car. How could she not? He was ready to do anything for her, he was putting her on a pedestal.

They made the home run.

Then, she remembered the bar they had visited, The Third Base. What a progression! It was a happy progression for her, not in a physical but in an emotional way. It heralded a closeness, a oneness of two lives together. The sex act itself remained pretty much meaningless, even absurd for her. The oral sex seemed very disgusting to her and she refused to participate in it. The intercourse did have some pleasurable sensations, but they were drowned in the inevitable discomfort of doing it for the first time, not fully aroused, and in a car. She did not have an orgasm, did not even know what it was. And when he ejaculated, she felt she was filled with something dirty that needed to be washed away as soon as possible.

Still, it was a birthday to remember, but not the way she came to remember it. She got pregnant. Big mistake. She in school, he with a part time job. What kind of life would they have? But the mistake had been made, it could not be undone. A solution had to be found. She consulted Rashid who had a quick answer. She remembered his actual words, "Get rid of it. Can't afford it." She could not believe her ears. Get rid of their love child? Can't afford it, like it was a commodity? Finally, she could see how Rashid thought. The two of them were on two different wave lengths, no communication was possible. She left him in tears. They were the tears of anger, frustration, even fear. No, she did not mourn the death of her love for Rashid. This was the point where she started seeing men as exploiters, controllers, and manipulators. She modified her stance and reserved these attributes for grown men only after she found out from the sonogram taken of her womb at the neighborhood clinic that the fetus growing within her body was male. She rationalized that the child in her womb was totally innocent, a product of love. Because Rashid did not want to be burdened, she decided to leave him and go it alone. She started taking a different route to school, avoiding Rashid's apartment building.

This was how it ended.

Was there a middle in it somewhere? She wasn't sure. The ending of her first and only love affair, at age 16 no less, was so sad that now she did not even like the beginning. It occurred to her that there was something sensible in arranged marriage after all, the decisions were made by older, mature people, and rationally, rather than emotionally. She had learned about it in school while studying the cultures of the world. But it was totally irrelevant for her life. What was relevant was the fact that her love affair had ended, and she stood at the end of a road not knowing where to go.

Bitter, angry, and confused, she approached her mother for advice, the only person she could trust and rely upon. Her mother listened to her story quietly and sympathetically, then said, "Go school. Baby, I takkare."

Robinson could not say a thing in response. She let the tears of gratitude roll down her cheek. They were also tears of sadness because she was going to be a welfare mom, something she had vowed not to be. 'For a short time only,' she consoled herself.

She did give birth to a boy and named him Jeremiah. She thought it was a proper Christian name, also befitting a black boy. No Muslim crap in her family. She was angry enough not to ever let her son know about his father and his religion, and determined enough to find a decent life for herself, her baby, and her mother.

Right after graduating from high school, Robinson went looking for a job. All she could find was hourly work in fast food joints. It was fine because it supplemented the meager family income, but it was not a job, not a profession. She kept looking for something better. One day she found it advertised in the newspaper, 'Correctional Officer' for the state prison. Had it not been for the eligibility requirements printed so boldly that no one could miss them, she would have ignored the ad thinking that the job was beyond her qualifications. She had everything asked for, high school, good health, and no criminal record. The qualifications required seemed to be minimal, so minimal that almost anyone could be eligible. She, out of curiosity, asked the clerk at the state employment office the reason for it, and was told that it was so because the prison had difficulty hiring correctional officers. She did wonder momentarily if it was so because the job was dangerous. So what if it was? She would deal with any danger that might be there. After all, what danger was there that she had not already faced and survived? She applied for the job and got it. She was surprised and elated at the same time. Surprised, because, in spite of the lowered standards, she could not imagine the prison hiring a black woman with no real work experience. Elated, because now there was a future for everyone in the family. Whatever, the job certainly offered food on the table and promise of advancement and financial security in the future.

She had plans for a better life for everyone in the family. But they had to be implemented slowly, with improvement in her finances. First she would have to establish herself with her son, then bring her mother to live with them.

After receiving her first paycheck she went looking for an apartment, of necessity, a furnished apartment. She found one in a black, run down, and depressed neighborhood. It was furnished all right, with scratched and unsteady furniture, torn and dirty mattress and curtains, and barely functioning kitchen appliances. It also required a six-month lease. Fine. It would give her time to save some money which, in turn, would enable her to move to a cleaner, safer, and more respectable neighborhood.

She moved out of the home, her growing up place. Everyone cried for different reasons. Her mother for losing the last of her family. Robinson for moving away from her familiar surroundings and for leaving her mother alone. Even Jeremiah, only two, no one could figure out why.

But it had to be done for the start of a new life. She promised her mother that she would visit her often, bring groceries and other life's necessities to her, until it was feasible for all of them to be together. She acted on her first two promises right away, the last would have to wait for the right time.

By the time her lease was up, she had decided not to live in an apartment. They were restrictive, crowded and dirty, had no play area for small children, and were noisy. There was always someone above, below, or adjoining, making all kinds of noise, banging on walls, stomping on floors, screaming and fighting, crashing things, and playing the radio, stereo, or TV at the highest possible volume. There was one sound she just could not take. The sound of rhythmic creaking of a bed and the occasional thumping of a head or hand on the wall, accompanied by groans and grunts, squeals and sighs. Certainly not a healthy environment for a growing child. So she opted to rent a single wide trailer which was free from all these drawbacks. And she found, to her surprise, that it was not any more expensive than her apartment to rent. But there was a problem. It was not furnished. She had a little money saved, but it was not going to be enough to buy everything she needed. Another surprise, she found that credit was easily available to her simply because she had a steady state job. She hit the thrift shops, and garage and yard sales, where she used her cash, and bought inexpensive but functional furniture and appliances on credit from department stores.

This was her home. She not only furnished it, she made it pretty with lace curtains, silk flowers, and pink and lavender wall paper. She also got a lot of toys and books for Jeremiah.

By this time she had already completed her six month probationary period and was a permanent employee with all the benefits. Things were certainly looking up.

She acquired all the tactics to make her position strong. One of the most critical was to support the prison's position on every issue, right or wrong. It was not a matter of loyalty, it was a matter of survival. The most important prison position she had to support was about inmates, that they were scum of the earth, dredges of society who needed to be kept in place and treated like sub- human organisms. There were rules for the prisoners, most of which, in her perspective, were an excuse for punishment. She had to be constantly on watch for their infraction so disciplinary action could be taken. Sometimes it was necessary to invent an infraction for the sole purpose of punishing an inmate. She was not to call them in respectable terms such as Mr. or Miss, and even though the policy required that the prisoners should not be abused verbally or physically, she was encouraged not to follow this policy while making sure that no documentation of violating the policy existed. Also, except when physical restraint was being applied, she was not allowed to touch the inmates, partly for safety reasons, primarily to treat the inmates like untouchables. All this was easy to do. Soon she learned to despise them.

She gave her all to her job because it had the promise of a future she had often dreamed of. Also because it offered her something she could never dream of having, ever; power over others, power to shape others' lives in significant ways, power even to decide if one should live or die. Especially men. She began to feel like a part of the elite ruling class which controlled the destinies of its subjects. From powerlessness to absolute tyranny was taking her ego to dizzying heights. Walking tall in the yard or standing on observation posts in her brown uniform and shining badge, she often imagined herself like an erect penis, ready to violate the inmates in any way imaginable. Penis represented power.

A small but very important soldier was the way she saw herself, and acted her part proficiently. That certainly got her noticed and rewarded. She moved up the ladder swiftly, becoming a Correctional Program Officer, CPO, in a record three years. Her first assignment in the new position was in the Administrative Segregation Unit, headed by Deputy Warden Humberto Martinez.

She loved her position. It freed her from shift work which had played havoc with her sleep cycles. Now she could work 8 to 5, Monday through Friday. She had more money. Most importantly, she had specific inmates on her caseload. This allowed her to acquire power over individuals rather than on hordes of inmates whose names she did not know. This also gave her an even greater sense of authority, a more pronounced sense of omnipotence.

Her first batch of inmates included Schultz.

She knew what Schultz thought of the blacks in general. It didn't particularly bother her, not even when he had nicknamed her, 'Black Bitch'. After all, a lot of whites thought like him, and she had learned to ignore it as so much hogwash. But she did despise him more than other prisoners, simply because he had singled her out for emotional assault. She was getting tired of it.

Once she even thought of putting in for a transfer to another unit where she would deal with the garden variety of creeps, not with a bigot who seemed to carry a personal vendetta against her. But that would be running away. She couldn't run away from life's problems because they would just chase her wherever she went. She would have to stand up to the menace and fight. Also, no one else she knew, equally abused by Schultz, was running away. Why should she?

She stayed on, reveling in the ego boosting authority, yes, but also enjoying the financial security she had achieved. Soon she would be able to buy a two bedroom house and bring her mom in. Her mom deserved a decent life after having endured the indignity of poverty for so many years, almost all her life. She would also be a great addition, especially for Jeremiah. She had cared for him for a couple of years after he was born, and she would again be able to do the same, maybe more. Free from the responsibility of running a home all alone, she would be able to devote most of her time to her grandson and help him grow to be a fine young man. And, for Robinson, the burden of looking after her son while working full-time in a stressful environment would be lessened.

Not that she wanted to relinquish all her responsibilities toward her son. No way. She loved her son even though she hated his father. It was actually quite easy to do. She never recognized the father part, the father did not exist. Jeremiah was an extension of herself, not so much physically as spiritually. So much so that she was able to accept his masculinity. She could hate men but still love her son, even his manhood. While bathing and playing with him, she would often hold his penis in her hand, feel it grow stiff, and be amused by it. Amused, not disgusted. She wondered if her son's erection was sexual. 'Naw,' she told herself, 'he's too young for that.' Sexual or not, her son filled the void in her life created by her lack of any close male contact.

She was happy. All her free time was spent with her son, whom she called her own flesh and blood as if, in his creation, there was no contribution by anyone else. Her son and her job pretty much defined her life. Her son was her future and her job was a means of getting there. She had charted the course of her life and had moved on it quite successfully, all by herself. She was determined to continue doing it, even to the extent of depriving her son of life with a father.

She remembered a conversation she once had with Jeremiah.

He had asked, "Where's my father?"

And she had answered, "Around."

"Where? Can I see him?"

"No. He doesn't want you," she responded in exasperation.

As soon as this conversation had ended, she had realized that she had not given an answer. Instead she had just dumped her emotional baggage on a child. Surely, it was likely to make him feel rejected, unloved, worthless. Probably, lead to a low self-concept, and create psychological knots which would be impossible to untangle later.

To correct her mistake, she had quickly added, "But I love you and your gramma loves you."

She never knew if her answer satisfied her son. She believed that it did.

And she did another thing to make her son not think of his father. She took on the role of a father.

She would buy all the trendy clothes and toys for her son that she had missed herself as a child. At home, she would play games, and 'hide and seek' with him. She would spend hours helping him with his erector sets. They also horsed around. She loved to tickle him and be enchanted by his giggles. She would take him to the park, run with him, play ball with him, and watch him swing.

She recorded the memories of her son growing up in photographs. She herself got in some of them when she could persuade her mother, her friends, neighbors, even a stranger, to photograph her with her son using her cheap camera, because she could not afford one with a self timer. She had an album of these pictures. The two of them looked at them often and tried to recall when and where they were taken.

They even slept together. They were virtually inseparable.

At least once a month she would take her son to a picnic. At that time she would specially invite her mother. Three generations together was a special bond she had been able to create. She hoped that it would last forever.

* * *

While Robinson was sitting and watching the mental film of her past life, there walked in Phil Bottillo.

Bottillo was also a CPO but in a minimum custody unit. Of Italian parentage. Short, dark, and muscular, in his mid 30s. He had met Robinson in one of the prison wide CPO meetings and had liked her right away for what he saw her to be. 'She was attractive but seemed unaware of it. She was smart and quite aware of it. She was tough and unafraid and wanted everyone to know it. She was quite polite and courteous with her superiors but didn't seem to like it. She carried with her an air of independence like she did not need or want anyone, yet wished to have someone to need and want her. Beyond all that she had a shadow of sadness following her; it was there in everything she did and said. Most likely because of the burden of being a single parent.' Bottillo felt he could fill her void.

And his own too. In his younger years he had a few dates, all pretty inconsequential. The girls wanted fun, and he had no money with which to meet their wants. The same scenario played out in his young adult years, only with a slight twist. The women wanted someone who could provide them with the luxuries of life, and he, a lowly CPO, was barely eking out a living. Robinson didn't look like a woman who was hunting for a rich husband. She seemed to be satisfied just being a mother. A good mother invariably made a good wife, he believed. So he pursued her in a low key manner to give her a chance to respond to his overtures without feeling pressured.

He started talking to her, occasionally calling her at home. In the beginning they talked about work, then progressed to social and political issues, and eventually their personal lives became a matter of conversation too. They became friends.

They even went out a few times. One could say they had dates. Yes, they touched, but it was the touch of buddies. Beyond that there was no physical intimacy, not even a kiss. Their relationship was purely non-sexual.

Bottillo would have preferred their relationship to have been more intimate than that, but did not let his desire mess up what they did have. He knew Robinson had changed a lot in her relationship with him, but she needed more time to trust him with her life. He could wait.

The relationship with Bottillo was a major progression for Robinson. Still having a bitter feeling for men in general, she, nonetheless, began to see that not all men fit the mold. She saw Bottillo as an exception. He had never demanded anything from her and was always there for her as a friend. Finally, she had abandoned her social isolation created by bitterness of her failed romance and had now embraced a new life in which she was comfortable with a man for emotional, if not physical, togetherness. So that Bottillo did not act under any illusions, she wanted him to know all about her. For this purpose she took him to meet her mother a couple of times and let Bottillo see, with ease and without apologies, the poverty and unstable family she grew up in, and also the kind of life she was leading, a life of struggle, financially, socially, and career-wise. And she also told him how she came to be a single mother. Incredulously but happily, she noticed that Bottillo still liked her, liked her probably for what she was rather than for what he wanted her to be.

It was this Bottillo who stood in front of her, calling, "Stella!"

Robinson's brain and its pondering got a jolt. She opened her eyes and was surprised to see her caller.

"What are you doing here?" she asked.

"I should be asking that question. I called your office. No answer. The unit office didn't know where you were. So, I decided to check all the likely places."

"But why?"

"Just wanted to know how your were coping with the Schultz threat?"

"What threat?"

"You don't know? It's all over the place."

"I've been busy. So what is it?"

The answer would surely lead to more conversation, so Bottillo decided to sit down. He looked around and found a wobbly resin chair. He dragged it, placed it in front of Robinson, and sat in it. Then he told her about Schultz's threat.

That threat made Schultz more menacing to Robinson than ever before. She was sure she would be one of his targets. It worried her not so much for herself but for her son. What if she was seriously hurt or killed? What would then happen to her son? Her mother would take him, but still she shouldn't be dumping all her responsibilities on her mother who had already done enough.

She had to find a way to protect her son. Think, think. But no solution came to her mind. Nervously she got up from her chair, walked across the room, came back, and threw herself into the chair, dejectedly. This time she was very careless and sat on the protruding spring which pinched her behind. She jumped up and yelled, "Fucking chair!"

"I haven't heard you swear before," commented Bottillo.

"My life hasn't been threatened before," explained Robinson.

"We need to find a way to protect you and your son."

"What? Any suggestions?"

"Yeah. Leave the prison, get another job."

"That's funny. Do you have any idea how hard it is for a black female with just high school to find a decent job? Before I came to work here, all I did was hourly work in fast food places. Fried hamburgers, washed dishes. That's what would be available to me. Is that what you want me to go back to?"

"Of course not."

"Then what? ... Listen, here I have it made. I can provide a halfway decent life for myself and my son. I have already moved up, and there is a possibility of further advancement. Soon I will be able to buy a modest house and bring my mom in with me. Where else do you think that's possible?"

"None of that will happen if you get killed."

"Okay, suppose I go back to frying burgers, what makes you think that Schultz will leave me alone?"

"Schultz is against the system. He is against you because you represent the system. You leave the prison you become meaningless to him."

"I can't believe you would be that naive. The AVs have been known to go after their enemies no matter where they are and what they are doing."

"I know that. But, don't you see? You are not Schultz's enemy, the system is. You leave the system, neither you nor your family is of any importance to him."

"So, I go back to my ghetto. Is that what you are saying?"

"There are other possibilities."

"There are? What?"

"We get married." Bottillo mustered enough courage to say what he had been thinking of saying for a long time and had not found a proper opening for it.

Robinson's brain was aflame, 'Here's a man for you again, a penis wielding, devious man, to get you under him. Fuck you Bottillo. Why can't you just be a friend and give me a friendly advice?'

"Fuck you, fuck you," she spoke loudly without realizing that she was in the officers' room where she could be heard by other staff. Fortunately they were alone at the time.

"There you are swearing again. What's gotten into you?"

"Nothing, Phil, nothing. ... It's just that what you are saying is not a solution."

"Why not?"

She did not want to give the real reason. Somehow she did not feel like deflating the ego of a man who had tried to be her friend. She still gave a compelling reason, "Then Schultz will go after you as well."

"Not if I also quit the job. We will go some place where no one knows us. I am sure I can get a decent enough job to support the three of us, or the four of us if you include your mother."

That sounded logical. Her anger and frustration had subsided a bit in the face of a truly friendly, maybe even loving, gesture. Except the marriage part. "I'll have to think about it," she said noncommittally. There was a time when marriage was sacred to her. Rashid had changed all that.

"We don't have much time."

"I know, but my mind isn't working very well right now. Give me at least until tomorrow, please."

Bottillo could see that what he was asking was a major decision, something that would change the entire course of Robinson's life. Yes, she deserved at least a day to think it over. But he saw the situation as so dangerous that waiting until the next day did not seem reasonable. So he pressed, "By tomorrow it might be too late. I am ready to give my two-week notice today."

That sounded like manipulation. Bottillo was using the danger of the situation as a ploy to get her to agree to his suggestion.

She could not be manipulated. So she said what must be said, even though it was hard for her to say it, "Sorry Phil." Realizing that her answer might seem ungrateful, she added, "Please don't take it wrong. But I can't turn my life around just like that. Good-bad, right-wrong, this is all I got, and I got to hang on to it."

"Well, there is no persuading you to change your mind, is there?" Bottillo sounded disappointed.

"No," said Robinson with determination.

"In that case, would you at least move out of your trailer and get an apartment? With people around you in the same building, you would be a lot safer."

Robinson chuckled. Where did he get his ideas from? An intelligent man who thought like an idiot. But she countered him in a friendly manner, "Do you have a clue what they are like?"

"Yes. I live in one of them."

"You may live in one of them, but you don't have the perspective of a woman with a child. You know, I lived in an apartment for a while after moving out of my mother's place. No more, never. You know why?"

"No. Why?"

She told him, then added, "Also you seem to forget that an apartment is not the only place where you have people around you. I got neighbors too. Besides, if Schultz is going to get me, he will get me no matter where I am, in a trailer or in an apartment."

"I suppose you are determined to be oppositional."

"No, I am not. You don't seem to understand my reasoning."

"I understand your reasoning but that doesn't comfort me, because I see the menace to be far greater than you do. By the way, do you know that Schultz's word has already reached his men who will soon be gearing up for attack."

"No. Where did you get that from?"

"The grapevine."

"You believe in gossip?"

"It's not gossip. It's real. I tell you, it's real."

Robinson believed him primarily because of the way he said it. Then she became angry. Not at Bottillo. He was just a postman, bearer of bad news. She became angry at Schultz. Not afraid, only angry. She metamorphosed into a raging volcano, "I'm gonna cut off his dick and shove it up his ass."

"Your thinking is weird Stella, really weird. I guess I should leave it at that, but I can't." He sounded frustrated.

"What are you gonna do?"

"From this day on until Schultz is executed, I am gonna check on you."

"Check on me? I'm not a child."

"You behave like one."

"Oh yeah? So, how are you gonna check on me?"

"I will come over to your place every evening. I won't bother you. I will just make sure there is no suspicious activity and that everything is all right. If for some reason I cannot come some day, I'll call."

"You serious?"

"Yes, I am. And I want you to call me if you notice anything out of the ordinary. Right away. Promise, you will."

"I will," she promised. This she could do. Not that it was necessary, but it would please Bottillo. She might not be in love with the guy but she liked him.

"Okay then, starting tonight. What time do you get home?"

"About six on weekdays."

Bottillo got up. "I'll come or call at about eight then, give you time to settle. What should we do for weekends?"

"I'll call you in the morning and give you my plan of the day, and you can call me in the evening or come over. To check on me," she said mischievously.

"Yeah, to check on you, unless we are going out," Bottillo gave the difficult conversation a lighter tone.

He got up, waved a good-bye, and left the room. He smiled as if he had been able to conquer a small part of Robinson's heart.

But Robinson's heart was fluttering. She still was not sure about her feelings for Bottillo. She believed from her past experience that men could be sneaky; they would charm you with their lies, get what they want from you, then trample on your desires and dreams, and dump you in the end like so much garbage.

Another part of her heart jumped and protested, 'This is all true but not quite. Not all men are alike. Bottillo could be different.' Robinson sat looking at Bottillo's image left behind in the air.

She had to finally admit that Bottillo cared for her, cared a lot. He was willing to go to any lengths to protect her. At that moment she wanted to trust Bottillo and love him. She might even marry him. Her family might have a new addition, and then there could be more. Who knew? At that thought she smiled within. All of a sudden, she had a vision of the sun rising and the flowers blooming.

But then Schultz might end all this before it began. Who knew?

This thought was very disturbing to her. So she got up abruptly, threw her paper cup with some coffee still in it in a trash can, and went to her office to occupy her mind with work. But she could not concentrate on anything, could not even think of what work to do. All she could do was pull and push filing cabinet drawers randomly. This lasted only a few seconds. She threw herself in her chair and slumped. Once more her life jumped in front of her for attention, for analysis. She felt that all her life she had suffered a lot because of giving in to life's threats rather than fighting them. Not any more.

Miraculously, there stood Schultz's image facing her. Surprise, surprise, Robinson did not feel intimidated. She was enraged instead. 'I'm gonna kill him,' she vowed. 'And when I do, the administration, instead of punishing me for the crime, will probably recognize my contribution and give me a promotion.'

She got carried away with the thought to the point that she forgot that it really was not a solution, it might even be a problem. Killing a physical giant like Schultz would not be easy, might even be impossible. Then, her enemy was likely to fight back and she herself might get killed in the process. Assuming she succeeded in killing Schultz, a big assumption, she would still not be safe because, most probably, his men would exact their revenge from her, and if, in the unlikely event she escaped that fate, she would be prosecuted as a murderer, not rewarded and promoted.

Still, her disturbed mind was prompting her distorted thinking, so much so, that, to her, killing Schultz was an idea with merit.

She sat in her chair contemplating various ways of implementing it. It was a mental exercise, a wishful thinking. She did not believe that she had it in her. She did not think that she could actually kill someone. Like a mystery writer, she still enjoyed creating that perfect murder in her mind. She was amazed at how many ways there were to do it. She could poison him, stab him, garrote him, slit his throat with a razor blade, electrocute him, stick a hat pin in his heart or trachea. Of course, many of the murder weapons needed were contraband in the prison, but there were ways of sneaking them in. And to render Schultz's brute strength ineffective, it would have to be a surprise attack of a kind that would kill him before he had a chance to react. She reveled in the fertility of her imagination. Then it occurred to her that it may not be all fiction, maybe she could actually do it. People had been known to do things out of their character, particularly when there was an urgent demand for them.

And so, she decided that she was not going to hide or flee. Instead, she would just kill the son-of-a-bitch herself. All she had to do was to choose the best way.

CHAPTER SIX

LOOKING FOR A NIGHTMARE

RAJIV GOPAL WAS upset. He felt insulted at being called 'A fucking Indian'. In his opinion, most Americans resented and hated foreigners, particularly the Asians, Africans, Mexicans, and South Americans. Why should Schultz be any different?

As a psychiatrist he knew that hateful behavior was emotional, not logical, and he should not be manipulated by it. Yet, he could not help the way he felt.

His sense of insult was magnified manifoldly by Martinez's order to write a psychiatric report on Schultz with a predetermined diagnosis. He couldn't refuse to write a report, but he wasn't going to do it unprofessionally. That meant he needed to study the inmate's medical and institutional files, conduct a clinical interview with him, and give him some psychological tests, before putting down his findings on paper. He proceeded with the distasteful task.

He went straight to the medical records office and found that there was no file on Schultz. Ironic! One healthy enough not to need any medical care was scheduled to die. Whatever, Gopal was relieved; one less task to perform. Next, a visit to the institutional records office.

As he was getting out of the medical unit, a guard at the gate asked rather jokingly, "Dr. Gopal, aren't you going to give Schultz a lobotomy or something?"

Gopal didn't understand the question and asked, "What are you talking about?"

"Something got to be done about his threats."

"Threats? What threats?"

"You haven't heard? I guess, we got the word while you were in the clinic." The guard then told him about it.

Gopal became thoughtful, uneasy. His discomfort, which had started in the program review room, magnified in Martinez's office, now multiplied a thousand times. He walked mechanically without being aware of his location in the universe, although his body carried him in the right direction.

He maintained reasonably good control over his emotions while requesting Schultz's file from the records clerk. He kept his control even while reading the file in a study cubicle. But after that his sense of disquiet, which had been chasing him all along, overtook him, overpowered him, primarily because of what he learned about the Aryan Vision and Schultz's role in it.

The first he had heard about the AV was during orientation for new employees. This two-hour lecture was on prison gangs with information about their nature and operation, and how to deal with them. Gopal was startled at the mention of 'Aryan Vision.' He thought it referred to a gang made up of people from his homeland, India, since most of the Indians considered themselves Arya, and had done so for millennia. Yet, what did Indians have to do with gangs in the USA? After the lecture he found out that there was no connection. Actually, the AVs did not consider any nonwhite person as an Arya. They did not know that their revered symbol of white supremacy 'Swastika' was a Sanskrit word from India which had been used as a mark of 'good luck' in many Asian and some European countries for thousand of years. In the AV movement Gopal saw prejudice as a parasite without any root of its own, growing out of an existing truth, using it to support itself, and eventually killing it. A very disturbing revelation.

He saw the AV marching toward its destination, 'white supremacy.' the journey looked real, and the desolation it left behind appeared real, too. In his mind, the journey would continue and so would the desolation. But the destination? It was a fantasy, it really did not exist.

Yet, it was being pursued by Schultz with courage, determination, fearlessness, and ruthlessness, even with a willingness to sacrifice himself.

Was he abnormal, a psychological aberration? To his horror, Gopal found that the answer was 'no', because Schultz was doing what the rest of mankind was doing. Everyone was trying to dominate everyone else, mostly through violence, living in a make-believe world of personal superiority in terms of race, religion, skin color, and what not.

Gopal did not want to believe that he was like that. To dissociate himself from the rest of the wretched mankind, he decided to forget about it and concentrate on the task at hand; conduct a clinical interview with Schultz and give him a couple of personality tests. First he made a photocopy of the Pre-Sentence Investigation Report (PIR) for use in writing his report, then returned the file to the file clerk, and headed toward the ASU.

With trepidation, because he expected a hostile reaction from a subject who clearly was not afraid of anyone or any consequence.

With anger, because he didn't like being attacked for being an Indian.

With fear, because with the knowledge of Schultz's threat he had developed a sense of doom for himself and his wife.

With frustration, because he did not know what to do about his situation.

His situation?

* * *

Ironically, Gopal himself was to be blamed for his 'situation'. It had been his choice to come to the USA and get specialty training in psychiatry and to chase the American dream of money and material possessions. Before he succeeded in getting any of that, he got something else, something totally unexpected, something wholly unimaginable, something absolutely vile.

It was the hostility and insult.

People didn't want to rent an apartment to him because he was dark skinned. They asked him if there were houses in India and if people there wore clothes. They mocked him for being a vegetarian and advocated that he should eat meat and become civilized. They suggested that he should change his name to something more pronounceable like 'Roger'. They encouraged him to become Christian and abandon the Hindu cult of stone worshipers.

Gopal put up with all that and continued to work toward his goal. In the process he did something for which he could not excuse himself, ever. At the time, however, he thought it to be a smart move, one that would be instrumental in getting him where he wanted to go.

Actually, it was not his move, not initially. He was drawn into the game, and once he was enmeshed in it, he adopted it as his own.

The game!

Gopal was doing his residency in a hospital with a psychiatric wing. There he noticed that a nurse, Christi Comora, showed more than a professional interest in him. She would ask him, sometimes jokingly, often times teasingly, a few times suggestively, personal questions like, 'What do you do with your free time?', or 'Don't you ever need a woman?' Not knowing how to answer, he would just evade the questions by lying that he did not have time.

One day she became very direct and asked him to have dinner with her. She even offered to cook a vegetarian meal, no less. Why? Why was she interested in him? He had nothing, no money, no position, no prestige, no nothing. No looks or build either. Only 5'6", non-athletic, a little on the plump side, well done roast brown, droopy eye lids, bow shaped lips, chubby cheeks, and a round face which tapered at the chin. Not ugly, not particularly attractive. So, why? Maybe she was just a nice person!

He tried to size her up. She looked to be in her mid 40's, a good 10 years older than he. Rather plain, permanently tan, endowed with pretty dark brown hair and eyes, slim in a muscular way, strong, and energetic. And she didn't seem to be a bigot.

He agreed to the dinner but in a restaurant. His treat. It seemed too much to be with a woman alone in her place the very first time. It was fine with her.

After that first dinner, natural progression took over. Within a few months they were going on regular dates, but no sex. He didn't know how to bring up the subject and hoped Comora would provide an opening of some sort.

She did when one day she suggested that they live together to save money. He knew it was not about saving money, or if it was, only a little. It was about sex, for sure, and possibly something else. Love? Couldn't be. She had never alluded to love, even jokingly, and he himself never felt he was in love with her. He enjoyed her company but never entertained the thought of spending his life with her. Marriage was out of the question. He had plans of going back to India, and he knew no American woman in her right mind would accompany him to what she considered to be the wretched land of the poor.

Coming from a sexually conservative country, he found Comora's suggestion rather destabilizing. He also found something exciting in breaking the taboo. Besides, she was right, it would be easier on his finances. Once more he agreed with her suggestion. Once more with a little modification. He asked her to move in with him. He could not break the bondage of a patriarchal society.

The first night together, he lay still like a log, didn't know what to do. Comora took over. She undressed him and went down on him. The licking of the shaft, and the sucking of the glans and testicles. In no time he was moving his buttocks vigorously, and in just under a minute he was ejaculating in her mouth. He knew what an orgasm was like, but it was something beyond anything he had experienced before. After a few minutes she was on top of him, letting him smell and taste her vaginal secretions. He had new stirrings in his groin area. No, he was not going to be a passive recipient any more. He turned her around on her back, got on top of her, and into her. He was transformed. This time it took him longer to finish. When he did, she moaned, twitched, and thrashed her body. He was in ecstasy.

A few months passed and ecstasy dissolved into disillusionment. He realized that he, not Comora, had to make a lot of adjustments, like putting up with the sight and smell of meat, cooking and eating with the shoes on, Christian books and paraphernalia, and that incessant country-western whine.

Living with Comora had not helped him financially either. Actually, he was worse off than before, because Comora was not contributing any money to the household. He did not know what she did with her money and he could not ask. His cultural background dictated that, as a man, household finances were his total responsibility, and he undertook it. It would have been easy to manage the budget if it were left entirely up to him, because he could be frugal and spend money only on essential needs, like a low rent apartment, basic food, minimal clothing, inexpensive transportation, and occasional cheap entertainment. But Comora was always demanding the finer things in life which were beyond his means.

Plus, his workload at home had increased. Comora seemed to be more interested in her job than in home. She hardly ever cooked and didn't like the food he prepared. He could see that she liked to eat out, and he accommodated her about once a week, staying with Denny's, Village Inns, and the like, on a day when both were free. This didn't seem to satisfy Comora who wanted going out to be a special occasion defined by lavish eating and upscale entertainment. Other days, he noticed, she would pick something up from a fast food joint on her way back home from work or would microwave a frozen dinner, looking quite unhappy. He, more often than not, ate alone. He also cleaned house, did laundry, and shopped, because, according to Comora, she wasn't born to be a housekeeper. To top it all, Comora didn't appear to be interested in sex anymore.

Suddenly he was faced with a new problem. The hospital administrator called him to tell him that he would have to let him go. Why? Because it had come to his notice that Gopal was living with nurse Comora, which was unlawful cohabitation. He was also told that 'Immigration' would be informed about it and he would be deported.

Business meddling in its employee's private lives? Gopal didn't understand it, but he had to accept it. Obviously, that was how things were done in this country

Gopal felt the earth shifting from under his feet and his heart sinking. He knew he was singled out because he was a foreigner. Selective enforcement of law was another means of discrimination. He would have to find a solution to this problem. He could not allow it to destroy his life's ambitions. His furiously churning mind suggested a possible way out, marriage or separation. That is, if he was not going to be prosecuted for the acts already committed.

He presented these options to the administrator who thought marriage, not separation, would legitimize his relationship with Comora and would make any administrative action against him unnecessary. The answer made his heart settle a little.

A separation would have been best for Gopal. It would have rescued him from Comora. But, since it would not save him from deportation, it was not an option. He would have to ask Comora to marry him. What if she refused? His heart jumped with a start and kept on throbbing furiously for a long time. Kept on throbbing until he asked himself, 'Why am I treating the possibility of refusal as a fact? Why worry about something which might not happen?' These questions calmed him down.

That night he talked with Comora, told her about his meeting with the administrator, and asked her to marry him. Clearly, it was a marriage of convenience without any pretense of love. To his surprise, Comora readily accepted his proposal. Immediately, Gopal wondered, why? Why did she want to help him? Was there something in it for her?

He was so engrossed in his questions that he was startled when Comora pointed out that the marriage would allow him to become a citizen of the United States.

Becoming a citizen had never been in Gopal's plans, but the suggestion was intriguing. He wanted to stay in America after his residency, work for a few years, and make a lot of money before going back home. For that he would need to find a hospital or clinic willing to sponsor him, which was not going to be easy. With marriage to

Comora he would not need to go through this rigmarole. He would get a green card right away, become a citizen later, and stay in the country as long as he desired. What could be better?

But the situation was not all that rosy. He would have to put up with Comora. So what? He had made many adjustments in his life, let there be one more.

Yet, he could not see Comora as his wife. To him, a wife created and cherished a home, raised a family, and fought the battle of life alongside her husband. Comora did not meet the criteria. Once more, so what? He needed this marriage. Afterwards, he would divorce her, get rid of her. The thought was distasteful. It made him look like a selfish monster, which he probably was, but didn't want to believe.

Then he remembered his suspicion that Comora was probably agreeing to marry him for her own selfish reasons. He didn't know what they were, just yet. This lessened his own sense of depravity.

They were married within a month, in the city hall. Gopal thought it was boring and degrading, having to seek permission from the government. But he went through the formality anyway because there was no other choice.

Comora became Gopal, Christi Gopal. A few months later Gopal got his green card.

After completing his residency he got a job as a psychiatrist in a psychiatric hospital. His money woes eased considerably, but only for a short while. Christi quit her nursing job and began demanding a big house in a rich neighborhood, a luxury car, designer clothes, frequent outings, and grand parties.

Gopal wanted these things too, yet not quite the same things. His tastes were radically different from those of Christi.

He wanted a brick house built around a fountain in a courtyard like a Spanish hacienda, and she wanted a wood structure, totally enclosed with gabled roofs, porches, and front and back yards.

He wanted a Mercedes, S-Class, and she wanted a Cadillac.

He wanted tailor-made cotton, wool, or silk clothing, and she wanted designer labels.

He wanted to eat in ethnic restaurants, and she preferred steak houses.

He wanted academic gatherings, and she went for catered garden parties.

He wanted to listen to classical music and her choice was country western.

He was in a cultural war with Christi, not conducive to peace and tranquility. Still, the relationship, although dysfunctional, continued primarily because he accepted the reality of being in a foreign country and made adjustments, most of the time giving up his own wants and needs.

Then came the money crunch. More money was going out than coming in, and Gopal was heavily in debt. Every month he dreaded the inevitable bills. Not the kind of life he had envisioned. He had dreamed of money and a comfortable life. He got money, but the life was anything but comfortable.

Worse than all this was Christi's new life style. Before their marriage she was absorbed in her work, now in social events. To Gopal, because of his Indian upbringing, these events were unfamiliar, therefore, unattractive and dull. Also, after working full time at the hospital, Gopal didn't have time or energy for them, but he was required to be a gracious escort. He would be with Christi, yet far apart. Effortlessly polite to everyone, yet strained. He felt he had a home but no family life.

Day after day and night after night Gopal's discontentment increased. One night it reached its climax.

They were in bed, he on his side, she spooned behind him, her favorite sleeping position, probably because it prevented him from making any sexual overtures. Sometime during the night their positions shifted in such a way that they were face-to-face, Gopal enclosing Christi in one of his arms. The feel of a soft body against his hands and chest woke him up and aroused him. He started caressing her sexually.

This woke her up. She flung her arms to get him away from her. Her knuckles hit his right eye. He screamed, covered his eye with his left palm, and bolted out of bed. Behind him he heard her say, "That's what you get for being horny in the middle of the night."

He was incredulous. She showed no sympathy for his injury which she had caused and then blamed him for it. Without saying anything, he went to the bathroom to examine his eye. The cornea was red but there was no detectable injury to it. The conjunctivas felt traumatized. No sign of any internal injury, any internal physical injury. There was plenty injury to his feelings. He would have to detach himself from Christi.

He spent the rest of the night on the living room couch. In the morning, when Christi came to the kitchen for her programmed-to-brew coffee, Gopal informed her, "I am going to fix a spare bedroom for myself."

"Fine with me," she said nonchalantly.

Gopal watched her get her coffee and take a seat at the breakfast nook overlooking a garden. Gopal followed her, sat facing her from across the small glass-topped table, and asked a question which had been nagging him for a long time, "It's obvious you don't like me, then why did you pursue me?"

She answered in a curt and brutally honest way. He listened attentively while she summarized her motives in between her sips of coffee.

"I was a janitor's daughter and grew up in poverty. Naturally, I wanted to marry a rich man. Couldn't find any in my own social circle which consisted of losers. After becoming an RN and getting a job in a hospital, I tried to get doctors interested in me. A few did. They fucked me and left. This went on for years. I started thinking about giving up my dream and finding someone at my level. I was 38 then, an old maid already. Then I saw you. I had heard that Asians, Africans, and Latinos were always drooling over a white pussy. I had heard right. I got you."

She stopped for a few seconds. For what? Obviously for what he got next, a bombshell. "I might as well tell you that it was I who went to the hospital administrator and complained about you?"

"Complained?" Gopal asked.

"Yeah. I told him that I agreed to live with you because you promised to marry me. Now you were going back on your word."

"But we never discussed marriage."

"That's exactly the point. I wanted marriage, legal right over everything you had. The administrator took pity on me. You know the rest. Yes, laws about cohabitation do exist but they are never enforced. The administrator used them to get you to marry me."

That was when Gopal abandoned his plan of separate bedrooms and decided to leave Christi. "So, you got everything you wanted from me, but no more," he said. Immediately after that he got up, went to the bedroom, put on his street clothes, picked up his briefcase, and walked out of the house, a free man, never to look back.

Within a few months they were divorced.

Gopal let Christi have everything, the house, the car, the bank account, just so he would have nothing to do with her, ever.

He started living in an apartment, thinking he would be happy. He wasn't. He felt lonely. Strange! Being lonely had not been a factor in his life before Christi. Painful as it was, living with her had given him a sense of togetherness. He pined for it, not the dysfunctionality of it though. That was when he decided to go back to India to find himself a real wife. One who would not only provide him companionship but would also help obliterate Christi's memory. Then, together they would go after the American dream. He called his parents on the phone to tell them that he was coming home and why. This was critical because his parents had to look for a wife for him.

Gopal went home and found Satya. He learned about her from his mother who had chosen her for him.

Twenty-two years old, she was an only daughter of a General in the Indian Air Force. Very pretty, 5'8" tall, slim, with a strong athletic body, wheat complexion, big expressive eyes, oval face, lips pursed in a permanent smile, and long black hair. And, she had a blending of feminine and masculine features. As a young girl, although quite feminine in looks and demeanor, she exhibited some tomboyish attributes like climbing trees, swimming in the canal, racing bikes, and playing cricket. As a grown-up, although quite adept in cooking, cleaning, budgeting, and managing a house, she showed little interest in a typically female career of teacher or doctor, and invaded a traditionally male territory by becoming a civil engineer. All this was most likely instilled in her by her father, who was looking for the son in her that he did not have. That was probably why he also taught her to fly planes, from two seater propellers to fighter jets; and to handle firearms, from small pistols to machine guns.

Gopal was intimidated and did not think he wanted a masculine woman for a wife. But his mother calmed his fears by explaining that Satya was not masculine by any means, she had only discarded illogical and stupid traditional male/female roles, which was actually a good thing, rather progressive. If there were any lingering fears still, they were dissipated when, following the protocol, Gopal went to see Satya in her home for the first time.

He found her polite, courteous, and very self-assured, and felt comfortable with the idea of spending his life with her. He communicated to his parents his willingness to marry Satya. Soon after that he got the word that Satya had also accepted him. He was pleased.

They had learned just enough about each other to agree to be life partners. There would be more to learn in the future, a lot more.

The marriage ceremony took place a couple of months later. Three days, hundreds of guests, nonstop celebration with songs, music, dance, and festive food. And no seeking permission from the City Hall.

The first night together.

Gopal walked into the room, decorated for the couple, and saw Satya sitting on a bed canopied by fragrant jasmine flowers and rose petals. Her head hung, shy eyes fixed at her henna colored feet. Attired in a bright colorful silk sari and weighed down with gold and diamond jewelry, she looked like a precious doll, a beautiful flower arrangement. He felt unsure of himself, did not know how to approach her. After a few seconds of indecision he sat beside her, and, being careful not to disturb even a strand of her hair, lifted her veil and saw her round sandalwood face embedded with almond eyes. He smiled and saw her smile too, a very faint smile like breaking of the dawn, opening of a pomegranate bud. In his clumsiness, all he could do was ask if she was hungry. She shook her head, 'no'. He offered her a drink then. She said nothing. He took the silence to mean, 'yes'. He poured two glasses of a mixed fruit drink, Rooh Afza, and gave her one. She took it but sat there watching him. He asked her to drink. He knew she would not unless he did. He scanned her face with his twinkling eyes and found an uncomplicated simplicity which immediately put him at ease. He took a mouthful of drink and made a funny gurgling sound. Her mouth broke into a wide smile. After they finished their drinks, he put away the glasses and suggested that they go to bed. She quietly walked toward the bathroom like a sweet pea waving in a gentle breeze. He changed into pajamas and, following the traditional reservation of the left side for the wife, lay on the right side of the bed. She came to bed, dressed now in a simple cotton sari, and lay on her side. He turned around, got his left arm under her neck. She snuggled against his chest. With his right hand he lifted her chin and placed a tender kiss on her lips. She just lowered her eyes. He stayed awake a long time savoring his blissful state. He sensed Satya was awake too. That physical closeness sealed their lives together. Neither felt pressured for sex. It came naturally a few days later.

During the next few weeks Gopal learned several new things about Satya.

Satya loved to fly but for personal travel and pleasure only. Contrary to her father's desire, she had no interest in becoming either a commercial or a fighter pilot. She had no business or military ambitions. So far as shooting was concerned, it was exclusively for entertainment. She would never use a firearm to kill anyone, not even a fly. And a career was of secondary importance to her. She would work as a civil engineer only if there was a financial need for it. Her primary interest lay in making a home for her family. She saw it as a full time occupation and as one that was honorable and important.

And she wanted to make a home in India in concert with the wishes of her in-laws. Each person had a different reason for this, based on whatever information or misinformation they had acquired.

Satya didn't want her children to grow up being selfish, disrespectful to elders, drinking, drugging, smoking, and engaging in casual sex.

Gopal's father thought that money was not everything. Really important was a comfortable, peaceful, happy, and secure life along with a profitable private practice, which was possible only in India.

Gopal's mother thought that her son needed to save himself from American women like Christi, who were nothing but whores, not able to stay with one man for any length of time. Also, he was likely to be killed in America, because the men there were violent and crazy.

Gopal vetoed everyone. He rejected every reason given. He wanted money, a lot of it, and it was available only in America. Out of his respect for his parents and his wife, he didn't say anything to contradict them, but felt they were being unfair to America, their ideas were based on prejudice and half truths.

He came back to the USA, Satya reluctantly following him. He did not go back to his old place of employment where everyone knew him as Christi's husband. He found work in another psychiatric hospital in the same city. He did consider moving out of the city, but only briefly, because he thought his job search would be easier in a familiar place. It wasn't as clean a break with his painful past as he wanted, but it would do.

It didn't do. His past was still chasing him, or rather Christi was, or perhaps he only thought she was. Because of what he saw in a shopping mall one day.

He and Satya were window shopping and ended up in the cosmetics area of Macy's. They were examining various perfumes. As Gopal was putting a dab of Opium on the back of Satya's hand, he saw a reflection of a woman in the mirrored wall behind the counter and in front of him. Just for a fleeting moment Gopal thought it looked like Christi and turned around to see if she was there. There were many women walking and examining merchandise but no sign of Christi. Probably someone who looked like her, he thought, and tried to dismiss his perception. Unsuccessfully. Waves after waves of unsettling thoughts kept pounding his mind.

He never talked to Satya about Christi and she never asked him about her. He treated it as a dead subject. Raising it would only cause a stink, which he was not willing to deal with. Whenever Christi popped up in his consciousness, he would squash it and divert his mind to something else, anything.

That's what he did. Went through the motion of shopping and tried very hard to keep his feelings hidden. He must have done a pretty good job, because Satya behaved like everything was quite normal.

At home, sleep eluded him. He got up and went to the living room, picked up a novel, and pretended to read. He was still thinking of Christi. What kind of power did that woman have over him? Power enough to disturb his sleep? He knew he did not love her, did not want to be with her, or see her, or hear about her. He should have found a job in another city, in another state, far away from Christi, but it was too late. Still, he wanted her completely out of his life. So why couldn't he get her out of his mind? Maybe she was hidden in his inner psyche from where she was going to destroy him. Was he in the realm of metaphysics or in the realm of the weird? Maybe he was just being paranoid.

Whatever, Christi had to go out of his life. But how? The only thing he could think of was to replace the thought of her with something tangible, firm, and sensually engrossing. So, he got up, went back to bed, and wrapped his arms around Satya who moaned in her sleep.

It helped. As the days passed, Christi's memory, particularly her image in Macy's, faded and life became routine, comfortable.

Next, he got himself in heavy debt. He borrowed money, a lot of it, to support his dream of a lavish lifestyle. He bought a sports Mercedes for himself and a BMW sedan for Satya, and sunk a big chunk of money toward building a big house.

Satya went along with his decisions while objecting to the expenses. She could not squash his dreams. Even agreed to take over the house project, mainly because she did not like the apartment they were living in and found it cramped. She wanted something spacious, the kind she had grown up in in India. While Gopal was working, she went out looking at properties. She found one out of town, on a rural route, almost in the wilderness, the closest home being about a mile away. She liked it for a number of reasons; it was big with about 3,600 square feet of built up space on a two- acre lot, it afforded quiet and privacy, it was free from city pollution, and most of all it was reasonably priced. The low price was primarily due to its away-from-the-city location, its somewhat rundown condition, and the desperation of an 83-year-old owner who was moving into a nursing home. It was all positive for Satya who wanted to be in the country and liked the opportunity to fix up the house to her own taste. Gopal let Satya do whatever she wanted to do with the house, except for two things: the house had to be electronically fenced and alarmed for safety, and there would be handguns kept strategically in the bedroom, living room, kitchen, and bathroom. A virtual armory, so what, they were put in all those places for easy access, if and when they were needed.

Satya had no problem with the electronic fence but she did not want any guns in the house.

Gopal explained, "It's for self-protection in a very violent country."

"I wouldn't use a weapon even for self defense. I know how to shoot, and I am very good at it, but I have never shot a living thing."

"So, why did you learn?"

"To humor my father. I learned to fly fighter planes too for the same reason."

"Fighter planes?"

"Yeah. He would take me to the base and teach me. Against the rules, but nobody minded."

"I don't think you will have any need to fly fighter planes. But, guns. It's a different story. We need to be realistic. Idealism goes only so far."

"What good are ideals if we don't live by them?"

They soon realized that all this arguing was futile and decided to make a compromise. They agreed to keep the guns in the house only to be used by Gopal, if needed. Satya would have nothing to do with them.

After securing the mortgage for the house, Satya obtained a loan from their bank to finance the remodeling. Although all design decisions were made by them together, Satya was the designated supervisor of the project, simply because Gopal's job responsibilities allowed him little time for anything else. Soon after that, Satya hired a building contractor and gave him six weeks for the completion of the work. In order to meet the deadline, the contractor had several tasks going simultaneously; roofing and landscaping, plumbing and electrical work, putting up sheet metal inside and exterior wall siding, tile laying and carpeting, door and window installations and yard fencing.

While the remodeling was going on, Gopal found a new job as a psychiatrist in the state prison. It paid almost twice as much as he was making at the psychiatric hospital, and it required only a brief interview to be hired. Maybe because the job was considered dangerous and no one else wanted it. Satya thought so too. He still took the job, ignoring the potential risks, because money still colored his thinking. And, at this time, with heavy debts hanging over their heads, it was also needed.

The work on the house finished, it was time to furnish it. Again Gopal contributed his ideas and even accompanied Satya on shopping trips, but left it up to her to make final decisions and carry them out.

Completely remodeled and fully furnished, the house looked impressive and expensive. And safe.

They came to live in it without any fanfare. Gopal did not want to invite his old friends from the hospitals where he had worked for the same reason he did not want to be in their company, the Christi connection. He had made no new friends at the prison where he had worked only a few weeks. Clearly, being new in a foreign country, Satya, too, knew no one to invite.

At the threshold Satya asked Gopal, "Wait. We must pray before entering the house."

"Pray? I don't know what to do or say."

"I don't know the ritual either, but we will improvise. Just copy me."

They knelt side by side, put their foreheads on the threshold and said, "Devi Laxami, give us prosperity. Brave Hanuman, protect us from harm."

They smiled at their clumsiness, but were sure that the invoked god and goddess were listening to them. They entered the house holding hands.

The house became a stimulus for more material wants for Gopal. He bought some custom clothing, Rolex watches, and platinum jewelry to complete the image. Satya knew, it was not just for personal enjoyment, it was for an appearance of prosperity to those who might come to visit them in the future. She did not like it, and hesitated to approve the expenses, but relented after watching her husband's child like excitement.

Once settled, Satya told Gopal how she felt about their situation and what she would like to do about it. They were overextended financially and they would have to tighten their belts. Also, if something happened and Gopal lost his job, she would have to be ready to bring in money. That meant she would have to secure her civil pilot and civil engineer licenses. To get a civil pilot's license, she would need to pass some tests and would have to provide proof of a minimum of 150 flight hours, for which she would have to enroll in a flight school. To get a civil engineer's license, first she would have to take some college courses since the work done in India would not be recognized, then would have to get through a number of tests and a lengthy licensing procedure.

Gopal had no problem with her plans.

The American dream had been realized. The search for it, ironically, had brought Gopal face-to-face with Schultz.

* * *

With each step closer to the ASU, Gopal was becoming more anxious.

No one had ever threatened him with death until now. It was so real and so devastating that he felt lightheaded. For the first time in his life, he was afraid of death and afraid of what would happen to Satya after he was gone. He had dragged her out of India into a foreign country, over the objections of everyone, including her own, and now there was a possibility that she might be left alone. Of course, she could go back to India and live with her parents or in-laws. Or, she could stay in America, find a job, get remarried, and lead a productive and even a happy life, which wouldn't be a difficult thing given the fact that she was bright, highly educated with marketable skills, and extremely capable of handling day-to-day affairs. Yet, deep down he felt that without him she would not survive. He loved his wife and did not want her to face a dismal future. It was his responsibility to shield her from harm. How would he do that if he were not around? Male ego aside, he felt concerned. And guilty.

But neither concern nor guilt could remove the threat he was facing. It had to be removed. Either that or leave the country. Somehow the second alternative still did not have sufficient power of persuasion. He really wanted to stick it out until ready to leave. And he did intend to leave in a few years, after he had amassed some wealth.

The events of the next few hours changed all that.

Gopal went to interview and test Schultz.

All dangerous inmates had to be interviewed in their cells. The interviewer would stand outside the cell at least three feet away from the bars or window. Of course, this compromised the privacy, but who cared about an inmate's civil rights. There were exceptions, of course, when the inmates had to be brought out of their cells. For privileged talks with an attorney in a private room, for daily one-hour exercises in the outdoor pens, or for program reviews in conference or meeting rooms. In such situations the security was maintained by increased restraints on inmates, either on their bodies, or around their environments, or both.

Gopal stood in front of Schultz's cell and asked, "I have been asked to prepare a psychiatric report on you. Could I talk to you?"

Schultz used his back and thigh muscles to lift himself from the concrete floor, walked up to the cell bars, and started unzipping his jeans. Being new to the system, Gopal did not know what was coming. So, he just stood there, confused. This was a mistake. Schultz pulled out his penis, aimed it at Gopal's face, and soaked it with a torrent of urine while spitting disdain, "Go fuck yourself."

Gopal retreated quickly from Schultz's unique brand of welcome, but it was not enough to save his pride.

A guard standing nearby commented rather casually, "We get this treatment all the time. Pay no attention."

Gopal heard the comment, yet did not hear it. The interview was over and there was no need for any tests, not under the circumstances. Then he rushed to a nearby bathroom to clean himself.

He stood in front of the sink but could not even turn on the faucet. He was shaking with humiliation and anger and needed to sit down. He stumbled into a toilet stall and slumped on a seat.

Gopal did not see the urine shower from Schultz as just an act of defiance, he saw it as an expression of hate so intense that it could set the world on fire, as an act of war. Could it lead to another world war? Was he exaggerating the whole thing, being a bit dramatic? No, he did not think so. All major wars in the past had started with trivial incidents, which harbored delusions of grandeur of immense proportions. Even if it did not involve countries and massive armies, a man-made disaster was about to take place. Many lives could be consumed, even of those who just stood and watched, including his own. He had not thought that he would ever be selected for sacrifice at the altar of racial hatred. He felt like everything around him was falling apart.

All of a sudden, another part of his brain intervened. Maybe nothing was falling apart. Maybe he was overreacting and nothing was going to happen to him. Maybe the prison would be able to diffuse the Schultz threat, after all Gopal wasn't the only one; three administrators had also been threatened. Maybe Schultz would die, someone would just stab him, shoot him, strangle him. Or, maybe the state would hurry up and execute him. Maybe even he could do something to expedite Schultz's demise. No idea came to his mind at the time. Maybe later.

He consoled himself; the whole thing was unreal, and it could not affect him in any meaningful way. He didn't need to be afraid.

Yet, there was a flutter in his heart, the kind he felt when in a dream, finding himself falling from the sky, about to crash on the ground. He never did crash, woke up before meeting the ground, but his heart continued to pound long after that.

He was afraid again. All his consoling thoughts evaporated. His fantasy bubble did not float for long, it burst quickly. Who was he kidding? The administrators would be trying to save their own skins, they couldn't care less about him. The execution could only be delayed, not expedited. And, who would go up against Schultz to eliminate him? He himself? That would be a laugh. He was not a fighter. He might use a weapon in self defense, but that would be the extent of his heroism.

He was now more dejected than before, and quite sure that he was going to die. This was a hell of a day and the next one would be a hell of a day too. And so would be the next, and the next, and the next, continuously, until he was killed. He must do something about it. But, what?

Escape? Go to another part of the country where no one knew him, and find another job? Immediately he canceled the idea, if the AVs wanted him they would find him anywhere in the US. He must to go back to India, AVs won't go there. He would save his skin and make Satya happy. For the first time he realized that money and material things were not that important. He had been stuck to them like crazy glue. He needed to take a lesson from his scriptures which taught not to obsess about material things, otherwise there would be nothing but frustration, dissatisfaction, worry, unhappiness, pain, and suffering of all kinds.

The finality of this decision was somehow dispiriting. All endings are. It also heralded defeat. So what? He never was a fighter. Escape could not be a dirty word if it assured safety. To make it sound nicer he would just call it 'strategic retreat'. They did that all the time on the battlefields.

His mind was churning, trying to decide what needed to be done for this retreat.

He must quit his job right away, give his two-week notice. He would have liked to quit immediately, but there was no sense in it since it would take him at least several weeks to manage his affairs before leaving for India.

He should also sell his house, cars, furniture, jewelry, books, clothing etc. Well, he could take small but expensive things like jewelry and cameras with him, and sell the rest cheaply or give it away. The house would have to be sold; it couldn't be given away because of the huge amount of money invested in it. And it would take some time, at least a few weeks, if not months. But he didn't have to be in the US for that, a real estate company could handle the sale.

And he needed to make flight reservations to India. He should be able to secure seats right away by paying premium prices for the tickets.

So, he told himself, 'Go back home, tell Satya the whole story, and start packing suitcases. Of course, also do all the other things that need to be done.'

Still, there was this nagging realization that even while preparing to leave he could get killed. What to do to protect himself and his wife until they were safely on the Indian soil?

Call the police? On what basis? Just suppositions?

Hire private body guards? Could be very expensive. And finding the right ones would take considerable time.

He needed to calm down, not assume that assault from Schultz was imminent and immediate. Deal with it rationally and realistically, if and when it came. In the mean time, do all that he needed to do for escape to India.

Still, the possibility existed that he could get killed before that happened. The fear just would not leave Gopal.

He must increase the value of his life insurance policy from the present half million to a million and add a double indemnity clause, to give Satya at least financial security. Once they were in India, the policy would be allowed to lapse. He must call his insurance agent, add that to the list of things to do right away.

Of all the things on his list to do, talking to Satya about all this was the most difficult task. How would she take it? Would she panic? Fear of an impending disaster could do more damage than the disaster itself. But she had to be told. How else was she going to assist him in his move to India and how else was she going to prepare herself for widowhood, if it came? He decided to do what he would have told any of his clients to do under similar circumstances; tell Satya about the Schultz threat in a matter-of-fact way and explain to her the logic behind his decision to move to India, and to increase the life insurance amount. If she were to exhibit psychological trauma he would decide then what to do. Most likely she would take the whole thing in stride. She might even be pleased at the prospect of going home, after all she did not want to come to America in the first place.

Having made the decisions, Gopal felt more in control of his life and his heart calmed down. He got up from the toilet seat, went to the sink, removed his tie and jacket stained with urine. His shirt was also a little tainted but there was nothing he could do about it. If washed he would be wearing a wet and wrinkled shirt and making himself look ridiculous. Just wear the shirt the way it was, no one would detect urine if he maintained a distance from them. He cleaned his face, neck, and hands as best as he could with soap and water. Then he folded his jacket inside out, hung it on his arm after taking off his tie and putting it in one of its pockets, and walked briskly toward his office. There was determination in his steps although some uneasiness lingered in his heart. He was sure that everyone in the prison knew about his urine bath. To save his dignity, he avoided glances and ignored greetings from everyone.

As soon as he got to his office he picked up his brief case and left right away. He was going home. All the tasks he had assigned himself could be done from there. To hell with this place.

When he got home, he wanted to go to the bathroom immediately, but could not. Satya was right there in front of him with a film of anxiousness covering her face. "I heard the door," she said, then asked, "Something wrong? What happened?"

Gopal answered in a voice heavily weighted down with shame and humiliation, "Yes, something happened. But first I need to take a shower."

He walked past Satya straight to the bathroom, took off his clothes, put the suit and tie away to be sent to the cleaners, and discarded the rest in the laundry bin.

In the shower he soaped and cleaned himself and repeated the process several times, but could not wash away the insult and abuse. Finally, he gave up.

When he emerged in the living room in his bathrobe, he found Satya waiting for him with freshly brewed tea, worry lines still visible on her forehead. Gopal sat beside her on the couch and, in between the sips of the tea, told her everything that had happened to him that day. At the end of the story, he asked, "So, what do you think about my decision?"

Satya answered with a question of her own, "You sure you want to go to India? Of course, it would be great, but I also know how much you want to work here."

"Yes, I do want to go, and I have already told you why. ... Now I think I better take care of my prison related tasks. You could help me with the other things."

"I'll make the calls right away," Satya assured him.

He got up and walked into his den.

Gopal sat at his desk and started with his letter of resignation. The main body of the text read, *"Due to some personal reasons I have decided to resign my position. Please treat this letter as my two-week notice."* He put the letter in an envelope and addressed it to 'The Administrator, Health Unit'. He would hand deliver it the next day.

Then he wrote his psychiatric report on Schultz. In the absence of a real clinical interview and psychological tests, it was hard for him to diagnose the subject. However, what he had gathered from the PIR told him that the subject was not mentally ill. He just had antisocial tendencies, expressed selectively toward those he did not like. With his family members, close friends, and other AVs his behavior was quite normal. Gopal wrote his report which, in essence, said, *"The inmate refused to cooperate and urinated all over me. He appears hostile toward authority and exhibits antisocial behavior."* The report would be delivered to Martinez the next day but not by him. He would give it to the secretary for copying, filing after creating a file since Schultz did not have one in the Health Unit, and sending the original to Martinez. The report certainly did not conform to Martinez's dictates but, at this stage, Gopal couldn't care less.

When he came out of the den, he found Satya ready to talk to him. They sat down in the living room couch, side by side.

"You know, I thought I would be happy to make those calls. They meant we were going home. But, I wasn't happy. Actually, I was depressed."

"I was too. After all we are losing our home. ... Anyway, so what did you get done?"

"I contacted our real estate agent. He promised to list our house by the end of this week and get it sold as soon as possible. After that I called our life insurance agent. This was a very difficult thing to do, asking him to increase the value of your life insurance policy to one million and add a double indemnity clause. It was like I was planning your death for my own benefit." At this point she started to cry.

Gopal wiped her tears and consoled her, "It is just good planning. No need to be emotional about it."

"I know, still..."

"Okay, so what else?" Gopal did not want to dwell on the depressing topic much longer.

Satya spoke in a subdued tone, "The agent said that he would have to get the okay from his head office although he did not see any problem, and that he would call us as soon as he got the approval."

"Good, so everything is taken care of."

"In a way. ... I also called our travel agent."

"Isn't that a bit premature?"

"Maybe. But, we can always change our dates."

"What dates did you give him?"

"No dates. I just asked him to issue two tickets, one way, to New Delhi, unless we saved some money by buying round trip tickets. I told him to keep the dates open."

"Good move. Anything else?"

"Well, I had also thought of calling the local newspaper and putting in an ad for an estate sale, but canceled the idea. I thought we should wait until we knew our departure date."

"You certainly got a lot done."

"Yeah."

The 'yeah' was so sad that it cast a curtain of gloom over Gopal. He said rather dejectedly, "It seems like the end of our journey without reaching the destination."

He got up slowly, like he had a heavy weight on his back and dragged his feet toward the back porch. Satya followed automatically.

They sat silently on a concrete bench, watching the empty sky. For Gopal the whole experience was draining and anticlimactic. He had put so much into building a home, and it was destroyed by the vileness of one angry man. He was sure Satya felt the same way.

He also felt like a coward for securing safety through escape. Still, he tried to put a positive spin on it and saw his whole life ahead of him with the prospect of climbing many mountains, crossing many deserts, exploring many skies, and fathoming many oceans. All this with Satya beside him.

At this time he was willing to let Schultz have a technical victory. He didn't care.

Yet, there were dry tears and silent cries.

CHAPTER SEVEN

COMDER WAS A PARROT

WITHIN A FEW hours after Schultz was locked up in his cell, everyone in the prison was talking about his threat. Some staff, not familiar with the AV operations, pretty much dismissed it, calling it ranting and raving. Others took it seriously. Certainly the program review board members did. So did the inmates. The AV inmates went even one step further. They took it as an order for action. One of them, Samuel Haney, decided to inform the AV officers about it. This he had to do, just in case the others failed in their duty.

But Haney was more than just a postman.

* * *

He was many things in different places and at different times.

One, he was a 'Little Darling'.

An only child, he had the dual responsibility of continuing the family and being a torch bearer of family values. He was married but there were no children to continue the family, not yet. But family values were his life, ingrained in him, since he was a baby, by his father, a Protestant preacher of an all white congregation. The core of his family values was 'The Covenant', that God had promised this earth to the whites to rule, and had allowed them to do anything, anything at all, to further this cause.

Two, he was a 'Mad Scientist'.

Ever since he started to walk and talk, he was breaking things and trying to put them together. His father saw this scientific experimentation as messing with God's creation, and did not like it. His mother, however, saw it as quite consistent with the covenant. She explained, "Science gives us the tools we need to rule the world. That's why all scientists are white." The family knew for sure that all nonwhites who posed as scientist were liars. As a grown man, Haney studied molecular physics to secure knowledge and skills essential to build sophisticated bombs. What for? He didn't know, but there must be some good use for them. There were times when he thought that if there were no coloreds, there would not be a need for the covenant and no cause for racial conflict. Did he want to use bombs to solve the problem which God should have not created to begin with? No, no, he could not kill anyone, not in his character. Still, building bombs, or at least thinking about building bombs, fascinated him. His father also thought that maybe his son's attraction for explosive devices had something to do with his desire to get rid of the coloreds. If that was so, it was not a good idea since coloreds were needed for service tasks. Still, it was all right if his son wanted to do it. Even though Haney had not built any bombs, while in college everyone knew about his intentions, which earned him his nickname, 'Mad Scientist.' Later, building bombs by manipulation of molecules became his main hobby. He knew he did not have the equipment, money, and space for the kind of experiments that were needed, but he still messed around with his theories and conducted some crude tests in his garage.

Three, he was an 'AV Poster Boy'.

Because of his high intelligence and education, Haney attracted attention of one of his father's parishioners who was an AV member and wanted the membership to go beyond uneducated blue collar workers. When Haney was in his late teens this parishioner approached him and suggested that he become an AV member because, as he put it, "The group needs smart young men like you to realize the terms of The Covenant." His ego inflated and his life's ideal championed, Haney became an AV member, one who stood above all others. Working for the AV cause became his life's mission, something no one outside the AV organization knew. He was well respected and even revered by other AVs and was always consulted by the AV leadership before making any major decisions.

Four, he was a 'Family Man'.

Becoming part of the AV organization brought him another reward, a wife, one he could have not found anywhere else. Sure, in his college years he had dated many girls but did not consider marrying any of them. He could tell from the way they talked that they did not share his ideas about The Covenant. It would be a hell of a life with someone who did not subscribe to his philosophy. Then he met Emily in the AV headquarters. She worked there as a secretary. That meant she was devoted to the AV cause. And she was single.

Haney found her very pretty, with smiling pursed lips and expressive eyes. And very bright. She was the only one in the whole organization who could understand him if he inadvertently happened to use a technical or scientific term or phrase.

In the beginning he just watched her. Then one day it occurred to him that she would make a perfect wife. That was enough for him to go to her and ask her to marry him. No dates, no engagement, no formalities. And she just looked at him with comprehension and said, "Yes." Later, after they were married, she told him that she had been watching him eyeing her and knew that it was just a matter of time before he would approach her with a proposal, and she had been ready to accept it.

His life with Emily was very comfortable because, he felt, they were compatible in thought and action. She was his right hand in the truest sense of the term.

Five, he was a 'Soldier'.

In a way. After his marriage, Haney got more involved with the AVs. Knowing the nature of the AV operations he was sure that there would be armed conflicts and he wanted to be prepared for them. Also, he wanted the AVs to have the kind of knowledge and expertise they needed in fighting their opponents that would give them an edge. So, he studied military warfare and became something of an expert in it. Then he started advising both the leadership and membership about offensive and defensive strategies in conflicts with the government or other groups antagonistic to them, and about effective ways of carrying on their crusade. He even delved into the production, storage, and use of weapons.

Six, he was a 'Professor.'

After earning his doctorate in molecular physics, he got a teaching position in a university and became a professor. He was a brilliant researcher and published several scholarly articles in respected scientific journals. Also a knowledgeable teacher, he was well respected by the academic community. He loved his profession. At the university, and even in the community, he maintained a typical persona of a high brow intellectual. He was always well groomed and conservatively dressed. A briefcase filled with papers, magazines, and books was always part of him, and he moved, almost always, in the company of other professors and students. His vacations were invariably in tandem with professional conferences. He was often seen reading and writing. Sometimes he would throw a party to which only his colleagues were invited. He was friendly with his neighbors but did not socialize with them. Even though six feet tall and quite muscular, he was mild mannered and looked harmless. Often people thought of him as one of liberal bent. No one knew about his double life except the AVs, his parents, and his wife.

Seven, he was a 'White Snot.'

He got this nickname in the prison, given to him by the coloreds, probably because he was white and snotty towards them. Prison! Haney never thought he would ever be arrested for anything, what with his being a respected professor and all that. He got careless with his bomb experiments, and one day his garage blew up. No one was hurt, but the fire and smoke prompted neighbors to rush to their phones and call 911. Haney knew he would be arrested and prosecuted, but didn't want his wife to suffer his fate. So, before there was any response from the fire and police departments, he instructed Emily, "Keep silent.

You didn't know anything about it. You need to stay free to carry on the AV mission." It worked. While the fire fighters extinguished the flames, the police arrested Haney and left Emily alone. The explosion was suspicious enough for the police to get a search warrant for his house. Not only explosives but also firearms were found, all unlawful. Plus, there was evidence of his and Emily's AV connection, such as names, addresses, and phone numbers of known AVs, the record of phone calls made to many of them on a regular basis, and the AV literature. This, however, was not illegal and was ignored. Haney pleaded 'not guilty' on the grounds that it was his hobby to collect guns and just professional inquisitiveness to experiment with explosives. No one believed him. Still, he got only five years, partly because the prosecution could not prove any harmful intent and partly because he had no prior record. The nature of his crime and sentence qualified him for minimum custody. Within days he got his nickname and found it amusing rather than insulting. Being incarcerated ended his double life, because now everyone knew what he really was, an AV. All other aspects of his personality were seen as secondary, or even camouflage. So, he openly started promoting the AV cause in the prison. He would even carry out the AV activities by circumventing and defying those prison rules which were designed to thwart them. Consequently, he was able to bring many inmates into the AV fold. And, he became the major communication link between the AVs in the prison and outside. This worried the prison authorities and they tried to strangle his postman role by scrutinizing all his conversations, face-to-face, written, or telephonic, and ending them whenever it appeared he was delivering or receiving information regarding AV activities. The efforts were largely unsuccessful, because Haney disguised his content in such linguistic jargon, symbolic phraseology, and deceptive stories that it was beyond the comprehension of the guards watching him. Out of frustration, his calls and visits would be interrupted, and letters confiscated. The prison finally realized that this would end only when Haney was released, and, ironically, wished for it to happen soon. It seemed like the wish would be fulfilled. Haney was not a trouble maker, not really, not like killing someone or plotting escape. He was accumulating time credits for good behavior and was destined to complete his sentence in a little over two years. From the day Schultz issued his threats, Haney, the 'white snot', had only a few months to go.

* * *

Haney called his wife on the phone, collect, a privilege minimum custody inmates had. Knowing that his conversation would be monitored by the prison communication center, he made it sound like a normal, innocuous, family chat.

"Hi, sweetie, how's going?"

"Hanging in there. And you?"

"Waiting to come home. In the meantime, keeping busy anyway I can. So, I started something new, writing children's stories. They are fun, short, and easy to write. I wrote my first story just yesterday. Wanna hear it?" This was his way of camouflaging the intent of his communication, hoping that Emily would be able to decipher it.

"Sure."

"Here goes. Comder was a parrot. He lived in a rain forest with other parrots. One day he left his forest to see what was outside. He found a village. There was a mango orchard. The fruits were ripe and inviting. He went to peck on one. It was sweet. He had not noticed a man named Wardo sitting under the tree, sleeping, with his back resting against the base of the trunk. Wardo was awakened by the noise made by Comder with his chirping and fluttering of wings. He did not like his fruits being eaten by a parrot. He threw a big net and caught Comder in it and then he put him in a bamboo cage. Comder was very unhappy and angry. He was not used to confinement. So, every time Wardo came near him to put food and water in his cage, he would poop on him. He would also stir the water and the bird seed furiously with his beak and claws, and let them hit Wardo. That made Wardo very angry. Now both were angry at each other. Wardo decided to punish the naughty bird by putting his cage in a remote corner of a dark room. That made Comder more angry. He would constantly chirp and flap his wings loudly in the hope of attracting the attention of some other parrots or birds flying by. A week passed. Then his efforts paid off. His friend Profy, who had been searching for him far and wide ever since his disappearance from the rain forest, happened to fly to the place where Comder was captive. Profy heard the parrot noises coming from the dark room and recognized them to be those of Comder's. He also knew what they meant, 'Get Wardo, and get me out of here.' Profy flew back to the rain forest and told other parrots about Comder's misfortune. They all decided to follow Comder's orders. They got together, thousands of them. They flew in army formation toward Wardo's home. They found him resting in his courtyard. Together they attacked him and also his family. They pecked at and clawed those people and bloodied them from head to toe. Within a few minutes all the wounded died of their injuries. Then the parrots found the cage in which Comder was imprisoned. They attacked the cage and tore it apart. Comder was freed. He thanked Profy and his army. All of them flew back to the rain forest. They lived happily ever after."

After a pause, he asked, "What do you think?"

"It sucks. As a children's story, it really sucks." Haney noticed that the answer was quick and given without hesitation. What did it mean? That the writing was really bad. In that case Emily was focusing on literary quality and his communication had failed. Or, maybe it meant, 'I got it, but to keep the prison from getting it too, let's just pretend that it's a piece of literature.' That's what he wanted, that's what he hoped, and that's what he assumed it was. So, he continued the pretend game.

"It sucks, how?"

"It has too many big words, the sentences are long, complicated, and poorly organized. The story is totally implausible. Who would believe that parrots can kill humans and destroy a bamboo cage, just with their beaks and claws? There's also too much violence. Besides, it's not original. It reminds me of Hitchcock's movie 'The Birds'. You are a writer of professional articles. I expected something better."

"But this is my first draft," Haney said defensively. "All right, I agree, it's bad writing. But, what do you think of the content, the story?" He had to direct Emily's attention to the import of the story, just in case she had missed it, just in case.

"I don't know. I'll think about it and give you my thoughts next time you call me."

"Okay. Now, be good."

"You, too."

"I have to. Don't want to end up in solitary like Schultz."

Immediately the line went dead.

In a few minutes a guard came over to Haney, accusing, "What do you think you are doing?'

"Talking to my wife. Why was I cut off?"

"For talking about Schultz."

"I wasn't talking about Schultz. I was talking about not going to the dungeon."

"Oh yeah? Like we don't understand. ... Your telephone privileges are suspended for a month."

"That's not fair."

"You misuse the phone, you don't get to use it."

"I protest. I didn't do anything wrong."

The guard just walked away without responding.

Haney had to insist that he was innocent and had to express his disapproval of prison rules. Not because he thought he was innocent or the prison rules were wrong. Simply because this was what one did in the prison, always.

And he knew, the prison held the opposite view, the inmates were guilty and the prison was right, always.

Haney was sure that his wife would know that Comder was George , the Commander, Wardo was Karcher, the Warden, and Profy was he himself, the professor, and she would be able to take the message to the AV bigwigs. Within a moment it occurred to him that if Emily got the meaning the prison would get it too. He dissipated his concern quickly, 'No, they couldn't. They were too stupid to understand any dialogue which contained words with more than two syllables.' Of course, it was his disdain for the prison talking, and he knew it. All prison officials were not that stupid and, after going over the tape of his conversation with Emily, some of them would surely get the purpose of his 'children's story'. So what if they did? George's command was open and known to everyone. It was open warfare now anyway.

At that point Haney felt like a fool. Of course, he had already reasoned as to why he should communicate to Emily, something already known to everyone. But he had a hard time figuring out the reason for his use of such a transparent disguise as a clumsy children's story to do it. In the end he found one; in the prison everyone automatically tried to hide true meaning of everything they did or said, whether or not it was necessary. Besides, at the time it seemed like a perfect avenue of cryptic communication. Besides still, it was a fun thing to do.

So now Haney was confident, Emily would let the staff in the AV office know about the Schultz order when she went to work there and, in no time, the message would reach the acting Regional Commander, Stewart Goodwin. After that the cannons would boom.

This was all speculation, of course. Haney did not know the specific purpose of Schultz's declaration of war because it was never spelled out, and he had no clue about what the AV leadership would actually do.

But he felt justified in what he had done. He saw himself in the battleground where he had to act on his own judgment at the spur of the moment, without waiting for instructions from his superiors.

Like a good little soldier.

CHAPTER EIGHT

FOUR MUSKETEERS

Stewart Goodwin was the acting AV Regional Commander. It was his responsibility to carry out Schultz's orders. After getting the message from his reliable sources, he pondered over his course of action. The task seemed to be too big, too difficult, and too dangerous for him to tackle alone or even in conjunction with someone else. So he decided to delegate the responsibility. That's what the leaders did, didn't they? He moved on to put together an action team consisting of people better equipped for the challenge.

Even though he would be involved in the operations only peripherally, he would still be doing some thing important, supervising and directing.

He was proud of what he was doing. Not carpentry, which he did freelance for a number of builders. It was his unceasing, untiring struggle to make the white race the most dominant and intimidating power in the world. Where did he get the motivation for it? Even he himself did not know. Maybe it came from the socio-environmental forces around him over which he had no control.

***

The forces!

First was his mother. The mother who had put him up for adoption after birth. She had just left him in the hospital and walked out. Her reasoning: she had become pregnant as a result of a rape, didn't believe in abortion, but could not financially care for the child. Goodwin didn't understand the reasoning. What's the difference between discarding the child from within the womb and discarding him after he was out of the womb? He never forgave his mother for abandoning him. It would have been better if she had aborted him, at least he would not be in this world wondering about his abandonment. He felt worthless.

He was born addicted to cocaine. This was the second force. The doctors figured the mother used the drug during pregnancy. It took them several days to detoxify him. The drug must have damaged him in some significant way, because his physical development was retarded. He looked sickly and unattractive. There was some question about his mental abilities also, but no one was certain.

A third force became operational when the Catholic church took him and placed him in an orphanage. His physical health began to improve, and in a few years he was a robust kid, not big and overpowering, but energetic and strong. Not his mind though. Not really retarded but close to it. On top of that, he had developed some mental health issues, anger and bitterness. Symptoms of low self-esteem also began to emerge. One critical symptom was that he never felt he could do anything. Whenever the nuns gave him an assignment, his usual response was, "I can't do it. Don't know how." The church thought his mental health might improve in a regular home and tried to find one for him. But no one wanted him, a boy who was sickly and addicted to cocaine in the past, and who was angry and self-deprecating in the present. A feeling of rejection was added to his mental health woes. And he was only five at the time.

In a few years he encountered the fourth force. He was being raised as a Catholic. He could not tell the difference between Catholicism and other religions, but that was not the point. The point was that he was expected to do the things and live a lifestyle he could not relate to: constant prayers, respect for the nuns and priests, wearing of uniforms, doing chores around the orphanage, receiving beatings for any infraction of rules. He wanted to be like other kids in the community. Like them he wanted to play, run around, do mischief, go to public school, wear jeans and T-shirts, study all kinds of subjects without a dose of religion, and yes, get punished sometimes, but only in the form of scoldings and detentions. He became hateful toward authority.

The fifth force hit him when he was about 16. By that time he was living in a dormitory within the church compound. A priest told him that the church wanted to prepare him to go to Africa and help the priests there in conversion of the natives to Catholicism. This meant several years devoted to learning about the people of Africa and methods of approaching them, and finally learning all the tricks used to convert them. He knew little about Africa and asked, "Why Africa?" The answer came quickly as if rehearsed, "They are poor and uncivilized. They practice wrong religions. We have an obligation to save their souls." The answer did not satisfy him. Why waste time and effort working with such worthless people? Besides, he did not think he could do the job even if he wanted to. The task seemed to be too big, hard, and complicated to him. He began to feel rebellious.

By the time he was at the threshold of adulthood, he felt he had to do something other than what was dictated to him day in and day out.

He wanted to get away from the church and from everything it represented. It would have been easy to do, the church gates were open during the daytime, and there was no strict watch over anyone. Surviving on his own, however, did not seem to be easy. He could think of nothing but stealing and begging to support himself, and he was not sure of his competency in either. He had tried it in the past and failed. The memory of that fiasco was still vivid in his mind. He had stolen a ham sandwich, a piece of cherry pie, and a loaf of bread from the kitchen and had taken off. In one day, all his food had been consumed. At night, he had ended up in a city park to sleep. It was cold and he had nothing to warm him. The next day, cold, hungry and tired, he had tried to beg, unsuccessfully, in the parking lot of a supermarket. His white cotton shirt, blue tie, khaki shorts, white socks, and black shoes had gotten in the way. He had no idea how to steal. While he had been trying to find a way to survive the next hour, let alone the rest of his life, he had been spotted by the police. When the police had threatened him with jail, he had admitted to what he had done. He had been brought back to the church. As an adult, however, he felt more confident but still not confident enough to actually leave the church premises.

He was kicked out instead. After he refused to go to the dark continent for the cause of spreading Christianity, the church felt betrayed. On his 18th birthday he was told that as an adult he was on his own. Was that the sixth factor shaping his life? He did not know. However, being forced out into freedom turned out to be a blessing in disguise.

With a little money he was given by the church, he rented a room in a rundown hotel for the discards of society, and talked to other tenants about ways of making a living. He got a lot of advice, as diverse as getting a college degree and becoming a gigolo. Some even told him to fuck himself. The easiest and most practical advice he got from some people was to get hitched to a builder and get some on the job training. In the beginning, he would make survival wages, and hoped that later he might become prosperous, depending upon his knowledge, skill, motivation, and hard work.

He followed the advice and became a carpenter.

It was on a work site that he was initiated into the AV organization. One of the fellow carpenters was a member, who told him about it and its philosophy and asked him to become a brother. The philosophy seemed to be the philosophy of kick-ass empowerment. Goodwin liked it, a lot more than he ever liked the Catholic philosophy. It was like a sumptuous meal for the hungry. All his life, his self worth had stunk like a sewer, suddenly it smelled like roses, all because he happened to be white. He did not hesitate even for a moment to answer "yes". A month later he was one of them.

Within the next few years he got married to the widow of a coworker who was a mason and got killed accidentally when a scaffolding he was on collapsed. And in a couple of more years, he became the father of a boy and a girl. Having become a member of the American middle class he felt elevated, important. Along the way, his low self-concept began to dissipate, at least he did not feel worthless.

A few years later he had an opportunity to hear George Schultz at the AV national convention. The 'We Bleed White' speech really stirred him. He became Schultz's disciple, not in any formal way, just in his mind. He even settled in a city where Schultz lived. Moving was easy for him with his carpentry skills, because construction activity was everywhere. He made sure to make himself available for any operation Schultz was involved in, and excelled in his tasks.

And then he became Schultz's heir apparent. This was how.

One day one of their commanders, Jeff Borchert, walked into the AV office with a scream for help, the kind of scream that did a fire dance on his forehead without any sound. Goodwin was roaming around, having had no job that day. Borchert spoke with suppressed fury, "A nigger family has moved into my Lake Shore development and a Filipino is signing papers as we speak. It will ruin me. I'll lose all my white customers."

Goodwin took a few friendly steps toward him, put his right hand on his left shoulder, and said, "Don't worry. We can scare them off."

"Yeah, then some others will come. I don't want them even thinking of living in my housing project. And, I can't say 'no' cause of these stupid federal laws, you know that equal opportunity housing crap."

"We can fix that too."

Borchert relaxed, "You can?"

"I can't, but we can, you and I and other brothers together, I think. Give me a couple of days and I will come up with something. I will have to run it by Schultz, though, before doing anything, you know."

"I was hoping to find him here. That's why I came."

"Well, he is not around. I will be happy to handle it, if that's okay with you."

"Sure, I just want this problem solved."

"All right. ... Now tell me about the family. How many are there, their ages and whether they are male or female."

"There are five of them, husband and wife in mid-forties, three kids, one girl about 10 and two boys a few years older than her."

"All right. I'll call you."

Goodwin came up with an idea even before the day was over. He called Schultz, told him about Borchert's predicament, and requested to meet with him to discuss his idea about how to solve it, because talking about it on the phone was not safe.

Schultz agreed to meet, but only for five minutes, saying that he was too busy with other more important matters.

They met in a bar, and Goodwin laid out his plan, "Kill the bastards, burn their house down, and spray paint the driveway with words, 'Niggers and such not allowed here', to put fear in the hearts of any nonwhites even contemplating buying a property in Borchert's development."

Schultz quickly approved it, provided Goodwin was willing to take the responsibility of carrying it out.

This was the first time Goodwin was made leader of a project, and by Schultz, no less. His mind was dizzy with excitement.

Right after Schultz left, Goodwin thought it important to talk to Borchert right away. It was a little after 9 according to his watch, late enough for Borchert to be home. He called him from a pay phone and said, "I'm at The Graveyard. Come here right away. I have good news for you." He figured it was not too late for anyone to leave home and go to a bar.

Once seated face-to-face in a booth, Goodwin first gave the good news of Schultz's approval of his plan, then gave a summary of it." He though Borchert would be ecstatic at his brilliant idea.

He was wrong.

"You crazy?" Borchert expressed his disappointment. "We could get killed ourselves or end up in prison."

"No, no, no. If done right, no one will even suspect us. Police will, of course, accuse some innocent slob of the crime and convict him to look good in the public's eye."

"Done right? How can something like what you are suggesting be done right?"

"Leave it to me. ... Just give me the key to the house. You must have one, right?"

"Yeah, unless the owners changed the locks."

"Go there when someone is home. Tell them that you need to check the locks, cause there have been complaints of keys sticking in some units. At that point, ask them if they have changed the locks. Most likely they have not, most people don't. So, If the locks have not been changed, use your own key to pretend-check its function. If they have been, ask them to loan you their key for a minute and develop a sudden need to use their bathroom. Once alone, get an impression made of the key on chewed up gum. ... carry some chewed up gum. After that, pretend-check its function and give it back to the owners."

"Then what?"

"You give me the key to the house or an impression of it and I will take it from there. By the way, do you think the house is alarmed? We need to be prepared for that, if it is."

"No, it's not. It is not an upscale neighborhood, you know that. Just lower middle class people who can't afford an alarm system."

Of course not. Even Goodwin's house did not have an alarm system.

"That makes our job easier. ... From this point on you know nothing about the project. Since this shit is gonna fly in your housing project, you will be scrutinized. Therefore, you shouldn't be involved in the operation. Safer that way. But, you will owe us one when the job is done."

"Oh, if the job is done I'll owe you big time. Anything, I'll do anything. Just ask."

Goodwin got the key the next day. It was the original key as he had guessed it would be.

A day's mulling over the problem yielded a plan, sort of. It required three men besides himself. The ones chosen by him had the attributes he considered important for his operation; intelligence, bravery, and devotion to the cause. Plus they had the experience of working with Schultz, at least once. They were Wade Searle, a software engineer, Chris Huddy, a geophysicist, and Herman Daboob, a personnel director. The very qualities for which Goodwin had chosen his men, and their highbrow professions, intimidated him. So, he called each one individually, and hesitatingly gave essentially the same pitch, something like, 'I am Stewart Goodwin. I have not had pleasure of working with you, but I have worked with Mr. Schultz, and you might know my name.'

Each one confirmed that he was familiar with his name and asked the purpose of his call.

He intimated in words like, 'One of our brothers, Jeff Borchert, is in trouble and needs help. I have a plan but it needs several people. So, I am calling you for help. Could you please meet me at The Graveyard tonight at eight to discuss my plan.'

Everyone agreed, agreed at least to meet and discuss the project.

Goodwin positioned himself near the cash register to greet each arrival. He had not met any one of them, but had seen their photos and was sure to recognize them.

The first one to arrive was Huddy, a tall, around six-four, athletic man with an oblong face and unruly hair. Although dressed casually, he looked imposing, a bit ferocious, certainly not like one pursuing his kind of profession. Goodwin got him a Bud, Huddy's choosing, and engaged in small talk while waiting for the others. Next came Searle, a big man, six feet tall, about 250 pounds, displaying bushy eyebrows and a severe facial expression, but looking very professional in a three-piece suit. Goodwin greeted him also cordially, and offered a beer. Searle chose Heineken and got into the small talk already in progress. Within a couple of minutes showed up Daboob, comparatively short statured at five-eight but with bulging muscles and big body mass, dressed incongruously in a white shirt, striped blue-brown tie, dark navy blue slacks, and black shoes. He opted for a Miller.

Goodwin ended the small talk abruptly and suggested, "Shall we?" Everyone got ready to follow him. He led them to a secluded round table in a corner, away from the chatter of the crowd gathered in the main lounge or around the two pool tables. Once everyone was settled around the table, somewhat stiffly, he said, "I feel privileged to meet you. I am a lowly carpenter by trade and find myself humbled in your presence."

Huddy leaned forward and asked pointedly, "Okay, so what did he do?"

Goodwin was taken aback by the question. He had not thought that 'Jeff Borchert is in trouble' would be taken to mean that he did something that got him in trouble of some kind. An explanation was needed. He offered that, along with his idea of what needed to be accomplished to prevent any future movement of the colored population into the white neighborhood. He also informed the group that he had the key to the house. All three visibly relaxed.

Searle asked then, "So, what's the plan?"

"I have one, preliminary. I hope you like it. I have cleared it with Mr. Schultz." The last sentence was meant to communicate that the plan was final and no one should look for any flaws in it.

"Let's hear it," chimed in Daboob who had been pretty silent all this time.

All eyes were focused on Goodwin, expectantly.

Goodwin gave a summary of his plan, "We go there, eliminate everyone in the family, and leave a message for other coloreds to stay away." A moment later he added, "Details will be worked out. We will change things as the circumstances require, but the main body of the plan will remain intact."

Searle was quick to approve the plan, "Brilliant. This is actually exciting. We have all done many daring things, some of them with Schultz, but nothing like this. Eliminate five blacks in one attack and secure a neighborhood for the whites forever. Big job, big pay off. ... What do you guys think?"

Huddy was not so enthusiastic, but he too gave a subdued approval, "It's certainly a major project, dangerous too. But, for the sake of our brother Jeff and our cause, I am in."

Daboob joined the company, "Sure, let's do it. We need to further our cause whenever we have a chance."

They agreed to carry it out four days later on a Tuesday, thinking that on a weekday there would not be any parties or teenagers making out in the cars in the neighborhood and they would have a smoother ride, so to say.

But, Huddy had a concern, "Being absent from our homes precisely at the time of our adventure could draw attention to us. Even our families could become suspicious of us."

Once more Goodwin had an answer, "Tell your families that we will be male bonding in the wilderness for four days, Saturday through Tuesday, and be back home Wednesday. Let's actually do it for show, except on Tuesday night when we'll do our planned thing. Use the same reason to get leave of absence from work. Include Wednesday in your leave request. I don't think we will be in any shape to go back to work that day. We all have some vacation time coming. Right?"

"That should work," confirmed Daboob and others shook their heads in agreement.

Goodwin had, de facto, become the leader, and his inferiority complex had gone down considerably. He brought the discussion to a close, if not the meeting itself, by saying more authoritatively, "Let's meet in the AV garage next Saturday morning at seven. Is that okay?"

"Yeah, I think so," said Daboob. Everyone agreed by not saying anything.

Goodwin then directed more firmly, "Bring with you wilderness survival gear. I will reserve a car ahead of time along with other needed equipment and arms for our adventure. But, we will travel in my car together to wherever you guys want to go for some fun and relaxation."

"We can decide where to go and what to do on Saturday," suggested Daboob.

That settled, everyone finished his drink amidst light talk about baseball and went home.

Saturday morning they all gathered at the appointed place and within ten minutes of the agreed upon time. Goodwin pointed to his car and said, "Let's load our gear."

For four days they had a mini vacation. Everyone did whatever he pleased but mostly they hunted, fished, cooked, cleaned, and badmouthed the government and the coloreds. No one talked about the project for which this mini vacation was a prelude. Tuesday evening they drove back into the city and stopped at the repair area of the AV garage.

Goodwin went into the back yard and brought out the car he had reserved. It had a totally beat up body, torn up interior, and broken instrument panel.

Huddy looked at it with raised eye brows and said, "We are traveling in this?"

Goodwin calmed his fear, and probably everyone else's, by saying, "Don't be fooled by its appearance. It runs good, has a reliable engine, and all important instruments work well. You know, in the end it will be destroyed. I took it so as not to waste a good one."

"No, we, I certainly, didn't know about it. What other surprises are there?" Huddy demanded.

"There are no surprises, just details. You know, it's impossible to finalize every step ahead of time, because we don't know what we will run into. Some things will have to be improvised while we are on the job. But I'll tell you whatever I have been able to plan so far."

"This is going in the dark. I don't like it. I will feel better if you tell us now what we will do."

Searle interjected this time, "Goodwin is right. We can't have the details in advance. Not realistic. … It's like going in the battlefield. At the time when we leave camp, all we know is we are going to fight the enemy. Everything else is dictated by what we encounter."

Huddy kept silent, which suggested that he understood but was still uncomfortable.

Goodwin opened the car's trunk and showed everyone four .45's with silencers, a can of WD-40, four flashlights, and a can of white spray paint and said, "Each one of us will have one of these guns for our protection and for executing the enemy. WD-40 is to spray the locks and any other areas which are likely to creak. I'll use the spray and the key to get in. Flashlights are for us as needed since we will be working in a darkened house at night. The white spray paint can is to write a message in the driveway, 'Niggers and such not allowed here'. This last thing will need to be done by whoever drives this car. Any volunteers?" The question was a diplomatic move since he did not want to take the responsibility of saddling someone with a low tier job.

Daboob raised his hand, "I'm a bit rusty at combat. I'll fight if I have to, but I think driving the getaway car would suit me best at this time."

Huddy, visibly jittery, complained, "All this is fine, but it's still not clear who will do what and when and how? I am really getting nervous about this half-cooked plan."

"All right, I'll give you all I have." Goodwin moved his eye focus from one person to the other, as if to say, 'Please bear with me, work with me.' Then he moved back a few feet, looked all his companions in their faces, and said, slowly, deliberately, and respectfully, "Mr. Daboob will take Mr. Searle and Mr. Huddy in the AV car and I will follow you in mine. We will drive to an undeveloped area not far from our destination."

"Why? And, what area is that?" Asked Daboob.

"That's where I will leave my car and ride with you to our destination. The reason for it will become clear in a moment. When we reach the house I will spray the lock with WD-40 and use the key to open the front door. Searle, Huddy, and I will go in." As soon as he said it he realized that he had dropped the use of Mr. for his companions. 'To Adopt a more lateral role?' he wondered. He was glad that it had happened unconsciously and would put him on equal footing with the members of his party. After all he was their leader.

He paused to see the reaction on the faces of his companions and found nothing discernible. They seemed to be waiting for him to finish telling them about his plan. So, he continued, "While we are inside the house, Daboob will quickly spray paint our message on the driveway, then sit in the car and wait for us. Inside the house, Huddy will disable the electric supply and cut the phone line. Then we will go to the bedrooms, I to the master bedroom, Huddy to the boy's room and Searle to the girl's. After executing the family we will pile clothes in the kitchen, master bedroom, and living room, and set some of them on fire. We will start a small fire so that it will take at least fifteen minutes to spread throughout the house, giving us enough time to get away before neighbors call 911. We will rush out to the car and Daboob will drive us back to where my car is parked. We will destroy the AV car and get away in mine. If we exclude driving time, the whole thing shouldn't take more than five minutes."

Thought lines formed on Huddy's forehead, or were they worry lines? Perhaps worry lines, because he brought up a concern, "What if someone in the neighborhood is an insomniac or someone coming home late, and happens to see us and our car from his window?"

Goodwin countered, "The car has phony Canadian plates and its ID number has been scratched off. It will be destroyed in the end, anyway. So, no one can trace us from what the car looks like. And, let's cover our faces with handkerchiefs so that no one can get a good look at us."

Searle quickly approved the plan, "Brilliant. Any fingerprints, anything we might leave behind in the house or car will all be gone. Nothing left to link us with the executions and fires. Brilliant."

But, Huddy had another concern, "What if we are stopped on the road? How do we explain the phony plate, scratched off ID, and guns in the trunk?"

"We play innocent. Say, 'We found it abandoned and are taking it for parts. We didn't even know it had guns in the trunk. ... You see drug dealers use such cars all the time and abandon them. The cops will probably seize the car and, if this happens before our operation, we will abandon our plan for that day. If this happens after our operation, and seems like the police already have the description of our car, we will just have to fight our way out with the police. Let's hope nothing like this happens."

Huddy was not satisfied, "How do we explain the car key. The drug dealers abandoned the car with keys and guns inside? Who will buy that? Also, our real identities will become known to the police and we will be sitting ducks if we venture on to some other project in the future and get caught. At this time we have no police records and we are safe."

Daboob came up with a solution, "Let's not use the key. Throw it away. Hot-wire the car. And, guns? Just say, 'We don't know why they left the guns behind. Maybe they got spooked by something and ran away in a hurry.' Whatever, nothing is foolproof. We have to take chances and deal with the situations as they come up. Huddy, you worry too much."

Emboldened by Daboob's support Goodwin said, "Anything else I can clarify? If not, let's go." He moved toward his car, signaling, 'Get on with the task. No more dawdling.'

The plan didn't quite work they way it was envisioned.

They got to the targeted house without any incident and entered through the front door, swiftly. The sound of the key turning in the lock was so faint that even they themselves could not hear it, thanks to WD-40. A faint glow from some kitchen appliances helped Huddy rush through the house to the backyard where he used his flashlight to find the electric control center and phone box. He turned off the electric main and cut the phone line.

Using their flashlights in the darkened house, the group moved toward the bedrooms. All of a sudden they heard a gun shot coming from the master bedroom and saw Huddy fall. Clearly the master bedroom occupant, most likely the head of the house, had sensed that there were intruders and was defending himself and his family against them. Clearly Goodwin's plan was in tatters, and the AV team had to improvise. Goodwin and Searle rushed toward the master bedroom with their guns blazing only to encounter a locked door. The shooter must have locked himself in, probably realizing the futility of standing up to a bigger force. At the same time they heard children's noises and cries from the other bedrooms. Goodwin ordered, "Searle, you go make the kids shut up, and I will handle the bastard inside the bedroom."

Goodwin had to drop his glowing flashlight on the floor and balance the heavy gun in his hands. The flashlight gave out enough illumination for him to get his bearings. He located and shot at the doorknob, and then kicked the door. The flimsy plywood door gave way easily. Goodwin rushed in the bedroom shooting at anything that seemed to move, one at the window trying to get out and the other trying to crawl under the bed. That must have been the husband and wife.

When he got out he saw Searle in the hallway who said, "All quiet."

Goodwin answered, "Okay. Now, I will get Huddy to the car and you torch the drapes, any drapes."

He grabbed Huddy by his shirt collar and dragged his unconscious body on the floor and out the front door. While doing this he noticed that Searle had set the living room drapes on fire.

Once outside Goodwin saw lights going on in many homes around him. He also saw their message sprayed on the driveway; Daboob had done his job and now he must help him. He called out loudly, "Come, help." The cry was meant for Daboob without the use of his name. After all, who else was there to help him? Goodwin didn't care at this time if he would be heard and recognized by anyone. He just needed to get out of the area with his companions, and fast.

Daboob rushed over to him and Searle. The three men lifted Huddy and threw him in the back seat.

Goodwin instructed, "Searle, you sit in the back and I will take the front seat."

Searle lifted Huddy's legs and sat holding them in his lap. Goodwin jumped into the passenger seat and Daboob took control of the steering and floored the accelerator.

No one said a thing until they got to where Goodwin's car was parked, in less than five minutes. Quickly, they transferred Huddy to the other car.

Goodwin removed the gas tank cap of the AV car, used his cigarette lighter to set fire to the upholstery inside, and yelled, "Let's get the hell out of here."

He got in the driver's seat of his car, Daboob in the passenger seat and Searle in the back seat, this time with Huddy's head in his lap. Goodwin took side streets and drove carefully, suppressing the urge to go fast, hoping to avoid any cops or emergency vehicles responding to the 911 calls made by the neighbors of the house, which they had just visited, not in a friendly way.

They made it to the AV garage without incident and relaxed in the safety of their environment. Relaxed, not really, but their heartbeats and breathing had slowed down considerably.

What should have been the successful end of the operation, wasn't, not quite.

Still something else had happened, something great for Goodwin, although not anticipated or expected. He was fully recognized as a leader, although none had articulated it. He said to Searle and Daboob, "Let's clean up here, in the bathroom. Burn our blood soaked clothes in our indoor incinerator and change into clothes we had with us on our trip to the mountains. I will take care of Huddy and you two go home and keep mum."

While Searle and Daboob were cleaning up, Goodwin placed an emergency call to Schultz from the phone in the garage office, "Need a body mechanic in the garage."

Not that he expected anyone to be listening to his phone conversation, but it did not hurt to be careful in the words he used. He hoped his need was understood. It must have been because the response to his request was a firm, "Right away."

He sat in the garage office waiting, with Huddy lying in the back seat of his car, hopefully, still alive. He was still waiting when Searle and Daboob came to say goodbye, about fifteen minutes later.

Before leaving, Searle said, "You did a hell of a job. Count me in for anything in the future."

Daboob followed, "He told me how well you handled the unexpected. I, too, would love to work with you. Just holler."

"Thank you guys. I couldn't have done anything without you," he said modestly, although he felt anything but modest. His chest was puffed up and he felt elated.

After that he sat waiting. All of a sudden he began to sweat, wondering if Schultz was going to see what he had done as a debacle.

About an hour later, he heard a key turning in the garage door lock. He got up to meet his visitors, his expected visitors. When the door opened he saw Schultz, himself, with a man whom he presumed to be a doctor, one of many the AV employed in confidence.

"Here," he said and led them to his car and pointed to the back seat.

"You got a place where I can work?" asked the doctor.

"Yes," Schultz said, "a place, not very good but a place."

Turning to Goodwin he said, "Let's move him in the spare room where we change clothes."

Goodwin and Schultz lifted Huddy and carried him to a spare room filled with dirty clothes, garage equipment, a huge stained stainless steel sink, and a cot. They placed their patient on the cot.

Schultz said to the doctor, "This is the best we can do for now."

He walked out, Goodwin followed.

That was the anticlimax to a very eventful night.

He sat with Schultz in the garage office and told him what had happened while the doctor worked with Huddy. A few minutes later the doctor came to them and, to his relief, declared that Huddy was conscious and would live, that he had been shot in the stomach and a bullet had to be extracted, that he had lost some blood and was weak, and that he would need constant medical care to recuperate and would not be able to work for a while.

After the doctor left, Goodwin and Schultz went to see Huddy.

Schultz leaned over Huddy and said, "I am sorry you got hit but Goodwin saved your life and still got the job done. Now you are going to stay in our infirmary until you are well. I'll call your family and tell them that you're on an assignment and will be back home in a few days."

Turning his eyes toward Goodwin, Huddy mouthed slowly, "Sorry buddy for grilling you. But, from now on I'm your man, anytime, anywhere, for any job you want me."

All Goodwin could say was, "Thank you."

Schultz turned to Goodwin, came close to him, put his right hand on his left shoulder and said, "A hell of a night you guys had"

Goodwin just shook his head. He was not sure if Schultz was commending or condemning him. He looked at him and saw a face drawn firm as if weighing a heavy load of judgment. Within a few seconds, he heard him say, "You did great. Not only did you put a great team together you got it to work with you, actually for you. That's amazing, considering that this was your first leadership job and the guys you chose are already established leaders. Also, you got the job done. Sure, we took a hit but that's part of the warfare. You proved yourself and I'll remember this. Now go home."

In the morning on TV, Goodwin saw the news, a special bulletin, giving details of the horror drama in which he was the principal actor only a few hours ago. He saw it with amusement and trepidation. Trepidation came when the reporter announced that the house had not completely burned down. Goodwin was concerned that some clues might have been left behind which could lead the police to him and his companions. He was a bit relieved when the reporter said that the getaway car had been located, but it had burned beyond any kind of useful identification.

Next few days the media was abuzz with this news and speculated that the heinous act was committed by one of many white supremacist nut groups, but they could not pinpoint any. A few days later the whole incident was forgotten, at least in the minds of the public.

The crime, as the police called it, remained unsolved. That boosted Goodwin's standing in the organization. It went up several notches when it was noticed that the interest of the colored to buy property in Borchert's development had gone down to zero and remained at that level even after a year.

No wonder Schultz chose Goodwin to succeed him after he was arrested and sentenced to death. Goodwin, a one time loser, became the Regional Commander of the AV .

* * *

Naturally, Goodwin was responsible for the execution of the order given by Schultz from the prison and communicated to him by Emily Haney.

He got busy with the selection of his warriors. It wasn't easy. Most of the AVs did not meet the needed criteria to conduct the kind of warfare he had in mind.

His men had to be smart. They had to be educated, not necessarily with college degrees, but at least high school. They had to look clean cut, very conservative, both in grooming and clothing. They had to be young and energetic, very fast. They had to have facility with arms, had to be able to draw quickly and shoot their target accurately. They had to be ruthless and not squeamish about carrying out the assignments which would be brutal, very brutal. They had to be free of a police record. They had to be totally, absolutely loyal to the organization, and would never betray any of their colleagues. They had to be able to work as a team, be able to support and protect their team members. The lead men had to be Commanders and their associates had to be the members who were willing to sacrifice anything and everything for the AV cause. While selecting people from within the organization was risky, it was also necessary because he could not fully trust people from the outside, no matter how supportive they might be of the cause.

It was an impossible task to go through the membership roster and find people who met his qualifications and then to interview all of them for a final selection of four. The only feasible way was to find his men from among those he already knew personally. He knew quite a few but none more intimately than those he had selected for his team for the housing project so many years ago. He thought about those men, including Borchert who had been asked to stay away from the action for strategic reasons. He thought of them fondly and somewhat nostalgically, since he had not interacted with them in a long while, in a very long while. As he pictured them in his mind, he realized that they all met most of his qualifications and that all of them had offered to work with him in the future. All of a sudden he had his team, at least in his mind. Now he needed to contact them and get their agreements to work with him on this new and very important project.

He went to a pay phone, one he had never used before, to call them. He reasoned that his home phone and pay phone he had used in the past might be tapped, and he himself might be under surveillance. Recently, he had seen some strangers in his neighborhood who would appear, drive around, then disappear, only to reappear, without any apparent business in the area. Sheriff Belford's men? They were always watching him and other AVs.

This was Friday. With each person, he used pretty much the same language, something like, 'Hi. This is Goodwin, remember me? ... Remember the last time we worked together?'

Everyone answered, "Yes" but Borchert added, "I didn't get to work with you, but I know the work was done for me. I remember that."

"Well, that's wonderful. Now, I need you again. Hope you don't mind helping out your old buddy."

Of course, no one minded. Must be because, Goodwin figured, it was good to be needed, better if it was going to pay off an old debt. Besides, who would not want to help out some one at the top. He asked his men to come for a meeting on Sunday. It was short notice but the task was urgent. Also, Sunday was the day when all of them were free from their job duties. The meeting time was nine in the morning, and the place was the secret AV headquarters hidden in the mountains. One couldn't be too secure, he figured.

The gathering was much like the ominous rolling of the clouds in the sky that day. The men came separately but arrived at about the appointed time.

They gathered in a huge cave which was furnished with all the necessities of survival for those running from the police; food, clothing, cots, sheets, toilet, shower, refrigerator, stove, cooking utensils, radio, TV, and heating and cooling. In the middle of it there was a 5-foot long teak wood table with coffee and donuts on it, and a bunch of wooden chairs that were scattered around and made comfortable with cushions on them.

As they came in, one at a time, Goodwin gave them a bear hug and intimated how happy he was to see them again. He took them individually to the table and offered to pour them some coffee.

Once everyone was seated around the table, Goodwin started in a friendly way, "Lousy weather, huh?"

"Yeah, but that's okay. We have faced worse, and not just the weather," said Huddy nonchalantly.

Goodwin thought he was referring to being shot during the last job with him. So, he said, "True enough, but this may be the worst of all. ... Do you know why we are here?" Goodwin's tone had changed. Yes, these were his buddies, at one time they had all worked together, albeit under his direction, but now he was the formal boss. He was in command and needed to talk with authority. No, he did not quite think along those lines, all that just crossed his mind. Others must have noticed the change in his tone, too, because their postures changed from just friendly to respectful friendly.

"No," Searle answered and others agreed by their silence.

"I got a message. Originated with Haney, you know, the White Snot, about a week ago," Goodwin informed. "The best I understand, George Schultz wants revenge against the warden and some other staff. I think they are the program review committee members."

"How do you figure that?" asked Daboob.

"By understanding the contents of a story Haney told Emily. George has been locked up and he wants to punish, no, actually kill, the warden and his cronies. I think the cronies must be the program review committee members, because the message came right after that meeting. We know who the committee members are. They are always the same, the Warden, the Deputy Warden, the CPO, and the psychiatrist. Even if they turn out to be the wrong targets, so what, a few innocents always die in a war. Let's start with these four people and we will correct our mistakes, if any, as we go along."

"You want us to hit these targets?" asked Daboob for confirmation.

"Yes. You have been chosen for the task because you are the best. But, if anyone is not up to it, tell me now, because later, there is no backing out. You already know that."

"Sure," spoke Borchert for everyone, "but what do we have to do?"

"Punish them. How you do it is up to you. You know your trade. No one, least of all I, can tell you how to do your job. The only thing I can tell you is that in the end there shouldn't be anyone left to tell tales. That's something we have to remember."

"So, are we supposed to go after our targets as a group, or what?" asked Borchert totally perplexed.

"No. Each one of you will have a separate assignment. Here goes: Chris Huddy, Robinson; Herman Daboob, Karcher; Jeff Borchert, Martinez; Wade Searle, Gooo...paaal. Got it?" Goodwin struggled with Gopal's name, dragging every vowel to its pronounceable limit.

"Who are these people?" asked Huddy. "Except Karcher I don't know any of them. Does anybody?"

Before anyone could answer, Goodwin said, "I'll tell you. Of course there's Karcher, the Warden. He lives with his wife on prison grounds behind the prison walls and gate. Very difficult to reach. Robinson,

Stella Robinson, is a CPO. She is a single mother. Don't know where she lives but should be easy to reach. Humberto Martinez is Deputy Warden of the ASU. He lives in a prison supplied house on prison property but outside the prison boundary and gate. Quite easy to reach. You may have to dodge the security, of course. The full name of Gooopaaal is Rajiiiv Gooopaaal. I don't know how to pronounce his stupid name, but he is the psychiatrist. Lives somewhere in the city or outside the city, don't know."

"This still doesn't help us. I don't know what they look like, where two of them live, what do they drive? Do you have their photos, any useful info?" Huddy continued with his skepticism and concern.

'Same old Huddy,' thought Goodwin, 'Same old questioning Huddy.' Then, he answered the question, "No, I don't have their photos. You will have to find out yourself where Robinson and Gooo...paaa...l live. Other details about them, I can get. I have a mole in the prison."

"Who?" Borchert jumped in with his question.

"I can't tell you. Very few people know who he is. You know, for safety's sake. So I, I will contact him to get the information you need. But let's not use him as an open post office. It could expose him in no time. Locating your target with the information I have provided is part of your job. We will use the mole when absolutely essential, when there is no other way to get the information we need."

"So, our mole is a man?" asked Huddy.

"You see, just a little talk and his identity is already unraveling. That's why I don't want to talk about him."

"Yeah, ... okay," said all four in unison.

"Now back to business. This is how I suggest we go about it. First, cancel everything. This has priority. We have to move fast before our enemy gets wise to our intentions and tactics. For all I know, it might already know about Schultz's talk and be ahead of us. ... Now, each one of you, work out your plan, ask me what you need by way of help in manpower and weaponry, transportation, whatever. And move. Okay?"

Everyone agreed by their silence. If there was any dissension against the plan, no one let it be known. In the AV organization you did not question orders and instructions, you followed them.

"After the job we celebrate," Searle announced confidently and jovially like it was a football game and they were assured of victory.

"Of course, but remember," Goodwin peppered the enthusiasm with a dose of reality, "each assignment is dangerous, so be extra cautious. It goes without saying, expect some casualties."

As he said it, the word 'casualties' sent a shudder through his spine. 'Through the spines of the four warriors also?' he wondered. The word just came out of his mouth, probably because it represented reality. But, he and his Brothers had always denied reality, the possibility of it. To them, only the enemy died in the war. Now that reality could not be denied, it was sobering, even frightening. Yet, he did not want to look weak. Cautious, yes, weak, no.

"Never underestimate the foe," Goodwin added a warning.

Everyone else nodded in agreement.

"That reminds me," Goodwin continued, "I have seen some strangers in my neighborhood. The enemy may already be on our tail. I think we are under watch. What does that mean?"

"That the enemy knows, or at least suspects, that we are on the move," answered Borchert.

"Precisely. So, be discrete, be very discrete. They figure out your movements, you're done. Our whole operation could die, too. So, watch for any suspicious characters and behave like an average guy, even when carrying out your assignments. It's the appearance that's critical, not the reality."

"Thanks for the advice," Daboob said.

"Yeah, thanks," the other three echoed.

"Now, listen," Goodwin directed. "Go to the ammunitions depot and pick out your weapons. All of them have been bought on the street and can't be traced to us, that is if you run into trouble. Select your vehicles from the garage, those that are appropriate for your tasks and carry phony Canadian or Mexican license plates. The IDs of such vehicles have been scratched out. While using them on the job, don't carry any ID including driver's license..."

"What happens if we get stopped for anything, minor traffic violation or routine check for drugs or illegals?" Huddy interrupted.

"Just tell them you forgot your driver's license at home. It can be produced later in court."

"If it's okay to produce it in court, why can't I carry it with me? Avoid hassle."

"What if you get hurt or killed on the job? It's to prevent identification, or at least make it difficult for the police. It protects the organization and other brothers."

Borchert continued to raise his concerns, "But the car will put us in jail right away."

And Goodwin had answers for everything, every good leader had to have them. "The car? Tell them you found it abandoned. Tell them you hot-wired it and are taking it home for parts. Drug dealers often abandon them." He remembered that he had used exactly the same explanation when using an AV car on the housing project job. How did it matter that it was the same logic, it was valid then and it was valid now.

"What if they don't buy our story?"

"So, you go to jail. Someone will bail you out. Then we will fight in courts. You have no record and you weren't doing anything illegal when stopped. There won't be much of a case. ... Still, let me tell you. We have thought of solutions to many problems. But we can't anticipate all eventualities. In the end, you will have to use your own head to deal with the situation. Okay?"

No one said a thing. After all Okay was an order, not a question.

The conversation so far was very low key, almost subdued, totally inconsistent with the seriousness and ferocity of the task ahead. A lot of questions and some concerns, but no enthusiasm, no excitement. Yes, there was commitment, but, it appeared, for the sake of a debt which, they probably felt, had to be paid. Goodwin looked at his team. It seemed like a wimp brigade. Was it the same team he had worked with in the past? Was it up to the challenge? Can it pull it off? If it failed, he would fail. Putting together a more responsive team crossed his mind. The idea was canceled right away. There was no time for that. Besides, he had done a very good job of selecting the right men, they met his criteria. He just needed to put some fire in their bellies, his job as a leader.

So, he said, "Remember, 'We Bleed White'. This is a crusade, a war we must win. I am counting on you. You have helped me in the past, please help me again to get the work of our organization done. So, go, put together your team of warriors from our membership. Make sure none of them has a police record or tattoos, and each wears his hair short, no shaved heads. Discuss your plans with your team members only. The fewer people who know about it, the safer it is for us. When the action starts, stick together, support each other, but dissociate yourself from anyone who gets caught, injured, or killed. All this to assure that the police don't come knocking on our doors if any thing goes wrong. Any questions?"

Did he notice some stirring in the groins of the warriors, some testosterone flowing? Imagine? Hope?

He didn't expect any questions but he got one anyway, from Searle.

"Yeah, I got one. You said not to discuss our plans with anyone. But, what about Albert Schultz? Shouldn't he know what we are doing?"

"Of course. And, I will take care of that."

After answering the question, Goodwin turned to his group and gave one last instruction, "Remember also, while you remain in total control of your assignments, all the time, you need to let me know, whatever way you can, about any difficulties you run into. Also, seek help. And report to me when the job is done."

Talk over, it was time for action. Goodwin felt he had done a fairly good job of deciding what needed to be done and how.

Others apparently felt that it was time to go home. They got up.

Goodwin shook hands with each Commander and made an emotional plea with him, saying something like, 'I am where I am all because of you, and I am doing my job the best way I can. But, in the end, it's you who make it happen. I and the Aryan Vision count on you.'

Each person gave his solemn promise to support the operation.

After that it was time for the goodbyes.

Goodwin watched the four AVs, Commanders of their assignments, march out of the cave, hopefully with big aspirations, towering confidence, and great excitement. However, he was not quite sure if the victory would be theirs to celebrate.

When alone, Goodwin drove into the city, went to a pay phone, and called Albert. Of course, informing him about his brother's orders and the AVs move in response to it was a polite thing to do. It was also strategically important; Albert might be able to give him some information about George which could be helpful in the upcoming operations. But, he wasn't going to talk about any of this on the phone which most likely was tapped. He just wanted to use the phone to set up a meeting, a face-to-face meeting, where the police would not be able to listen to their conversation, even if they knew the location and the time of their talk.

So, when the phone was answered, he said, "Hello. This is Stewart Goodwin. I trust you know me."

"Yes, I do. You the man who took over from George?"

"That's right."

"We haven't had any contact in the past, so I reckon, this must be important."

"It is... Could you meet me in the city park, say in two hours. I'll be sitting alone on the bleachers around the baseball diamond."

"I'll be there."

After meeting at the agreed upon place, Goodwin suggested, "Let's walk and talk in case my call to you was intercepted and the bleachers are listening."

Albert nodded his agreement.

Once Goodwin was sure that they were out of hearing range of anyone and anything, he said, "You must have guessed, this is about George."

"I thought so."

"First, I got a word through the usual channels that George wants some prison officials punished."

"But why?"

"We don't know. We just follow orders. But, I think the prison may be abusing George. So, we are moving. Just wanted to let you know."

"Abusing? Anything I can do?"

"No. We have always known that George doesn't want you involved in anything we do. You have a family to take care of."

"Yeah, that's true. But he is my brother."

"Of course. Still, this is something better left to us. Trust me on that."

"All right. Thanks for the info."

"There's one more thing."

"What?"

"I wonder if there's something George might have done or said to you which could help us."

"There are a couple things which have certainly puzzled me. I don't know if they would help you."

"Tell me anyway. What?"

"During one of my visits to him he had said, 'When I feel down I think of the good times we had together, like our birthdays'."

"I don't know what that signifies, if anything."

"I don't know either. And, once he asked me to send him copies of our family photos. He specially wanted his portrait, wallet size. To look at when sad."

"Everyone likes family photos."

"Yes, but why his own portrait? And wallet size?"

"Huh, that's puzzling."

"If you can figure out what these two things mean, let me know. Will ya?"

"Sure will."

"Well, I hope your operation goes well. ... I am still worried about George."

"We'll protect George, I promise."

"Thanks."

They parted company.

Goodwin was satisfied with the outcome of his meetings. Now he must wait for the news from the battlefront.

He headed home.

In spite of an apparently successful meeting why was there a furious flutter in his heart?

CHAPTER NINE

KILLING IS FOR THE BRAVE

WITH AN OFFENSIVE strategy already in place, it was time for defensive moves. Right away. So, as soon as Karcher came to his office the day after the Schultz episode, he ordered his secretary, "Find Mr. Martinez, Ms Robinson, and Dr. Gopal. Ask them to come to my office this afternoon at one for an urgent meeting." He would have liked to meet with the program committee members immediately, but it was necessary to allow enough time for his secretary to locate them, and also allow enough time for the staff to rearrange their schedules and prior appointments, if there was a conflict. This was Friday. If he had waited until Monday for the meeting, no one would have felt pressed for time. But this was a critical matter to be attended to as soon as possible.

The secretary got busy. Karcher sat behind his desk piled with incident reports, inmate complaints, staff grievances, and a proposed policy to ban smoking in all common areas in the prison, all in need of review. All could wait.

About the appointed hour of the meeting his secretary announced the arrival of all three staff members, one after the other, within a matter of five minutes. Karcher received them formally and directed them to a couch to sit on. Once all his staff were settled, he occupied his plush chair behind a cherry wood desk.

He looked at his crew, a Mexican, a black, and an Indian. A pathetic sight in his opinion. But what could he do? Might as well work with what he had. He started the meeting, "Thank you all for coming at such short notice. But it's important."

Everyone kept silent, anxiously waiting to hear what it was all about.

"I am sure you have heard of Schultz's threat."

Total silence still, meaning, 'Yes'.

"That means war. That means some of us could get hurt."

No one said anything, meaning, 'Don't bother us with the obvious. Come to the point'.

Karcher did, "I want all of you to take precautions. Sheriff Belford suggests that all of you carry a gun on your person at all times except when on prison grounds. Be extra vigilant. Take defensive action if you see any strangers lurking around you and notice any unusual activity. Watch where you go, what you do, and whom you talk to. And don't be predictable."

Everyone developed a questioning look, meaning, 'Predictable, how?'

Karcher understood. "Get rid of the routines, go to different places for shopping, recreation, etcetera. Take different routes for travel."

All three relaxed their glances, meaning, 'We understand'.

"Also secure your cars and home."

Karcher turned to face Martinez directly and said, "Mr. Martinez, since you live on prison property, although outside the actual boundaries, I have the authority to increase security in and around your residence. I will also try to have steel bars placed on all your windows and doors, but don't count on it. By the time the request is made and the action is taken, it might be a year or longer. But there is something we can do right away. Ask Mr. Jordan to set up a 24-hour patrol in front of your house. I will have a memo in your hands by this evening confirming this order. Then he turned to face Gopal, "All this applies to you too, even though you are leaving us."

Martinez looked at Gopal in disbelief and said, "You resigned?"

Gopal explained, "Yes. Some family matters. ... By the way, this morning I had my report on Schultz delivered to your office."

"I haven't seen it yet, but thanks. I appreciate…"

Karcher interrupted and addressed Gopal, as if the exchange between Martinez and Gopal had never taken place, "I understand your need to resign. Not all of us are fighters."

Gopal, in a dismissive tone, said, "There's something I wanted to say to you, too. May I?" It seemed like he, ignoring the implication of Karcher's comment, was ready to speak his mind about the situation freely, even critically, now that the threat to his job was gone.

"Yes, of course," Karcher gave permission with a great deal of reluctance and resentment. He did it out of professional courtesy, not because he cared about Gopal or his ideas. Actually, he was quite unhappy over the fact that a colored foreigner, who was subordinate to him, made a considerably higher salary than he did, simply because he was a psychiatrist. Psychiatrists, like all the other mental health therapists, were a bunch of idiots who only attempted to find excuses for criminal behavior and were always trying to save law breakers from just punishment. Of course, he was the one who had hired him, but against his better judgment. The Search Committee had recommended Gopal for the job, and he had no say in the matter.

Gopal seemed to ignore the emotional underpinnings in Karcher's permission and said quite matter-of-factly, "This Schultz business worries me. I think people are going to get hurt."

"So, Schultz deserves to get hurt." Karcher felt that permitting Gopal to speak did not mean agreeing with him.

"I think the staff will get hurt, too. Your life could be in danger also."

"I appreciate your concern. I really do. Thank you." Karcher said irritably, then took a few seconds to shift the focus of his response from phony appreciation to outright rejection, "Dr. Gopal, I am aware of the danger. That's why I called this meeting. We need to take precautions, but we don't need to be afraid. You probably don't know that we, Mr. Martinez and I, have served in Vietnam. We know what danger is. It doesn't bother us."

"Still, why invite it? what purpose does it serve?"

"To control gang activity."

"I don't see it working. What we are doing will only make them react violently. It's the ego thing."

"You are right about the ego. I'll crush theirs."

"Perhaps in the prison, but they have connections outside. They are likely to take revenge."

"The police will deal with them."

"It hasn't worked so far."

"Do you have a better idea?" Karcher was getting angry, and it showed in the way he enunciated his words.

And Gopal seemed to be getting bolder, maybe because he had nothing to lose, "The way I see it, the gangs provide a sense of belonging to those who see themselves as social rejects. They thrive on their perception of society as an enemy and draw their power through violence against it."

It was like an incomprehensible treatise to Karcher, but he was not about to admit it. "So, what are you saying? Succumb to them?"

"No, change their perception. Give them a sense of belonging. There are psycho-social techniques to do that."

"Dr. Gopal, no offense, but that's bullshit. The only thing these bastards understand is a big fat log up their asses. I know you mean well. But, it's life in the trenches, kill or get killed. In time you will learn that."

As he said this, it occurred to him that there was not much difference between himself and Schultz. Both were adamantly hanging on to their values which were surprisingly the same, power. Both were willing to fight for it till the end. Neither was willing to back down, compromise, or run away. Neither wanted to look like a coward.

Also, did both refuse to see that when the war was over neither would be a winner? That the fury of conflict would have devoured them all? The questions and the implied answers were distasteful to Karcher who turned his head toward Martinez and Robinson, supposedly part of his army. They were good workers, obedient to a fault, and clearly on his side. He could depend upon them to accomplish anything and use them to further any ends he had in mind, particularly the ones for which he did not want to risk his own life. Not Gopal. Although he had not seen Gopal violate any institutional rules, he still saw him as an outsider who did not fit in with the prison culture. Gopal was a psychiatrist, always talking about treating the inmates rather than punishing them, even after the urine treatment he himself got from Schultz. 'The guy is totally insane,' mused Karcher. He was not sorry that Gopal was leaving, but was frustrated, because surely the shrink would be replaced by someone else just like him. Whatever, he decided to treat him as a non-person. 'Fuck Gopal, who needs him,' the words vibrated inaudibly under his breath.

He addressed his trusted audience, "Dr. Gopal will not be here to face the criminals. He can afford to be benevolent. We can't."

"What do we do?" asked Martinez. Was he hoping to earn a few reward points through his compliant attitude?

"We do what we have already decided to do. Only, make sure that no one, except the personnel involved in the operation, knows what's going on."

"That would be hard to do. People talk."

"I know, but do the best you can. And keep me informed about the progress."

"Yes," said Martinez, "I wanted to tell you that I have Ms. Robinson's incident report and Dr. Goapl's psychiatric report. Mr. Jordan is putting together a disciplinary court. Everything is in order, and in just a few days, Schultz will be convicted and his isolation will be legitimized. 'Worse fate than death' will be awaiting him there, in installments. Mr. Jordan is in charge of that too."

"Good work. Thank you. Anything else?"

"No. But I have a question," said Martinez.

"What?"

"You had said something about Schultz not needing a lawyer?"

"Yes, dead people don't need legal protection. But keep him alive until I decide it's time. I want him to suffer. I want him to know who is the boss here. I want him to know that his threats are not going to make us run and hide."

As an afterthought, he quickly added, "Remember, not a word of this goes out. It is against the prison policy and the state law to talk about anything that goes on in the prison with anyone outside our circle ... even after you are outside the circle. And, in case something does leak out, you know, walls can have ears, we'll deny everything." He made sure that Gopal understood the inevitable severe penalties, if he let his tongue loose, under the wrong assumption that having resigned his position he had nothing to fear.

Gopal sat like it was no news to him.

Martinez played his role, the servant role, "Of course not. ... And, we'll do exactly as ordered. But, I need help. Could I make a request?"

"Absolutely. What?"

"Could we promote Mr. Jordan? He has a very difficult and delicate task on his hands. Make him Assistant Deputy Warden. My unit doesn't have that position right now. With a promotion, Mr. Jordan could be expected to have greater motivation to do the best job possible. Also this will give him clout over other staff to get their cooperation in accomplishing the task when needed."

"Creating a new position is easy, finding money for it is not. But you are right. I will find a way to do it. So, go, get the paperwork started."

"Thank you, sir."

Total silence once more.

Karcher broke it, "Thank you all for your support. We will win this war, I am confident. This will be a lesson for other creeps like Schultz, in fact, for all the gangs in the prison. They will know I run this place, not they."

"Yes sir," said Martinez. Robinson echoed the words. This was the first time she had spoken. She appeared intimidated by the company of all the big shots. Gopal, on the other hand, just sat, lines of incredulity forming on his forehead.

Karcher looked at all three staff intently and said forcefully, "Let me repeat, take precautions." He kept silent for a moment as if he had something else to tell but was trying to find a right way to say it. He must have found it, because he said, "Never underestimate your enemy. Start taking defensive actions immediately and take offensive action as needed. We will relax only when the threat is gone. And I am going to make sure that the threat is gone, and soon. I don't want to be looking over my shoulder forever."

Did he really believe it? Was it possible for him, or for anyone, to eliminate all the thousands of AVs?

Disturbing although the questions were, the bravado was still reassuring to him, and he believed that it was reassuring also to everyone in that room, except perhaps Gopal who did not count.

In the battlefield, didn't the commanders always lie about the invincibility of their troops and the certainty of victory over the enemy? Didn't these lies always make the lowly soldiers feel brave and be willing to die for the causes they never understood? Even for the causes which never existed?

Karcher was not sure if his cause was understood by his troops, but he believed that it did exist.

He got up. That meant the meeting was over, and the war had started. The war, the seeds of which had been planted only a day ago.

CHAPTER TEN

THE DEAD ARE NOT STRONG

As she walked out of the Warden's office, Robinson could see the danger much more clearly than before. Protective measures must be taken and right away.

She went to her office, sat in her chair, and wondered, 'What measures?'

Schultz's image materialized before her eyes, a menacing image. Yet, this time she did not think of killing him. She could see it was useless. Even if she could manage to kill him, and the 'if' remained huge, she would not be safe, the AVs would get her. Gopal was right about the revenge factor. The previous day's bravado had been replaced by today's fear. But fear was not going to save her, either. There had to be something else. She could not think of anything. Just follow Karcher's advice, and do a number of things.

Get a gun. A small caliber gun for easy handling and storage in her purse, the glove compartment of the car, and the night stand. This she did not want to do with a small child in the house, afraid of an accidental shooting and death. But this risk she had to take in favor of overall security.

Watch if she was being followed. She assumed that tracking a tail was not easy, impossible if the tail was smart. All she could do was remain watchful and hope to spot the tail, if there was one, and take evasive action. She would have to do it all the time.

Stay in populated areas when not in the privacy of her home.

The decisions made her feel secure, a bit relaxed. But she knew nothing was foolproof. She was a target and she could be killed in spite of all her precautions. What would happen to Jeremiah then? She must find someone to raise him. Find someone now, before it was too late. Who was there to take over such a big responsibility and carry it out faithfully? She could think of only Bottillo and her mother. She canceled Bottillo right away. He was a man, and she still had trouble trusting a man fully. Of course, he was no Rashid, not a good-for-nothing garbage dwelling rat Rashid, but he was still a man. She had overcome her bitterness and mistrust of men to the point where she could see Bottillo as a friend, but not as a lover, husband, or as a guardian to her son. Men had penises which they used to violate women, it was a power rod for abuse. Often they used it disguised as love. It was subtle rape. Rashid did that, so would Bottillo, if she allowed it to happen. Also, she could not see a man, any man, no matter how sincere, as capable of raising a child all by himself. That left her mother. She must talk to her about it as soon as possible. Today. The matter was too important to wait even until the next day, Saturday, one of her two regular mother-visiting days.

That done, she was able to concentrate on her work. At the end of the day she recalled her decisions regarding safety.

As she drove out of the prison parking lot, she looked around for any possible tail. There were a couple parked cars with people in them, most likely there to pick up some staff who did not drive. She did not detect a tail. This would have to become a habit, an automatic behavior, and it would become so, if she continued to do it.

She went to Jeremiah's preschool and parked her car on the street filled with children, parents, and school staff. 'Good girl,' she praised herself for remembering to stay in peopled areas. This, too, would become an automatic behavior with practice.

After she and Jeremiah were buckled up in their car seats, she fought traffic to get to a sporting goods store to buy a gun. She found a gun exactly to her liking, small caliber, small size. She felt it in her hands and immediately had a sense of power. If anyone dared to come near her and her son to hurt them, she would blow off the head of the creep. Okay, so her small caliber gun could not do that, but it could still kill. Kill. She had no doubts about her ability to do that. After all, the prison had given her high marks in target shooting during weapons training. She put the gun in her purse. It would become part of her attire, except in the prison where it was not allowed. And when sleeping, she would keep it in her night stand drawer, fully loaded. This, too, would become a routine.

The only thing left now was to talk to her mother about taking care of Jeremiah if something happened to her. She drove towards her mother's house, anxiously, stopping on the way at a supermarket for groceries.

She parked on the street and got out with her son. She stood beside her car, holding Jeremiah next to her, and looked at the house which had always been her home, even now when she did not live in it. She was born here, grew up here, gave birth to her son here, in this dilapidated house. It looked like it was a million years old. The paint had peeled away exposing the wood shingles, the ones which still remained. The porch sagged and it was necessary to know where to step. The roof was more patched up than a circus clown's outfit. The screen door hung precariously on only one of its three hinges. The fixtures in the bathroom were all cracked and the toilet was always backing up. The kitchen was carved out of the living room. In the way of appliances, it had a tiny refrigerator which barely kept the food cold, an electric hot plate, a toaster oven, and two cabinets whose panels had long disappeared. There was also a wobbly dining table which was never used because it could not support the weight of any eating utensils. The living room sported a worn carpet whose original color was impossible to discern. It did have a new sofa and a 19-inch color television, both Robinson's gifts to her mother. There was another gift from her, a single bed in the bedroom.

Robinson had left that house physically but her spirit still lived there. She frequently came to visit it in the guise of seeing her mother. No, that was not quite true. When she came, her mother was always the reason for the visit. But there was also the anticipation of visiting her own spirit, and the reunion was always a happy one.

The confines of this two-room house were filled with many sad moments, the ones that touched the fates of her brothers and father. But there were happy times, too, which eloquently spoke of her mother. Thanks to her, Robinson had been able to carve out a destiny for herself and her son which promised happy, safe, and secure days ahead. Had promised. Now that promise was being threatened, and she was running back to her mother for protection.

"Let's go see Gramma," said Robinson to her son. She balanced the grocery bag in the bend of her left arm and extended her right hand to her son to hold. They walked to the front door. Jeremiah knocked. There was no door bell.

In a moment there was shuffling of feet behind the door before it opened. She heard her mother welcome them with a spatula in her hand, "Ma babies. Come in, come in." Apparently, she was at the stove fixing dinner. She put the spatula on the arm of a nearby sofa next to the door, and spread out her thin arms to take her guests in.

Jeremiah squealed, "Hi Gramma," and beat her mother to those arms.

They entered the house. Robinson put the grocery bag on the kitchen floor, kissed her mother on the cheek, and said, "Sorry Mom, to just barge in like this, unannounced."

"You come any time. It's your home. ... But, it mean, you don't come tomorrow?"

"I will, if you want me to."

"No, not necessary. You got other things."

"Yeah, well, I will be back on Wednesday, our regular visit day."

"Okay. So what's today? Something happen?"

"Yeah. I need to talk to you about it. But later." She started putting the groceries away.

The topic got changed. "Look at all the food. We eat good cause of you. ... Dinner will be ready soon," her mother commented.

A couple of hours later they had their dinner on the living room floor, Southern fried chicken, potato salad, grits, and biscuits topped with gravy.

Then it was time to talk. Talk about solutions to her problem. Robinson said to her mother, "I need to discuss something, something serious, with you, alone."

"I'm always here for ya," agreed her mother

"You watch TV," Robinson instructed her son. "Gramma and I will be in the bedroom. Okay? Just for a while."

Jeremiah got his nose in the TV. The women retired to the bedroom.

As soon as they sat at the edge of the bed, Robinson started, "There's trouble in the prison. If something happens to me, promise, you'll take Jeremiah."

"Trouble, what trouble?"

"There's this mad man, threatening staff. I'm on his list."

"Why you? You didn't harm no one."

"He is crazy. That's all. ... You have done so much for me. This will be the last favor I ask."

"No, nothing will happen. Not to my baby."

"Maybe not, but just in case."

"God will protect you and Jeremiah. God protects everyone."

Robinson was not so confident of God's power or even His willingness to protect everyone, but she had to share her mother's faith because that would give her mother the power to protect Jeremiah. What else was there any way?

Robinson felt bad that she had to do this to an old lady who had already paid her debt to life many times over. But she knew her mother who, even though old and frail physically, was strong in every other way. Her black ghetto culture had made her strong, had made all women in that culture strong. Men there only pretended to be strong. Robbing, killing, dodging police, and abandoning families was not being strong. It was being stupid. Women raised their children all by themselves, living on welfare, fighting off the burglars, drug dealers, gangsters, and rapists. They weren't afraid of anyone, not even the cops. Robinson saw herself as a product of the same culture with the same attributes. That was why she was able to complete high school while raising her son, although with her mother's help, find a job in the prison, fight her way up to a respectable position, help her mother financially, and dream of buying a home where the three of them could live together. Yes, she was tough and strong because she was her mother's daughter.

But, dead people are not strong. That's why she needed her mother.

The women were silent for a while, then Robinson's mother said, "Get another job."

"It's not easy to get a decent job for a black woman with only high school. You know that. Besides, even a new job won't solve anything. He would chase me wherever I go. ... I hate it, I really hate to burden you, but I have no one else to go to. I have a friend who would take Jeremiah, but I feel more comfortable with you. Promise Mom, please promise."

"You have a boyfriend?" Her mother asked like it was welcome news.

"No. Just a coworker, a good friend."

"Oh!" The enthusiasm subsided. Now back to the problem, "It's okay. It hurts too much to think it happening. But don't worry. Jeremiah will not be an orphan, if I don't die first."

"You won't," No sooner had she said that than she realized that it was a lie. How could she predict it? But she had to have hope, some kind of hope. That's all it was, hope. So, she added, "Thank you."

That settled, Robinson was relaxed.

So relaxed that she forgot about the Schultz threat and began talking about the money she was saving for a down payment on a house for all three of them to live in as a family.

So relaxed that when she was ready to say 'Good night' to her mother she imagined Bottillo waiting for her on her trailer steps.

What was happening? Was she falling for Bottillo? She had to admit that she did not see him as a typical man. He was a good friend and a typical man could not be a good friend. All of a sudden, she wanted to see him, see him badly and tell him the arrangements she had made for Jeremiah, and also tell him how much she appreciated his caring for her. Maybe she would even hug him and give him a kiss on the cheek. And, one day when this ordeal was over and they survived, she would say 'yes' to his proposal. She smiled at the thought. Although still cautious, she was beginning to slip on a smooth, wet rock.

Whatever. As she drove home, she was happy. Her happiness grew and the Schultz threat receded in the back of her mind with each passing day.

Five days later it changed.

This was Wednesday, her day of visiting with her mother. As usual she drove out of the prison and right away noticed a car appearing in her rear view mirror every now and then. It was either dark blue or black, hard to tell in the fading daylight. She had gone, maybe a couple of miles, when it came to her that she had seen this car outside the prison gate as she was getting out. At the time it meant nothing, there were always cars on the street in front of the prison gate. But to see it again, and apparently following her, was disconcerting. She didn't feel to be in any kind of danger since the car was not making any threatening moves, still, while steering with one hand, she checked her purse for the gun with the other. It was there and she felt reassured.

She continued driving carefully while keeping an eye on the tail, if it was one. She made her usual stop at the preschool to pick up her son. Back on the road, she looked in her rearview mirror and did not see the dark blue or black car behind her. She admonished herself for being jumpy and directed her car toward a supermarket to get groceries for her mother. After coming out of the supermarket parking lot, she once more looked left, right, front, back, for the car which she had suspected of being a tail and felt relieved at not seeing it. After stopping at the curb in front of her mother's house, she turned her head back, once more to look for the tail and saw none. Now she was sure she had let her imagination run wild. Feeling calm, she got her son and grocery bag out of the car, climbed a few steps to the porch, and knocked on the door.

"It's open," came the reply.

She, followed by her son, entered the house filled with the smell of food.

The dinner and talking about the usual plans for the future took about two hours. Then the usual hugs, kisses, and goodbyes.

As she drove home, that black or dark blue car came into her rear view mirror again. It could not be coincidence. She became nervous but not enough to start crying, or driving erratically. At one point she thought of going to the police but discarded the idea quickly. The police could not possibly help her. A dark blue or black car, which may or not be following her, would not provide sufficient information and compelling evidence of a crime for the police to act upon. She maintained her precautionary stance and kept her car in the populated and lighted areas. Still, her heart was skipping beats and her whole body was trembling. She also felt chilled and feverish. Now she wanted to rush to the safety and security of her home, and her foot went heavy on the pedal. When she reached her home she noticed that the car following her had stopped on the road about 50 yards from her trailer park. It actually scared her.

She hurriedly pulled Jeremiah out of the car, slammed shut the doors, and ran toward her trailer. And, bumped into Bottillo sitting on the steps. In her edginess she had not noticed his car parked nearby.

"What's the rush?" he asked.

"There's a car following us," she answered breathlessly.

"Where?"

She pointed toward the road, "There. It's black or dark blue."

There was nothing on the road, just a faint glow of the street lamp.

"Let me go, see. Give me your gun. ... You got a gun, right?"

"Gun?" In her almost panicky state she had forgotten that she had a gun. While pulling it out of her purse and giving it to Bottillo, she said, "Some good it will do me. I can't remember I have it."

The comment was not meant to elicit any response and it didn't. She saw Bottillo snatch the gun from her hand and run toward the main road. She and Jeremiah went inside the trailer. Bottillo's presence made her feel somewhat composed. Without bothering to turn the lights on, she threw Jeremiah and herself on the couch in the living room, sitting stiffly upright in the dark, and waited for Bottillo's return. Bottillo's safe return. Did she sense danger for him? Of course, she did. So, when she saw him at the entry door, safe and sound, her stiff posture slumped and her heart jumped up a few feet with elation. "Found anything?" she asked.

"Nothing. No parked cars. A few drove past me though, not the color you described." He came close to Robinson and gave her gun back to her.

"I must have been hallucinating," Robinson commented.

"Maybe not. In any case, it was good that you were watching. ... So, how do you feel?"

"Shook up."

"I bet. ... Want me to stay?"

"No, that won't be necessary. I have the gun. I will be okay."

As she said this she became aware that her son was sitting beside her listening. She had kept her son completely in the dark about all this threat business purposely, so as not to scare him. Now it was out. Her fear had made her careless. Oh well, she would give her son a watered down version of the problem. That would explain to him what was going on without frightening him.

Bottillo didn't appear convinced that she would be okay. So he asked, "You sure?"

"Yeah, I'm sure."

"Okay. ... By the way, where were you? It's rather late, isn't it?" No, there was no accusation, no frustration, or anger at having to wait at the steps, or even an attempt to control. Robinson saw it for what it was, a caring rebuke.

"This is the day I visit my mother. You know that," she answered in a subdued, informational tone.

"Oh, your mother! I totally forgot."

"That's okay."

"How's she?"

"Well, she is fine. And, I arranged for her to take Jeremiah if anything happened to me." No need any more to keep this conversation secret from her son. She looked at Jeremiah to see how he was reacting and found his eyes big with fear.

Robinson pulled her son to her bosom and said, "Don't worry. There's nothing to worry about."

"You giving me away?" Jeremiah had begun to sob.

"Of course not." Robinson knew she had to do some explaining to her son but not at this time. Quite unprepared for the response, she just said, "I am making arrangements for you if I die. We all die, you know."

At that Bottillo intervened, "You are full of gloom and doom."

"No. It can happen."

"Anything can happen. But, we don't have to think of the worst."

"I am not thinking of the worst. I am planning."

"Some planning. Saddling an old lady with the responsibility of your son! I would take Jeremiah if need be. You should know that by now."

Robinson could see that Bottillo was hurt. Other than her mother, he was the only one who cared for her, and she hurt him, rejected him, did not appreciate all he was doing for her.

All of a sudden she began to cry. Jeremiah too.

Bottillo thought it was because of him. It had to be, who else was there? "I am sorry. I didn't mean to…"

Robinson did not hear what Bottillo was saying. She felt that he would certainly leave her if she failed to recognize his love for her one more time. So, she disengaged herself from her son, got up, threw her arms around Bottillo, hid her face in his neck, and sobbed, "Don't leave me, please don't leave me." She was not aware of what Bottillo was saying and that she was interrupting him. Her defenses had broken down, her vulnerability had been exposed, and her gratitude had spilled over for the man who loved her.

A new relationship was born.

How did it come about? Robinson had never been expressive toward him in the past. Did it confuse him? But, he looked pleased. And, Robinson realized that there was a spark in her heart after all, a spark that would light a candle which would illuminate a home, their home. She held Bottillo close, and he reciprocated. For how long, she did not know, but it felt natural, very natural.

Then she noticed being gently guided back to the couch and being made to sit down. She allowed it to happen. She even allowed Bottillo to sit between her and Jeremiah, saying nothing.

The crying had stopped.

For Robinson, the life had taken a new hue, a bright hue, and it was there to stay; and, there was light, the dark room was filled with a million stars.

That night Bottillo stayed in the trailer. With Robinson. In her bed.

CHAPTER ELEVEN

FLY ME TO THE MOON

GOPAL IGNORED KARCHER'S hostile and aggressive posture. He was leaving the damn place soon, as soon as his house was sold, to the safety of his country. Only if he and Satya could survive until then. They would if they took the necessary precautions, and, he reluctantly admitted, the ones suggested by Karcher were really good.

That day when he got home in the evening, Satya announced, "Our insurance agent called. Wanted to know the reason for our requested changes in the policy."

"What did you say?"

"Told him the truth, that you worked in a dangerous place, that's why."

"Then?"

"He called back a few hours later and told me that his head office had approved our request at a considerable increase in our premiums."

"Well, I expected that, but how 'considerable'?"

"He didn't know. Said we should get a written confirmation in a few days which will also tell us about our new premium."

"Good, and…"

"And the real estate man called. Our house has been listed for sale, MLS…"

"MLS?" Gopal interrupted.

"Multiple Listing Service. I didn't know what MLS meant either. He explained. There would be several different agents showing the house. He hoped he would have some prospective buyers within a week."

Gopal put his briefcase beside a wall, loosened his tie, threw himself on the sofa, and said, "That's good news." In a subdued voice. Somehow it did not seem like good news. There was a painful pinch in his heart, and he knew why. This house, which had grown out of love, would have to be abandoned.

Satya sat beside him and echoed his sentiments, "It's sad though. Leaving a place that we put so much into. Today I have been wandering around the house feeling dejected. It was like I was viewing a dead body in a coffin before closing the lid. Morbid, isn't it?"

"Oh well. We will build a new house, one bigger and better, in India. Leave the past behind. Think of the future," he spoke like a therapist.

Satya added to this positive spin, "That's right. There are so many good things about going back to India. A better house is only one of them. Not having to keep and carry guns is another. And we will be relaxed."

"I'm already relaxed, ever since I made the decision to leave this violent country. And you know what? I am not going to worry about anything any more. I want to enjoy whatever little time we have here."

"I know one thing we could enjoy."

"What?"

"Fly. Let's rent a small, two-seater propeller and go up in the sky."

"That would be great. Just us and the wind."

"I will call an aircraft rental agency tomorrow. See, if I can get a plane for this weekend."

"That would be heavenly. I have wanted to see you fly. Let me know as soon as you get a plane. If I am at work at that time, call me there."

"Okay."

Gopal slid forward, locked his arms above his head, and sighed contentedly. And thought.

If nothing else, his marriage was going smoothly. He remembered his life with Christi which was a constant tug of war. He was happy that it was over. Was it really over? All of a sudden his contentment was gone and he was doubtful, disturbed. He remembered that face in the mirror at Macy's. Christi's? She seemed like a bead in the string of evil that was choking him. Maybe she was still around and plotting to destroy him, just like Schultz. Two different people, unknown to each other, but with the same goal.

No, this would not happen. He would escape, escape from the clutches of all his enemies. They won't have a chance.

He calmed down and took his mind to the intoxicating smell of flowers, softness of white clouds, silkiness of a gentle breeze, and the smoothness of water on a placid lake. That was Satya.

His life with Satya was comfortable. He enjoyed being with her, so much so that he would even go grocery shopping with her. And he liked to please her by doing little things for her almost every day; bringing a gift, usually something inexpensive like costume jewelry, cosmetics, candy, spending time with her in the mall, looking at things she might enjoy, and often buying something like clothing, shoes; taking her to movies, comedy clubs, or concerts, once a week. All this and more he would do in spite of her weak protestations that they needed to save money and not spend it on unnecessary things.

A comfortable life did not mean total absence of conflict. After all they were two different people with individual personalities. She would get annoyed over his messing up the bathroom right after she had cleaned it, or over his use of his shoe heel instead of a hammer to put a nail in the wall. He would get upset over her straightening his desk in the den and making it impossible for him to find his things, or over her refusal to give him money to buy frivolous things like car ornaments. These irritations of daily living, however, were just that, irritations.

Now that he was going back to India, life would get even more comfortable and exciting. He would be able to enjoy the movies, music, food, clothing, and festivals he had grown up with. In a low cost country he would be financially secure. Most of all, his children would not have to grow up in a culture of selfishness, greed, and violence. He admonished himself for not having seen all this when he had decided to come to America over everyone's objections. He had been robbed of his intelligence and foresight by the glare of money and materialism. Not any more.

That night when he snuggled in bed with Satya, he was very peaceful. More peaceful than he had been in a long time.

The next day, late in the afternoon, Satya came running to him, "We got a plane. For tomorrow."

"Good. It's Sunday, my day off, too."

He was excited like a child with a bag of candy.

With Satya at the controls, Gopal had the most joyous flight of his life. They flew over the city and over their house, then ventured out toward nearby cities. They never climbed above 5,000 feet, did not want to give up their fun of watching the landscape and activities below. Their speed never exceeded 100 miles per hour. At that speed it was not necessary to keep their windows shut tight. The wind caressing their hair and singing in their ears made the whole experience very romantic. Slicing through the infinite blue expanse, dissociating from the mundane world underneath, was liberating. All the flights in commercial jets did not even come close to the thrill Gopal experienced in this tiny aircraft.

A couple of hours later, the fight ended, safely.

Gopal was so excited by the experience that he wanted to repeat it within a week and often thereafter. Satya toned down his enthusiasm by pointing out the fact that it was very expensive and would be impossible to afford in India. They finally agreed to do it occasionally when their finances would allow it.

Encounter with reality, however, did not dampen Gopal's sense of thrill. It stayed with him through the weekend, through the next work day, and the next.

Maybe that's why the next Wednesday, on his way back home from work, only three days after his journey to the moon, he had not noticed a Jeep following him behind the dust clouds created by his Mercedes on the dirt country road.

CHAPTER TWELVE

BRING IN THE SAINTS

MARTINEZ GOT UP and slowly walked out of Karcher's office. Although Karcher's recommendations made him feel a little at ease, there were still those pesky worry waves rushing through his whole body. If his staff noticed it, it would not be very reassuring, might even increase their heartbeats. He took a deep breath, calmed down a little, and walked to his office.

Sitting in his chair, he pondered over ways of protecting himself and his family. Family actually came first. If he were to die in the war, so be it, but no harm should come to his wife and children.

He needed Jordan again.

This time he picked up the phone and dialed Jordan's number himself. When he heard, "Hello," he said, "Please come to my office immediately. It's urgent."

Jordan appeared before him in less than five minutes. After he was seated, Martinez started, "First, the good news. I have recommended you for a promotion. Warden Karcher has agreed to create a position of Assistant Deputy Warden for you. I am taking care of the procedural details." It was a very important strategic move; reward Jordan before saddling him with more responsibility.

"That's a pleasant surprise."

"Well, you deserve it. You have earned it."

"Thank you, sir."

"Now, I need your help in another matter. It is about security around my residence. It needs to be increased. Warden Karcher's idea, and I agree. As you know, my residence, although on the prison property, is outside the prison perimeter, beside a road available for travel to anyone. It is, therefore, very vulnerable. I want you to devise a twenty-four hour security plan for it. I am not talking about an electronic alarm system. I want at least one armed officer in front of my house at all times, who could respond to any danger immediately. You don't have to worry about the back of the house because that is flush with the prison boundary. You may use prison personnel for this purpose."

"It will be hard. We never have enough security officers to adequately cover all our territory."

"I know. You know. But in the prison we have learned to do with nothing. Get this done. I know you can. Just one person at a time."

"Okay. I may have to loosen security in some areas. I will make sure they are not critical areas."

"Of course."

"How long will it go on?"

"I don't know at this time. Not long, I hope. I will let you know when we can relax."

"All right. I will get on with it right away."

Jordan left.

Martinez sat and wondered if what he had done was enough and realized, not quite. He would have to do some other things Karcher had talked about. He already had a pistol from his army days, which had not been used in a long time. So he must do some target practice with it. All other precautions did not require any equipment, just vigilance and appropriate defensive action. He also must alert his family to the danger, give everyone tips about how to protect themselves. He wished Lupita would learn to use a gun and keep it on her person, but knew she would not. She had seen his gun and was scared of it. Maybe she really did not need it, after all she never went anywhere without him, and at home she could make sure never to open the door to any stranger. The children, boy 10, girls 8 and 6, were too young to be even near a gun, let alone use it. But, they could use simple common sense to protect themselves. He should talk to them. He was a little concerned that this might cause fear and panic which would render any attempt at protection ineffective. The concern quickly evaporated when he decided to approach the whole thing matter-of-factly and calmly.

That evening after dinner, while sitting on the couch in the living room, he talked with his family, "Listen. There are some people who want to hurt us. So, be careful. Never walk alone. Keep an eye on your surroundings. If you notice anyone following you, memorize what he looks like and run back home. Except us, don't tell anyone where you are going and when, and what you are going to do. If anyone tries to entice you to go with him or tries to grab you, scream, fight, call others for help."

He had hoped his family would take the message rationally. He was wrong. His family appeared devastated by the news. At least the children. They started to cry. Lupita gathered them in her arms and said, "Don't be afraid. Our saints are watching over us." She wiped their tears but they continued to sob.

Martinez was irritated, 'How are the saints going to protect them?' But he kept his feelings to himself, expressing them was not going to help the situation in any way. Instead of showing his irritation he needed to allay their fears. So, he said, "There's no need to be afraid. There will be an armed guard outside our house around the clock."

The announcement should have been soothing and comforting. But it was not, even to himself. An armed guard could be manipulated, bribed, waylaid, or killed. He tried to hide his anxiety, did not want his family to be more afraid than it already was.

Then he realized that he was wrong about his family, at least about Lupita. He was amazed and impressed at how calm and stable she looked. She probably was afraid, too, and might even be shaking inside, but outwardly she was a pillar of strength. And the children? They didn't look afraid either, not any more. They had their heads resting on Lupita's breasts, looking peaceful and secure. His mind flashed back to the day when he was leaving to join the army. It was exactly the same; the safety of a mother's breast and the invocation of saints. He knew at that moment that there was nothing more protective and more powerful in the world than a mother and her saints, nothing.

So, he added, "And yes, our saints will protect us too."

A few days later, Wednesday in fact, Martinez noticed a Chevy Blazer with two men cruising down the street in front of his house. Noticed because of the way it was moving, slow, slower than the other traffic, and steady, and it seemed like the driver was intently looking at his house. Casing? Maybe, maybe not. A lot of people slowed down in front of the prison building for a curious look at modern man's house of horrors.

'I shouldn't be paranoid,' he told himself.

CHAPTER THIRTEEN

DISPENSING JUSTICE

Jordan stepped out of Martinez's office, stood in front of his secretary, and asked, "You got something for me?"

"Yes. I was going to call you. Here they are."

Jordan took the incident and psychiatric reports from her and went back to his office. He had two equally important tasks to perform, call a disciplinary court for Schultz and arrange for security around Martinez's house. Which one to do first?

Security seemed more important. He did a mental examination of every guard who worked for him for reliability and sincerity and came up with a list of eight names, Ibarra was included primarily because of Martinez's orders. He called them for a meeting in the unit conference room that same afternoon. Those who had the day off were contacted by phone and asked to come for this emergency meeting. Those who could not be reached were dropped from the list. Finally he had a task force of five.

Jordan presided. He explained, "We have a new and additional responsibility to protect our Deputy Warden. His life has been threatened. It goes without saying, it is critical. You are the most dependable security-conscious personnel I can think of. So, you have been chosen to do the task."

He paused for his audience's reaction. Everyone sat stone-faced which was eloquent in its message, 'Go on.'

Jordan got it. "Now, this is what you will have to do. Each one of you will be assigned to stand guard, armed with a high powered rifle, in front of the Martinez residence, continuously for eight hours. Our usual shift times will apply, 11 to 7, 7 to 3, and 3 to 11. Your meals will be delivered to you, and while you are eating the delivery person will replace you. If you need to go to the bathroom, or get sick, or have any other emergency, immediately use your radio, get in touch with me or whoever is the Shift Commander at that time, and ask for a replacement. Wait until the replacement arrives before leaving your post. While you are on duty, watch for any unusual activity; any person or car lingering in front of you, any sudden loud sound or distraction, any weapons, any threatening move by anyone. If you notice any such thing, call the tower guard nearest you right away and report the problem, then ask for back-up. Take defensive action if you are threatened or attacked. Make sure your weapon is loaded and ready to fire throughout the period of your duty. Use your own judgment in how to protect yourself and the Martinez family. Don't be trigger happy, however. Fire only if you sense imminent bodily harm. This is very important. We don't want any innocent person to get hurt or killed. Any questions?"

"You think there is real possibility of violence?" asked Ibarra.

"No, I don't. What we are doing is taking a preventive measure. I think the people who want to harm Mr. Martinez will stay away when they see an armed security guard. But, you never know. There are some stupid people out there. So, violence remains a possibility. You can actually thwart it by your vigilance and prompt defensive action. Like, if you suspect danger, shoot around the person rather than at him and scare him away. If the attack is directed at you and you have no chance to take cover, you may have to shoot him. You have to protect yourself, otherwise you won't be able to protect anyone else. Okay? Use good judgment, it goes a long way. Anything else?"

"Yes, sir, when do we start?" Still Ibarra.

"Right away. I am going to work out a week's schedule for now. I will make sure no one has this duty more than once within a 24-hour period. There will be a new schedule every week, prepared one week in advance. This will continue as long as necessary. You will get your assignments in your mail boxes. None of you will start until tomorrow morning. I want you to have enough time to get physically and psychologically ready for it. I also need time to prepare your schedules. So, I will do tonight's duty myself, from 11 to 7."

After the meeting was over, Jordan prepared a one-week schedule to start with. He made copies of it and placed them in the mail boxes of his 5 crew members. He also called and communicated this information to the guard who was to relieve him in the morning, in case this guard was not able to check his mail box by the end of the day.

The day was almost over but his work was not. He started to make a list of disciplinary court members. The rules required at least three members, all prison personnel representing both the security and program areas, but none from the unit where the accused was housed. He wanted all three staff to be willing to convict Schultz, no matter how weak the case or how strong the defense. Being security staff himself, it was not difficult for him to find such employees from the security area. He quickly decided to invite the Deputy Warden of the maximum custody unit and the Shift Commander of the medium security unit. The program area was a different matter. It would look good if he could find a program staff who was also willing to convict Schultz, have a unanimous verdict. But if he could not find one, it didn't really matter. The two security staff would constitute the majority and their decision to convict Schultz would prevail. After scanning the personnel in education, vocation, religion, and health fields, he found a psychologist who was new, and who, having been there only six months, he reasoned, would be easy to manipulate.

Then he picked up the phone. The first call he made was to the selected Deputy Warden, "Sir, I am calling to seek your help in a matter of extreme importance."

"What matter?"

"Schultz. You know Schultz?"

"Of course, who doesn't?"

"Sir, Mr. Martinez and myself would be greatly obliged if you could find time to preside over a disciplinary court created to convict, I mean to hear a case against, Schultz. I will be the prosecutor."

"When?"

"Tuesday, at 10 a.m. in the ASU conference room."

"This is Friday."

"Yes, sir. It is short notice but its urgent."

"Isn't this about Schultz's outbursts the other day?"

"Yes, sir."

"This doesn't give any time to the accused to gather his witnesses and engage an attorney."

"We are sure he would not want any. He's so arrogant and cocky."

"What if he does?"

"Then we will change the date. We do not want that, of course. Mr. Martinez, under Mr. Karcher's orders, wants it done immediately."

"I understand the need, but we must follow the procedure. Assuming everything goes as planned, I will be there. I am looking at my appointment book and see no conflict. Let me and the other court members know if the court date changes."

"I will. Thank you, sir."

Next, he called the chosen Shift Commander. The phone was answered immediately, "Hello."

"Hi. This is Tommy Jordan. How you doing?" Sharing the same job title, the two had a more informal conversation.

"Good. And you?"

"Up to my neck in work. ... Need your help."

"At your service, any time."

"Next Tuesday at 10 in the morning, in the ASU conference room. I need you to be a disciplinary court member to convict Schultz." This time Jordan let his real intentions be plain, no formalities with a buddy-colleague were needed.

"Okay. You got it."

Now came the difficult part, just a little difficult. Jordan called the Health Unit and asked for the psychologist he had picked out for the job. He had to wait a couple of minutes before he heard, "Hello. May I help you?"

Program personnel were a different breed, hated by the security staff for their treatment orientation, but treated with restrained respect because of their higher status in the chain of bureaucracy. "Yes, sir. This is Tommy Jordan, Shift Commander, ASU. We need your help."

"Anything I can do."

The response told Jordan that there wouldn't be any problem with this guy. He said, "We need you to be a member of a disciplinary court for George Schultz. I believe you know the inmate."

"I have heard the name, but do not know the person."

"You can look at his file, if you want. He is a real pain."

"What would I have to do? I don't know anything about disciplinary courts."

"Not much. Just listen to the charges then vote to convict him. If you desire, you can ask him some questions also."

"Just convict him, guilty or not?"

"That's the idea. You know, we staff stick together. Besides, I am sure you will find the evidence against Schultz overwhelmingly damaging. So, can I count on you? This will be an experience." This was another hook which, Jordan was sure, would drag the psychologist into his fold.

And it did, because the psychologist agreed, "Yes."

"Thank you. So, I will see you in the ASU conference room on Tuesday at 10 in the morning. Okay?"

"Let me see if I am free." After a few seconds, he said, "I have to do a psychological evaluation at that time."

"Reschedule it. It shouldn't be a problem." Jordan knew the psychologist was in his grip and he could order him around, not really order, but prod him, sort of.

"Right. I could do that."

"See you then, And, call me if you have any questions."

"I will. Thank you."

It was six in the evening when he was done. Surprised and pleased that he was able to find all the chosen disciplinary court members by the end of the day. Tired already, he faced all night guard duty, his own doing. Still, he did not mind. He was willing to take extra responsibility. That was the way to promotion. Although promised, the promotion could easily slip away if he did not keep his boss happy.

He headed home. There was enough time for dinner and a short nap.

At 11 p.m. he was in front of the Martinez residence.

It was boring. Except for an occasional car passing or a dog barking, there was nothing to see or hear, or even do. Just be there, stand, sit, and pace.

Still, anything could happen, any time.

CHAPTER FOURTEEN

RISE LIKE A TSUNAMI

Three days passed since George Schultz had issued his threat and nothing had happened.

All this time he remained confined to a cell without any of his personal possessions, and with the bare essentials of a set of clothes on his body. The furnishings consisted of a mattress, a blanket, a toilet, and a sink. He was escorted to a single exercise pen outside the building three times a week, each time for an hour. The rest of the time, he sat in his cell, waiting for something to happen, from the prison or from the AV side, something, anything. Sometimes, when he got too bored, he tore the mattress and blanket to pieces for entertainment.

Technically, he was not in isolation, in reality, he was.

He could not believe it. The prison did not need this much time to put together a case against him. They made up charges and cooked up evidence when there was no case. Here he had provoked them with plenty of ammunition. Still, no action. What was going on? What was taking so long? Not that he was anxious to go to isolation, a few grades steeper than the isolation he was in. He knew for sure that that was the fate for him. It was just that when something didn't happen in a normal way, it meant something abnormal was going on. And, that couldn't be good news for him.

Whatever, he had learned to deal with adversities. Soldiers had to be prepared and ready for any eventuality. He was already putting up with the damn meat loaf and water. Getting sick of it. Sometimes he would just throw the tray back at the guard who brought it. Better to go hungry than eat that shit. He had already lost some weight. In the stepped up isolation, when he got there, he would lose some more. He would probably have to endure some pain too, real pain, the kind that churned your stomach, made your eyes bulge out, made your ears ring, and made you dance on your butt uncontrollably. He would endure all that and survive the persecution, the abuse, because he knew it would be temporary and a tool in his secret escape plan. And after he was free from this hell, he would create a bigger hell for these self-righteous, smug, and self-congratulatory idiots. He would rise like a tsunami and devour everyone who had ever tried to stand in his way.

So what if it was taking longer than normal! Sooner or later he would get what he wanted. He was certain that his threat would work. It would have already spread throughout the prison. One of his AV brothers would have communicated it to other brothers outside who would be planning to march. They would eliminate these assholes who had been manipulated into taking punitive action against him. Manipulated by him. He wanted punitive action, had purposely invited it, because it would assure his freedom. How? Only he knew.

Sometimes, he did get depressed and could not help but wonder if the end was near. Then, he would become philosophical. It really did not matter what happened to him. Everyone and everything, including his enemies, would come to an end. What mattered was the present and what he did, before the end came. What he did was a crusade which would continue until the goal was achieved, maybe not in his life time, but it would be achieved, with the help of others who would follow him. In the process, there would be sacrifices, there would be suffering, and there would be death. A lot of blood would be spilled. He recalled his 'We Bleed White' speech of so many years ago. It was certainly true, not literally, but in a metaphysical way. The prison was a small stage for his bleeding warrior role, his real arena was global.

But he did not want to die in the execution chamber. He would die a warrior's death, fighting his enemies. That's why it was so important to escape. And escape he would, and, in the process, cheat the prison of its chance to execute him.

His concern over the prison's inaction, however, evaporated when on Monday he was served with a notice of a court hearing against him.

He was charged with:

Using offensive language, swearing, and cussing.

Threatening staff with bodily harm.

Assaulting a prison official, throwing a food tray at staff, and spitting and urinating on staff.

Disrupting official business, a meeting.

Destroying state property, tearing mattress and blanket.

The notice included the date, time, and place of the disciplinary court meeting. It informed Schultz of his right to defend himself and present his witnesses, or have an attorney represent him. He was warned that if he failed to be present, the case would be discussed and the judgment passed in his absence.

Schultz knew that the charges were accurate enough but the process was phony, because the prison staff had already decided what they were going to do. The whole thing was a farce. He tore up the notice and threw it away. By his actions he had, in effect, waved his right to witnesses and an attorney.

The next day, a few minutes before ten, two guards came to take him to the disciplinary court. He agreed to go with them, happily. The prison was playing right into his hands and didn't even know it. He was ready to spit venom at the court, receive the maximum punishment possible, and move one more step closer to liberation.

He extended his arms through the bars to be cuffed. After the handcuffs were on, he pulled his hands back. Then the door was opened. One guard stood attentively ready to subdue the prisoner if he misbehaved while the other guard put chains around his legs and belly. The belly chain was tied to the handcuffs. The guards, one on each side, held his arms at the elbows, and guided him out toward the conference room. Schultz shuffled along, quietly and obediently, surprising not only the guards but everyone else they passed.

Upon entering the conference room Schultz found all the principals of the disciplinary court gathered around a table, waiting for him. Each had a yellow legal pad and a ballpoint pen on the table in front of him. The guards guided Schultz into a resin chair placed directly facing the court. Schultz scanned his surroundings. Except for a bunch of chairs scattered around, the room was bare. He looked at the court and recognized two of its members, the Deputy Warden and the Shift Commander. He had spent time with them in their units in the past. The psychologist was new to him. He had never met him but had seen him walking around and heard about him from other inmates who had gone to see him for what they called 'psychological mumbo-jumbo'. In addition to the court members, there was also Tommy Jordan, seated on the left side of the court about five feet away. The guards, who had brought Schultz into the room, took seats away from everyone, remaining vigilant and ready to respond to any request from the court.

Before starting the proceedings the Deputy Warden turned to the psychologist and said, "Would you mind taking notes of the proceedings? We don't have a Secretary"

"No, not at all, but I don't know how. I'm new here," said the psychologist looking rather uncomfortable.

"I'll do it," offered the Shift Commander. He pulled the legal pad in front of him and poised his pen on it for attack.

"Thank you." The Deputy Warden acknowledged the offer.

That settled, the Deputy Warden turned to Schultz and started, "Mr. Schultz, thank you for coming."

Every time Schultz had a meeting with staff he heard that sentence. These retards had a formula for everything, even talking. He said nothing.

The Deputy Warden ignored his silence and said, "I am the Judge today. The other two gentlemen along with me constitute the court.

Mr. Jordan here is acting as the prosecutor. He will read the charges against you.

Schultz looked at Jordan who impassively pulled out a sheet of paper from a file folder he was carrying and read the charges.

The accused remained silent.

The Judge asked, "Mr. Schultz, do you dispute any charges?"

Instead of answering the question, Schultz asked a question of his own, "Who put together this kangaroo court?"

The Judge responded with a great deal of restraint, "The policy requires three neutral staff to constitute the court. That's what we have here." He didn't really answer the question. Schultz knew why. He knew the routine; the Prosecutor always called the court, and how could the Judge admit that?

Schultz sneered, "Neutral my foot. You want neutral, bring people from outside the prison. And, this Jordan. He works in my unit, damn it."

"They are neutral because they have not witnessed the crimes you have been charged with, and they do not work in your unit, so have no direct authority over you. Besides, this is an internal matter. We cannot bring outside public in here. Yes, Mr. Jordan is not neutral. He can't be, he's prosecuting you. But, he will have nothing to do with the judgment. He won't be voting."

"Whatever the fuck you idiots do, I don't care," spewed Schultz with disdain.

"So, do you plead guilty or not guilty to the charges?" asked the Judge.

Schultz fixed his hostile gaze at him and said nothing.

The Judge returned the stare and said, "Mr. Schultz, you do not need to be hostile to us. We are just doing our jobs."

When Schultz still did not answer, the Judge repeated his question, and added, "If you do not answer, the court will assume that you are pleading guilty."

This time Schultz simply said, "I wanna go back to my cell. I know what you guys are doing. Just do it and get it over with."

"In that case, the court notes that Mr. Schultz pleads guilty. That makes any questioning or expression of any opinions by anyone quite unnecessary. I will go ahead and pronounce the judgment and the sentence."

"Just one thing," Schultz interjected and surprised everyone.

They all looked at him in a questioning pose, but the Judge also asked, "What?"

"Just let me keep my family photos."

"Isn't that jumping the gun? You haven't heard the sentence."

"I don't give a fuck about your sentence. Just let me keep my photos. If you don't, there will be hell to pay, I promise you that."

"Mr. Schultz," Jordan explained, "the point we are making is: why demand something which may not be taken away? So, please calm down. Still, I must point out, we are not intimidated by your threats."

Schultz didn't say anything, but his angry eyes said everything.

The Judge took on his presiding role, "Mr. Schultz, you're, herewith, found guilty as charged and sentenced to isolation for a period of 30 days. In isolation you will have no communication with anyone except your attorney, and that, too, only if the request comes from him. Any other communication will be at the sole discretion of the staff. You will have no personal property of any kind. But, I don't see any reason why you should not be allowed to keep your photos. Mr. Jordan, would you please make sure that Mr. Schultz's photos are not taken away from him?"

"Yes, sir," Jordan agreed.

"You will receive meals three times a day," the Judge continued.

"The same fucking meat loaf, yeah?" asked, or rather commented, Schultz.

"Whatever your Deputy Warden decides. You will be given a change of clothing every other day. You will be allowed solitary showers and exercise three times a week. If you require medical attention, you can tell the guard assigned to your area, and it will be provided. The medical staff will have the final say in this matter. If you misbehave, the period of isolation could be extended to 30 more days, or even beyond, at the sole discretion of the ASU Deputy Warden. Mr. Schultz, do you understand the sentence?"

"Fuck you," Schultz answered.

All this time the psychologist sat twitching his face, looking amused and curious, and occasionally shifting position in his chair.

The Deputy Warden said, "Let's sign the papers and get back to our units."

The Shift Commander pushed the papers toward him.

The Deputy Warden threw a cursory glance at the notes, made sure that the recording format had been followed, and that all the essential information such as date, time, place, names of the accused, prosecutor, and court members, charges, verbal exchanges, court decision, and sentence, had been noted. How could it be ready right after the proceedings? Most of it must have been put together in advance, he was sure. It was done all the time. The Deputy Warden signed the document at the bottom, dated it, and passed it on to the other court members, who also signed it promptly.

Formality completed, the papers were delivered to Jordan.

The court adjourned.

The guards put their hands under Schultz's armpits, pulled him out of the chair, and carried him away.

Schultz got exactly what he wanted, photos, and another step closer to freedom.

He was taken straight to an isolation cell, 6' X 8', furnished with faint indirect lighting, a futon-like mattress and a blanket made of so-called indestructible material, a recessed toilet, and a water spout. This wasn't much different from his previous cell except for very limited sights, sounds, and smells. He had been to isolation many times before and knew how to deal with loneliness. Besides, he was never really lonely, his family photos and his heartbeat were his constant companions, his true companions. But Schultz knew this isolation would be different. There would be torture which few would see and only he would feel. He had made himself ready for it, after all he had worked very hard to invite it.

He hoped that his brother remembered 'Birthdays'.

CHAPTER FIFTEEN

THE FIRST VOLLEYS

From the day the task was assigned to him, it took Jordan about a week, five days to be exact, to decide what needed to be done with Schultz to satisfy Karcher and Martinez. He remembered, 'worse fate than death awaits Schultz'. Karcher's words, but communicated to him by Martinez.

It was a three-stage plan, initially, more to be added later. Each stage was separated by a few days. The length of the interval depended upon the speed with which Schultz recovered from the previous treatment. It was important that Schultz should receive a string of attacks without being killed.

Now he had to find a staff who could implement his plan. He needed someone who could maintain secrecy, could communicate with him without creating any suspicions in the minds of other staff, could move about normally while carrying out the brutal assaults, could act with such finesse that no clue of any kind or documentation of the operation was left anywhere. Also, that he was not queasy in the stomach and faint of heart, and had enough knowledge of anatomy and physiology to be able to cause extreme pain without killing the victim.

He thought of several guards including Ibarra. None of them had the qualifications needed. Of course, many of them could be trained, but there wasn't enough time for that. So, in the end, it was he who would have to carry the burden.

Besides, he wanted to be the master of this project.

He called Martinez who had to be kept informed of all the details of this business. "Sir, the operation we talked about is ready to be launched. Could I come and see you, tell you about it, confidentially."

"Of course. Come now."

The meeting was short. Jordan said, "The plan involves gradually stepped up bodily assaults which will cause extreme suffering but no death. I have not decided what those assaults specifically will be but I will call you after completion of each stage and tell you what I did. Or, would you like to know the means of punishment beforehand?"

"Not if it is going to delay the task."

"Yes, sir. Calling you or seeing you to get an okay before carrying out the punishment would slow down the process considerably."

"Okay. I really don't want to know what you do until it is done. That way my office will be protected. No one could accuse me of not stopping something I did not know anything about."

Jordan didn't like it because it meant that if there was any leak, he would be blamed for abusing Schultz on his own without knowledge of and permission from his superiors. But, that was the way of bureaucracy and he had to accept it. So, he said, "Yes, sir." After a moment of contemplation, he added, "One more thing, sir."

"Yes, what?"

"I would like the do the whole thing myself. I have not been able to find anyone else right for the job. I don't have time to train anyone, either."

"That's all right. Just make sure our asses are covered."

"Yes, sir. And sir, for the success of the project, Schultz needs to be in a cell which is totally isolated. I don't want anyone, any guard, any inmate to be able to hear or see what is going on."

"Of course," Martinez agreed.

"So, I need your permission to clear the area in which Schultz has been placed."

"I will get you a written permission before the day is over."

"Thank you."

Martinez was satisfied with all that Jordan had told him, yet not quite.

"Where's Ibarra in all this?" he asked.

"He has been assigned to Schultz's area."

"That's all?"

"He is the most reliable and trustworthy person we have. Of course, he will have a bigger role to play, a little later, once he becomes familiar with the operations and I've had a chance to train him."

That training card again, and it worked. "All right." Martinez agreed reluctantly. He definitely wanted Ibarra to be a major player but also understood the need for him to get properly trained.

The next day, Jordan, before going to visit Schultz, walked over to the unit office, peeked into the video monitoring area and said, "The camera in Schultz's area will be off while I am there. Every time. Don't be alarmed. I will turn it back on when I leave."

"How will we account for the lapsed time?" asked the staff monitoring the video.

"Repairs, or maintenance."

It was afternoon. No staff had any routine business with Schultz at this time and he would have a free hand without anyone knowing what was happening. He walked briskly, quietly, and maintained a serious countenance. Stopping in front of Schultz's cell, he looked in through the bars and said, "Mr. Schultz, are you thirsty?"

Schultz was pacing in his cell at that time. He stopped, probably because of the stupidity of the question, and threw a question of his own back at Jordan, "What the fuck are you talking about?"

"I will show you."

Jordan retreated a few paces, turned right, walked a few more paces to a wall and turned off the monitoring camera. Then he took a few more steps to a fire hydrant. He pulled out the hose, dragged it to Schultz's cell, placed the nozzle in the observation window, aimed it at Schultz, and turned on the water jet with a non-lethal force. It threw Schultz against the wall. He tried to regain his balance but slipped on the wet floor and fell. He tried to launch a few choice invectives at Jordan but no words came out, just a whiff of air from the mouth.

The water treatment continued for about 30 seconds. Then Jordan stopped the jet and pulled out the nozzle. A moment later Schultz regained his breath and yelled, "You broke my ribs, you bastard."

Jordan ignored Schultz's exclamations. He put away the water hose, turned on the monitoring camera, and quietly walked away, leaving Schultz where he fell.

When he got to his office he called Martinez and simply said, "Sir, stage one of the project completed. Incident report on its way."

Then he wrote the required incident report, the main body of which said: *The inmate was hosed down to maintain hygiene. He slipped on the wet floor and fell. No injuries were noticed.* It would tell Martinez what actually was done.

The last sentence of the report was to protect himself. If later the injuries were found, it would be thought that Jordan, not being a medical person, just did not notice any. Of course, this was an unlikely scenario, because Schultz was not going to have any opportunity to communicate with any one in any way, and he himself wasn't going to flap his lips.

Stage two came a couple of days later. It required a blow torch. Jordan visited the vocational training area of the prison and borrowed one from the instructor for a day. Then he went to visit Schultz. Same demeanor as during stage one. Same instructions to the video monitoring staff. Same precautionary turning off of the monitoring camera. This time he found Schultz lying on his mattress facing the bars, eyes open. Jordan asked, "Are you cold?"

"Cold?" Schultz sneered. "What do you want to do this time? Burn me?"

"You're smart. You can figure out what's coming."

Jordan turned on the blowtorch. Through the observation window, he aimed the stream of fire at Schultz's mattress, only about three feet away, which caught fire immediately. Schultz jumped up and crouched in a corner instinctively, although he must have known that the corner did not provide any protection to him from fire. The flames leaped from the mattress and licked the walls of the tiny cell and scorched almost everything within it, including Schultz.

"You burned my skin, you asshole. I'll make you pay for it."

Jordan said nothing. He just watched the mattress and the blanket burning. He also watched Schultz abandoning his corner, taking off his clothes, throwing them on the burning mattress, then placing himself under the recessed water spout, and turning it on.

Jordan had an amused smile on his face at the sight of naked Schultz under the flowing water. About half a minute later, he turned off the blow torch, smashed the glass encasing of the fire extinguisher on the opposite wall, took out the equipment, and started putting out the fire. When it was over, there were charred walls, burned pieces of clothing, mattress and blanket, and soot covered Schultz.

The stage one after-action was repeated. The monitoring camera was turned on. Jordan called Martinez and reported, "Sir, stage two of the project completed." This time he did not feel a need to mention the incident report, it was implied.

But, the incident report was prepared, had to be prepared. It said in essence: *The inmate attempted suicide. He set himself on fire. I don't know how he got hold of matches. I think that he probably hid a match or two in one of his body cavities before being placed in isolation. I happened to be in his area at that time. Fire was extinguished promptly by me after discovery. The inmate received minor surface scorching of the body. I offered medical attention which he refused.*

After filing the report, Jordan walked over to Ibarra who was on gate duty. "There was a fire in Schultz's cell. I put it out. But the place needs to be cleaned," he said.

"I will be happy to do it right away. But I will need to be relieved of my duty here."

"No, you can't do it right away. It's very bad. The cleaning might take a full day. I will change the duty roster and assign you to Schultz's cell area, tomorrow. I will instruct the unit office to move Schultz to another isolation cell for just one day."

"Do I need help or can I do it by myself?"

"You might be able to do it yourself, I don't know. You know, this is a secret operation, so I don't want someone else involved. But, if you need help, let me know. I will see what I can do."

"All right, sir. Is this part of the same project Mr. Martinez talked about? I was wondering when I might be able to help you?"

"Yes, it is. And, you are helping me."

"Thank you, sir."

Jordan really did not want to use Ibarra but was giving him some unimportant and menial job to keep Martinez happy. He didn't want anyone to help him with the project, not with the important parts, and wanted to keep all the rewards for himself.

The employee time-clock told Jordan that it took Ibarra a better part of the next day to clean the cell. There wasn't much stuff to throw away but the floor, toilet, and sink had to be scrubbed clean, and the walls and the ceiling, after washing, had to be painted. It was hard work but Ibarra was able to do it. He most likely wanted to do it, needed to earn some reward points for himself, too, Jordan surmised.

The following day Schultz was promptly moved back to his original cell, all clean and smelling of nauseating fresh paint. Jordan noticed that Schultz began to decorate it in his own way; scratching the walls with his nails, peeing all over the floor, and defecating on the new mattress and blanket.

Schultz had only one day to do the interior decorating before he got interrupted by Jordan who decided it was time to move on to stage three. This time he needed to actually enter the cell. Again the pre-action steps of stage one were followed. The video monitoring area was instructed of a temporary failure of video feed in the Schultz area and the monitoring camera was turned off. His stage one demeanor was also maintained. Except, he came prepared with a can of pepper spray. Standing in front of the cell he looked inside and made a visual examination of the place. He saw Schultz leaning against the wall in a sitting position, eyes closed, thinking or meditating. He held the can in one hand and put the key in the door lock with the other. The rattle of the keys and the clang of the door must have startled Schultz who opened his eyes, and seeing Jordan entering his cell, exclaimed, "Now what?"

Jordan attacked him with pepper spray before he could do or say anything. He could imagine what it did to Schultz; the pepper on his still irritated and traumatized body from the fire must have made him feel like he was being eaten alive by a million sharp stinger insects; also his eyes, nose, and mouth must have burned like hell, in spite of his trying to protect them with his hands.

Schultz screamed while twitching all over. Jordan shuffled on his feet slowly and got himself behind Schultz. Then he kicked his victim in the back and made him fall on his posterior. Before Schultz could recover from this assault, Jordan was out of the cell locking the door.

Schultz hollered behind him, "Wait till I get hold of my attorney!"

"Attorney my foot," Jordan minced his words as he turned the video camera back on and walked back to his office.

The obligatory call to Martinez, "Sir, task completed. Other steps still being examined."

This was followed by the obligatory incident report, the substance of which was: *I needed to enter the inmate's cell to make a routine search. I asked the inmate to come up front to be handcuffed. He refused. So, I had to enter the cell and use pepper spray to restrain him.*

As he was leaving the unit, after sending his incident report to Martinez, he noticed that the video monitor was motioning him to stop. He did. The video monitor came to him and said in a whisper, "What happens if someone notices that every time Schultz is hurt the video camera is off?"

"We should accidentally lose or destroy all the tapes which have time gaps, and a few other innocent tapes, too. We don't want anyone to think that the only tapes lost were the ones involving Schultz. Do we?"

"Of course not."

Jordan was satisfied with his handiwork, although all that had been done through three stages didn't quite qualify as 'worse fate than death '.

Apparently, Martinez was not satisfied because Jordan got a call from him after he had submitted his last incident report, "We need more."

Jordan agreed. Had to. Superior's orders.

CHAPTER SIXTEEN

CHAMELEON

It was dinner time at the Karchers. Not the kind they normally had. It was filled with tension. Karcher noticed that Carolyn was silent throughout the meal, but the folds on her forehead and twitching of her lips told of her suppressed anxiety, or anger, perhaps. He did not know what it was about but was sure that it had to do with him, and that made him uneasy. Not knowing what changed the usually pleasant countenance of his wife into something from a suspense film, he was at a loss to say anything. He ate in silence, hoping for an opening of some sort from any direction, so that Carolyn's mystery posture could be unmasked.

It came from Carolyn after they had retired to the living room with their cups of coffee. Karcher occupied one side of the couch but Carolyn chose to sit in a chair facing him. 'Purposely?', Karcher wondered.

"What's this I am hearing?" she asked.

"What are you hearing?" Karcher asked in return.

"That our lives are in danger. All because you decided to punish an inmate who was impolite to you."

"Who is telling you all these lies?"

"No one is telling me anything, not even you. I overheard the porters talking among themselves."

"And you believe them?"

"I am only telling you what I heard. Now, you tell me what the truth is."

"The truth is that an inmate by the name of Schultz has become a serious security threat and has to be isolated. I don't know the specifics of what the staff are doing, but I am sure they are following prison policies."

"You saying you had nothing to do with it?"

"No, I am not saying that. I ordered my staff to discipline him. That's my job."

"And your job has brought us in conflict with the AVs. Schultz is an AV, everyone knows that."

"Such risks come with the territory. I don't go looking for them."

"Then why don't you leave this job?"

"We have gone over this before. I like the job and I intend to stay with it until I retire."

"Retire now, early. We will manage financially. Or get another job, less risky."

"Get another job? At my age? Maybe minimum wage. Retire? Yes, I can retire. It's not the money. Damn it. A man has to have satisfaction in life."

"And you are not satisfied unless you hurt others?"

"No one is hurting anyone. It's the system, that's how it works. If someone gets hurt, it is not any individual's fault."

"The system? You are the system."

"I am only part of it."

"So, you would rather let the system destroy us?"

"You are exaggerating. No one is destroying us." Karcher was lying, of course, as he recalled his conversation with Sheriff Belford. But, he had to lie to calm Carolyn. This battle at the home front needed to end so that he could devote all his energies to defeating the AV.

Carolyn didn't seem to believe him. "How can you say that? The AVs have vowed to kill several staff including you. They might even go after me and our children. That's the word. It's everywhere."

Karcher was still standing his ground, "You are listening to too many rumors. Yes, the threat is there, but it will not hurt us. I have already taken the necessary precautions."

"Precautions? And you didn't tell me? You..."

"I did not want to worry you." Karcher interrupted.

"Okay. So, what precautions?"

Karcher summarized his conversation with Belford, something he had not wanted to do. What was that he had told Belford? 'It will only worry her. I'll tell her later when necessary. Until then, I'll do all that needs to be done, to protect us. After all, it's my responsibility, my burden.' Well, it looked like it was finally necessary, so he told her. He felt it would make Carolyn feel safe, take away all her worries and anxieties. It did not.

Carolyn retorted, "You call it precautions? It's more like a war strategy. I can't use a gun. I won't use a gun."

"You won't have to. I will. Besides, these precautions go into effect only if we are attacked. And, I promise, it won't come to that. I will destroy these AVs before they can say 'Heil Hitler'."

That was the wrong thing to say. The bravado spelled war.

Carolyn became caustic, "Very cute! You tell me. Has anyone ever been able to root out evil by evil?"

What was he going to do with Carolyn? Karcher wondered. He needed her. He needed her strength, her love, her support to accomplish his mission. Instead he was getting flak. But, more than anything else, he needed her on his side. He must try another tack.

He put his coffee cup away, got up, and sat on the floor beside Carolyn's chair. He wrapped his hands around her legs and said, "Don't be angry with me, please! Just try to understand. We are faced with a situation we have no control over. I didn't create the AVs and their hatred toward the prison staff. I also did not write the prison policies and procedures, but I have to enforce them. I know this creates a climate of conflict. Not my doing, that neither. All I can do is to find a way to protect my staff and my family. I am doing the best I can. I need you beside me at this juncture, not against me."

He sounded like he was going to cry. No, it was not phony. This time he had truly become emotional.

Carolyn carefully placed her coffee cup on a nearby side table so as not to spill its contents. Then she held Karcher's head in her arms and said, "You are right. I am sorry for arguing with you. We will weather this storm together. I promise."

Just then the phone rang.

"I will get it," Carolyn said. She relaxed her arms. Karcher got up and moved back to the couch. Contented, happy that he had Carolyn back. He could still feel her arms around his head.

Carolyn went to the kitchen to answer the call. She said, "Hello. Karcher residence."

She silently listened to the message for a few seconds then said, "Yes, Mr. Martinez. He is right here."

Karcher heard her and knew right away that he was needed on the phone. He came to where Carolyn was and took the phone, "Yes, Mr. Martinez?"

He intently listened to Martinez describing the just completed three-stage treatment of Schultz, then said, "This is not enough." He didn't want to say anything more lest Carolyn learned about the operation. After getting the okay from Martinez he hung up.

"Trouble?" Carolyn asked, standing next to him.

"No, no trouble. Schultz is acting up and the staff are trying to restrain him. That's all."

"That sounds routine. Then why did Mr. Martinez call you at home?"

"I guess what he is doing isn't working. He needs my advice."

"But you didn't give any."

"I have to think about it. I'll take care of it tomorrow."

Karcher was behaving like a great, accomplished actor. He could change color like a chameleon. In the prison he was a raging tyrant, at home he was a meek dove. He hoped that Carolyn would not be able to peer into his other side.

To make sure she didn't, he moved close to her, held her in his arms, kissed her gently on the eyes and the lips, and mumbled, "I love you, and I will protect you and our children with my life." As he said these words, he believed them to be true. That was not acting.

Carolyn must have thawed at her husband's gesture, because she said, "And I need you, too."

The two bodies just melted into each other.

CHAPTER SEVENTEEN

BUTTERFLY, BUTTERFLY

It was Thursday, a normal weekday for Robinson, hurried. She woke up around six. After completing her bathroom chores, she started coffee, walked back into the bedroom and shook sleeping Jeremiah, "Rise and shine. Come on, let's get going."

Her son rubbed his eyes and protested, "Too early."

"No, it's not." She picked him up, put him down on the floor, and gently pushed him into the bathroom.

"Don't dawdle there," she instructed and went into the kitchen. She served herself some black coffee and waited at the dining table for her son whose bathroom visits were always short, no more than 10 minutes long.

Her son came and took a chair. "I don't want to go to school," he complained.

"Like always," she said smiling. Then she got up, poured some corn flakes and milk in a bowl, and put it in front of him.

While he ate, she fixed a couple of slices of toast for herself.

Breakfast done, there was not much talk afterwards. They were busy getting dressed and getting their things together, Robinson to go to the prison and Jeremiah to go to the school. They were in the car to tackle the world by 7:30.

Robinson took her son to the preschool, gave him a kiss, and told him, "Be good. Mind your teacher."

Jeremiah returned the kiss and ran inside the school.

It was all routine. Fun routine. Routine that Robinson wished would define her life forever.

She drove on to the prison.

It was all routine at the prison, too. Classification meetings, disciplinary hearings, updating of records, program reviews, answering mail and phone, talking to the inmates with all kinds of requests and gripes, and one-thousand-one other tasks. But it wasn't the routine Robinson wanted to define her life. It was ego enhancing livelihood, something important but not fun.

Locking her office and driving out of the prison was also routine. And so was her going to the preschool to pick up Jeremiah who was waiting for her outside the building with a teacher's aide.

"I hope he was no trouble," Robinson made a polite gesture to the aide.

"He is a delight to have, Miss Robinson," the aide reciprocated.

Social courtesies over, Robinson prompted Jeremiah to jump into the car, buckled him up, put his things in the back seat of the car, got in the driver's seat, and drove toward home.

"Have a good day?" she asked her son, rubbing his head with her right hand while steering with her left.

"We practiced writing. Someone stole my pencil. I had to borrow one from Miss."

"I will get you another. What else did you do?"

"Worked in the garden."

"Was that fun?"

"It was, but the story time was most fun."

"Story time?"

"Yes. The teacher told us stories. I remember one. Wanna hear it?"

"Sure."

Jeremiah recited the story, haltingly, in a child's voice:

"Once upon a time there was a potter. He lived in a small village with his wife and son. He loved them very much. He made very little money and was very poor. Sometimes he did not have enough food for his family. That made him very sad. One day he told his wife, 'I must go to the city. I can make more money there. I'll be back soon. Until then you take care of the home.'

"The wife had no choice. She agreed.

"The potter went to the city. He went from person to person asking for a job. But, no one had work for a potter. He slept on the sidewalks and in the parks and went hungry. Several days passed. He became very weak and could not walk. One day he was lying on the grass in the city park. He was waiting to die. He was sad because he would never see his wife and child again. He wanted to find some way to let his family know that he would not be coming. Then he fell asleep. In his sleep he noticed a butterfly fluttering around him. He thought the butterfly might help. He called it, 'Butterfly, butterfly, I'm dying. Please go to my village and tell my wife and my son that I will not be coming home because I am dead, but I love them, and will love them forever.'

"The butterfly understood the message. It answered, 'Don't lose heart. You will see your family again.'

"The potter was happy to hear that. But he did not know how he would see his family again. In a few minutes he died. The butterfly immediately turned him into one of its own, and said, 'Butterflies can turn dead people into butterflies. Now, come with me and drink some nectar. You will become strong. Then we both will fly to your village. I think you know the way.'

"The potter liked the plan. On the way, the two butterflies met other butterflies and asked them to join them in their journey. They did. All of them carried pollen and seeds with them. When they reached the potter's home they found that his family was very weak and sickly. They did not have enough food to eat. The butterflies then dropped the pollen and seeds around. Many plants grew. Soon there was a lot of food for the potter's family. Everyone became healthy.

"The potter noticed that his family was still sad. They missed him. He decided to change that. One night when his wife was asleep, he went to her and told her, 'I am your husband. I died in the city. I could not come back as a human. But I am here as a butterfly. I have brought all this food for you. From now on I will look after you. I want you to go to the village blacksmith. I have heard that his wife was bitten by a snake and died recently. Be friends with him and marry him.'

"The wife took the advice. She married the blacksmith and lived happily with him and her son for many years. When she died the potter remembered how he had become a butterfly. He then used his powers and turned his dead wife into a butterfly too. The two of them flew away together into the forest."

Robinson listened to the story without interruption. She was surprised that Jeremiah told the story in the language of grown ups. But then, she figured that this must have been the way he heard it from his teacher and must have a good memory to remember. By the time it ended she was already parking her car in front of her trailer home.

"Good story, and you told it so well, too," she said to her son.

In her mind she did not buy it, not quite. These stories always ended on a happy note. This was not the life she knew. Where was her butterfly? In her life story, she was the butterfly, testing her own tiny wings against the ruthless storms raging around her. She had survived so far, pretty much on her own. How much longer, she did not know. Maybe indefinitely, maybe until her next breath.

Then she remembered Bottillo. Could he be her butterfly? He had been coming by her house and calling her as he had promised. Lately he had even been sleeping with her. She looked forward to his calls and visits. And now he had a key to her trailer. Even though she still did not want to marry him, it had become a future possibility.

As she got out of the car and helped Jeremiah do the same, she wondered if Bottillo would come that evening, with a bottle of wine, perhaps. It would be nice and relaxing, if he did.

At that moment she felt that she had a wonderful relationship. There was, in fact, a butterfly, her butterfly, looking after her.

She climbed a few steps to the porch. Jeremiah followed.

She inserted her key in the lock.

Did she feel a presence behind the door? It could not be Bottillo, could it? No, it could not. His car was not there. Then who? What?

Probably nothing.

She turned the key.

CHAPTER EIGHTEEN

GET YOUR HOLES PLUGGED, BITCH

Huddy worked out his strategy only a day after his assignment. The task would be accomplished in three phases, the assembling of the force, the stakeout, and the kill. It probably would be several days before the final climactic moment arrived.

It took him two days after the AV meeting to assemble his force of two, three including him. It was easier than he thought it was going to be. He contacted a man, Travis Torte, he already knew and had confidence in his abilities to carry out his ruthless orders. After explaining the task he said, "As you see, I need one more person. Can you think of anyone suitable?"

"Sure," Torte spoke, "I brought a young man into the organization a few years back. I think he can do the job. Sonny Madrill is the name. You may have heard of him."

"No, I haven't. Any experience?"

"No, not really. But he is mentally prepared for something like this. And he is good at following orders."

"Well, I trust your judgment. Get him on board. Like yesterday."

Torte brought in Sonny Madrill, his trusted apprentice.

On Tuesday evening, Huddy had a short meeting with his team in a coffee house in which he explained the 'how' of the operation followed by a couple of instructions, 'Meet in our garage on the day of the kill. At about one. I have reserved a car, you know, with phony license plates. Bring your gun. You will be more efficient with your own equipment. We will try not to use it, don't want to leave a lot of clues. But you never know. We might need it."

Madrill asked, "But why are we doing this?"

"Because George Schultz wants it," Huddy answered. "He is apparently pissed off at the program review committee. That's all I know and that's all you need to know. And, no word of this to anyone else." He ended his non-answer with the exhortation, "Let's go get her."

What he intended to do to Robinson needed to be done in the privacy of her home. So, not only did he need to know what Robinson looked like but also where she lived. Huddy knew a few AVs who were on Schultz's visitor list and figured they must know her. The next day he contacted one of them. The same day in the evening they planted themselves in front of the prison gate sitting in a dark blue sedan, and waited. The helper pointed out Robinson when she drove out of the staff parking area. They followed her.

It was tedious, boring, and tiring, particularly after a full day's regular work for a living, to follow her to the places she went; the preschool, a supermarket, and a dilapidated house in a depressed black neighborhood.

Now he knew Robinson was not alone. Most likely she had a son, who else would she be picking up from the preschool? And some relatives or friends, who else would she be visiting? This complicated matters a little. He would have to do something about her son, like killing him too. Couldn't leave him alive. He looked old enough to be able to tell the police what happened to his mother and to remember the faces of those who did it. And, these people she was visiting would have to be eliminated, too, if they got in the way. The task, all of a sudden, seemed a lot bigger than he had originally imagined it to be.

He wished he didn't have to do all that and was not sure of his ability to plan an operation of this magnitude. For that matter, he wasn't sure of his ability to carry out the execution of even one person. After all, this wasn't his main occupation, and he had little experience with it. In the past, he had participated in only one venture of this sort in which his role was pathetic, to say the least. He was supposed to eliminate the enemy, instead he himself got shot and had to be rescued by his friends. With that to boast on his resume, he was worried that he would make some serious mistakes, and might even jeopardize the whole operation. Still, he could not see himself as shirking his responsibility. He decided to do all that needed to be done and some more, if he had to, and in the best possible way. That just went with the territory.

Huddy parked about 50 feet from the house and sat, engine cut off.

"Why are we sitting here?" asked his companion.

"Waiting for her to come out so that we can follow her home."

"Isn't this her home?"

"Obviously not. Didn't you see her knock on the door? Who knocks on his own door? She is visiting someone."

"I see. ... But, wouldn't sitting here draw someone's attention to us? The last thing we want is trouble with blacks on their own turf."

"You're right about that. Two whites just sitting in a parked car in a black neighborhood does look suspicious."

"Yeah. If someone asks us what we're doing here we wouldn't know what to say."

"Let's go to that hamburger joint then. You see it, half a block down the road? We order something to eat. A good excuse to stay there as long as we need to. I think we can easily keep an eye on Robinson's car from there."

It worked. They ate a couple of hamburgers, drank several sodas, slowly licked soft ice cream, visited the rest room several times, and talked about nonsense. No one questioned them. They were customers, so what if they were white.

After about two hours, Huddy became concerned, "Any longer and we will look suspicious even here. What the fuck she is doing?"

"Maybe she is staying here overnight," answered the companion.

"We can't sit here all night. Let's go, try it another time. I will do it alone, now that I know what she looks like and what she drives."

They got in their car and started driving away. The kids playing in the street, however, slowed them considerably. They hadn't gone more than half a block when Huddy saw Robinson in his rear view mirror. She was getting in her car with her son. What luck! He wouldn't have to waste another day tailing her. He slammed on the brakes, pulled to the curb, and waited with the engine running for Robinson to pass him, if she drove in his direction. And she did. After she was several cars ahead of him, he pulled out into the street and followed her.

About half an hour later, he saw Robinson pull into a trailer court. He stopped on the street shoulder and watched her. She parked in a one-car carport, got out of the car, pulled her son out roughly, and shut the car door violently. She looked very anxious. Huddy thought maybe she had spotted his car. Then he saw her bumping into a white male sitting on her doorsteps and exchanging a few words with him, acting like she knew him but did not expect him. Then she took out something from her purse and gave it to the man. She unlocked the door to the trailer nervously, got inside dragging her son, while the white man ran toward the street with something in his hand. A gun? Time to scram. Now that he knew where she lived, no need to hang around any longer. Time to really scram.

Huddy floored the accelerator and disappeared from the scene in a flash. He slowed down a couple of blocks later. No one in front of him or behind. He relaxed and asked himself, 'What's the scoop?'

Then he asked his companion loudly, "What's the scoop? Do you know?"

"We know where she lives."

"Yes. But she seems to have a boyfriend, a bodyguard. This complicates matters. To do what we need to do we need her alone. In her home."

"I don't know what your plans are for her. But that bodyguard, boyfriend, or whatever, clearly does not live with her. You watch her place for a few days, throughout the day, find out her routine, then do whatever you need to do when she is alone, or with just her son."

"It delays our operation, but what's a couple of days?"

Huddy started his stakeout by himself. Faster and convenient that way. He did that for the two following days, Thursday and Friday. To be inconspicuous, he left his car at a supermarket near Robinson's trailer court at about 6 in the morning, and took a bus to her place. Then he stayed at the bus stop pretending to be waiting for a bus or just being a homeless person. He did take a bus and went away for a few hours after Robinson left with her son, clearly to go to work. He came back to the bus stop at about 4 in the afternoon, again staying there most of the time until about 10, with short breaks for bathroom visits and dinner in a fast food joint within walking distance. In the end he got what he wanted. The woman left her trailer in the morning at about 7:30 and came back by about 6.00 in the evening. Her bodyguard/boyfriend came to visit her at about 8:00, then on Thursday, he stayed for about two hours, but on Friday he stayed on, spending the whole night there, but not on Wednesday, probably because that was the day when Robinson had gone to visit a run down house in a poor neighborhood.

Huddy didn't have time or patience for a longer stakeout, which did not seem to be needed anyway. He knew now that the best time to hit Robinson and get away would be between six and eight in the evening, after she came back from work and before her bodyguard/boyfriend showed up. Also, he would have the whole day, from the time she left for work until she came back, to set the stage.

The window of opportunity for the actual operation was very narrow, only two hours, and even narrower if he allowed for unanticipated changes in his victim's routine. Huddy felt that he could complete his task within the available time period, but he would have to work very fast and be very efficient. He did not like the feeling of being squeezed in by time and blamed Robinson's bodyguard/boyfriend for it. A thought of eliminating him did cross his mind, but was quickly rejected. The man was not a target and going after him would unnecessarily delay the operation. It would have been nice if he were not there, but the fact that he was there simply meant that Huddy would have to work around him, treating him as a non-person, not caring to know who he was or even what he looked like.

But, he mused about the relationship, 'The bitch is fucking a white guy. All the more reason to eliminate her.' He chose next Thursday for the kill. That would give him the whole weekend and three weekdays for planning and pre-operational arrangements. He hoped nothing would go wrong. He knew that hope often got modified or destroyed by reality, but did not want to think about it. If he did, hope was likely to be destroyed, even before reality was encountered.

Huddy met his team in the AV garage as planned. Each person left his car there, and all three got into a previously reserved, dark blue Buick. Huddy drove with his two fellow executioners occupying the passenger seats. They arrived at Robinson's trailer park about four hours before her return time and parked on the street, choosing a place where his car blended with others, becoming inconspicuous. Everyone got out.

Huddy opened the car trunk and retrieved his supplies; a crow bar which he hid in his jacket sleeve and a lot of duct tape which he put in his pant pockets. He felt he was missing something but could not think of what it was. With an uncomfortable feeling, he quickly reached into the glove compartment of his car and pulled out his handgun, looked at his fellow travelers, and asked, "You got yours?"

"Yes," both answered simultaneously.

"Okay. Hide it inside your clothing and don't use it unless I order," he instructed.

Then he looked around to make sure no one was watching them. Satisfied, he motioned his troops to follow him and strolled over to the back of Robinson's trailer. He used the crow bar to remove a piece of skirting and all three crawled inside, very quickly, very smoothly. They felt secure in their hiding place. So they took their time removing floor boards and climbing inside the trailer. They found themselves in a bathroom.

Not wanting to attract any outside attention, they did not turn on any lights, did not open any drapes, used no radio, TV, or any other sound-producing appliance, avoided even flushing the toilet after answering the call of nature, talked in whispers, and walked stealthily. They agreed to ignore the phone if it rang, no one was supposed to be there. But only until six, after which the receiver would be taken off, to give an impression to any caller that Robinson was home but on the phone. No suspicions would be aroused that way, not until they had gone away. They ate what they found in the refrigerator and the cabinets and made themselves comfortable. They weren't concerned about leaving their fingerprints, which could not be matched with any prints in the possession of the police, since none of the men had any police record. To pass the time they nosed around.

Finding a photo album they poured over it. There were photos of a growing child, a beaming mother in many different poses and roles, cooking, having a water fight with her son, and playing with him in a park. A few photos, also of her with a white guy, just portraits. Looking at these photos they forgot their mission, but only for a short while.

When it was close to six, they got ready. They took the phone off the hook and positioned themselves on the left side of the entrance so that they would be invisible behind the panel when the door opened. Their timing was good. They did not have to wait long for the key to turn in the front door lock.

As soon as Robinson entered with her son, Huddy grabbed her from behind and Madrill duct taped her mouth giving her no chance to scream. Torte did the same to the child all by himself. They used additional tape to tie their victims' hands and feet and threw them on the living room floor with a thud. No need to worry about the noise any more, it would be considered normal by any one who heard, believing that Robinson was home. As Robinson fell, her purse flew from her shoulders and landed a few feet away from her, spilling its contents; make-up, a notepad and a pen, some money, and a gun. Torte reached for the money and the gun, exclaiming, "Some bread and steel, man."

Huddy admonished, "Don't take anything. We are not thieves."

Torte backed away. Huddy quickly went to the door and locked it as a precaution against any friendly neighbor just walking in. Then he looked at Robinson and announced, "Get your holes plugged, bitch."

He could see terror pouring out of Robinson's eyes. What was she thinking? That they would kill her, mutilate her, torture her, rape her?

He saw terror pouring out of the child's eyes too.

Good, the bitch and her son needed to feel terror. Not just anticipating what was going to happen, but actually experiencing it.

Huddy chose three usable orifices in Robinson's body to violate. Two were easy, but the mouth? The tape would have to be removed. What if she screamed alerting the neighbors, or what if she chomped down on the penis and chewed it up? He decided to do it in two stages, mouth being reserved for the second, when she would be immobile.

Huddy uncovered himself below the waist, lay on his back, and masturbated himself to stiffness. Madrill and Torte tore off Robinson's uniform and underclothes. Torte exclaimed, "O la la, sexy," at the sight of her black panties with red initial 'S' and 'R' and black bra.

"Shut up," Huddy chastised.

"Sorry," Torte apologized and became more focused on the task. He, with Madrill's help, hoisted Robinson over Huddy, face to face. They folded her legs at the knees and pushed her down. Her dry vagina was stretched painfully as a lead hard penis punctured her.

"Okay, it's your turn Madrill. Get into her from behind," Torte said.

"Is it necessary?" Madrill asked hesitantly.

"We have gone over it, damn it. You're not quitting on us now, are you?" asked Huddy.

"No. But she has been humiliated enough."

"There's never enough humiliation. Now get on with it," Huddy ordered.

"I can't do it. It's nasty. I don't dig shit."

"All right. Do it with a broom or something."

Of course, an order had to be obeyed, code of the organization. Madrill quickly brought a broom from a closet and thrust it into Robinson's anus, rupturing it, blood trickling down her thighs. Torte slapped Robinson hard as she tried to free herself from the painful position.

The sustained attack from three sides soon took its toll on Robinson, and she fainted. At that point the broom was pulled out and she was separated from Huddy and thrown on her back on the floor. Torte now took his turn. He unzipped his jeans, pulled out his penis, and stimulated it to hardness with his hands. Ready for the assault, he took off the tape from Robinson's mouth.

Madrill knew what was coming and he objected again, "She is unconscious, man. How do we humiliate an unconscious person?"

"I will tell you how. I am gonna revive her, then violate her. Someone, I prefer Huddy, to sit next to her abdomen, and hit her stomach hard with a fist to open her mouth, if she tries to bite me." Torte went to the kitchen sink, got some water in a glass, and splashed it on his victim's face. He continued to do so until Robinson's face twitched and eyes opened. Then, he straddled her at the neck area, and tried to stick himself into her oral cavity. Robinson started to whimper and refused to open her mouth. At that point, Torte signaled Huddy who punched her in the stomach. The mouth opened automatically and a blast of air came out. Torte took this opportunity and thrust himself into Robinson's mouth. Still, it was hard to go in and the penis was scratched and bloodied by the stubborn teeth. Yet, the task had to be accomplished. And, it was. No sooner had he entered her than he extricated himself from the body.

None of the men ejaculated, that was not the purpose.

Huddy quickly taped Robinson's mouth again and also her nose. The three attackers stood there watching her suffocate. Reflexively, she heaved her breasts, twisted her facial muscles, and made some gurgling sounds. After a minute or so, all that stopped. The three violators used paper towels to wipe blood and other organic fluids from their bodies, and put on their clothes.

Before leaving, however, Huddy said to no one in particular, "Do something with that kid. He has seen and heard a lot."

Torte responded to the call. He briefly looked at the bulging, questioning, scared, and pleading innocent eyes of the child. Then, he gritted his teeth to chew down any compunction and stomped on the child's face a few times, pulverizing it, blood spurting out of every orifice.

Right away he noticed blood on his boots and complained, "Fuck."

"Stop whining. Wipe them on the carpet," instructed Huddy.

Madrill looked at the crushed face of the child and began to shake like he was going to faint.

"What's the matter, man?" Torte asked while rubbing the soles and sides of his boots and the pant ends on the carpet.

"How could you?" Madrill could barely get the words out of his mouth.

"When we go, we go after the whole clan," answered Torte.

"A child? Someone totally neutral in the conflict?"

"Snakes are snakes, babies and all."

While Torte justified his actions, Huddy rushed over to the bathroom and flushed the toilet, now that its noise was not a concern any more. A dirty toilet was not civilized. Bloodied dead bodies in the living room were a different matter. They were the result of a war, and a war was civilized.

Mission accomplished. Huddy was pleased that they did not have to use their guns, and the whole operation was smooth, efficient, and quiet. He collected the crow bar and unused duct tape, and the three warriors left as unhindered as they had come in. This time through the front door, fearlessly, like they were leaving after a friendly visit. And, they left the door open. There was nothing to hide except themselves and they would be long gone before anyone found the carnage. Huddy looked at his watch. It was only 7:08. They did good, time-wise, also.

They had gone past only two trailers when they encountered a man coming toward them with a bag wafting Chinese in one hand and swinging a six-pack in the another.

Huddy wondered if he was Robinson's boyfriend. Wondered, because he never had an opportunity to see him up close. Wondered still, because the man's height, build, and walk seemed similar to those of the man he had seen the other day in front of Robinson's trailer. Wondered also, because he seemed like the man he had seen in several photographs in Robinson's album. And, he had arrived at about his usual time, although a bit early. Whatever, be cool.

"Hi," the man greeted them pleasantly.

The AVs did not want to be greeted, they only wished to get away from that place as fast as they could. They also did not want to act guilty and draw attention to themselves. Huddy, as the leader, took upon himself to handle the situation. "Howdy?" he answered.

"Haven't seen you before?" the man asked casually.

Even though their hearts jumped to their throats, they outwardly remained calm. Huddy answered, "We are from out of town, visiting friends."

"Of course."

"Nice meeting you," Huddy said cordially and walked past the man. Madrill and Torte too, although without speaking.

The man looked at their backs and returned the courtesy, "Same here."

No sooner had the words come out of his mouth than he said, looking at Torte's boots, "Looks like your friend stepped on something. Ketchup?"

Huddy controlled his annoyance and fear as best as he could and answered humorously, without stopping or turning, "Probably did. He is always stepping into shit."

They wanted to run, but the judicious part of their brains ordered them to walk. They did, but as fast as they could.

The encounter with the man shook the confidence of Huddy in their safety, and made him realize that they had been careless in a number of areas, particularly in leaving their fingerprints. In a restrained voice through clenched teeth, he said, "Fuck."

"What?" asked Torte.

"We forgot to use gloves."

"So? We have no police records. Police can't match our prints with the ones they have on file," said Torte.

"But now they will. Anytime in the future, if we are picked up for anything, we will be easily connected with these murders."

"We will have to be careful not to be picked up."

"Shit happens. You know as well as I."

"Too late to worry about it now. Let's go," Torte prompted.

"Yes. Let's go," Huddy said, but he kept wondering, 'Could it be his inexperience which made him forget the gloves? Or, could it be that using hands without gloves just came naturally and the gloves never entered his mind?'

Still, it was clear that a serious mistake had been committed.

He knew but didn't want to know. At the time, he just wanted to disappear.

In the car, Huddy noticed Madrill craning his neck back toward the trailer, looking disturbed. A bad sign. He also noticed Torte leaning back in his seat and sighing deeply with relief. A comforting sign.

Ignoring both, Huddy just revved up the engine and sped away, very angry at his mistake.

CHAPTER NINETEEN

FROM HELL TO HELL

BOTTILLO CALLED ROBINSON a little after six to ask her not to bother with dinner as he was on his way with some sweet and sour pork, egg rolls, fried rice, and some beer, figuring there was some milk in the refrigerator for Jeremiah. The line was busy. He called two more times, line still busy. 'What the heck, just go there now, a bit early, before she starts fixing the evening meal,' he instructed himself.

He got to the trailer court a little after seven, parked in the visitor parking area, and walked toward Robinson's trailer, carrying dinner. On the way he came across three strangers walking briskly in the direction of trailer court exit. He exchanged friendly greetings with them and remembered the humorous comment by one about ketchup on the boots of another. Simple courtesy, of course. Yet, it did not feel quite right. He looked at the three backs quickly moving away from him and shook his head at something incomprehensible about the movement, attitude, and speech of the three men. It was like something that did not gel. The men seemed to be out of place, like a piece of jigsaw puzzle in a wrong spot. He was not normally suspicious of people unknown to him, but he certainly had an uneasy feeling about these strangers. All of a sudden he thought he knew who they were and was alarmed.

He ran over to Robinson's trailer and rang the bell, three times, out of a sense of decorum. No answer. He knew Robinson was home, her car was parked in its usual place. Why wasn't she answering? Even if she were in the bathroom or just indecent, her son would answer. But there was dead silence. Dead? His heart jumped a few feet. Hurriedly, he pulled out and used his key to the trailer. He didn't need to, the door flew open. He entered while screaming, "Stella, you okay?"

What he saw froze him on the spot. The ghastly scene made his head spin. The food and beer slipped out of his hands and spilled all over the floor. He stood shaking from head to toe. He wanted to scream and cry but no sound came out of his mouth. It was hard for him to believe that a tough talking, tough acting woman, strong, self assured, and independent, was lying there in a heap like offal. If the AVs wanted to desecrate her private temple and destroy her self-worth they could not have done a better job. Then he remembered the three men and his discomfort about them. They had to be the ones who committed this horrible act. Suddenly, he was filled with anger, which helped him gather his composure. He ran out to find them, catch them, kill them, and worse. He forgot that he had no gun and was no match for three strong killers. He looked and looked, but there was no sign of them.

Even though he had come to see Robinson earlier than his usual time, he blamed himself for not being there sooner. His eyes welled up and he felt a marble stuck in his throat.

Somehow, he recovered himself from fainting and realized the need to call 911. Now, slowly and resolutely, he walked back to the trailer and looked for the phone. He found it on a table next to the living room couch, receiver off the cradle. Now he knew why he had been getting busy signals. He pressed the hook to get a dial tone, then dialed 911. After giving his name, he begged hysterically, "Send someone, please."

"Calm down, sir. What's the problem?" the operator answered.

"Two people murdered."

"Are you at the scene?"

"Yes."

"We have the location of your phone. The police and ambulance should be there in a few minutes. Please stay there to meet them."

"Okay." Then, he slumped on the floor.

He sat looking at the two bloody and mutilated bodies. Jeremiah's face had lost its contours, all features were distorted, misshapen, and misplaced, and a piece of duct tape loosely hung from a part which must have been lips. Robinson's face, although intact, was covered with rippled, traumatized muscles, pieces of duct tape firmly placed over the mouth and nose. He gently removed the duct tapes, very gently as if it might hurt her, slowly moved his hands over her bulging eyes and closed them. Then, he sat next to her, cross-legged, lifted her head, put it in his lap, and mumbled gently, "We should have gone away." Not accusingly, but sadly.

He sat. The fading evening glow turned black, but he sat. In the darkness of the room he saw ghosts, evil ghosts, circling him. But he sat, unafraid, resigned to die himself at their hands. But, they faded away. A few minutes later the police arrived. An ambulance also came at their heels.

The officer in charge approached Bottillo and said, "I am officer Clyde Hefferly. Did you call 911?"

"Yes."

"And you found these bodies?"

"Yes."

"How did you get in?"

Bottillo felt he was being treated as a suspect but was too grief stricken to indulge in self defense. He simply answered, "I have a key. But the door was unlocked."

"You have a key?"

"Yes. We, Stella here and I, are friends, we work together at the prison. We are CPOs."

"I see."

From the way the two words had been uttered, Bottillo felt that Hefferly understood the nature of his friendship with Robinson. He also noticed a change in the officer's speech, from hostility to compassion, from suspicion to understanding. All because he worked at the prison? Of course. They were both in the same law enforcement business, brothers in trade. How often, after being stopped for speeding, was he let go by traffic cops with just a verbal suggestion to drive safely, after spotting his ID hanging from his shirt pocket or jacket lapel, announcing him to be a prison employee?

He acknowledged Hefferly's expression by his silence.

Hefferly then went on to say in a friendly tone bearing admonishment, "Looks like you disturbed the crime scene."

"I am sorry. I didn't know..."

"Never mind. You seem to be in shock. Do you need any medical assistance?"

"No."

"Then why don't you rest in the ambulance while my men do their work? You don't need to see the police procedures. They aren't pretty. ... Stay put though, I need to talk to you."

Bottillo put his hands under Robinson's head, lifted it carefully, moved it slightly to a side, and put it down on the floor. Then he got up. He was wobbly on his feet. The room reeked of death. What was he going to do?

He did not have to answer. A paramedic and a police officer came, helped him out of the trailer, and into an ambulance. The paramedic asked, "Would you like a tranquilizer?"

"No," Bottillo answered. He just wanted to die.

"Rest then. If you need anything let us know. We will be in the trailer, working."

The paramedic left but the policeman stayed behind keeping watch over Bottillo. 'What? Was he a suspect?' He was too grief stricken to analyze police behavior any further. He sat in a daze. What he had tried to prevent had happened. Now what? Somehow it felt like his life had ended with that of Robinson's. Still, he needed to look beyond the tragedy. Look at his own life. What kind of future was there for him without Robinson? And what about Robinson's mother? She should know what happened from him, rather than from the impersonal police or the news media. Then there were the AVs. They must be punished. But, how? He had no immediate answer but was determined to take revenge.

His train of thought was broken by the arrival of officer Hefferly.

"How you feeling?" the officer asked sympathetically.

"Confused, angry, depressed," Bottillo answered.

"I can understand that. Obviously you had a special relationship with the victims." Hefferly sat beside Bottillo. He pulled out a small notebook and a pen from his shirt pocket and started taking notes.

"Yes, I cared for her very much."

"Could you tell me what happened, what you saw, heard? Anything? It would help us solve the case."

Not being in a comfortable frame of mind, Bottillo kept his narration very brief. He related everything he knew starting with the program review committee meeting. When he came to describe his meeting with the three strangers, he was interrupted by Hefferly who looked agitated, "Hold it there. What did they look like?"

Bottillo described them the best way he could, making it a point to mention something red, most likely fresh blood, on the boots of one man.

"That's a critical fact and we didn't know about it. We could have caught them by this time. Now it may be too late."

Bottillo knew that Hefferly was not accusing him of anything, he was self-musing. Yet, he felt guilty and kept silent.

He saw Hefferly pull out his radio, dial a knob, and speak into it, "This is Officer Hefferly. Alert all units in the field right away to stop and search any car with three adults, one short and two tall, one with fresh blood on his boots. The suspects may be armed and dangerous, so tell the officers to take extreme precaution. Ten-four."

Bottillo hoped that the killers were still on the road and one of the patrols would spot them, arrest them, and bring them to justice, which meant get them a death sentence.

He was still daydreaming when he heard Hefferly ask him, "What else can you tell me?"

Bottillo summarized what he found and did after leaving the three strangers until the police arrived. He made it a point to emphasize that he suspected the AVs behind the crime to avenge their leader's abuse in the prison. In the end, he asked, "Do you know how they got in? There was no forced entry."

"But, there was forced entry. You did not see it because it was in the bathroom. ... Not a word of it to anyone, though. You understand that?" That's where the officer stopped.

Bottillo figured that Hefferly did not want to tell him anything else about the case and wanted him to keep confidential everything he did know. So he confirmed, "Of course not," then asked dejectedly, "But, what are we going to do?"

"We are already doing it, looking for the men. We will find them."

Bottillo did not share his enthusiasm. He sat feeling depressed.

After a few minutes of silence he heard Hefferly again, "Do you know if Ms. Robinson has a family? Anyone who should be notified about this tragedy?"

"Yeah. Her mother. If Stella has any other family members alive, she never told me about them."

"Know her address, phone number? .... We can find all that out after we examine Ms. Robinson's belongings. But, your help will make our job easier."

Of course, she must be informed about what happened to her daughter and grandson. He was thankful to Hefferly for bringing up the issue but did not think the police or any bureaucratic machinery, for that matter, were appropriate for the task. So he said, "Yes, I know her address and phone number. But I think I should take this sad message to her. I could comfort her in a personal way."

"But, are you up to it? I mean, it is a very difficult task."

"I don't know if I am up to it, but it needs to be done and right away, before the media get wind of it."

"The media already know. They have access to 911 calls. But, they will have to contact us for details, and we do not give out any information, certainly not names, until the family has been notified."

"Still, I think I should leave now. I don't want to be here when the news media arrive."

"Okay. I will arrange an escort for you."

"No please, I need to talk to her alone, personally."

"The police will not go inside the house. I just want to make sure you get there safely and come back safely. In your condition, it is not wise to go alone."

It sounded quite logical, but Bottillo felt that Hefferly did not want him out of his sight. Did he suspect him of the crime? Well, if he did, he would just be doing his job. Bottillo did not take offense and simply agreed to the suggestion, "All right."

But he was aghast when Hefferly, after talking on his radio with someone in police headquarters, said to him, "The escort will be here in about half an hour."

"I can't wait that long."

"I have no one to spare. The station has to find someone and send him here. Normally there would be two officers, but in your case we will manage with one, and even finding one is proving to be difficult. Just half an hour. After all, It's not an emergency."

"For me it is." Now Bottillo was upset. Out of frustration and anger he said, "Sorry. You will have to arrest me to prevent me from going." No, he did not want to say that. Arrest would have been a worse choice over waiting for half an hour. The words just came out of his mouth.

"If I wanted to arrest you, I would have done so already."

"Then let me go."

"All right. This is what I'll do. I'll relieve one of my officers to drive you to this place you need to go to, and bring you back afterwards. I can manage with one less officer for half an hour until relief arrives. But, I need the address where you are going. And, could I have your address and phone number also? Solving this case pretty much depends upon you."

Bottillo gave Hefferly the required information and asked, "What happens to the bodies?"

"There will be autopsies. Mandatory in such cases. After that they can be claimed by the mother."

"What if she is not able to? Can I?"

"We will have to consult our legal department. But I don't think there would be a problem, so long as the mother does not object."

As he got in the police car, Bottillo glanced at the trailer which had been cordoned off by yellow tape announcing, "CRIME SCENE". To him it announced 'Final Separation'. He felt like crying. His eyes did not, but his heart did. If only Robinson had listened to him! But this was not the time to find fault with her judgment.

As he sat in the moving car, he was confused about his emotions. There were so many, intermingling with each other, that he was not sure how he felt. But he knew one thing. Sadness at the loss of a dear person and anger at the perpetrators of the offense, together they were an explosive combination. He did not want to explode and tried to calm down. He did not explode but could not calm down.

At that time, more than anything, he wanted revenge.

But before revenge it was time for... for what? To comfort Robinson's mother on her loss. Even before that, he would have to give her the bad news. He wished he could do it without making the old lady fall apart. If she could not handle the shock there might not be any opportunity to comfort her. How was he going to do it? He realized he could not plan for it. He would just have to do it, and do it in whatever way he could.

When the police car reached the destination, Bottillo said to the officer, "I don't know how long it will be. If you need to go, go, give me a phone number where I could call you when I'm ready to leave. Or, if you can't come, I'll catch a cab."

"You take your time. I'm on duty and I'll wait."

As Bottillo got out of the car, his courage to face Robinson's mother began to fail. He just stood in front of the house, almost paralyzed. Then he let his mind push his heart in the direction of the front door. He knocked feebly.

"Who is it?" The words slid through the torn screen.

"Phil. Stella's friend." The nature of the relationship had to be mentioned for Robinson's mother to understand who he was. After all, she had never met him and might have not even heard his name.

"A minit."

Slowly a frail shadow emerged behind the screen. It put its hand on the door knob, turned it, and pushed the door open. "Comin," it said.

Bottillo followed Robinson's mother into the living room where Blues floated out of a radio. He sat on the couch while she occupied a rocking chair facing him.

"How's ma babies?" she asked.

How was he going to answer that question? What was he going to say? The words totally failed him. He sat there with his mouth half open. A moment later his face sagged and tears started to form in the corner of his eyes.

The message was communicated. No words were needed.

"Ma baby boy?"

The tears spilled out of Bottillo's eyes.

Robinson's mother sat with trembling lips and unblinking eyes. She did not ask how, when, where, and why. They were irrelevant questions.

Both sat silently, burdened by their grief, for how long, neither knew.

"Let me take you to a hospital," Bottillo finally managed to suggest.

"No," she answered, emphatically, although the words were barely audible. "I die here."

Bottillo sat with her. He tried to talk, she would not say a word. He made some coffee, she would not drink. After a while Bottillo saw that she had closed her eyes. Looked like, she had fallen asleep.

Obviously not. There were tears. They had broken the eyelid dam and were flowing freely. The stone mask had finally cracked.

Bottillo remembered something Robinson had told him. Her mother never cried. In her long life of only 56 years, she had endured much, but never cried. Not when her first boyfriend had abandoned her after she became pregnant with his child. Not during birthing pains. Not when her husband was shot dead by the police. Not when her three boys left her, dividing their time between the streets and the prison. Not when her daughter fell prey to a conniving young man. She had turned into a stone sculpture, but with a bleeding heart.

Not any more. The stone wept, not the tears but blood, draining her heart.

For a long time, she sat in the same place.

Bottillo offered again, "Could I get you something to eat, drink?" No answer.

Bottillo looked at her face intently and noticed that the lips and the cheek muscles had stiffened, and the eyes were dry and unblinking. He knew. Still, he checked her pulse. Now he was sure.

The radio continued to play the Blues.

Bottillo sat on the floor, his head in his hands. If his heart were a jet engine, it would have exploded into a million pieces.

CHAPTER TWENTY

CLEANSING GUILT

As Huddy drove from Robinson's trailer court, Madrill was thoughtful, contemplative. He wasn't sure that he wanted to be a soldier any more.

Was this the only killing? Were there others planned or already carried out? He had heard rumors among the AV rank and file that several state prison staff were to be executed. How many? And how many more children would be sacrificed on a whim or as a matter of convenience? He did not see himself as an AV any more and was angry at anyone who was. He thought about the man they had met in the trailer court after the completion of their mission and hoped he would help the police unravel the AV plot and catch these baby killers. Then he thought, why wish for someone else to do what he wanted done? He must do it himself.

His stream of thought was broken, when Huddy stopped at a convenience store after about half an hour's drive and said, "I need to report the success of our operation to Goodwin."

"From here?" Torte asked.

"Yes. I don't want the cops connecting us to him if his phone is bugged."

"But if his phone is bugged wouldn't the cops go after him when they hear about what we did? Then it would be easy for them to find us."

"Relax," said Huddy, "I'll only say 'Job's done'. Anyone listening would think it's about some building project. Goodwin is a carpenter, you know." He got out of the car and went to a pay phone.

Torte leaned back in his seat, but Madrill was anything but relaxed.

Huddy was back in a couple of minutes. All he said was, "Goodwin got the message."

The car was moving again. It screeched to a halt inside the huge AV garage. Everyone got out.

Huddy faced his companions and said, "Well done. Now keep quiet like you don't know anything about it. And Torte, go wash your boots now. They are a dead giveaway."

"Damn boots with nigger blood," Torte cursed and went to the washroom to scrub them clean.

Madrill said nothing. He pretended to be fascinated by a dozen or so cars in the garage while deciding what to do to stop further killings.

After Torte was back, Huddy said, "Let's go home. Clean up, get some grub, and sleep. Remember, today did not happen."

All three got in their own cars and drove away in different directions.

For Madrill, today did happen and it changed his life. Until today he was willing to take other people's lives for the principles he had been taught, now he was willing to give his own life for the principles he had just acquired. You could not kill a child for any reason. So, he determined to defy the AVs, no matter what the cost.

After getting home, he immediately hit the shower without even saying hello to his sister with whom he lived. He felt dirty, not because of his contact with a black woman but because of what he had done to her. He came out of the shower still feeling dirty. The water could not cleanse his guilt. Something else had to be done, but what? There was no immediate answer. He had to think. Coming up with a plan was so important that everything else became secondary, including the evening meal. He went to the kitchen where his sister was cooking. He told her, "Don't prepare anything for me. I am not hungry."

"You sick or something?" asked his sister.

"No. Just tired." In part, this was a truthful answer.

He went to the bedroom and sat in a chair thinking. A few minutes later it came to him, a perfect plan. At least he thought it was a perfect plan.

He picked up the phone and dialed the number for the state prison.

An operator answered, "State prison. How may I direct your call?"

"Warden Karcher please."

"He is gone for the day. Please call tomorrow."

"It can't wait till tomorrow."

"Tomorrow at eight, please. Ask for extension 3000," the operator said mechanically, like he was not hearing Madrill.

Madrill got angry. Here he was trying to save the lives of the prison staff and they were giving him a brush off. "You're not listening to me. The Warden's life is in danger. I must talk to him right away."

That made the operator alert. "What's you name, sir?"

"My name is not important. Just connect me with the Warden."

"Hold on," said the operator.

About a minute later Madrill heard the operator again, "Thanks for waiting."

Immediately after that, he heard, "Hello, this is Warden Karcher. Who am I talking to?" He also heard a tape recorder turned on. It did not particularly bother him. So what if they found out who he was through a record of his voice? He would have already completed what he had set out to do.

"What I have to say will interest you. My name is irrelevant."

"All right. Go on."

"AVs are after some prison staff members."

"I know that. You're wasting my time."

"It's not a threat any more. Robinson is gone. Stella Robinson and her son have just been killed."

"I know that too. The news is on TV, radio, everywhere." Still there was a detectible tremor in his voice. Caution? Fear? Anxiety? Worry?

"But you don't know the killers. I do. I was there. What happened disgusted me so much that I am willing to risk my life talking to you."

"How do I know you were there?"

"What if I told you Robinson was wearing black underwear. Also 'S' and 'R', bold, in italics, were embroidered in red on the left front of the panties. You want to check it out?"

"Can't right now, can I? Let's assume you're for real, what do you want?"

Madrill felt insulted that Karcher would not trust his altruistic motives. But what he had to do was beyond ego. So, he simply said, "I don't want anything for myself. I just want this madness to stop."

"How?" Karcher sounded interested.

"I don't know the size of the operation. But I do know one thing. The operation is directed by Stewart Goodwin, Regional Commander of the AV. That's who you need to catch, if you want to stop this mayhem." Madrill felt guilty a second time that day, this time for betraying the organization. How much guilt would he have to carry?

"I know who Goodwin is. But, why are you talking to me? Why didn't you go to the police? Why not try to stop Goodwin yourself?"

This time Madrill got angry at Karcher's suspiciousness, "Are you kidding? In our organization we obey our leader, we don't question him. If we do, we are considered traitors and executed. And police! I can't believe you would be such a dunce. If I go to them, they would take their sweet little time investigating my information. In the meantime people would get killed. It's you and your people whose lives are in danger. You are the one who needs this information."

"How do I know you are not setting us up? We go there to apprehend Goodwin and we are ambushed." Distrust. Doubt. Would they ever end?

"If you don't believe me, it's your problem. I answered the call of my conscience. There's nothing more I can do. Goodbye," said Madrill with exasperation and hung up.

Madrill had thought that this talk with the Warden would make him feel better. It did not. He felt dejected.

X

Sonny Madrill's life had been a classic tale of disappointments and failures. He never understood, why was he born, or even his older sister, Susan? He knew, of course, that his parents paired and the children popped out. What he did not understand was why did they do it, when obviously they did not want them? His father hardly ever noticed his children because, when he was not working, he was almost always on drugs, crack being his favorite. When he did notice them, he beat them up and called them names for no apparent reason. His mother was an alcoholic who hardly ever bothered to cook and the children pretty much subsisted on convenience foods that they could find in the refrigerator or pantry. Their ragged clothes and old shoes with worn-out soles and heels told them that they were poor. Not because of any real lack of money; his father earned decent wages as a mason. It was the drugs and the booze that kept the family in poverty, but strangely the children were blamed for it; they were the burdensome 'extra mouths' to feed.

Madrill was never what they call bright. He was often put down by his classmates as dumb. He was also roughed up by bullies. His short stature, 5'3", did not help either. All of these factors together led to his very poor self-concept.

He found solace in his sister. She was his protector. When they were little, they would huddle together away from their parents' sight. When he would get home, after being molested by neighborhood kids or school bullies, he would find comfort in his sister's arms. The huddling continued even when they entered their teenage years. The physical closeness brought emotional security which he could not bear to let go. They even slept in the same bed. The parents were too aloof from them to notice, and the children would keep the pretense of having separate bedrooms and sneak into each other's bed during night when the house was quiet. After completing high school, his sister moved out of the house taking him with her. She got a job as a secretary, and he fried hamburgers in a fast food joint. They got by financially. Emotionally, they could have not been more content.

Madrill liked his sister but did not like himself. He became moody and withdrawn. Several times he thought of committing suicide. His life had no meaning, and he did not want to be a burden on his sister forever.

All this changed one day. He was on his break, sitting on a concrete bench in an outside eating area. He was sipping a coke when a man came and sat on another bench facing him. The man looked to be several years older than he and quite opposite of him in almost every respect. He was big boned, muscular, and rugged, and his face showed maturity and confidence. Madrill had seen this man many times before when he came to buy his lunch. He looked at him curiously.

The man said, "Hi." He sounded friendly.

Madrill responded, "Hi." Just courtesy.

The man said, "I am Travis, Travis Torte."

"I am Sonny Madrill."

The reciprocal introductions, social formality. What next?

"Yeah, I see your name on your uniform. Looks like you don't have many interests. You just work here."

"So," Madrill was a little miffed at the man whose words felt like a put-down.

"I didn't mean to offend you," Torte tried to smooth out the wrinkled situation. "I was only making an observation. I thought you could use some friendly company."

"Like what?" Madrill's curiosity was piqued.

"Like a club I belong to."

"A club?"

"Yeah. Sort of. It's a group of patriotic people. We use our free time doing exercises and playing games. We also learn to use firearms. You never know when we may have to defend our country."

It sounded interesting. But? There was always a but. "Why do you want me? And what will it cost me?"

"Nothing. There is no cost. Like I said, you could use some company and excitement, and of course, we would benefit from having a nice young man among us."

Madrill did not see any subterfuge, any con game. All he saw was a sincere offer, mutually beneficial. Still, he acted cautiously and said, "Let me think about it."

"Absolutely. Take your time. Let me know when you have decided. You can find me easily. I buy lunches at your place."

There was no hard sell either.

"All right."

Madrill discussed this with his sister. She immediately suspected the man belonged to one of those white supremacist groups; they were always recruiting young men for their organizations. Her feelings were neutral toward them. She told Madrill, "You decide. If you join them, it will give you something interesting to do. There is only one problem; once in, you can't get out. Also, sometimes they do violent things. This is what I have heard."

"Well, I will ask a lot of questions, and if I am satisfied, I will join."

His sister said, "That's reasonable."

Next day when Madrill saw Torte he told him he wanted to learn more about his group.

He found out it was the Aryan Vision. The more he learned about them the more he liked them. For the first time in his life he felt he would not be a weakling to be pushed around and abused, a poor slob to be spit upon. He would be someone, something. Even though physically small and not very strong, he felt he would be powerful, particularly with a rifle in his hands. He didn't care much for the white cause and fighting for it, but it was a means to his self realization. He decided to join the organization. Torte sponsored him and became his mentor.

As an AV, Madrill participated in many dangerous missions, including a few bank robberies which, in his way of thinking, were essential to raise money for the organization. None of that compared to what he was asked to do under the leadership of Huddy. When the task and his role in it were explained to him, they seemed all right, even exciting. At the time.

X

During the operation, however, the perspective changed. Humiliating and killing a defenseless black woman, for the simple reason that she was a member of Schultz's program review committee, did not seem exciting or justifiable. Then stomping on the head of an immobile child was gruesome and inexcusable. The image of the physical abuse he endured as a child flashed on the screen of his mind, and he became even more disturbed. Perhaps he had not been brainwashed as well as the AVs would have wanted him to be.

Sitting in his bedroom, the more he thought the more he realized the absurdity of the plan which only a few minutes ago had seemed perfect to him. What he had done was totally futile. His contact with the prison Warden would not remain secret. Sooner or later he would be found out to be the rat that he was and would be executed. Of course, that was the risk he had been willing to take when he had decided to talk to Karcher. Now, after the talk, he became aware that the purpose for which he had taken the risk would not be accomplished. The killings would not stop. So what if the police arrested Goodwin? Someone else would take his place and carry on the unfinished business. He also saw that the prison and the police would retaliate, and many AVs would die too. When he had joined the AV, he had seen dying as a sacrifice for a noble cause. Now he saw dying as dying, accomplishing nothing. The fight to be supreme had been going on for thousands of years and would continue as long as humans existed. The resulting suffering had also been going on and would continue. It was endless.

Enough was enough. He had suffered enough emotional trauma. No more.

That was when he made another decision. He wrote a note to his sister:

Dear Susan,

Goodbye is a hard word to write, but I have no choice. I can't explain it to you, but I am through being an AV, and you know what that means. For years you have protected me from harm. You can't do that any more. I got to go. I am sorry.
Sonny

He put the note on the table next to his chair.

Then he took out his loaded handgun, which he had carried with him on the just completed mission, put its opening under his chin, and pulled the trigger.

CHAPTER TWENTY-ONE

THERE'S A MOLE IN MY SOUP

KARCHER SAT THINKING about the suggestion he got from his anonymous caller. It might work. Connect Goodwin with the Robinson murder, charge him with being an accessory to a crime, then offer him a plea: he would not be charged with any crime if he stopped any further attacks upon the prison staff. Sure, it would not bring Robinson's killers to justice, but who cared about a black woman and a black kid? The main thing was that it had the potential of stopping and even eliminating any AV threat to him and still giving him a free hand to punish Schultz any way he wished. It would also eliminate any threat to his remaining staff. Not that he much cared for either Martinez or Gopal, the two brown, sorry excuses for human beings, he still needed to save them so that the AVs could not chalk up any more victories. Anyway, for this plan to work he would need the cooperation of the police and the prosecutor. No problem. He could surely count on Sheriff Belford, and the prosecutors traditionally sided with the law enforcement officials anyway.

A better scenario, however, would be to completely destroy the AV organization. Not because he disliked their philosophy, actually he agreed with it. It was just that they were a threat to his survival. This war was not guided by philosophical values, it was guided by the motives of power and domination. Better or not, this scenario was not going to occur.

The first idea had its own problems. He couldn't ask the police to file charges against Goodwin without any evidence of his involvement in the Robinson killings. If only his anonymous caller were willing to be a witness, which did not seem likely. He wished he had a private army, which could be used to invade Goodwin and force him to do his bidding. He did have an army, of sorts, under his command, and a lethal one at that, but its reach was limited to the prison. He was beginning to feel frustrated. It was like he was within a few feet of the summit but had no means left to conquer it. He needed help.

Again? What happened to the help he was promised by Belford a few days ago? The surveillance of the AV principals, the protective watch over the threatened prison staff? Well, the help was there but it did not work. Robinson still got killed. And her son too, an innocent entity, simply because he was present.

Still, he must talk to Belford. Tell him about the anonymous call he had received. Something in it might help Belford come up with a better solution this time. But it was past ten at night, so Karcher decided to wait until morning.

Sleep evaded him pretty much all night. In the morning he sat, sandy eyed, at the kitchen table, drinking coffee prior to getting ready to go to his office. He opened the morning paper and there it was. The Robinson murder was headlined prominently on the first page. There were photos of the victims. He felt sorry for them but did not have any feeling of sadness or loss. It was like war, you surged ahead pretty much ignoring your fallen comrades, sometimes even walking over them.

He got to his office by eight and waited until eight thirty to call Belford, giving himself enough time to get his coffee and settle down in his chair. He hoped Belford did not have any early morning meetings to make him unavailable.

He hoped correctly. Belford answered his phone call, "Hello, hello, Sheriff Belford speaking."

"Hector! This is Karcher. Got a minute?"

"Always, for you. It's about Ms. Robinson, isn't it? I feel terrible, terrible. We did everything we could. Tailed the known AV officers, although couldn't provide protection to your staff. We don't, don't, have enough men to go around, you know. Couldn't tap Goodwin's phone either. Needed a court order for that which we couldn't get without any damning evidence, evidence, against him."

Karcher felt like he was getting a list of excuses, but getting irritated over that wasn't going to help him. He needed to stay calm. So, he said in a non-emotional tone, "Actually, this last thing may not be a problem any more. I called to tell you that a man phoned me last night, claimed it was his conscience calling. Said he was there when Robinson was killed. Warned me of more killings and suggested we go after Goodwin to stop further bloodshed. This should be enough to get a court order to search Goodwin's house."

"Yes, if this man, this caller of yours, is for real, real. Do you believe him? What's his name?"

"He didn't give it. Of course, I didn't expect a killer to give his name."

"So, you actually talked to one of the killers, killers. There were three you know."

"Well, I wish he weren't anonymous. He would have made it easy to catch the other two killers. Imagine catching three AVs for murder. It might have prevented them from continuing their misadventure."

"True. Still, how do you know, know, he was not some prankster?"

"A prankster? No way. He offered proof that he was there. Said, Ms. Robinson wore black panties with italicized bold letters 'S' and 'R' embroidered in red on the left front. The media does not have this information, I don't think, but your men do. If they can verify this proof, then this man is genuine."

"I can verify that. His description of panties, panties is accurate…"

"Okay, so he is our solid lead."

"Then we need to use him. Even if we can't find him, we can use his voice, voice. You have a record, I mean tape, of this, his, conversation with you?"

"Yes. It's routine. But, how will that help?"

"It will help us get a court order, order, not only to tap Goodwin's phone, but also to talk to him and search his home, home. Maybe we will find something which will lead us to the killers. Get it over to me, the tape, tape."

"That will certainly solve all our problems. Once you find them you will be able to convict them rather easily, right?. They will get death. Not only that, it might put Goodwin away, too, for a long time, ending this nightmare. Thanks. I will have the tape delivered to you immediately."

Karcher hung up the phone, walked out of his office, stood in front of his secretary, and interrupted her typing, "Get yesterday's tape of phone conversations over to the Sheriff, Mr. Belford. The evening conversations only. A copy."

He went back to his office and sat in his chair brooding. Of course, it would be great if getting a court order with the tape worked. But, would it? It might not. So, he must explore additional ways to contain the AV. He must not lose heart.

The most urgent thing seemed to be to secure his fighting force and keep its morale up. He had to win the war.

So, first he called Martinez, "You heard?"

"Yes, sir."

"The war has started. We don't know how it will end, hopefully without any more casualties on our side."

"Yes, sir."

"Now this is what I want you to do. Increase your security and raise the heat under Schultz, so that he begins to beg for mercy."

"Will do."

After directing Martinez, Karcher called Gopal, "You heard about CPO Robinson?"

"Yes. That's what I was afraid of."

"Now that it's here, the war, I mean, we have to face it."

"I don't think I am up to it. I am a healer not a fighter. Call me a coward but I am very unsettled."

"I am unsettled too. That's to be expected. But, we can't let these criminals win. If we did, they would be emboldened and would do more horrible crimes. We have to stand and fight while protecting ourselves."

"As you know, I have already submitted my resignation. I am out of here in a few days. I am sorry to be such a craven, but what can I do?"

"I am sorry that you decided to leave, but I understand. Still, I called you to suggest that you increase security around you and your wife. Considering the circumstances, this is very important. I certainly would not want you to become a casualty of this war."

"Thank you for your advice. But, I don't think I will be a casualty. You see, I have decided to leave the country in a matter of a few weeks, if not days."

"Good luck."

Karcher was pleased that Gopal was leaving. He would have one less colored worker while the AVs would have one less possible gain. It was a win-win situation for him, and a long term one, if he could find a white psychiatrist to replace Gopal.

After he put down the phone, Karcher wondered if there was something else he could do. And it came to him, rather quickly. Diplomacy. Use it in addition to the punishment Schultz was receiving and which, under his orders of a minute ago to Martinez, would be increased. Maybe it would calm everything down, like a cease fire, would give him time to work out new and more effective strategies. And, if the diplomatic maneuvers failed, then he would take some stronger physical measures against Schultz. At the time he did not know what they might be.

Karcher went to the ASU, straight to Schultz's cell. He dismissed all guards in the vicinity and used the house phone to ask the video monitors to turn off the video recorder in Schultz's area for a few minutes, until instructed to turn it back on again. After that he stood looking inside the cell, through protective Plexiglas, at Schultz lying on his mattress, appearing uncomfortable, most likely from the wounds he had recently received from Jordan. He said in a conciliatory tone, "I have an offer. You call off your men and I will make your life easier."

Schultz expressed surprise, "Oh yeah?"

Karcher saw him turn on his left side, apparently to have a better view of him and also to find a position in which he did not have to lie on his wounds.

"You know how it is. This whole thing just seems so senseless. You and I want the same thing, white man's rule. So, why fight? Call it off, otherwise people will die needlessly."

"That's news, you being on my side. I don't believe it one bit."

"Believe it or not. You would still want to consider my offer for your own sake."

"My own sake? What's in it for me?"

"Like I said, I could make your life easier. Looks like you could use some medical attention. I can have a doctor or a nurse here in no time."

"Here? Not in Health Unit?"

"For security purposes. Besides your injuries do not require a stay in an infirmary or a hospital ."

"That's bullshit, man, and you know it."

Karcher did not think his offer would be rejected so quickly. Maybe, Schultz thought the barter wasn't equal. He must try something else. "Then you tell me?" Still negotiating. Karcher thought maybe, just maybe, Schultz's demand would be something he could live with.

"I want out of here, this hell hole. Yes, I want to see a doctor but in a clinic or a hospital. I also want to see my brother and my attorney."

This was too much. Let Schultz communicate with the outside world and expect a media field day about abusive treatment of prisoners in no time. Karcher would not agree to that, "Sorry, no dice."

Schultz remained silent for almost a minute. To Karcher that meant he was considering asking for something less. He began to sense an upper hand in the negotiations.

But Schultz did not ask for anything else. Instead he said, "You obviously don't want me talking to anyone outside. But, if I were to agree to your deal, wouldn't I have to communicate with my people then?"

Karcher answered, "No, you won't. I will give you pen and paper. I will dictate the terms of the truce, you will write them down and then sign the document. You will address it to someone who has the power to implement it. I will have it delivered."

"You think I am an idiot? You think I will really give you the names and addresses of my contacts? Sign a written document selling out for a little medical treatment? Forget it, just forget it."

"We already know your contacts and their addresses, at least the big contacts. ... So, are you ready to sign the truce document?"

"I won't sign anything. But if you really want a truce, you will have to agree to my conditions." Schultz held his ground.

Karcher quickly examined Schultz's tough stance. It could be because he perceived Karcher's desire to negotiate as a sign of weakness. Negotiations were about making your best move and taking advantage of the opponent's weaknesses. He could not fault Schultz for that. By the same token he could not fault himself, either, for playing his own hand shrewdly. So, he said, "I will agree to your conditions if you ask me something I can grant."

"Then I suggest you find a really big piece of log and stick it up your ass," Schultz said defiantly.

Karcher remembered, wasn't it an expression that he had used for Schultz while talking to Gopal just the other day? How ironic!

That was it. Negotiations had broken down. That put Karcher in a fighting mood, no sense being civil any more. He spoke angrily, "You blew your last chance. Let me tell you, you haven't seen anything yet." Karcher turned to leave.

Schultz spoke to his back, "And let me tell you, I know why you are here. You are losing the war. You don't even know who to fight. How could you fight an invisible army? You don't know who will hit you when and where. You already lost Robinson. Afraid of more casualties? So, you come here waving a white flag."

Karcher was alarmed. How did Schultz know about Robinson's murder? Maybe Schultz overheard some guards talking about it carelessly. That did not seem likely. Jordan had to have carefully selected very responsible staff who would not engage in loose talk, not in inmate areas. The other possibility suggested the presence of a mole. Of course, all staff were screened for gang affiliation before appointment. Still, the procedure was not perfect. It was a serious matter, even frightening. But he did not want Schultz to even guess what he was thinking. So, he kept on walking as if he never heard Schultz's words, which were bouncing off the thick stone walls and echoing loudly in the hollow spaces.

Before leaving the unit he waved at the video monitor and told him to turn the video recorder back on in Schultz's area.

As he walked to his office, it hit him. God, what did he do? He went to negotiate with Schultz out of fear. The victorious did not negotiate, losers did. He told Schultz what he never wanted him to know.

But then he saw Schultz made a mistake too. He overplayed his hand. Now Karcher knew a number of things, although still with question marks:

Schultz wanted to get treatment outside his cell in a clinic or hospital. Why? For possible escape? Could not be. The security was always tight

Schultz also wanted to see his brother and his attorney, why? For assistance in escape or for filing lawsuits against the prison? Not likely. The prison had a way of listening to the privileged conversation between the prisoners and their attorneys, and Schultz, for sure, would know that. Besides, he was already communicating with the AV, and could communicate with his brother and attorney too, through the mole, without prison permission and get whatever assistance he needed for his escape plans or for filing a lawsuit against the prison.

Lack of answers made his position weak. Actually, weaker. If his position had not been weak, he would have not gone to see Schultz. He would have to get some answers, otherwise his position would remain weak. Since no answers were available immediately, he decided to postpone their search for a later time.

Now what? If he could not persuade Schultz to stop the war he would have to force him to do so. Truce by intimidation, torture. Truce achieved this way would end the hostilities and put Schultz in the hospital. The prison administration, having provided medical treatment to Schultz, would be free from any lawsuits. And, with the end of the conflict both sides would feel like winners, both the staff and Schultz would no longer fear that their lives would be snuffed out by their enemies.

Of course, like all humans, he rationalized his desires and actions, and became blind to the disaster his decisions were likely to cause.

He made his move.

First, he wrote a memo for general circulation, very simple, very direct, very forceful:

Any staff found talking about anything not directly related to their duties, near any inmate, will be immediately terminated. They may even be prosecuted under applicable laws. No exceptions.

He gave the memo to his secretary for typing and distribution.

Next, he called Martinez and ordered, "I have already told you, but I must repeat: Force Schultz to seek a cease fire. I have tried to talk to him and that did not work. Also, there is a strong possibility of a mole, an AV mole among us. You see, Schultz knows about Robinson. It could be because of staff's loose talk around him, but I doubt it. Even if I am wrong about the mole, it won't hurt to hunt for it. I think it's in the ASU. Find it."

Martinez did not appear so sure about the mole, "Sir, if there is a mole Schultz would have used it to safely communicate with the AV instead of yelling in the corridors and hoping the prison gossip would carry the message."

"You don't understand. A mole is used only when there are no other avenues. This protects the mole. So, go find it."

"Yes, sir."

Karcher leaned back in his chair and took a long breath. Having taken the actions, he felt better, more in control of the situation.

CHAPTER TWENTY-TWO

THE DEAD MAN TALKED

Hefferly came to his office late, about 11 in the morning, looking tired, droopy, and even sleepy, and was immediately attacked by the pesky media reporters. The previous night, at the Robinson crime site, he had been able to evade them by just saying,, "Later, after we have finished our work." By midnight, the crowd of newsmen had thinned out, most likely because they realized that it would be a futile wait. But, the next day it was a different story. To satisfy the public's need to know, he made a brief statement, "Ms. Stella Robinson and her son were murdered in their trailer home last night at about six p.m. Ms. Robinson was sexually assaulted and killed by suffocation. The child was crushed to death. I can't go into the details, nor is it necessary. The assailants remain at large. However, I am confident we will catch them. That's all for now." He did not say anything about who might have committed the crime or why, primarily because he did not know the answers to those two questions.

Sure, Bottillo had implicated the AVs, but without any solid proof of their involvement, it was speculative. For that matter, Bottillo himself might have committed the crime for a motive only known to him and might be inventing the AVs to divert suspicion away from him. While it was a possibility, Hefferly discounted it right away for several reasons. First, the intruders came through the bathroom and, Bottillo, with a key to the trailer, did not have to. Second, the nature of the crime suggested the involvement of more than one person and Bottillo was alone. And, it did not make any logical sense that Bottillo allowed his companions to flee and made himself a scapegoat. A better scenario would have been for him to scamper away, too. Then, there was a third reason which was most convincing. Bottillo had not tried to hide anything, give any wrong information, evade any questions, or run away from the police. He had gone to see Robinson's mother with a policeman and had come back with him. When asked for the address of his destination and his home address and phone number, he had given them readily and correctly. Hefferly, suspicious by profession, had checked out the 'correctly' part. He had called Bottillo's home number and had been assured after getting an answering machine which announced Bottillo's absence in his own voice. Then, he had called the prison and had received the confirmation that Bottillo did, in fact, work there as a CPO.

Then he felt guilty after receiving a call from Bottillo's escort a little after ten informing him about Robinson's mother. At that point he cleared Bottillo of any suspicion and told the officer to stay with him as long as necessary.

Soon after that, he had placed the crime scene investigation in the hands of his senior assistant and had gone home around one in the morning.

Now, sitting in his office, a bit away from the hustle and bustle of the outer building areas, Hefferly was going over the evidence gathered at the Robinson murder scene, trying to make some sense of it, only to come up with a lot of questions. On the face of it, it looked like a sex crime. But there were things which argued against it. Why was there no ejaculate? Why was she humiliated and not just violated? Why was she killed after the rape? Why was she tortured by suffocation? And if it was to prevent her from identifying her attackers, then why did they leave their fingerprints all over the place? Also, why was her son murdered, crushed so brutally? No, it was not a sex crime, it was, like Bottillo believed, a hate or revenge crime. And, that would also answer most of the questions, except the one about fingerprints. It could have been bravado, a hallmark of the AV. Or, the killers didn't have police records and felt they couldn't be identified. They forgot that they would have the fingerprints in the police records now.

Anyway, the motive seemed to be clear. But it still did not solve the crime.

The mystery of the crime, however, began to unravel in a most unexpected way.

One of Hefferly's assistants came to him and said, "I think you should look at this." He put a file folder in front of him.

"What is it?" Hefferly asked.

"Yesterday evening, while you were investigating the Robinson murder, we got a call from a woman by the name of Susan Madrill about her brother's suicide. He shot himself. I covered that case. The body is in the morgue awaiting autopsy. The name's Sonny Madrill. According to his suicide note he was an AV member. Since I heard from officers who worked with you on the Robinson case that the AVs might be involved, I thought you should know about it. Because suicide is not a criminal case, the body, after autopsy will go to his sister, the only known kin, to do whatever she pleases with it. Maybe you want to see it, get fingerprints, or whatever else, before this happens."

"Good thinking. Thanks." Hefferly eagerly opened the file in the hope of finding something useful there.

As he read the report, it struck him as curious that an AV man committed suicide right after Robinson's murder. Could there be a connection, like his assistant had suspected? Start with the fingerprints. If Madrill's prints matched any of those lifted from the Robinson murder scene, it would establish his presence there and the AV connection. It might even help find the other murderers. He also thought of talking to Madrill's sister, just in case she had any information which would help solve the case.

If an AV-Robinson murder connection was established, he would need to talk to the AV operatives and even search their homes, cars, whatever. For that he needed a court order. And right now he had nothing on which to base his request for a search warrant.

Then he got a quick break in the form of a call from Belford, "Mr. Karcher had an anonymous caller last night. I have the tape, tape. It has everything you need to get a court order, to search Goodwin's home. Get on with it, it."

After he digested the contents of the tape, Hefferly was convinced that the caller to Karcher and Sonny Madrill were the same. To be absolutely sure, he decided to do a number of things: talk to Susan Madrill and ask her if she could identify the voice on the tape as that of her brother Sonny Madrill; show Sonny Madrill's photo to Bottillo and ask him if he saw him among the three supposed murderers he had run into; compare the fingerprints lifted at the crime scene with those of the suicide victim. If the results confirmed his suspicions, he would have one of the murderers, albeit dead.

But, the dead had been known to talk. This dead man too, most assuredly, would lead to the other two accomplices. Hefferly felt good. He decided to get on with it, like his boss ordered.

Excited, he picked up the tape from Belford's secretary, made a copy of it for his own use, then delivered it to the legal department with a request to secure a court order and a warrant to search Goodwin's home and property. He asked that it be done the same day, because after that, over a weekend, it would be hard to find a judge.

Next, he instructed his assistant to get Sonny Madrill's fingerprints and photo from forensics; compare the prints with the ones obtained from the crime scene as soon as possible, and put the photo on his desk right away.

Then he called Susan Madrill. He was not surprised to find her home, being distraught over her brother's suicide the night before, she would not be in any shape to go to work. But, would she be in any shape to talk to the police? Well, He could try, "This is officer Hefferly. I am sorry about your brother."

He only heard sobbing. So, he continued, "I would like to get to the bottom of it and I need your help. Could you spare a few minutes to talk to me?"

He got an appointment for one in the afternoon that same day.

After that he called Bottillo, who, too, was home probably for the same reason Susan Madrill was home. As soon as he heard, "Hello," he responded, "This is officer Hefferly. I am grateful for your help last night. But I have a few more questions for you. I hope you can find a few minutes for me. I am sure you would like to see the killers caught as much as we do."

Contrary to Hefferly's expectations, Bottillo sounded very eager to talk, "For that I will find time. When? Where?"

Hefferly thought for a moment about how long it would take for him to interview Susan and then arrive at Bottillo' place, and answered, "About four, give and take a few minutes. At your place?"

Susan Madrill lived about 20 miles away. He picked up the copy of the Madrill tape, secured a partner, and checked out a squad car.

As he drove, his mind was in high gear. Many questions popped up. Was Madrill the one who called the prison warden? Did he really call the Warden because of his conscience? Did he also commit suicide for the same reason? A conscience factor did not make a whole lot of sense. How could someone associating with the likes of the AVs have a conscience? But then, it did make sense. Maybe he was not fully brainwashed. And if conscience did play a role, did he go as far as leaving clues to facilitate the capture of his murder associates? If so, what clues were there? Or, perhaps he was forced to kill himself by others, like the AVs, who found out about his diminishing loyalties to them and feared his betrayal.

Too many questions and not many answers. Hefferly knew the answers would come as the facts emerged. 'Just collect facts,' he ordered himself.

It took him about half an hour to reach the Madrill residence, even with the emergency lights flashing on his squad car..

The door was opened on the first knock, there was no doorbell in the low rent apartment.

"Ms. Madrill?" Hefferly asked.

"Yes." Susan Madrill looked haggard with a pale face, puffy red eyes, and a weepy countenance.

"I am officer Hefferly and this is my partner," said Hefferly. Both flashed their badges.

Susan slowly shuffled her feet and moved to let the policemen come in.

After the two policemen and Susan were seated face-to-face in the living room, Hefferly started the interview while his partner took notes.

"I am really sorry for your loss, Ms. Susan. I appreciate your willingness to talk to us at such a difficult time. But, your help will help us solve these murders." Hefferly's mind was still on Madrill's connection with the Robinson murders.

"Murders? It was suicide." Susan sounded confounded.

"Yes, of course. But, we have a tape in which your brother confesses to be involved in the Robinson murders. I am sure you have heard about that."

"I have heard about the murders, yes, but..."

"I will play the tape for you. Could you identify if it's your brother talking?"

He played the tape. At the end he asked, "Does this sound like your brother?"

"Yes. But, I can't believe what he is saying."

"So, you didn't know anything about your brother's activities?"

"I knew he was a member of the AV. We talked about it when he joined. He also told me about everything. We had no secrets between us. That's why I am surprised that he did not tell me anything about this. ... As an afterthought, I know why. All the AV activities are secret."

"Do you know who he was with during the Robinson murders?"

"No. Like I said, he did not tell me anything about it."

"Why do you think he killed himself, your brother?"

"It's in his note, and also on the tape you just played."

"Could it be that someone made him commit suicide to hide something, some crime perhaps?"

"I don't know."

"Could it be murder because he was threatening to expose someone, something?"

"How could it be? I didn't see anyone around."

"Maybe someone sneaked in and out."

"But the front door was locked. I had to open it to let the paramedics and the police in. There is no other entrance."

"Maybe someone had a key."

"I would have heard if someone came in. It's a very small place, as you can see."

"Of course. So, you didn't see anyone. But, what did you see?"

"First I heard the gun going off in our bedroom."

"Our?"

"We have one bedroom."

Hefferly ignored the implication and asked, "So, what did you do?"

"I ran to the bedroom. There he was in the chair, dead, blood pouring out of his face and neck, right hand hanging down, and the gun lying on the floor below. I almost fainted."

"What did you do then?"

"What could I do? I screamed. Then I gathered my wits to call 911." At this point her eyes welled up.

"I am sorry for all these questions. But I was entertaining possibilities other than suicide. You see, on the tape, he doesn't say anything about killing himself."

"But it's clear he was distressed with what happened. Then he wrote the note which is very clear about his intentions."

Hefferly was fairly certain now that Sonny Madrill was the one who had called Karcher, that he was one of the Robinson murderers, and that he had committed suicide. From all indications, there were two other killers at large who must be found before they struck again. And strike they would, if they were after the selected prison staff as suggested by Bottillo. So, he changed the direction of the interview. Now it was more like a fishing expedition.

"Just a couple more questions. Did he go to work yesterday?"

"Yes."

"Where did he work?"

"At McDonald's."

"Which?"

"The one near us, on the highway."

"What time did he leave?"

"At six in the morning, his usual time."

"What time did he come back?"

"About eight."

"His usual time?"

"No. When he is on the early morning shift he usually comes back in the afternoon."

"Anything unusual about him last night?"

"He went to the shower as soon as he came home. That was unusual because he always announced his arrival to me before he did anything. I didn't pay any attention to it because sometimes people don't follow their habitual patterns. After his shower he did come to me in the kitchen only to tell me that he was tired and wouldn't eat his dinner, and went to the bedroom. That didn't look very unusual to me. I do that when I am tired."

"Did you ask him why was he late?"

"No. Sometimes he goes to the AV activities after work."

Hefferly smirked snidely within himself, 'Indeed he went to an AV activity after work!' Outwardly he asked, "Do you know any of his friends?"

"He had no friends that I know of. He wasn't very social. ... He was shy."

"I mean his AV friends?"

"No. Like all the AV activities all the AV identities are also confidential."

Hefferly realized that he had all he was going to get from Susan and decided to end the interview. "Thank you ma'm for your help. Here's my card. If you think of anything or need to reach me for something, please call me."

After leaving Susan, Hefferly drove straight to McDonald's, thinking that Sonny Madrill's coworkers might be of some help. He found the restaurant without difficulty. After he showed his badge and explained the purpose of his visit, the Manager was willing to talk. They sat in the dining area, face-to-face.

Hefferly asked, "Did Madrill work yesterday?"

"Yes. He came right on time. He was always a reliable worker. But he left early, at noon. Said he wasn't feeling well."

"Unusual for him?"

"Yes."

"And, did he have any friends?"

"He was friendly with everyone, coworkers, customers alike. He was a very good worker. But, did he have any real friends? No. He was kind of shy, you know."

"Yes. But, maybe he talked with someone more than others, someone special?"

"Well maybe. A customer, Travis's the name. Sometimes they would talk over a cup of coke or coffee, but always during his break, never on company time. He never shirked his duties."

"This Travis character. Do you know anything about him?"

"No, we don't meddle in our employee's personal affairs."

"If you ever see him, would you be kind enough to alert us? Take no action, just alert us. Ask your employees to inform you if they see him."

"Sure would."

Hefferly gave him his card and left. He was pleased. Maybe, just maybe, he had identified one of the living Robinson murderers. Now, to see what he could learn from Bottillo. But, he would have to go to the headquarters first and pick up Madrill's photo, hopefully waiting for him at his desk.

It was.

He did not make it to Bottillo' until after four-thirty. The side visit to McDonald's had eaten into his time. But, Bottillo was waiting for him patiently and invited him into his living room to talk.

After they were settled, Hefferly proceeded with his interview, in a kind of rehearsed formula format, "I am sorry about your loss. I know how fond you were of Ms. Robinson. I hope you were able to get some sleep, some rest."

"Not really. I stayed up with Stella's mother all night. You know, she died."

"She died?"

"Couldn't take the news, I guess. This morning I called a funeral home. After they took her body away, I came here. Been too depressed to go to work."

"I understand. Perhaps I can come back some other time?"

"No. It's okay. You're already here."

"I will make it short. ... Can you identify this photo?"

"He was one of them, one of the three. But, he looks wounded, dead."

"He committed suicide. It's in the papers, TV, but not big news, and no photo."

"How did you find him?"

Hefferly told him everything, including the lead on another of the trio, Torte. He expressed his firm belief that he would soon be able to catch the remaining two, still alive, Robinson killers.

Bottillo appeared to perk up on that, "Pleased to hear that. Anything I can do to help?"

"Yes, a couple of things. You could identify Madrill's body. We have already identified his voice and photo. The three identifications together will leave no question about his identity as one of the Robinson murderers."

"When?"

"Sooner the better. If you are up to it, we can go now. By the way, have you eaten? We could grab something on the way."

"Had lunch yesterday. Nothing since then, haven't been hungry."

"Try something. You need your strength."

"What was the other thing?"

"Help our artist to sketch the other two murderers."

"I can do that, too."

"Is there any way you could spare a few minutes tomorrow for that? Today is too late for our artist to be around."

"But tomorrow is Saturday. Will your artist be available?"

"If you have time I will ask him to come in, as a special favor."

"I am free. I have even taken the next week off. My mind is not on work. Helping the police avenge Stella's murder will keep me sane."

"Thank you. I will have our artist call you."

"That will be fine."

In a few minutes Hefferly and Bottillo were on the road. They first went to the morgue where Madrill's body was kept. Bottillo saw the body and said, "Yes. He is one of the three I saw in Stella's trailer court and in the photo you showed me earlier."

As they got out of the morgue, Hefferly asked, "Where would you like to go? For dinner?"

"Just home. I have food, if I get hungry."

Hefferly knew better than to insist. He took Bottillo back to his apartment.

It had been a long day and he wanted to go home too. Still, he went to his office to take care of the items which needed immediate attention.

First, he called the police artist who agreed to come to the police headquarters the next day to work with Bottillo. He gave him Bottillo's phone number and asked him to call and make an appointment, which he promised to do. Then he checked his 'in' box. There was a search warrant for the Goodwin residence. Even though it would be a Saturday tomorrow, he decided to go and hit Goodwin anyway, surprise him. He would take some comp time later. He also found the report from his assistant waiting for him; Sonny Madrill's fingerprints obtained from the coroner's office did match with some of those collected inside the Robinson trailer.

Hefferly mused, 'Funny, how a dead man could talk.'

CHAPTER TWENTY-THREE

DIGGING DIRT

Goodwin was happy and worried. Happy because Robinson had been eliminated and part of his project was complete. Worried because the AVs involved in the project might be found out. For several reasons. Huddy, after having talked with him briefly on the day of the Robinson murders, had met him in the morning, and while giving him details of the successful completion of his assignment, had also told him that there was a white man, most likely Robinson's boyfriend, who had seen them leave the trailer court. Then, there was the announcement of the Madrill suicide and the publication of his suicide note in the newspapers and on TV, which would implicate the AV, and soon the police would be digging into their operations, starting with his. He had always thought that the dead couldn't tell tales. Here, the dead man was screaming bloody murder.

Whatever, he decided to be prepared to deal with the police, when they came knocking on his door. Actually, it was not a real problem for him. All he had to do was to move and hide all incriminating information before the police came, and act dumb.

But, there were other serious problems, which he did not know how to handle.

First, there was Robinson's boyfriend. Who the hell was he, what did he know, and how much did he tell the police? All unknown to him. Even if this man knew nothing about the AV plans and operations, he certainly had seen the three operatives and could identify them. This made him dangerous and, therefore, he should be eliminated, and before he did any more talking. In order to do this, Goodwin had to find out all about him, such as what his name was, where he lived, what he did for a living, and other necessary details, and work out a strategy to get rid of him.

Then there was Madrill's sister. He was sure that sooner or later she would be approached by the police, and she might be able to lead them to the AVs. Being his sister, she probably knew a lot about Sonny Madrill and his activities, and by association, those of the AVs. This would have not been an issue if Sonny Madrill had kept silent, like he was supposed to. Considering the betrayal he had committed, he could not be expected to keep his mouth shut, not with his sister. There did not seem to be any choice but to extinguish her also, before the police had a chance to talk to her.

It was burdensome to have two more killings suddenly added to his list of the other three, and he wished he didn't have to carry them out. Maybe it was this wish which made him think that he would not have to arrange for the killing of these two people, if they were not real threats. Judging against the seriousness of the threat factor, Robinson's boyfriend could not be spared. He was already an established threat. But Susan Madrill was an unknown entity. To determine her threat level, he needed to find out what she knew. It sounded easy, but when he thought about how to do it, it became almost impossible. Yes indeed, how did one go about searching someone else's mind? Impossible or not, he had to do it, and had to do it now.

Faced with the inevitability of the task, he got an idea about how to do it. But not before he had cursed Robinson for having a boyfriend and Sonny Madrill for betraying his organization. Robinson, the horny bitch didn't need a white cock, she could have fucked herself with a dildo. And that bastard, Sonny Madrill could have killed himself quietly, he didn't have to blabber everything to the prison warden and leave a note for his sister.

In the absence of any solid information about Robinson's boyfriend, all Goodwin could do was speculate. This boyfriend could be a neighbor, a past acquaintance, a classmate, or a coworker. If he was a coworker, it was possible to find him through the AV brothers in the prison, but if he was someone else, it might be impossible to reach him. So, he decided to check out the coworker angle, and if it led to a dead end, only then he would explore other possibilities.

He got in touch with his mole in the prison and asked him to find out if Robinson had a colleague who was also her boyfriend. The mole did not have to find out, he knew. He told Goodwin that Robinson was close, very close, with another CPO, Phil Bottillo, although the relationship was not flaunted, simply because work place romances were not allowed in the prison. So, now Bottillo would be punished by death for having seen the Robinson murderers accidentally. Not right away, though. There were others, who were more important, in line. Still, he decided that the best way to bring about Bottillo' demise would be to have one of the AV brothers in the prison shank him or something.

And, the best way to read Susan's mind was to talk to her. First, he thought about going to her apartment and talking to her face-to-face. He immediately dropped the idea, fearing that the police would be watching the place and picking up and questioning anyone who came to see her, logically thinking that the AV connections might want to silence her, by any means, as a matter of precaution. No, he did not think the police would do that to protect Susan, they would do that as one possible way to catch the Robinson killers. He, therefore, decided to call her instead. What if her phone was bugged? He would cover his mouth, change his accent, adopt a phony name, and would not say anything that might arouse suspicion. What if she was in mourning and unable to talk? Give her till morning the next day.

It was Saturday, his day off. After breakfast he leisurely went to a convenience store, found a phone booth which afforded privacy, and dialed Susan's number, actually Sonny's, figuring that both had the same number.

When Susan answered, he said, "I'm Peter, Sonny's friend. Sorry about your loss."

"Sonny's friend?"

"Yeah. I met him at McDonald's where he worked. I ate there sometimes. Very nice fellow."

"He was kind of shy and not very social. That's why I was surprised when you said you're his friend."

"Quite understandable. ... Why do you think he did that? I never saw him depressed or anything like that."

"Don't know. Police were asking the same thing."

Police? Damn! It was a mistake not to call her yesterday when he had thought about it. If she knew something, she probably already told the police. All the more reason to continue the conversation, find out what she told the police. "Why police?" he asked.

"Again, don't know. Guess, all suicides have to be investigated. A state law or something."

"I suppose. What did they ask?"

"They had a tape. Wanted to know if it was Sonny talking on it. It was Sonny all right talking to Warden Karcher about the Robinson killings and implicating the AVs."

"And all this time I didn't know he was an AV."

"Of course not. It's confidential. But I'm his sister. I knew he was an AV."

"I suppose the police wanted to know what he did for the AVs as part of the murder investigation."

"Yes. But I didn't know what he did. I was no help."

"Well, Susan. I know it is difficult time for you, and wish you weren't bothered by the police. But they are doing their job. ... Is there anything I can do to help, anything you need?"

"No, thank you. I will manage. It's nice to know Sonny had some caring friends."

"Well, Susan, I will be calling you from time to time, just to say 'hi', and see if I can be of any assistance to you."

"Thank you. You're very kind. What did you say your name was?"

"Peter."

"I appreciate your call, Peter. Could I have your phone number?"

Goodwin hung up immediately, making it look like he didn't hear the question.

No, Susan was not a problem. Ignore her.

But that eyewitness had to go. Who was he? The police were keeping a tight lid on his identity. There had to be some way of finding him. But it might take a while. In the meantime he must secure his troops.

Right away he called Huddy, "Madrill screwed us, you know. He talked to the prison Warden before killing himself, the bastard. I just found out, the police have a tape of the conversation. Because of that and his suicide note, the police have linked us to the Robinson murders. I suggest you and Torte disappear."

"And draw more attention to us? Besides, isn't it unsafe calling me at home?"

"I am calling from a pay phone and your phone is not bugged. They don't even know you exist. But as the police investigate us further, they might find you. If you don't want to disappear, do something. Protect yourself and talk to Torte, too, about it. And let me know what you guys decide."

"All right. If necessary, I will disappear. So will Torte."

After that Goodwin rushed back home to get rid of everything he did not wish to fall into the hands of the police.

He was too late. The police were already there with a search warrant for his premises. Damn it. It was going to be a bad day, a very bad day. Still he tried to play it cool.

"What's this all about?" he asked.

"You know what it's about. Now move aside and let us do our job," Hefferly bellowed.

Goodwin stepped aside, hoping for police stupidity, which he was convinced of, to miss the critical documents. He went and sat at the kitchen table. His wife and children, all confused and afraid, gathered around him. He watched the police take over. They were from the big city but there were local cops also. He could tell from the shoulder patches of their uniforms. And they had come with guns. What did they think? That he would not let them in, barricade himself, and put up a fight? He wasn't stupid to do that. And they had a forensics team also. Looked like it would be a thorough search. What would they do? Take his toilet and carpet with them?

Goodwin lived in a typical middle class home with typical junk strewn all over the place; children's toys in the living room, dirty clothes on the bedroom floors, wet towels draped over the shower bars, toothpaste and lipstick marks on the bathroom mirrors, kitchen drawers filled with odds and ends, backyard cluttered with gardening tools with no garden to speak of, and dog shit and piss stains on the carpet and furniture.

He watched the search team go through all that, displacing virtually everything. They examined a lot of stuff, family photographs, letters, phone bills, payment records, check books and registers, all the AV literature, guns, phonograph discs, even his garbage. They also went around tapping floors and walls in search of cavities hiding incriminating evidence. They did not find any. All this amused Goodwin, because he did not think there was anything in all that to connect him with the Robinson case.

However, when they started checking his computer files, he was alarmed.

To distract the police he asked them, "Would you like some coffee and cake? Anything to make you comfortable?"

Hefferly looked a little guilty at the offer and answered politely, "Thank you, but we can't, against the rules. Besides, we're busy."

Goodwin could only hope that they would soon leave without finding anything damaging. His hopes were dashed when he saw one of the cops find a computer file of his regional AV address book with phone numbers. The cop made a copy of the file on a disc and seized the computer. Goodwin sat wondering what the cops would find in the address book that would wreck his handiwork, jeopardize everything he had accomplished so far, and might even send the current prison project into a tailspin.

He took a sigh of relief when Hefferly and his team were ready to leave. The words, "I am sorry to disturb you like this. Have a good day," from Hefferly were welcome, very welcome.

And yet, his heart was erratic. What would they do with his address book?

The good thing, however, was that the Goodwin home did not look any messier than before the search team had descended upon it.

CHAPTER TWENTY-FOUR

THE DARK SIDE OF GOD

WADE SEARLE MADE his move almost immediately after getting out of the AV headquarters. There wasn't time to lose. His action plan required only one other warrior, who could pass for a conservative professional. The ever combat ready membership, dressed in fatigues or camouflage clothing and military boots, sporting crew cut or shaved head, and displaying tattoos of Swastika, sword and crown, and American and confederate flags, was not cut out for the needed appearance. Searle did the best he could. Ignoring the appearance part, which could be created, he decided to pick the right person for the job, ruthlessness being the most important criterion. He found one, Arthur Ellsworth. But it took him two precious days to do it.

The next day, Tuesday, they got together, in a coffee shop for a brief preliminary meeting. Searle outlined the plan, "I want to kill Gopal in a most humiliating way in front of his wife. Then we will kill her too, not leaving any eye witnesses. Specifics will be given to you as we proceed. I want to do this in his house for privacy. It's also safer and more convenient."

"How are we going to get in?"

"We will get to his house on a weekday, in the evening, before he does. Tell his wife when she answers our door bell that we are her husband's colleagues from out of town and would like to meet with him for a few minutes."

Ellsworth snickered, "Who would buy that? And, would we ever look like doctors? Beside, we will need to know his routine to get there before him, won't we?"

"Yes, for his routine, we will follow him after we find out where he lives. Yes again, we will look like doctors with some preparation. And assuming his wife doesn't believe us, we will go to plan 'B'."

"Plan 'B'?"

"Wait outside, grab Gopal when he comes home, show him the gun, and make him take us inside. And, if that fails, we will kill him on the street. Dangerous that way, and doesn't humiliate him the way I want, but it gets the main task done. That's the way it is with contingency plans."

"All right. First thing, where does he live? Do you know? We don't need to know what he looks like, it would be him, in his home. Right?"

"That's right. Let's check the phone book first. If he is unlisted, like most prison employees are, we will follow him from the prison."

"Follow him? Then we need to know what he looks like."

"Not really. How many Indians are there working in the prison? So, any Indian looking person coming out of the prison parking lot would be Gopal."

"It would mess up everything, if we got the wrong person."

"Don't worry. Once we find his home, we will call the county recorder's office to get the name of its owner. It is public record. If it is not Gopal, only then we will try something else."

"All right. Let's start with the phone book."

Searle went to the cash register, borrowed a phone book from the clerk, and came back to his table. After a minute or so of searching, he exclaimed, "Hey, there's a Gopal, but it's with a 'C' not 'R'."

"Maybe he has his phone number listed under his wife's name. You know her name?"

"No."

"Let's dial the number and ask to talk to Dr. Rajiv Gopal. If our call is acknowledged, we will know it is the number. We can get the address from the phone company."

"Okay." So as not to have to check the phone number again, Searle wrote the number on a piece of paper napkin.

They paid their bill, returned the phone book to the cashier, and located a pay phone in the lobby.

Searle dialed the number. He got an answering machine, a woman's voice, without an accent, "Leave a message and a number. I will call you back." He hung up.

"What?" Ellsworth asked.

"A fucking machine. And, you know what? The woman has no accent and is really brusque."

"Maybe he has an American wife. Maybe we got a wrong number."

"But the phone book says Gopal."

"Why don't you keep calling until you find a live person?"

That settled, they left the restaurant.

Searle called the number several times with no luck, until late in the evening.

He heard a woman, sounding like the same one as on the answering machine, "Hello." Rough but civilized.

"May I speak with Dr. Rajiv Gopal, please?"

The woman's voice changed into searing lava, "The bastard doesn't live here any more."

The answer was not a simple 'yes' or 'no'. It offered a very different kind of information. Yes, Gopal did not live there, but the woman knew him and hated him, and therefore, could prove to be a promising lead, or even an ally in some way. It was an opportunity to exploit.

"Can you tell me how I can find him? His phone number, address?" Searle asked.

"Don't know. ... But, why do you want it?"

Searle detected a note of curiosity, a hint of interest in the woman's voice. So, he proceeded cautiously, to get her to reveal information he wanted without exposing his plans, and said, "A personal matter. Could you help me?"

Searle thought that the innocent sounding reply, containing a hint of a sinister motive, might get the woman to cooperate with him. Instead he heard, "Sorry," and a disconnect.

He was disappointed but not disheartened, and decided to find out Gopal's residence on his own. He also decided to keep the woman's phone number in his pocket. He might need to talk to her again, after all she was connected with the psychiatrist in some way.

He reflected on what he had done so far, and he was not happy. Three days had been used up, and he had accomplished precious little. He must quicken his pace. Tomorrow morning, check out where Gopal lived, then start following him to learn his routine. He would have three days before the weekend, enough for his purpose. On Saturday and Sunday, he would work with Ellsworth to prepare for the task and, if everything went according to the plan, he would execute Gopal and his wife on Monday. Man, it would be many days of work and, while thrilling, quite gruesome. He did not like it one bit. But he had no choice.

First thing first, find Gopal's residence. He went home, rested, ate his lunch, rested some more, then drove to the prison and planted himself in front of the gate, looking conspicuous like a person who was there to pick up some employee in need of a ride. It was 4 pm.

But it was about an hour and a half later, when he saw a red Mercedes with an Indian looking man drive out of the prison parking lot. Had to be Gopal. This must be his time to go home. Searle followed him. Proved to be a hard task to keep pace with the Mercedes in the thick of all kinds of vehicles from motorcycles to trucks and everything in between. It was like chasing a rocket in the midst of flying fighter planes, but he somehow managed to keep it in sight while maintaining a non-threatening distance. After a couple of miles out of town, the traffic thinned to nothing and Searle relaxed. The relaxation lasted only about half an hour. The Mercedes left the black top and whizzed on Rural Route 24, a dirt road, becoming invisible behind a cloud of dust and rock fragments spewed by it. The Jeep fell back about a quarter mile to avoid being pelted by the flying tiny missiles. The swirling beige cloud provided it a cover and a means to track its target. After about eight miles on the bumpy washboard surface the dust cloud dissipated, a sign that the destination had been reached. Searle slowed down, got off the road behind some bushes, and stopped. He pulled out his binoculars and took in the details; the Mercedes idling in front of a gate, the gate opening electronically within a few seconds, the Mercedes driving inside, and then the door closing automatically.

He found it to be a stately home on about an acre of land, enclosed by a six-foot brick wall with metal wiring on top, most probably electrified, fronted by a massive wrought iron gate, most certainly electronically controlled.

He drove past it at a normal speed so as not to arouse any suspicion about his motives in the mind of anyone who happened to be in the area, and was surprised to see a "For Sale" sign. Then, immediately it struck him as lucky. It would make getting inside the house a lot easier, and he would not have to use those cumbersome plans he had discussed with Ellsworth. He stopped, pulled out a piece of paper from his wallet and a pen from his pocket, and wrote the name and phone number of the real estate agency advertising the sale. He noticed that it was the same paper on which he had that woman's phone number who was using Gopal as her last name. Good! Both useful numbers in one place.

He spent the next day watching the house from a distance behind some low bluffs. He found that Gopal left home at about 6:30 in the morning, presumably to go to work in the prison, and came back home in the evening at about 6:30. A BMW came out of the home at about 1.00 in the afternoon and was back at about 5:00. Searle went home that night tired and bored, but happy.

His happiness was marred that night by the news announcing the Robinson murders. Not really by the news itself, since it proclaimed the AV victory. He was unhappy about the fact that Huddy got his work done before he could. Still, there was nothing he could do to expedite his plan. He would have to wait until Monday for his executions.

One more day of surveillance of the Gopal residence, and it was the repeat of the previous day with one exception. There was a car sporting the same real estate company name which was on the sign board in front of the house, most decidedly bringing prospective customers.

Searle was satisfied and pleased with the results of his effort.

By the end of the day, however, he was concerned and worried. From the TV news he found out that Madrill had killed himself and he was the reason the police had connected the AVs with the Robinson murders. Now his own operation did not appear to be as safe as he had thought it to be in the beginning. The Gopal murder would immediately be assumed to have been committed by the AV operatives, and the police would be after any AV they could find. Sooner or later, they were likely to catch him.

Yet, he could not just abandon the job and walk away. Besides, no one ever ran away, couldn't run away, from the organization. He might as well complete his obligation with courage and dignity. Afterwards he would worry about how to save himself from the police. One big consolation was that the AV organization was committed to saving and protecting all its faithful members, and he would not be alone in this game.

He called Ellsworth and instructed, "Ignore today's news. Focus on our project. It's time we got together again. Come to the AV garage tomorrow at about one in the afternoon for rehearsals. Bring a well fitting three-piece suit. Rent one if you have to. And, a briefcase to complete the professional look. We will also pick out a car at that time."

When they got together, Searle announced the change in plan, "Now we act as customers, in the market to buy property. We will call the real estate agent and tell him or her that we are investors and want to buy the house for use as a mental health retreat for some of our clients. The agent will take us inside to show us the place. That's all we need." He didn't have to explain the reason for the change in plan, it was obvious that they could more easily pass as businessmen than as psychiatrists.

"But then we will have another eyewitness. Plus the real estate agent would want to know our names. Maybe not our IDs, that would be impolite, but certainly the names."

"How about Al Bellamy and Syd Richards?" Searle smiled at his cleverness at coming up with phony names so quickly, then added, "And, eyewitness? As much as I hate it, we will have to kill the agent too. Collateral damage. What can I say?"

It was ballooning. From one it had grown to three. It was grisly, but what was the choice?

"Yeah! Still, It's a good plan," Ellsworth agreed.

"Now we rehearse," Searle suggested.

It was not a problem for Searle who was a software developer, a white collar worker. Still, he tended to wear casual clothing which needed to be replaced with more conservative attire. He put on a light brown suit, beige shirt, purple-gold striped tie, dark brown socks, and tan shoes. Ellsworth, however, was a different story. He was in construction and needed a complete overhaul. Searle spent several hours transforming him into something he was not, a white collar businessman. Stubble on the face was removed. Hair was cut short. Tattoos were no problem; they were on parts of the body which would be hidden under clothing. The usual dingy tee-shirt, jeans, and work boots were discarded and replaced with a dark blue suit, light purple shirt, red tie with blue polka dots , dark blue socks, and black monk strap shoes. Not being used to such attire, both looked ridiculous and ill at ease. So what? They needed to keep this clothing on and become used to it as much as they could in the short time they had before the event. They also needed to work on the professional comportment. Again, for Searle it was not a problem, however, Ellsworth's blue collar walk and talk did not conform to the businessman mode and had to go. But, doing this proved impossible and was quickly abandoned; they would just have to wing it. The rehearsal also included methods of restraining people and then executing them. They decided to rehearse one more day.

After making that decision they sat at a table. Searle pulled the phone sitting on the table toward him, took out his wallet, checked the phone number of the real estate company handling the Gopal residence sale, and dialed it, while Ellsworth looked on.

When the phone was answered, Searle said, "I am calling about a property you have for sale on Route 24."

"Just a moment sir, I will let you talk to our agent handling the property."

A few seconds later Searle heard a female voice, "Would you like to see the house?"

"Yes, of course, before deciding if it will meet our needs."

"What are your needs? What's your price range? I can make a list of other properties meeting your specifications, in case this one is not what you want."

"We want a large home on a big lot to serve as a mental health retreat. We are shopping for our psychiatrist clients who want something out in the country, peaceful, tranquil. Price is not an issue. We are more particular about features."

"You are a doctor? Doctors?"

"No, we are investors. There are two of us. We want to own the property jointly and then to lease it out to our psychiatrist clients."

"That's interesting. The house is owned by a psychiatrist, Dr. Gopal. You know him?"

"I know the name. We haven't met."

"Well, now you will. When do you want to see the place?"

"Could we do it this Monday, day after tomorrow? Or, whenever it's convenient to you. The sooner the better, though." Searle did not want to sound impatient while communicating the need for urgency.

"I am booked on Monday but I can reschedule some of my appointments."

"If it's not a problem..."

"No, no problem. How about in the evening about seven when Dr. Gopal would be home? You will have an opportunity to meet him and ask any questions which only he can answer. I mean, questions concerning the appropriateness of the property for use as a mental health retreat."

"I would prefer to see the home before meeting him. That way I will know what questions to ask him." He did not want to handle too many people at the same time. Get the two women, Gopal's wife and the real estate lady, in control before attacking Gopal. Two women if there was no housekeeper, and if the real estate lady did not bring someone else with her. If that happened they would have to find a way to handle all of them on the spot. They had to be prepared for any eventuality.

"Good idea. You will be able to examine the property without social distraction. Let's make it five then, about an hour before Dr. Gopal usually comes home. He works at the prison, you know."

"No, I don't know where he works. ... Yes, five o'clock would be ideal."

"Could you meet me in my office, say at four. I'll take you to Gopal's house. It's about an hour's drive."

"How about we meet you in front of the property at five? We know it's location." Searle needed his own transportation for a quick get away after the job was done.

"If you prefer. In the meantime I will call and tell Mrs. Gopal that I am bringing two prospective buyers. She would be expecting us. ... What are your names, sir?"

"Al Bellamy and Syd Richards."

"I am Penny. I will be waiting for you in front of the house. I will make sure to get there before you do. I don't want you to have to wait out in the street. You know the gate is electronically locked and the property fenced? Mrs. Gopal may not let you guys in without me."

"We understand. Of course, this security feature makes the property even more attractive to us. Anyway, see you on Monday."

Searle looked at Ellsworth. Both smiled, pleased at the way the things were progressing.

Only one more thing to do that day, pick out a car, suitable for big time investors. They chose a Lincoln Continental.

The next day's rehearsal was a repeat of the one on Saturday. They did not spend much time. In the end, it was not what they wanted, either in looks or in conduct, but they had to settle for whatever they could accomplish. Still, they were confident to pull it off, maybe with a hitch here and a hiccup there, but pull it off nonetheless.

Searle gave Ellsworth the last instruction, the last for that day, "Now, get here tomorrow at four in the evening. I will bring all the needed weapons. We will leave our cars here and drive out in the Lincoln. After the job's finished we will come back, return the Lincoln, get in our cars, and go home. From that point on, forget there was a Gopal and that we had anything to do with him. And remember, your name is…?"

"Syd Richards."

"Absolutely. And, I am Al Bellamy."

They shook hands.

The way things were going proved to Searle that, without doubt, there was a God, and He was on his side.

CHAPTER TWENTY-FIVE

THE COLOR OF REVENGE

CHRISTI GOPAL WAS a happy woman. She had not been this happy for a long time. Not since her divorce from Rajiv Gopal.

Her mind made a quick trip back to the time when Gopal had left her. Divorce was imminent. Not only because Gopal wanted it. She, too, wanted to bring a quick end to the farce they had called marriage, but on her own terms.

She did not wait for Gopal to act, did not wait for the divorce papers to arrive. Instead, she prepared herself for the day when they did. She scanned the attorney section of the yellow pages and picked a female divorce lawyer, believing a counselor of her own sex would be more sympathetic to her cause and more understanding of her position. She made an appointment to see her.

After the introductions were over, the lawyer asked, "You want to file for divorce?"

"No. My husband is going to."

"I see. Do you want to contest it?"

"I don't know. I want your advice. Tell me what's best for me."

"Then, let me ask you a few questions. First tell me about him, who he is and what does he do, that sort of thing. Also tell me how the two of you met, and what brought this friction about. Anything that can help me understand the two of you and the nature of your relationship."

Christi narrated the story of her life with Gopal.

When she stopped, the lawyer asked, "Do you love him?"

"We are way past that."

"At this time what's most important to you in this relationship?"

"Money."

"Did you have a prenuptial agreement of any kind?"

"No."

"In that case you might want to hang on to the marriage. You will have a lifelong claim on all his earnings which are likely to grow. If he is a good money manager and a shrewd investor, the wealth could be substantial."

"Do I have to remain married to him for that?"

"Not necessarily. There's alimony. You could have lifelong security without having to do anything for it."

"Hey, that sounds good."

"At the surface only. You see, your gains will be limited. You lose everything, if your husband goes bankrupt or you get married. Also, if he leaves the country, there is no way you could collect a penny. Besides, you will have to remain single. And, the alimony amount would fluctuate based on his earnings."

"Give me your best advice."

"Go for the financial settlement. Get everything you can. Then marry someone wealthy and have access to his earnings also."

"Later I could divorce him too, get all I can from him, then go, marry someone else."

"Yes, this could be a serial enterprise. A really neat way to amass a fortune. Some of my clients are doing just that."

"It seems like prostitution."

"In a way. But aren't all marriages?"

"All?"

"Yeah. I think so. Anyway, what's your decision?"

"I'll take your advice. What do I do now?"

"Sit and wait for your husband to act. When his attorney contacts you, direct him... or her to me. ... And remember not to start living with someone before the divorce is final."

"No, of course not. I don't have anyone in mind right now anyway. But, I can dream, can't I? I do move in moneyed circles, thanks to my husband. I could start prospecting."

"That's your business. Dream and plan all you want, just don't get involved with anyone, not until the divorce."

"All right. Understood."

"So, let me make sure that we are on the same page. We won't contest the divorce, we will go for a financial settlement, and try to get as much of his wealth as we possibly can. Right?"

"Right."

Without contest, the divorce was a quick affair. Gopal, in his desire to be free, agreed to give Christi everything she wanted. She got the existing house, the cars, the jewelry, everything in savings, and all the investments. She gave up all claims on Gopal's future earnings. But she always presented herself to be Gopal's wife, ex-wife. It sounded impressive that she was once married to a psychiatrist. It was a status symbol.

She was excited about a new life waiting for her, a life of freedom, wealth, and adventure. She started going to parties and eyeing unattached men with money. It proved to be more difficult than she had thought it would be. Most single men she met had already burned out on marriage and didn't want any part of it any more. Others had never married and had no desire to go that route. Certainly, they all wanted to go to bed with her. She slept with every good prospect she could corner with no hoped-for results. It was like the pre-Gopal times had returned. After a few months, all she got was the title 'easy' and a bad reputation. She felt like a whore and began to think that the divorce settlement was not the best deal after all. She felt cheated.

In the meantime, due to her extravagant living, the settlement money was running out. She was beginning to have difficulty even paying her utility bills and buying the necessities of life. It looked like she would have to sell the house, move into a cheap apartment, and go back to nursing. The whole thing was utterly depressing.

As if that was not enough, she found out through the grapevine in the hospital where she used to work, that Gopal had come back with a wife after a few months in India, had found a job in the prison, and was doing great financially. She was jealous. It bothered her that Gopal's life seemed to be working, moving smoothly on its tracks. She wanted him to be as miserable as she was; rejected, rebuffed, used, and abused.

That was nothing compared to her jealousy of Gopal's new wife, particularly after she saw her in Macy's one day.

It was a chance encounter from a distance, a brief one at that, without any interaction. She was shopping for some clothes and saw Gopal at the ladies' cosmetics counter with a woman in a saree. There was no overt display of affection, but she could sense that there was a closeness between them. She glanced at the woman and surmised her to be Gopal's wife. She was struck by the clothes she wore, a purple saree and a gold blouse, all silk, both emblazoned with distinctly Indian prints in burned orange. Her eyes were drawn to her stature, tall, around five-eight, quite light skinned but not light enough to be confused for a white, slim but strong boned, glowing with youth of probably 26 springs. Devastating.

Christi was suddenly a changed woman. Not wanting to be face-to-face with someone despicable in her eyes, she quickly walked in a direction away from Gopal. Still she could not resist a last glance at him and his escort. She thought he saw her.

She went home consumed with hatred. Her mind churned with random thoughts, 'He gets rid of me and finds himself an Indian cunt. Then he brings her here to torture me. ... Come to think of it, he is doing this by using my gift to him, the green card. Ungrateful prick.'

Prior to that day, Gopal's new wife was just a vague concept somewhere in the back of her mind, now she was real. Real like fire that burned.

The thought drove her over the edge. She began hatching a plan for revenge, rather unsuccessfully.

Then, it was delivered to her unexpectedly. She could not believe her luck after her phone conversation with a stranger who was 'looking for' Gopal, and clearly not for a friendly chitchat. She could smell blood in the stranger's words, the way one could smell a coming tornado in the air. Maybe she would get her revenge without having to lift a finger.

And so, she was happy.

But, she was scared also. After the phone was silent, she could hear her heart screaming, thumping violently. What if something went wrong and the police connected her with Gopal's prospective visitors?

At the same time, she was excited. Something was likely to happen, something was going to happen, and Gopal, the shit-head, wouldn't get away with his vile deeds.

She anxiously waited for that 'something' to happen. One day, two days, several days. She checked the daily newspapers, watched TV, listened to the radio. No news of any kind about Gopal.

Still, she hoped the stranger would be able to do what she sensed he would do. With each passing day her hope faded and her anxiety increased.

Yet, she dreamed. Dreamed of her stranger, her avenger, doing to Gopal what she wished done.

And, she wondered, in the process, what would be the color of the blood that would be spilled? White, brown, or just red?

And, the color of revenge? Just plain ugly?

CHAPTER TWENTY-SIX

THE DANCE OF DEATH

Searle and Ellsworth arrived at the AV garage at the appointed hour. They wore the professional clothing selected for the task and carried no personal identification. Searle produced two sets of weapons and tools; 8-inch butcher knives, thin but strong polyester ropes, duct tape, and .45 caliber pistols. The last one, just in case. They hid their sets in briefcases and got into the previously chosen Lincoln Continental, whose vehicle identification number had been obliterated, and which displayed a stolen license plate. The car was on the road to the Gopal residence by 4:00 pm.

When they arrived at their destination, they found a woman already waiting for them, sitting in her car, in front of the house. Had to be Penny. They got out of their car, Searle taking the lead, Ellsworth following.

As they approached Penny, they saw her getting out of her car, she must have seen them coming. Face-to-face, Searle said, "Sorry to keep you waiting. ... I am Bellamy, this is Richards."

"No, you are not late. I came a few minutes early, I always do. Didn't want to disturb Satya while waiting for you, so I sat here. ... Well, nice to meet you. Let's go in now."

She led the way. At the gate she pressed the intercom button.

"Who is it?" An accented female voice. The words came out of a speaker.

Penny answered, "This is Penny with a couple of buyers. I believe you're expecting us."

"Yes, of course. Please come in. The gate's open now."

They entered the gate, covered a 100-foot long flagstone walk through beautifully landscaped grounds to the house entrance. The door was opened and there stood a woman in a red-purple printed cotton saree.

"Please," she said and directed them to the living room.

"Thank you," everyone said in unison.

Then Penny took over and introduced her clients, "Mr. Bellamy and his partner Mr. Richards to see the house."

"Pleased to meet you," Satya said. "I am Satya Gopal. Have a seat and I will go make some tea."

"Let's see the property first. Then, after Dr. Gopal comes, we will have some tea," Penny suggested.

Satya, by her silence, accepted the suggestion and moved aside.

It was all Penny now. "You already saw the front. Very inviting and peaceful. And the living room. Big, isn't it? You can hold a group of 25, 30 people comfortably. Let's move on to the next area. After we have seen the whole house, we can come back to any part of the house you want to see again."

She started to walk out of the living room when Searle jumped her from behind. Still holding his briefcase in his left arm, he put his right arm around her neck, tight enough to prevent her from speaking and loose enough to keep her alive, and said, "Be still and quiet, and you won't get hurt." Penny let out a puff from her mouth and started hyperventilating.

Searle dragged Penny toward the couch, put his briefcase on the coffee table, pushed its spring latch to open it with his one hand, and pulled out his shining knife. He placed the knife under Penny's chin and ordered, "Cooperate or die."

Penny slumped.

While dropping Penny on the couch Searle addressed Ellsworth, "You take care of the other bitch."

Ellsworth quickly copied Searle's movements and rushed at Satya, frozen in place with terror. He placed the tip of his bare knife at her throat and said, "Keep quiet and nothing will happen to you."

Satya pursed her lips and stood still.

Searle threw a glance around the room, and after spotting two straight backed chairs next to a writing desk, commanded, "You ladies, sit there."

He freed Penny while holding the knife menacingly as Ellsworth did the same to Satya.

Both women obeyed the order, shaking all over.

Searle stood before them and explained, "Contrary to what you might be thinking, this is not a robbery, and you will not be raped. Our business is with the shrink only. We will restrain you so that you don't interfere with what we have to do."

After that he put the knife back inside his briefcase and pulled out his string. First, he tied Penny's hands and feet with it, then he tied the middle of her body to the chair. Ellsworth once more copied Searle in restraining Satya.

Searle looked at his captives from a distance of about two feet. He saw Penny shaking, clearly in shock, and fearful for her life. All of a sudden, she started screaming, involuntarily. Not that there was anyone outside the house to hear her, but it was disturbing and unpleasant. Also, it was likely to alarm Gopal when he came home and force him to take evasive action. Who knew, he might even take aggressive action and foil the whole plan. So, Searle slapped her hard and said, "Shut up."

Penny could not. Searle slapped her harder and continued to slap her until she became unconscious.

Satya sat up straight, her eyes in sync with the movement of her tormentors. She did make a feeble protest against the abuse of Penny, "Why are you hurting her? She did nothing to you." The protest was ignored.

After silencing Penny, Searle and Ellsworth made themselves comfortable on the sofa, both facing the two women. It was clear that one woman was totally out of awareness of anything, but the other seemed to be as aware of everything as one could be. Searle wondered what Satya was thinking and feeling, then decided he did not care. After a few minutes Searle noticed something else about Satya. She looked shaken, and her face appeared clouded with disbelief, but she did not look scared. She sat firmly like a speaker on a podium waiting for her turn to give a speech. Her eyes were wide open and roaming as if hunting for something.

That was not reassuring to Searle. He jumped up and said, "I am going to kill them. What if this woman wakes up and they both start screaming just when I am doing my job, spoiling everything."

"No, just tape their mouths. At least let that funny looking brown woman see what we do to her man," Ellsworth made the sadistic suggestion.

It was appealing to Searle who said, "Good idea."

He pulled out the duct tape from his briefcase, used it first to cover Satya's mouth and watched her face contort with pain. He had no such satisfaction with Penny. Her stiff and unresponsive mouth, due to her unconscious state, was easy to tape.

He sat again next to his partner. The two of them waited, their eyes shifting, scanning various objects in the room. A framed wedding photograph of the Gopals caught Searle's eyes. It was sitting on the mantle of an unlit fireplace. Searle walked over and picked it up. He showed it to Ellsworth and said, "Funny clothes they wear!"

"Yeah. And why don't these funny faces stay in their funny slums? What the fuck are they doing here?" Ellsworth questioned.

Both snickered at the photograph and twisted their mouths like they had bitten into something distasteful. Searle threw it into the gaping hole of a trash bin.

They waited some more. A few minutes later Searle suggested to Ellsworth, "Why don't you go around, check the layout of the house, find out where the opening to the garage is so that we can wait for the shrink there. I'll keep an eye on the women."

Ellsworth did as he was told. He finished his task in less than five minutes.

Once more they sat on the couch waiting for another half an hour. Then they heard a car idling, a moment later the gate and the garage door opening electronically, and someone calling in an accented male voice, unmistakably Gopal's, "I'm home. ... Is Penny here? I see her company car parked in front."

No answer.

Searle and Ellsworth got up to meet their victim. They stood behind the door connecting the garage with the main house. The door opened and Gopal emerged. Searle threw a vicious punch at his face making him stagger and fall backwards. The sudden attack made him go limp. Searle and Ellsworth immediately grabbed Gopal's arms, one on each side, dragged him to the living room, and dumped him on the floor.

They could not have imagined what followed. It happened in a flash. Gopal snapped out of his daze, probably at the sight of Satya and Penny bound to the chairs, jumped to his feet, and screamed, "Who are you? What are you doing to my wife?"

Looking at his unathletic body, Searle would have not guessed that Gopal had it in him. So when Gopal quickly moved his feet like a kick boxer and struck Ellsworth hard in his groin area, doubling him over with pain, Searle was in shock. And before he could recover from it, he got hit by Gopal on the nose which immediately began to bleed like a drain.

While trying to regain their balances, the two AVs saw Gopal run over to Satya and start removing her ties. Searle could see that it would be a disaster if the woman got free. So, ignoring his pain, he swung on his feet and hit Gopal over the head with his fist. Gopal fell down. Searle kicked him in the ribs and kept on kicking him until he was subdued. He had forgotten all about his own pain and bleeding nose.

The room was filled with gurgling sounds coming out of Satya's taped mouth. No one heard them, everyone was busy, tormenting or being tormented.

Searle once more opened his briefcase, pulled out his knife, and some more string. He used the string to tie Gopal's hands behind his back, pulled him up by his hair, and shoved him against the sofa in a sitting position on the floor. Then he stood in front of him, put his knife under his chin, and ordered, "You're gonna suck it and swallow. You bite and I'll slit your throat." He unzipped the fly of his pants with his free hand, pulled out his limp penis, and stuffed it in Gopal's mouth.

He was satisfied with Gopal's clumsy obedience. Soon the penis was hard and in a minute or so the ejaculate was sliding down his victim's throat. Searle was surprised and disgusted when Gopal threw up on him. He pulled himself out and screamed, "Stinking bastard. He started to wipe himself with his shirt tail while ordering, "I don't care if you puke again, do the same to my friend."

But, Ellsworth refused, "No, no way. No way am I sticking it in his dirty, filthy mouth."

"That's okay. He got a taste of it anyway." After that, he wondered about Gopal, 'Was his humiliation more painful to him than his physical abuse? What did he want to do, kill me? Or just die of shame?' There were no answers.

Then, he looked at Satya. Seemed like she was going to faint, but did not.

After zipping himself up Searle said, "Just one more thing and we'll be gone."

He scanned the faces of his three victims and wondered once more, 'What did Satya and Gopal feel at his announcement? Relief that the end was in sight, or dread at what that 'one more thing' might be?'

Whatever. He revealed that 'one more thing' rather quickly.

He pulled out his knife again and, with a swift move, slit Gopal's neck under the chin. First a thin red line appeared, then the blood gushed out. Searle saw Gopal slump forward silently, his face sinking in a pool of his own blood, his body thrashing involuntarily for a few seconds, then lying motionless and contorted. With a satisfied grin on their faces, the two AV warriors watched him die slowly, quite unaware that the dance of death had only begun.

Searle felt a sharp pain in his head, like a sudden migraine, like a thousand fireworks exploding simultaneously. He heard pounding on the back of his skull and saw blinding light spread in front of his face. His body lost balance, swayed in a bizarre pose, and fell on the floor, as blood spurted out of his head and all the orifices in his face. All in less than a second.

Ellsworth heard the gun shot. He instinctively turned to Searle and saw his head explode in a fountain of blood. Instinctively again, within a fraction of a second, he turned his head toward the source of the gun shot. There she was, Satya, standing erect, firmly planted on her feet, like a ferocious animal, lips pursed, eyes blazing, face taut, a gun clasped in her hands, pointed to where Searle's head had been when standing. His reflexes paralyzed, Ellsworth stood motionless. Before he could fathom what was happening, he saw Satya turn slightly, ever so slightly, toward him, gun pointed at his face. He stood frozen. Then he heard the cracking of the gun again and felt his whole face disintegrate into a thousand pieces. He saw a burst of colors, then it was all black. His body performed a grotesque dance and fell on Searle with a thud.

Then, it was all still, all silent, like a frozen night.

CHAPTER TWENTY-SEVEN
THE SCREAM OF THE BANGLES

Satya thought that her prayers had been answered, when Penny called her to say that she was bringing two customers to see the house and told her who they were. It was welcome news; the house might get sold quickly, allowing her and her husband to go back to the safety of their country that much sooner. And, if that happened, the house would be used for mental health purposes, allowing Gopal's soul to live on in that place, even after he was gone from there. She hoped these investors would buy the house. But, after seeing the two men she felt there was something wrong with the picture. The men were tall, muscular, and coarse, not chubby and delicate like businessmen. Their clothes were clearly not tailored, which was inconsistent with the image of rich investors, and their walk and posture did not exhibit upper class sophistication. But she immediately chided herself for profiling them, she, an intelligent woman, needed to be more rational. Besides, she had been in this country only a few months; what did she know about the appearance, clothing, and demeanor of Americans?

But, when she and Penny were restrained and bound to the chairs, she knew for sure the men were not real estate investors. Who were they? Robbers, murderers, rapists, what?

Then she remembered the reason for selling this house. These men were the AVs. She was scared, terrified was more like it. More so when one of the men slapped Penny until she was unconscious. Mercifully for Penny, in a way, because she would not have to suffer whatever might come next. Being conscious, Satya would have to endure every indignity and suffering thrown her way. What would it be? Rape, torture, death? And, what would these men do to her husband? Kill him probably, and maybe commit more repugnant acts before that. But, why? What had he done to deserve this? All he wanted was to make some money before going home. Was that such a bad thing? Now it seemed like he would neither make any money nor go home.

Was there anything she could do to change the course of these events, to counter the AV attack? Or, would she just sit there, watch this horror unfold little by little. No, she would not. With that resolve her fear turned into anger. She would find a way to stop these horrible creatures. That was when she thought of the guns bought by Gopal for protection. One was in the drawer of the writing desk only a couple of feet away. Instinctively her eyes drifted toward it, but, not wanting to tip off the intruders to its significance, she immediately diverted her gaze and let it roam around the room. She wished she could reach it. Yet, wished not to reach it; she had never shot anything alive in her life and could not imagine doing it now. She was torn between the choices of killing or getting killed. Maybe it won't come to that, she rationalized. Maybe these people would just talk to Gopal and would settle with him whatever issues they had, without violence. More rationalization for not wanting to use the gun.

Right after that, she was sure that the end had come; one of the men had threatened to kill both women. It was averted on the suggestion of the other man to do it after Gopal had come, and just to shut the women's mouths with duct tape to keep them silent. What did they think? How was any sound from the women going to hinder anything they wanted to do? There was nobody to hear. They could kill them and nobody would know. While one man was taking out the duct tape from his briefcase, she felt like screaming just as Penny had done, but, realizing the futility of it, kept silent. Not only that, her screaming was likely to bring more physical harm to her, maybe death, and then there would not be any possibility of her being able to change the course of events in any way. Was she still considering using the gun? In her ambivalence she had no answer. And, in her ambivalence, she sat silently, even when her mouth was taped up.

But, she was seething inside. It built up to a rage when the men made fun of her wedding photograph.

That was nothing compared to what they did to Gopal when he came home. Why were they beating him? She was at a loss. Her husband was such a gentle man who, even though he bought a few guns, would not think of committing violence. And here, he was getting heaps of it.

Then she could not believe her eyes; Gopal actually kicking one man in the testicles and punching another on the nose. At that time her ambivalence had diminished to almost nothing, and she felt she could really kill them. She remembered her earlier desire to reach for the gun in the desk drawer, and now she understood why.

Immediately after that she was filled with relief and contentment when Gopal rushed over to her and started removing her ties. Maybe there was a chance for rescue. Even if there wasn't, she wished for both of them to die at that moment, making their short togetherness meaningful. She was filled with love for the man who was trying to save her while facing death himself.

Relief, contentment, love, all were obscured by terror as the intruders dragged Gopal away and one of them started to abuse him sexually. That was when she realized she must do something, particularly now that Gopal had made it possible for her by loosening her ties. She slowly began freeing her hands hidden behind the folds of her saree, the end of which was draped over the back of her chair. She succeeded in doing so in a few seconds, but kept her hands hidden and remained immobile. Maybe she still did not want to use the gun and thought that she and her husband would be spared after the abuse. But when Gopal's throat was cut, she was taken over by her primal force. An unknown power propelled her to do the unthinkable.

While the AVs watched Gopal dying slowly, she, in a flash, pulled open the drawer in the writing desk, took out the .357, and shot one man in the back of his head, and then the other man in the face, when he turned toward her. The quiet of the night was shattered, and the two AVs lay dead, one on top of the other.

Satya dropped the gun, pulled off the duct tape from her mouth, untied her legs, walked over to Penny, and freed her from the bondage. Penny fell to the floor, still unconscious. Satya, feeling somber, sad, and angry, went to the kitchen, where the nearest phone was, and dialed 911.

At that moment the realization hit her that she was a widow. She briefly looked at her glass bangles which had signified her marital status, not any more. She crashed her wrists on the kitchen counter and broke them. Then she started to cry. Tears flowing down her face, she shuffled her feet toward where Gopal lay. She sat beside him in his thickening blood, letting her tear drops wash his face.

She was still in the same place and in the same position when the police and paramedics arrived. Still, she sat there, face streaked with tears and wrists bloodied. She knew the police were there and were doing what they had to do, and they were trying to do it without disturbing her. She was also aware that they were trying to talk to her and ask her questions, but she could form no words to answer them. In the midst of it all, she noticed that the paramedics were leading her toward an ambulance while taking Penny out of her house on a stretcher. She was too numb to ask what they were doing and why. She was not sure if she wanted to be put in an ambulance and taken to an unknown place, perhaps a hospital, but she had no will to resist. Before crossing the threshold, she, however, turned to look back and saw her broken glass bangles lying on the kitchen floor, screaming about a shattered heart.

After that it was a blur until the next morning when she found herself in a hospital bed. She could see the present but the future was hazy. When and how was she going to get out of the hospital and go back to her house? Go back to her house? Would she be allowed by the police? Also, what was there for her any more? And, what about the days, weeks, months, and years beyond that? The haziness made her cry.

A nurse came in at that point. "I see you are awake. Would you care for some breakfast?" she asked.

Breakfast? Who cared for breakfast after what she had been through? She did not answer the question, instead said, "I want to go home." She wanted to go home in spite of all the questions still crowding her mind.

"Of course. Better check with the police officer. He is waiting outside wanting to talk to you. You up to it?"

"I suppose," she answered tentatively.

"You sure you don't want anything? A cup of coffee perhaps?"

"That would be fine. Thank you."

A police officer and a cup of coffee arrived together.

The police officer pulled a chair next to her bed, sat in it, and said, "Mrs. Gopal, I am officer Troy Sanderson investigating last night's tragedy. Could you relate last night's events?"

Satya covered everything from the time Penny pushed the intercom button at the gate until the time the police arrived on the scene. She also mentioned her suspicion that the killers were AVs and the reason why. Before Sanderson could ask any more questions, she added, "I'm sorry for shooting." Satya sounded sad and genuinely apologetic.

"You are not to blame."

"But I killed two people."

Now Sanderson looked confused, probably at Satya's statement which, at the face, was clearly weird. He must have ignored it because he did not respond to it. Instead, he said, "Thanks for talking with me. Your answers will help us bring the culprits to justice."

That was a mistake.

"What justice?" Satya began to cry.

"We will make sure the people behind this heinous crime are caught and punished." Sanderson explained somewhat irritably at the dunceness of this seemingly intelligent woman.

Satya wiped her tears and said softly, "But they are dead."

"There may be others behind the scene."

"How's punishing them going to bring my husband back?"

"It won't, but it would prevent them from hurting others."

"Why would they want to hurt others?"

Satya was exasperated because she could not see any purpose in punishing anyone. But, she saw exasperation on Sanderson's face also. Could it be because he saw punishment to be the only purposeful thing to do?

At that point Sanderson said, "That's all ma'm," and started to get up to leave the room.

Satya felt that the extreme divergence of their views on crime and punishment had probably forced Sanderson to abandon formality and to end the interview curtly.

Still, there was something important she needed to know and Sanderson was likely to have the information. So, before Sanderson could even get out of his chair, she asked, "How is Penny?"

"She regained consciousness in the hospital last night." Sanderson settled back in his chair.

"Is she okay?"

"She looked all right. I was able to talk to her."

"She couldn't have told you much. She was unconscious most of the time."

"Yes. She told me all that happened before she became unconscious, including the fact that these men had made an appointment with her to see the house. That was their ruse to get into your residence. The whole thing was obviously planned."

"I hope she gets over her trauma soon."

"I am sure she will, although I doubt if she will be able to work as a real estate agent, ever."

"Is she still here?"

"Yes. Under observation. And her husband is with her."

A haze of gloom covered Satya's face. "Where's my husband?" she asked.

"All bodies are in the morgue awaiting autopsies. When done, they will call you, and then you may claim your husband's body."

"Can I go home after I am released from the hospital? Wait for the call?"

"I'm sorry, but we have not finished our investigation. There is so much to do, fingerprinting, photographing, collecting of evidence, you know. Your house, as a crime scene, is off limits to everyone. For a few days anyway. Until then, stay with your friends or family."

Satya wanted to say, she had none, but did not. What could a police officer do about it anyway? She decided to stay in a hotel and asked, "Could you at least deliver my personal things. I don't even have a change of clothes."

"Yes, of course. What would you like?'

Satya gave him a list of clothes and toiletries.

"We will bring them here. It may take a couple of hours," Sanderson assured her.

"Thank you," said Satya and lay back. She would call a hotel after she got her things and then would demand a release from the hospital.

Sanderson left.

Half an hour later Satya's phone rang.

She was surprised. Who could be calling her? The police already talked to her. Who else would even care that she existed? Maybe the real estate company, or the insurance company. She answered in a voice weighed down with pain, "Satya."

"I am so sorry about what happened. I called you as soon as I found out from the police where you are." An unfamiliar female voice.

"Thank you," Satya said gently, "but do I know you?"

"How stupid of me, of course. I am Carolyn Karcher, wife of…"

"I know. Very kind of you to call."

"But, this is not just a courtesy call. I have discussed this with my husband and we want you to come and live with us until you decide what you want to do. I know you don't have a family here."

Satya was touched, but she did not want to be a burden on anyone. "I appreciate your offer. I really do. But I can stay in a hotel."

"I am sure you can. But I will be very grateful if you would accept my request. There is a lot I need to talk to you about. You know, I am fearful of losing my husband, too."

Satya heard Carolyn crying.

That made her decision. "All right."

"I will come pick you up. Give me about an hour."

"I may need a little more than that. The police are bringing my things here, and I have to check out of this place."

"That's all right. I will wait in the lobby."

Satya had a friend she did not know. She hoped that her new found friend would not lose her man and hear the scream of whatever represented her marriage.

She fell back in her bed. Her head was filled with a soft melancholic raag interspersed with the scream of her bangles.

CHAPTER TWENTY-EIGHT

MURDER FOR HIRE

DETECTIVE TROY SANDERSON left dissatisfied with the Satya interview. He learned nothing useful. But he excused her, after all she was traumatized which was why she was making those irrational comments. Anyway, he still needed to go over her statements, just in case there was something hidden, and check out other avenues.

He went over his notes made during his interviews with Penny and Satya, examined what the police had found in the Gopal residence, and deduced a number of things: It wasn't a robbery, no evidence of any attempt to take anything of value. It wasn't a sex crime, Satya and Penny were restrained but not sexually molested, and the sex act with Gopal was clearly for the purpose of humiliation. Satya suspected it to be a hate crime by the AVs and all the evidence supported her suspicions; the threats by Schultz against some prison staff including the Gopal and Robinson murders which were most definitely committed by the AVs. He called Hefferly and requested, "Could you share with me anything you uncover regarding the AV involvement in the Robinson killings? I think they are behind the Gopal murder as well."

"Sure will," assured Hefferly.

Even though the Gopal murderers were dead, the case was not solved. Sanderson wanted to know who they were, and if they were really part of a conspiracy as suggested by Satya. The fingerprints lifted from the crime scene did not help, they did not match any in the police records. Obviously their owners had no criminal history. Also they left no useful clues. Their wallets had only paper money and no ID of any kind, not even a driver's license, and they drove a car with no serial number and with a fake Canadian license plate. Their photos might help. If published, someone was likely to identify them. He ordered his staff to publish them requesting the public's confidential help in their identification. Then it would be easy to check out their AV connection. Sanderson was not sure if that would lead to the criminals. After all the Robinson murderers had already been linked to the AVs without any arrests or curbs on their activities.

There was something else, and it was puzzling. One of the killers had a piece of paper with a couple of phone numbers on it. Whom did they belong to? Could they provide a clue to the killers' identities? He decided to call these numbers and see where they led.

One led to the real estate office where Penny worked. No mystery there, the number was used to make an appointment with Penny to see, or rather enter, the Gopal residence. The other number belonged to a woman, Christi. What was most interesting was the fact that her last name was Gopal. There had to be a connection between this woman and the Gopal murder or at least there might be some clue to find the culprits who are still out there pulling the strings and causing these deaths.

Sanderson got Christi's address from the phone company. He took a partner, routine procedure, and went to see her, unannounced. When he rang the door bell he noticed someone looking through a peep hole and asking, "Who is it?"

"Police," Sanderson said forcefully.

The door opened, and there stood a woman looking scared. Sanderson and his partner flashed their badges. Sanderson took the lead, "Ma'm, we need to talk to you."

"About what?"

"It would be better if we talk in private. May we come in?"

Christi moved aside.

After they were seated face-to-face in her living room, Sanderson said, "It's about Dr. Gopal's murder. You heard about it?"

"Yes."

"You related to Dr. Gopal?"

"I was married to him. We are divorced."

"Did you know his killers?"

"No. I saw their gruesome photos on the TV. I never met them."

"Did you ever talk to them?"

"Yes."

"How did you find them?"

"I didn't find them. They found me."

"How?"

She told him what the killers had told her.

"Why did they want to talk to Dr. Gopal?"

"I don't know."

"How did they get his address? Did you give it to them?"

"No."

"Why not?"

"I didn't want to share personal information with strangers. Besides, I didn't know the address."

"You did not have any suspicion that they wanted to kill him?"

"No."

"Could it be that you are lying about some man calling you, looking for Dr. Gopal? Could it be that you hated your ex-husband and hired these men to kill him?" Sanderson decided to use the badger technique. It might make her confess. He wanted her to confess, whether or not she had actually done the deed. The badger technique was quite effective in making people confess things they did not do. And, Sanderson was not interested in the truth, he was only interested in a confession. Good for his career.

"I told you, they called me. I did not know them."

"Your phone number was found in the pocket of one of the Gopal killers. Maybe he kept it so that he could call you when the job was done." Badger some more.

"There was no job. ... Maybe they took note of my phone number from the phone directory before calling me. We do that with unfamiliar numbers."

"True, your number would be unfamiliar to them if this was the first time you contacted them." Keep badgering. Sooner or later she would break.

"I did not contact them."

"Not personally. Could be through an intermediary. Who is he or she?" Keep it up, keep it up.

"No one. There was no contract."

"Contract? Did you say contract? That's the word. How much money, and how was it going to be paid? Of course, the men are dead, but the intermediary probably is still alive. Right?" Keep accusing, she would slip.

"I meant contact. I had no contract with anyone. Please, I had nothing to do with the killing."

"Nothing? I think you hired the AVs to kill Dr. Gopal. We know the killers were AVs." Keep pressuring.

"I don't know any AVs."

"Everyone knows AVs." Contradict her, confuse her.

"AV? The Aryan Vision gang? Heard about it. Who hasn't."

"I think you are a member. That's how you could easily find these killers. Come to think of it, they may have done the job for free, hateful as they are of the coloreds." Keep attacking her with hypothesis after hypothesis. One of them was likely to hit its mark.

"I have nothing to do with the AVs either."

In spite of all his attempts Sanderson failed to make Christi admit to anything. Maybe she was not guilty and all her responses were truthful. Sanderson immediately discarded the 'maybe'. He was convinced Christi had something to do with the Gopal killing, she was not telling the whole story. How to get it? He did not know what else to do or ask. He also had no hard evidence against her, so he could not charge her with anything. Then, it occurred to him, he could detain her on suspicion of collusion. Lock her up for a couple of days and she was likely to squeal. If she still did not, he would get a search warrant based on the fact that her name was found in the possession of one of the killers. Then he would check her bank account, phone records, search her whole house, whatever, and secure sufficient evidence to charge her with hiring two people to kill her husband. He was sure it would work.

So, he said, "You know miss, I am sure you had a role in this sordid affair. Therefore, I am arresting you on suspicion of being an accessory to murder."

He went through the usual routine of reading her rights. In the end, he said, "Formal charges will be filed after our investigation is complete."

As he moved to put handcuffs on her, he could see that Christi was anxious, it showed on her face. He was pleased. After handcuffing her he said, "We're going downtown."

A day later Sanderson, armed with a search warrant, went to Christi's house. He went through it and collected a lot of 'stuff'. In the end, he had nothing. No evidence of any connection with the AVs, no large cash withdrawals from the bank, no phone contacts with any questionable characters. Just nothing.

Still, he was convinced of Christi's involvement.

CHAPTER TWENTY-NINE
THE TASK FORCE

Hefferly was still examining the stuff collected from the Goodwin house when he got the news of the Gopal murder. Soon after that he heard from Sanderson requesting to share with him any information he might uncover about the AV's involvement in the Robinson murders. He figured out the reason for the request. Of course, he would supply any information which might help his fellow officer in solving his murder case.

The most useful item to him appeared to be the regional AV membership list, and he poured over it. Thousands of names. All male which made sense, women only served the organization as menial and office workers. So far he had only two names to check. Sonny Madrill was there, as expected. Then Hefferly looked for Travis, and this being a first name, found a whole bunch of them, 9 to be exact. Maybe one of them had gone with Madrill to murder Robinson. But who? Check out all of them. Once he found the Travis, he might use him to find the last of the trio, and who knew, he might get a lead on the Gopal murderers as well.

He deputed two of his assistants to the task. Nine Travises shouldn't take more than a couple of days. The task involved checking out their identities, their whereabouts on the day of the Robinson murders, and obtaining their recent photos from someone in their homes. He was right in his estimate of the time needed to get the job done. There was only one Travis who could not be accounted for. And, he was missing, missing from his apartment. The neighbors told the officers that Travis lived alone, did odd jobs, and had not been seen for many days.

Hefferly checked the list of the AV membership again. The missing Travis was Travis Torte. Next step? Get a court order and check out his apartment. It took another day but finally the task was complete.

It looked like Torte had left in a hurry. There was half eaten food on the kitchen table and clothes were scattered outside the closet. The police collected everything they thought might be important. But they did not find the most important item, a photo or any other identification. What they collected looked like a pile of garbage. When the stuff was examined, a piece of paper was found in the kitchen trash can with the words, 'Huddy at 8'.

Who was Huddy?

Hefferly once more went back to the AV member list. Voila! There was a Chris Huddy, a Commander no less. Hefferly reasoned; the job was too critical to be given to anyone but to a Commander who, in this case, was Huddy. The Commander chose his men from the membership list and they were Torte and Madrill. That was the whole gang. Madrill was dead. The other two must have been alarmed at the police searching the Goodwin house and disappeared. How to find them? If they drove, which they probably did, the Motor Vehicle Department would have their photos and addresses. That was easily accomplished. Hefferly took the photos to Phil Bottillo who identified them positively.

Next he sent a couple of officers to Huddy's place.

The door bell was answered by a woman.

"May we talk to Chris Huddy, please? Miss?" asked one of the officers.

The woman answered, "He is not here. I am his wife, Sally."

"Where is he, Sally? We need to talk to him."

"Don't know."

The officers were surprised that Sally did not look at all worried about her missing husband. Did she know his whereabouts and was not telling? He looked at her closely. A young thing in her mid-twenties, most likely about 5'6" in height, with sandy brown hair, mischievous eyes, pouty lips, and flirtatious demeanor. No, she was not flirting, she was just acting that way, and shielding her husband. She was a very bad actress, he concluded.

"Don't know? Was he here yesterday, day before?"

"He was here Monday. No, hasn't been home since yesterday."

"And you are not concerned? Have you reported him missing?"

"Sometimes he has to go out of town. Part of his job. Sometimes he forgets to tell me. And then, it has been only one day."

"Oh yeah? Where does he work?"

"At Earth Research. You know…"

"We know. Thank you."

Hefferly thought of calling Earth Research but quickly abandoned the idea, the people there would not know if they were talking to the police or someone shady trying to get information about their employee. So, they went there.

The manager told them, "Chris Huddy has not showed up for work for several days. Didn't even call. It's not like him, so we thought there must be some emergency. But now it's worrying. Work on his project is lagging behind. We can't afford to be slack on a federal government contract. We're ready to fire him."

"Was he here the day the Robinson lady got killed? You know the Robinson case?" asked the lead officer.

"Oh, the Robinson case! Horrible, horrible. Who would do such a thing?"

"Yeah. So, could you check Huddy's attendance records?"

"Yes, of course." The manager disappeared from the office and came back after a few minutes with the answer, "No, sir. Huddy had approved leave for that day, Thursday, the day the Robinson lady was attacked."

"Did he come back to work the next day?"

"Yes, he did, and then again on Monday. After that, you know, we haven't seen him."

So, in the beginning, Torte and Huddy went back to their daily routine after the Robinson affair, smug in the belief that no one could link them to the crime, and bolted in a hurry when they realized that the police were on their tail. Now, the police had a new task, find their hiding place.

Hefferly reasoned that a Commander, Huddy, was chosen by the AV top brass to pick his help from the membership and plan and execute the Robinson operation. If this was true, then the Gopal murder was also led by an AV Commander, and other planned murders would be too. Hefferly decided to check out all AV Commanders and investigate the whereabouts of the ones who were missing. This was a manageable task since there were only 13 of them. He was sure this would help him identify the person responsible for the Gopal operation, and, through association, his assistant.

Sure, this was not Hefferly's job, but he was happy to help out, not only Sanderson but also the Department, by thwarting the murders of Martinez and Karcher. This would win him the Department's admiration, necessary for his future professional advancement.

Executing the plan was not easy, though. The 13 Commanders were spread out over hundreds of miles. He looked at the area codes of the phone numbers and found some of them belonged to several adjoining states. He would have to coordinate his work with all those state and local authorities. It was a big job for one person who might take days, weeks. He did not want to wait that long. This meant that he would have to get some officers who were experienced interviewers, give them the task, and get it done in no more than a few days.

Hefferly got busy.

In a couple of days he had found eight officers and the task force was operational.

Even thought it was a Saturday, Hefferly showed up for work. He would take some comp time later. Four pairs of officers were formed, 3 pairs to interview 3 commanders each while the fourth pair was required to interview four commanders. The interview assignments were geographically clustered so that each pair of interviewers moved within a small area and saved a lot of travel time. They aimed to get it done in two days.

While flashing their badges, the standard police pitch was, "I am officer _ _ _ and this is my partner _ _ _." The blanks were to be filled in with names. "We're investigating the murders of Stella Robinson and Rajiv Gopal. Could we talk to you?" If the Commander was not home, they asked whoever answered the door where to find him. Then the police hunted him down at his place of work or wherever else his family told them he might be. In some cases there was no one home and they had to make return trips.

Eleven commanders on the list were found. If they refused to talk they were told, "It is better that you talk now. Otherwise, we will be back with a court order which will only increase the hassle." All of them agreed to an interview. It was a total waste of time. All of them admitted to being AV members but denied any involvement in either of the two murders. They claimed to be working on the days of the murders, which, when checked later, was confirmed to be correct.

Still, it was not a total loss. Of course, the police already knew that one of the missing commander was Huddy. When they reached the home of the other missing commander, Wade Searle, they did not find him either. Instead, their call was answered by a woman who looked wilted, like she had not eaten in several days.

After introductions the lead officer said, "Sorry to bother you ma'm, but we would like to talk to Wade Searle, please."

In spite of her depressed countenance, she spoke angrily, "He's dead. You know that."

"No ma'm, we don't."

"How could you not? You published his photo in the newspapers. It was also on TV."

"We publish a lot of photos. Which photo you are referring to?"

"The one published on Tuesday. There were two photos actually. They were said to have murdered some doctor."

"Oh those! Ma'm we did not know their names. They had no ID. One of them was your husband?"

The woman just looked at the officers incredulously.

The lead officer continued, "So, why didn't you call the police station?"

"What for? I knew they would call me. You are here, aren't you?"

"Yes, ma'm. But we did not know one of the dead men was Wade Searle. But, you did. I still don't understand why you didn't call the police. ... Could we come in, ma'm? This is a sensitive matter."

The woman moved aside to let the officers come in.

After they were seated in her living room, the lead officer asked again, "Do you have a photo of your husband we could see? Just to confirm that it was your husband's picture that was in the newspapers."

The woman walked over to a corner desk, picked up a framed photo of a man, brought it to the officer, and said, "This is my husband, Wade Searle. ... By the way, since you keep asking why I didn't call the police, I will tell you. When I read that Wade had no identification on him, I knew there was a reason. I didn't want to call the police station and become the source of his identification."

The officer answered disinterestedly, "I see." Then he looked at the photo and said, "Yes ma'm, it matches. ... By the way, what's your name, ma'm?"

"Tracy," she said and grabbed the photo back. Then, she said angrily, "Why don't you arrest that woman who killed my husband?"

"But ma'm the evidence suggests..."

He was interrupted, "I know what the evidence suggests. I have read about it in the papers. But I don't believe it. My husband isn't like that. I don't understand." At this point she appeared distraught and unsteady on her feet.

She grabbed the arm of a nearby chair, sat in it, and started to cry.

The officer said sympathetically, "We don't either. Maybe someone put him up to it. Do you have any idea?"

"No." Tracy said in a voice that sounded like it came from a well.

"Could it be the AVs? We know your husband was a Commander among them."

"I don't think so. Don't know. He had some friends who seemed to be the AVs, they talked about all that white supremacy stuff."

"So, do you know the man who died with your husband?"

"Not really."

"But you do know him."

"Just that he came to visit us a few times and talked about stuff, you know."

"Yes. You know his name?"

"Ellsworth, something, Arthur Ellsworth, I think."

"Would you mind letting us see your husband's things, papers, mail, etcetera? Maybe we could get a lead on those who sent him to his death."

"No. Go ahead."

The officers found the AV literature which proved nothing. Such literature was freely distributed, and even many people who despised the AVs had it. Amidst other papers, there was a Certificate of Appreciation issued to Wade Searle for devotion, dedication, and hard work to further the AV cause, signed by George Schultz, the AV Regional Commander. That proved something. The police took it.

The lead officer, at that point, said, "Thank you for your cooperation. It was good that we found you because we would have not known who to give the body to. The autopsy must have been completed by this time. You may claim the body from the city morgue." Then, in a consoling way, he added, "We are going to find those people who exploited your husband and prosecute them."

Tracy said nothing. She sat there, head bowed, face strained and wet with tears.

The policemen waited for a few seconds, and when it was obvious that Tracy was not going to say anything, the lead officer tore the curtain of the uncomfortable silence, "Would you like us to take you to a hospital, help you in any way?"

Tracy answered in a subdued voice, "No, thank you."

Disappointed that they did not get any evidence of direct involvement of any big AV official in the two murders, the officers still felt they had accomplished something, got the name of Searle's accomplice.

After leaving Searle's home, the lead officer called Hefferly's office and asked to check the name Arthur Ellsworth in the AV list and give him the address and phone number. In one minute he got the answer, "The name is on the list." He also got the address and phone number.

The officers immediately went to the address. They would call later if no one could be found in the home.

They found Ellsworth's brother. As soon as they rang the bell, the door opened and a burly six-foot tall man emerged who yelled, "Yes?"

The officers identified themselves and said, "We are looking for any kin of Arthur Ellsworth. Are you a relation?"

"I am his brother, Randy" the man answered gruffly.

"May we talk to you for a few minutes about your brother? He was killed a few days ago, as you know. We are investigating the case."

Randy spoke in a hostile manner, "Why did it take you so long? He was killed Monday, right?"

"Yes. But, we didn't know who he was. No ID. Besides, why didn't you contact us once you knew about your brother's death?"

"Obviously my brother didn't want to be identified. Why should I help the police by calling them?"

The officers noted that it was the same response Tracy had given them just a little while ago. Amazing, how similar circumstance made the minds run on the same track.

They ignored the answer, "Could we come in to talk to you?"

"No. I mean, what for? Why don't you go downtown and prosecute that bitch who killed my brother?" Another echo of the Tracy conversation. Ignore, ignore.

The officers also ignored the hostility, better for public relations and securing information, and said in a conciliatory tone, "We are looking into everything. We want to find out who conned your brother into this."

The approach worked, as they knew it would. Randy seemed to calm down a bit and said, "It could be that guy who was with him."

"Do you know him?"

"No. But I know he is, was, an AV. I told my brother to stay away from those people, they are trouble. He didn't listen."

"How do you know?"

"I know. My brother was a member. He told me."

"Is there something which proves he was a member, like a membership card?"

"No. I haven't seen any card. But, once he got a 5-year service medallion from the organization."

"Could we see it?"

"Should be around here somewhere. If you don't mind waiting, I will look for it. ... Oh, what the heck, why don't you come in?"

The officers' tactics had obviously mellowed him a bit. He led the policemen into the living room which was small and cluttered, indicating it was a bachelors' den.

The officers sat and watched Randy open and close the drawers of the cabinets in the living room, and then they saw him go further inside the apartment. After about five minutes, he reappeared with a medallion which, along with the big 88, had Aryan Vision engraved on it.

"Could we have it? It might help us find the AVs who got him in this trouble," said the lead officer.

"It's no use to anyone now."

The lead officer took the medallion then said, "You may claim your brother's body from the city morgue. Until a few minutes ago we did not know if he had a family."

Hefferly got the field reports. Now he knew; the still alive Robinson murderers were hiding. Goodwin, after the search of his house, probably told them that the police were after them and they disappeared without even telling their families. He thought that the AVs were smart for acting before the police could make their move, and gave them credit for being fast and efficient. And he knew, with proof now, that the Gopal murderers were also AVs. Not only that, he had their identities.

Now, the main question was: How to find Huddy and Torte? He decided to put around-the-clock surveillance on Huddy's and Torte's residences. Sooner or later the killers would come to their nests, for closure, if nothing else. It would mean collecting their possessions and moving on. When that happened, he would arrest the sons of bitches.

The other big, probably bigger, question was: How to nail the big wigs in the AV organization, at least one, Goodwin, pulling the strings? Right now there was no evidence that Goodwin did anything incriminating. Although both the Robinson and Gopal murders were committed by the AVs, it could be claimed that they were committed by individuals who happened to be AVs, thereby shielding the organization from any liability or culpability. He would see, he would find a way.

Before calling it a day, he called Sanderson and gave him the news of his investigation related to the Gopal murder.

CHAPTER THIRTY
THE WALLS SQUEEZED IN

Sitting in her jail cell, Christi had nothing to do but reflect over what had transpired.

She heard about Gopal's murder from one of those morning news programs on TV. She surmised, it must have been done by the man who had called her looking for Gopal's address. He, along with his companion, was gone and done in by the Indian bitch. Now she even knew the Indian bitch's name, thanks to the news media. At that moment, she hated Satya but also feared her. Hated her for blowing away the two men who had inadvertently avenged the exploited Mrs. Christi Gopal, and feared her for being capable of doing just that.

Strange, she wanted Gopal dead, yet, at the news of his murder she started to shake violently. The reality was unbearable. When she had talked to the strange caller and felt that Gopal should go, it was a fantasy, as if it were an event in the dream world with which she had only a vague association. Someone did something to someone else, and it just so happened that she benefitted from it. But now that the act was done, she felt guilty. Shaking aside, she was not quite sure of her emotions. Fear? Anger? Shock? Incredulity? Sadness? Repentance?

Still, she felt like a murderer, as if she herself had lifted that knife and slit Gopal's throat. In a way, she had. She could have alerted the police after she had a feel for the intentions of her strange caller. She did nothing and, by her silence, allowed Gopal to be killed. She had to share the blame. She could not deal with that knowledge and continued to shake.

Her shaking was interrupted by the ringing of the door bell.

The police were there. Although unexpected, she should have expected it.

Afraid as she was of the situation, she did remarkably well with the police interview. For one thing, she did not have to lie much, only a couple of times. Still, the interview made her feel concerned. Her guilt must have shown on her face. Why else would she be arrested on suspicion of being an accessory to murder and taken to police detention?

She had not expected any of this to happen. Now, she might rot in prison for, who knew, how long? In the midst of prostitutes, drug addicts, child abusers, robbers, burglars, and killers. She did not think she could survive the ordeal.

Help! Where was it? There was no one she knew who would come to her rescue. No real friends. Perhaps, she should hire an attorney. But, how to find one? She knew only one attorney, the one who had handled her divorce and had given her bad advice.

It was all dark, hopeless. Sure, she finally got what she wanted, gotten rid of Gopal without lifting a finger. She still felt hopeless. Depressed. Suicidal. Maybe what she did was wrong, maybe it was her guilt feeling which was punishing her.

But then maybe not. Why was it wrong to want Gopal dead who had wronged her? He had wronged her not only by coming back to America, but also by coming back with a wife and by becoming more prosperous than before.

These thoughts made her feel less guilty. Even righteous. This led to the natural progression of feeling like a victim, particularly at being arrested.

When night fell, she sat sleepless on her bunk, totally dejected, and started to cry. The tears fell on the back of her folded hands. That was when something stirred in her. She had never cried in her life. She had faced many adversities, many hardships, but never cried. She had been a fighter, was a fighter, would forever remain a fighter. Let them bring charges. She would fight them. The feeling of confidence made her believe that the police actually had no case against her and, in the end, they would just let her go.

She lay down on her bunk and determined to hang tough and not allow anyone to break her. She felt better. Not only that, she was even able to sleep.

So, the next day when Sanderson came and took her to an interrogation room, she did not flinch. She knew that he would try to lean on her, make her confess to her involvement in Gopal's murder, but she also knew that he would not succeed.

She sat in a crumbly resin chair facing Sanderson from across a wobbly folding table, and heard, "I just want to avoid the hassle of a court case which will surely bring you a lot of humiliation and pain. So, why don't you work with us? Tell us how the Gopal killers came to know you. The truth."

"I have already told you."

"Tell me again."

She repeated her answer of the previous day.

Sanderson did not seem satisfied and said, "Listen miss. We have searched your home and found some very incriminating evidence."

What incriminating evidence? Christi was sure Sanderson was lying. She did not know for sure, but suspected that the police must have found such lies to be effective in making even innocent prisoners feel that there might be something they didn't know, which could be somehow used to prove that they were guilty. She was not going to succumb to them.

While these thoughts were going through her mind, she heard Sanderson add, "Tell the truth and we'll recommend that the court go easy on you."

Adding some sugar to the heat to make the deal palatable? Christi questioned the police tactic and determined that it would not work. She became angry, "I am not guilty of anything."

"If that's how you feel." Sanderson got up in a huff and left.

Christi was transferred to her cell.

The next day, to her astonishment, she was released with an admonition, "We are still investigating. Don't leave town."

It should have pleased Christi, but it did not. She was still a suspect, might still be hauled into a court and, who knew, might be found guilty. Even though she did not kill Gopal or participate in his killing, she had a motive. She felt the police already had an inkling of it. All they needed was some tangible proof to prosecute her and get her convicted. It was a nightmare.

She found another nightmare when she got home.

The place looked like it had been burglarized. Although she knew it had been searched by the police, Sanderson had told her so, it was still a nightmare. She faced a big task of cleaning it and getting it back in order. She might have to hire some help.

She threw herself on the couch, very perturbed because prison was still a possibility. The bravado of a few hours ago dissipated quickly. It was replaced with fear and anxiety. In addition, guilt began to raise its head again. She could fool others that she had nothing to do with Gopal's murder, but she could not fool herself.

Days passed. With each passing day her mental condition deteriorated. She often thought of her life with Gopal. What had she accomplished by using and even abusing him? In retrospect, Gopal was not such a bad man. He had his quirks, who did not? She could have made adjustments with them. Instead, she turned the marriage into a war. She had to win every argument, every time. Her wishes and desires had to take precedence, her beliefs and values had to dominate. It was the ego thing. In the end, she lost him. Sure, she got a lot of his money, but somehow it did not seem all that critical anymore. That money, almost all gone, had brought her temporary comfort but not happiness.

She had become a victim of greed, ego, and hate. Powerful tools with which to cut yours and other's lives into pieces and throw them to rot. Rot! That was it. Her own life, too.

Sometimes, she reflected over her present life. It stunk from the rot she had brought upon herself. She stopped socializing and meeting others. Did not want anyone to be near her, lest they run away from her decayed existence. She also stopped talking to anyone on the phone. What would she say? She could not talk about her life, could not bear to hear about other's filled with glorious happenings. She got occasional calls from tele-marketers, then it was quiet, deathly quiet, even in the midst of the TV howling, radio screaming, record player blaring.

Hers became a solitary life looking for some connection, never finding it.

She wandered around her house in her bathrobe most of the time, missing most of her meals. She had lost her appetite for everything, food, sex, shopping, partying. No, not everything. She drank rum and coke, all day long. While drinking, she talked to herself and got lost in the quiet after becoming unconscious. She dreaded going out. She stumbled most of the time and did not think she could drive anymore. She had her groceries and booze delivered to her. A few times she tried to go to a movie. She felt people were avoiding her. Why? Was it because of her haggard looks? Did she smell? Did the people think she was a bag lady? Did she appear like a thief, a robber? What? she did not understand. Movies abandoned, she chose to stay within the walls of her house. Soon, these walls began to close in on her, at least that was how she felt. Often, she had a smothering sensation. She could not breathe, the walls were squeezing her from all directions. She would scream and the walls would scream back. She would scream louder and louder and the walls would scream back louder and louder. She would get angry that no one would respond to her cries, would not try to rescue her from being squeezed by the mocking walls. In anger, she would tear her hair, slap herself, then fall down unconscious. She could not save herself from herself.

She was sure, no one was aware of her condition, no one cared to know. So, she was surprised when one day her door bell rang. She ignored it. The bell rang again. She shuffled her feet toward it in exasperation. As she was looking through the peep hole, she heard a pounding on the door. Seeing that it was the postman, she said, "Knock it off. You're hurting my head." She heard her own voice and it sounded strange, like it was coming out of a drum, a female voice which had a male resonance to it.

She opened the door. The mail man explained, "Ma'm, your mail box, it's full." Then asked in a worried voice, "Are you ill? Want me to call someone?"

Christi could imagine how she might have looked to him. She was not Mrs. Rajiv Gopal, an exuberant and lively lady, Mrs. Gopal the postman had known in the past. Now, she probably looked like a week-old piece of rump left on the kitchen counter on room temperature, still sort of red but quite brown, wrinkly, and decayed. She probably also smelled like rum and vomit. She could imagine her appearance, having seen it a few times in the mirror and becoming scared, eyes sunken, face creased, hair a bird's nest. What's more, clad in dirty clothes, she was staggering. No wonder the mail man thought she needed help.

"No. I'm fine," she said and immediately asked, "Where's my mail?"

"Here," the mail man said and gave her a handful of it. Then he said, "I think you are very sick. I will call 911."

Christi was admitted to a hospital. The doctors told her, "Your body functions are overwhelmed by alcohol. We will have to detox you first. Then we will refer you to a psychiatrist. You also look depressed."

A few days later, she was taking antidepressants and receiving counseling from her therapist. A combination of the two seemed to make a difference, and Christi began to become oriented to life.

Just before being released, she had a prerelease conference with her psychiatrist. She was told, "We think you had a severe depressive episode which led to your drinking."

"I don't know what I have."

"You don't need to worry about what you have. In fact, your condition is not serious. What happened, happened. Now, if you take care of yourself, you will be okay."

"How am I going to take care of myself? What am I supposed to do?"

"Well, we think you are still traumatized by your divorce. You still see Gopal as your husband. Because he is dead, you feel like a widow. You also think you had a role in his death. You feel guilty and want to punish yourself. So, you are engaged in self destructive behaviors."

The explanation had nothing to do with her question. So, she said, "I don't understand what you are talking about."

"All right. What we are saying is that you are going to continue with the medication we have given you, for a while anyway. In addition, you are going to see a psychologist, mental health counselor, someone, for psychotherapy."

Christi felt that even though these people interacting with her were for hire, the doctors, psychiatrists, nurses, they had helped her become a person again, had helped her gain some control over her life, and establish some connection with the world.

So, she agreed to follow their advice

A day after her psychiatric conference, she was released from the hospital. A few days after that, she started her psychotherapy sessions with a psychologist.

CHAPTER THIRTY-ONE
HAPPY BIRTHDAY TO YOU

Schultz was very happy with the way his talk with Karcher had ended. He already knew through his usual sources, but now quite sure, that his warriors were following his orders making Karcher nervous. Nervous enough to want to negotiate with him. Soon after that he learned about the Gopal murder. He was pleased that things were moving in the right direction and rather quickly. But he was also sad, a couple of his men had also taken a hit. He could not believe that a spineless cow of an Indian pussy could blow away two of his fierce warriors. Still, he had to accept the reality and go on. It was a war and casualties, even on his side, could not be entirely avoided.

Then he learned that Karcher had asked his staff to look for an AV mole. He laughed; they would never find him.

He figured that while the prison was distracted and demoralized by the murder of two staff members, he needed to communicate with his brother about his escape plan and obtain his help in carrying it out. There might not be a better time to do it. If he were to die trying to escape, so be it. No, a solitary cell in the prison or, for that matter, the execution chamber, was not the place where he wanted to die.

He thought and thought for several hours and finally hit upon a solution.

He would employ a carrier pigeon. Ruben Ibarra, who usually brought his lunch, came to his mind. A poor Mexican would be easy to manipulate, he figured.

That day when Ibarra came to him with his meat loaf and water, Schultz received his food without any fuss and cast his net, "Hey Ruben, could you do me a favor, a very small favor?" He felt safe talking with Ibarra about a proscribed subject because the video camera could only record the movement.

"No, no favors. We are not allowed to do any favors for inmates. You know that," Ibarra said and turned to go. Then suddenly he reversed himself, faced Schultz and yelled, "And, even if I were allowed to, I wouldn't do you any favors. Why should I, considering the way you have treated me, throwing food in my face? Do you have any idea how many times you have done that?"

"I know. I am sorry. It's nothing personal. I was just mad at the system. You understand that. No, I will never throw food or anything else at you, ever. I promise."

"Promise or not, I still can't do you any favors."

"But, please listen. It's really not a favor. I used a wrong word. It's more like a courtesy. Just tell my brother Albert that I am sending him best wishes for his birthday. That's all. There's money in it for you."

"Now you are gaming me. I am telling the warden about it."

Schultz had not expected even this much resistance. But the resistance itself forced him to demolish it. So, he said, "Go ahead. What more can he do to me that he hasn't done already? Only this will trigger an investigation. Guess, who would be the target? No matter what comes out of it at the end, people will talk. You will always be under suspicion."

Ibarra hesitated for a moment. There was truth in what he just heard. Schultz noticed the hesitation and knew that the guard was entrapped. This was the moment to strike, "Listen, all you have to do is give my brother the message. It's totally innocent. How's that going to get you in any trouble? Like I said, there's a reward in it, if you want it. So, what do you say?"

"No, no way," Ibarra held his ground. "You can tell your brother whatever you want to tell him yourself. By mail, or in person."

"I am in solitary. No communication allowed, except with my attorney. You know that. It would take a lot of time to arrange a meeting with my counselor. My brother needs to know about my best wishes now."

"In that case I am telling. I will tell Mr. Martinez that you were trying to bribe me."

"And I will tell him, or anyone else, that you were asking money from me for even serving food and water. And when I refused, you threatened to accuse me of bribing you."

"It will be your word against mine. You can well imagine who would be believed."

"Man, you live in a dream world. All accusations against staff are taken seriously, and bribes are a very serious matter. True or not, it will ruin your career. Even if they have no evidence of any wrongdoing on your part, they will still fire you on some excuse. No one will ever trust you. That's the nature of the beast. You want to test it out, be my guest. Or, why not do something nice without any negative consequences, and still get paid for it?"

Schultz could see that Ibarra was no dummy, and probably had noticed his insistence and threat, and knew the message could not be innocent. Ibarra probably also knew him well enough to be sure that the threats would be carried out. And, the mentioned consequences were most likely to materialize. Schultz was sure that Ibarra felt trapped. So, he added, "Why not take a safe approach. My brother will get his birthday greetings on time, you will get some money, a messenger's payment, not a bribe. And this will, then, be the end of our entire conversation."

"What's the number?" Ibarra asked.

Schultz was pleased that he had caught a bird which would fly at his direction. He mouthed the number quietly and warned, "Don't forget it. It's unlisted."

Just at that moment another guard appeared and said, "What's going on? Is there a problem?"

Schultz realized that he had been talking with Ibarra for a period longer than would be considered normal by the prison, and the subject of the conversation, if it became known to the authorities, would surely get both of them disciplined. Not sure how Ibarra would handle the situation, he intervened, "No problem. I was just asking when this fucking meat loaf and water crap would end, and Ibarra here didn't know."

"And, it took you guys this long?"

"I guess I kept insisting on an answer and he couldn't just walk away without saying something, even if it was 'no'. He is very polite, you know."

"Whatever, break it up."

Schultz watched Ibarra walk away meekly followed by the other guard. After that he put his food tray aside, leaned back on his floor mattress, still uncomfortable and feeling pain from the abuse he had received from Jordan, and reflected over what he had accomplished just now.

It was not necessary to employ Ibarra to communicate with his brother. Just like it was not necessary to employ the prison grape vine to ask the AV leadership to punish the program committee members. Both communications could have been accomplished easily through the mole. But his chosen means were critical for keeping the mole out of the picture. If the mole were identified, it would get him in trouble and would jeopardize the entire operation including Schultz's escape plans. Therefore, the mole had to be used in situations where no other safe method of communication was possible. Since Karcher had become wise to the presence of a mole and was looking for him, it was all the more important to do all that could be done to keep the mole's identity secret.

He was surprised at Ibarra's stupidity in finally accepting his request. The threats Schultz had made and the consequences he had specified for not doing what he had asked him to do were possible, but not unavoidable. But his surprise lasted only a minute.

He knew human nature which was more controlled by immediate rewards than possible dangers far off in the future. Ibarra was no exception.

Whatever, Schultz was pleased that he was one step closer to his escape. He hoped nothing would happen to derail his plan.

He smiled smugly. Then sat up and started to eat his meat loaf with relish for a change.

CHAPTER THIRTY-TWO

BLACKMAIL AND MORE BLACKMAIL

Ibarra could understand being blackmailed for something he did, but this was absurd. Maybe he should just go to his boss, tell him all about how Schultz was gaming him, and take his chances with the prison than getting caught in the sticky web knitted by a prison inmate. Considering that Martinez was promoting him, no matter what Schultz said, he would not be blamed for anything. Then the money flashed in his mind. How much could he get for the delivery of the message? He didn't know what would be a reasonable price. A quick weighing of the risk involved made him decide on a grand.

At the end of his shift, on his way back home, Ibarra stopped at a convenience store to make the call. He did not want his home number connected with this shady business.

Three rings and the receiver was picked up on the other end, "Hello."

Ibarra also heard a click and knew that it was the tape recorder turned on. He wasn't terribly concerned about that, since he was sure he could not be identified; he was using a pay phone and was not going to give out his name and address.

"Albert Schultz please," he said.

"Who's calling?" Ibarra heard caution. Apparently Albert did not recognize the voice and probably wondered how a stranger got his unlisted phone number?

"I have a message from your brother, George," Ibarra also responded cautiously.

"I am Albert. What's the message?" Curiosity in the voice.

"There's a delivery charge." Ibarra did not want to call it a reward which sounded illegitimate and demeaning, irrespective of the fact that what he was doing was just that.

"Sure. How much?"

This was too easy. Now, Ibarra was nervous, but his greed overpowered him. "A grand," he answered.

"You got it. What's the message?"

Ibarra was worried. If Albert was willing to pay a thousand dollars for a message he had not received, it could not be innocent. But he had come this far, there was no retreat. "I really didn't get it," he said shrewdly. The implication of the statement was clear: no payment, no delivery.

"I see. In that case, meet me at milepost 8 on state route 248 tomorrow night at eight. And, come alone."

The phone went dead.

It would be dark and deserted at the appointed time and the meeting place. Ibarra's nervousness was ballooning. He even considered forgetting the whole thing. 'Don't be paranoid,' a voice prompted him from within.

He kept his appointment. To play it safe, he carried his .45 with him.

He waited and waited. No one showed up. At about nine he gave up. Angry, he went to a pay phone and called Albert. "You didn't come?" Ibarra questioned.

"You think I am an idiot, meeting with a stranger in the dark in the wilderness with a grand in my bag?"

"But that was your idea. You could have chosen another place. Now, how do you intend to pay me?"

"I don't any more."

"Why did you ask me to meet you then?"

"Don't you hear? Are you deaf? I said, 'Not any more.' When I heard about a secret message from George I was excited, willing to do anything to get it. Afterwards I figured, I don't have to give you anything, and you are going to give me the message anyway."

"I am? You are gonna make me?" Ibarra mocked.

"Yes. Because if you don't, the prison is going to hear our conversation. It's on tape. They can easily match the voice on the tape with yours, that is, if you really work for the prison. If you don't, then you are a phony and don't matter to me. I am not bluffing."

Ibarra knew he had been taped, so he did not ask for any evidence. He became concerned, worried was more like it. Instead of getting paid, he was being threatened with exposure. He had lost the battle of wits, and it was time he played defensive. So, he asked cautiously, "How do I know that you will keep quiet after getting the message?"

"You don't. The tape goes to the prison for sure if you don't give me the message right now."

The curt reply hurt. Now, it was time to bargain, "Couldn't I get the tape in exchange?"

"Don't be stupid. The tape is my insurance that you won't do anything asinine. Besides, I can't give you the tape even if I wanted to. Since I am not meeting you, I can't give it to you personally, and I can't mail it to you because, I am sure, you won't give me your name and address." After a short pause, he asked, "I don't understand why you want the tape? It won't protect you, because I could always keep a copy."

Finding the situation hopeless, Ibarra decided to play it safe, safer than the alternative, and gave the message.

That's when he realized, how stupid he was that he had allowed to be gamed by Schultz. He also realized the value of the prison policy to inform the superiors about any gaming attempt by the inmates. Actually, he was going to do just that, but the possibility of making a quick grand had clouded his mind. At that time he wanted to shoot himself.

But he did not.

Instead he allowed the cloud over his mind to dissipate and began to think. He knew the situation was hopeless, the blackmail tape could be used any time and most likely it would be used, just for the fun of it, to tease him, to destroy him, or for all those reasons combined. Well, if he was going to go down, he was not going down quietly. He would do some damage, some real damage, to the blackmailers.

He would teach George Schultz a lesson for ensnaring him. He was determined to get even, determined to give that son-of-a-bitch a treatment that would make him sorry he ever messed with him.

Not only that, it might even persuade Schultz to ask his brother to destroy the tape.

Ibarra smiled at having discovered the last bullet.

CHAPTER THIRTY-THREE

A NOT SO WEASEL WEASEL

IBARRA CAME TO the prison the next work day, ready to strike back.

He should have gone to see Jordan, but chose not to. Jordan was not likely to approve his request to punish Schultz, primarily because it was his job, and he stood to gain from it in the form of a promotion.

Ibarra remembered his talk with Martinez a few days ago and was very sure that Martinez would be sympathetic to his request, and was most likely to approve it. Going to see Martinez, to talk to someone several rungs above the chain of command, of course, was not standard procedure. But then, his was not a standard request.

He went to Martinez's office and saw his secretary, "I need to see Mr. Martinez about something very important."

The secretary saw the serious look on his face and acquiesced by calling Martinez on the phone, "Sir, Officer Ibarra wants to see you. Says it's very important."

'Important' was a critical word in the prison bureaucracy. If something was declared important you had better attend to it immediately because, if you did not and it caused any problem, you were in serious trouble. So, Ibarra was not surprised when he overheard Martinez give the predictable response, "Send him in."

Ibarra entered Martinez's office hesitatingly and suddenly was a bit unsure of himself. He had been there only once before and at Martinez's request. But this time he was there to ask permission to do something which was against all policies and procedures. If Martinez granted his request, he himself might be in trouble with the administration. Ibarra obviously had been taking Martinez's interest in him for granted and assumed to be supported by him for any idea and action. As he crossed the threshold of the office of his supervisor's supervisor, his mind warned him in a flash, that no matter how much Martinez liked him, he was not going to jeopardize his own position to give a lowly guard a helping hand in his vengeance against Schultz. But, now he could not back out. He was here, and he had to tell something, something important. Wasn't that the reason he had given to the secretary to gain audience with his boss?

Once more, in a flash, his mind guided him, 'Make your request. You are in a pile of shit already. What more could happen? If you are denied, think of something else, later.'

By the time he sat down in a chair in front of Martinez, Ibarra was fairly composed, "Sir, I know it is against policy to jump the chain of command, but what I have to say can be said only to you."

"Go on," Martinez tacitly excused him.

"It has to do with Schultz. I have been delivering his meals for a while and so many of them have stained my uniform. I'd like to request an opportunity to give the bastard back his due."

"I don't understand. You are already on the team to punish Schultz. Hasn't Mr. Jordan explained your role to you?"

"Yes, sir, he told me that I am on the team, but he is doing all the work by himself. I am still only delivering meals."

"All right. I will talk to Mr. Jordan about you. ... I think you will have an opportunity to fulfill your wish. You see, the Warden wants more than what has been done to Schultz so far."

But Ibarra wanted the job for himself. That was the only way he was going to have satisfaction. He decided to become a bit bolder and said, "Sir, Mr. Jordan may not want to share the responsibility with me. He is good at what he does and may feel that no one else can do the job as well."

"But, it's still his responsibility, he has been made in charge of this operation. It's only appropriate that you talk to him. I am sure, after I talk to him, he will give you a major role to play."

That was not what Ibarra wanted. He made a last plea, "Sir, I know my place. I will do whatever Mr. Jordan and you demand. But, just for once, give me a free hand to punish Schultz. Just one chance. I will be able to show you that I am capable of supporting the operation. If you approve my request, I am sure Mr. Jordan would not mind."

"All right, let me think about it."

"Thank you, sir."

Ibarra thought it would be a while, at least several days, before he heard from Martinez. He was surprised when he did not have to wait even a day.

In the afternoon, he got a message on his radio, "Report to Mr. Martinez's office, now."

His first thought was, 'Am I in trouble because of my request this morning?' Whatever, he would handle it.

He sat in the same chair which he had occupied in the morning, anxiously waiting for Martinez to speak, not knowing if he would get his head chopped or be ensconced in a throne. Neither happened. Instead he heard Martinez inform him, "I have decided to act on Mr. Karcher's request 'to do more' right away. Since you volunteered, you get the job."

"What about Mr. Jordan?"

"Don't worry. I will talk to him."

"Thank you sir. I am here to serve you."

Martinez ignored the flattery through submission and said, "This time Schultz gets the cattle prod treatment. Can you handle it?"

"Yes, sir. Any special instructions regarding this, or do I have a free hand?"

"You have a free hand, just don't kill him. And it goes without saying, keep it to yourself."

"Yes, sir."

That day Ibarra stayed late to carry out his assignment. After collecting the necessary equipment, he marched swiftly. First, he stopped in the video monitoring room and informed the guard, "I will be turning off the video recorder in the Schultz area. I will turn it back on again when I am done. It's necessary to do something ordered by Mr. Martinez. Okay?" He knew, no questions would be asked by the Video Monitor upon mention of the Deputy Warden's name. Besides, such requests by staff were not uncommon. A video recorder was there only to record the events which made the prison look good, not bad.

Then he went straight to the solitary confinement area. He turned off the automatic video recorder, and then quickly unlocked the door to Schultz's cell, burst it open, and pounced on his prey. The sudden attack put Schultz at a disadvantage. He staggered and yelled, "What the fuck?"

Ibarra was not Schultz's match but he had the upper hand. He pushed him down and sat on his chest pinning his arms under his legs. He loomed over him menacingly with the electric prod sticking out of his uniform and announced, "This is what you get for messing with me."

Schultz, apparently finding himself in a bad spot, spoke in an appeasing manner, "What are you so angry about?"

"You know. Your mole told you already, I am sure."

Before he could finish his sentence he was hit with spit from Schultz's mouth. Now Ibarra was sure that Schultz knew all that had transpired between him and Albert Schultz. He also deduced that Schultz, realizing the failure of his appeasement approach, was ready to fight.

Ibarra did not bother to wipe the spit. The weasel was casting a lion's shadow. He was there to draw blood, take his revenge. He delivered a vicious punch to the left side of Schultz's face with his right fist, crunching his knuckles against the cheek bone. He expected Schultz to be subdued. Instead, he was surprised to feel one of Schultz's knees dig into his spine so viciously that he almost lost his balance. He noticed that Schultz was also trying to free his arms. This was unbelievable to him that Schultz was able to fight back with such strength even after all the physical abuse he had received recently.

'Not any more,' Ibarra decided, 'he will be a limp, wet noodle after I am through with him.' He intended to deliver the maximum dose of the medicine, just short of killing him.

He screamed, "You asshole," and lunged at Schultz. First he pummeled his face with his fists. He noticed that Schultz screamed in the beginning then whimpered. After Schultz appeared subdued, Ibarra took out the electric prod, turned it on, set the voltage at high, and administered the shock to Schultz's eyelids and mouth. Schultz twisted his face and ground his teeth. Ibarra then balanced himself on his right knee, brought his left foot on the right side of Schultz's face, and stood up crushing it. Schultz shrieked in agony. Ibarra, feeling confident that Schultz would not be able to counter his attacks, released pressure on his victim's upper body, moved down slightly, tore his pants and shocked his testicles, then plunged the prod inside his anus.

Schultz thrashed, flailed his arms, screamed, expelled the contents of his bladder and bowel, frothed from the mouth, then slumped with his eyes bulging out, and his tongue hanging down. Ibarra pulled the prod out and applied it to Schultz's feet but it appeared to be in vain. Schultz had fainted.

Ibarra left him there to recover by himself. He locked the cell door, turned on the video camera, went to an emergency phone hanging on the wall, and called Martinez, "Job done, sir."

He heard no reply and replaced the receiver. No incident report was prepared this time because he didn't know what to say in it, how to explain Schultz's injuries without implicating the prison staff. Besides, he was sure, everything will be hush hush.

As he walked out of the prison that evening, smugness showed on his face. He thought he had won the game.

CHAPTER THIRTY-FOUR

BREAKING SPIRITS

Sitting in his office chair in the early morning hours, Karcher pondered, 'It has been a week since Gopal's murder, and the police have not been able to make any arrests.' He cheered Satya for gunning down the two AVs. In his opinion, she had done better than the police. He did not have any particular sadness at Gopal's murder. Gopal, in his eyes, was just a war casualty.

But it was clear to him that he was losing the war. He had lost two principals on his force which meant only one thing: security measures were not working. He was not sure where the weak points were, but if he did not find and eliminate them soon he might be the next victim. He feared for his life. Something had to be done. But what? He could not find fault with his original strategy. He still felt that the way to a decisive victory was for Belford to rein in the AVs, and for him to subdue Schultz, something neither of them had been able to do so far. They needed to put some extra fire in their weapons.

He picked up the phone and called Belford to prod him, "You know Hector, we have incurred some heavy losses."

"AV, AV have too," Belford countered.

"Yeah. But, they are supposed to, not us. Our defensive posture isn't working. I think we need to go on the offensive."

"But, we need to find our target first. We, we don't have any."

"We have Goodwin."

"But, we have nothing, nothing, to tie him to these murders. We have searched his house. We found stuff, stuff, that proves that he is an AV. But, being an AV isn't a crime. His list of membership has helped us identify the murderers, but their crimes do not implicate Goodwin. We really have nothing, nothing."

"Nothing?"

"Nothing. We have Sonny Madrill who is dead, dead. The other two Robinson murderers, Huddy and Torte, are missing, hiding, hiding, I think. And, the men who assaulted Gopal, Searle and Ellsworth, are dead, dead. Man, what a woman, that Mrs. Gopal? Blew them away, away, just like that. An Indian woman, man, I can't believe, believe."

While Karcher shared Belford's appreciation of Satya's heroic act, he was not interested in it at the time. He wanted the problem solved. So, he asked, "You mean we have no leads?"

"Actually, we thought we had one, one, Christi Gopal. But, so far we have found no hard evidence to link, link, her either to the AVs or to the murders."

"So, what are we going to do?"

"At this time, time, I don't know. I am sure there will be another attack, but don't know, know, when, where, and on whom. All I can say, be on guard, guard."

That was not comforting to Karcher. He was sure that the situation was not comforting to Belford either. His Department was looking bad because the AV attacks were continuing, and he had not been able to make any arrests, not counting Christi's brief detention. Well, he could not do Belford's job for him but he certainly needed to do his. What had he done to control Schultz? Actually, he had done everything he could, but the outcome had been dismal. What now? What now?

He was still in a question mode when there was a call from Martinez, "Sir, Schultz has received his next dose, a big one, yesterday. He needs medical treatment, that is, if we don't want him to die."

"It has come this far? And, you are calling me now? After, what, ten, twelve hours?"

"We didn't know the seriousness of his condition until this morning. The guard who took his breakfast noticed him lying almost unconscious and bleeding. I took the first chance to call you."

"All right, thank you." Karcher dismissed Martinez. It was not the time to argue over what had already happened. It was time to think of future moves. A little contemplation, and he felt this to be a good time to negotiate with Schultz again. After his most recent treatment, he might be willing to agree to a truce. If a cease fire could be achieved, there might not be any need for further extraordinary security arrangements. Knowing that the cease fire, if achieved, would not last, he still pursued it. If nothing else, it would buy him time to strengthen his forces.

Karcher, once more, just like last time, walked to ASU, then to Schultz's cell and dismissed all the staff in that area. He did not bother with the video monitors, since he was not going to do anything but talk and the cameras were not equipped to record sound.

He looked inside Schultz's cell and saw him lying in a heap. Had it not been for his blinking eyes and heaving chest, Schultz might have been considered dead.

Karcher looked at Schultz like he was a piece of wood and said matter-of-factly, without a sympathetic note in his voice, "You really must see a doctor, Mr. Schultz. I believe you are hurt."

"What do you... think? Your men did it... you fuck!" The rope had burned but its arrogant twists were still intact.

Karcher swallowed his pride for the sake of negotiations.

Schultz turned his head to get a full view of Karcher, then he added slowly and forcefully, "You lost... another man?" It seemed like these few words took a great deal of effort to come out of his mouth. His speech was strained and barely audible.

Karcher was disturbed by the fact that Schultz knew about the Gopal killing, but did not want it to show. He ignored the comment, drained his face of all emotions, and made a last ditch effort to get his adversary to talk peace. "Time is running out," he said.

"What gives, man?" asked Schultz. He appeared like he was ready to compromise. Why? Karcher was clueless.

"I will call the Health Unit right away. All you have to do is call off your men."

"My... men?"

"You think we don't know? The AVs. Just a statement that says the war is over, and sign and date it. We will deliver it to Mr. Stewart Goodwin."

"You mean, confess? ... Fuck you." Schultz muttered faintly between his teeth.

"Well, they have to know."

"My way."

"How would I know that the matter had been taken care of?"

"No more attacks."

"And, if there are?"

"Get me."

Karcher thought the man was stupid. Karcher would do anything with him and in anyway he wanted. But, just to keep the dialogue going, he said, "All right, I am calling the Health Services right away."

"One more thing," Schultz interjected.

Karcher was surprised at the boldness with which the speech had been delivered, since all through this talk Schultz had been uttering very few words and in a very subdued manner, as if in pain. "Yeah?" he asked

"I want to see my brother."

"In the Health Unit, yes."

Karcher called the Health Unit on the radio, "We have an emergency. It's George Schultz. Yes. ... Yes. ... Send an ambulance. I will appreciate it if someone could see him immediately. Thank you."

He turned to Schultz and confirmed, "All set."

"My brother?" Schultz asked.

"I am calling him too, right now. What's his number?"

Schultz mouthed it slowly.

Karcher picked up a wall phone nearby in the hall and called the number. After getting a response, he said, "This is Warden Karcher. I have approved your visit with your brother George. You can see him in the Health Unit."

Schultz looked satisfied.

Karcher went back to his office, elated but still worried, not about the truce, but about the ease with which it was accomplished. Schultz must have some hidden agenda. 'What?" Karcher wanted to know.

And, Schultz seemed to know everything that was going on. He clearly had an upper hand in this regard.

Karcher was frustrated at not knowing who the source of Schultz's knowledge was. And, Martinez had not been able to find the mole, apparently. He decided to check with Martinez, whom he was going to call anyway to make administrative arrangement for Schultz to be moved to the Health Unit. He dialed Martinez's number, "I went to see Schultz to talk about a new truce and found out that he knows. Damn it, he knows everything. Where's the mole?"

"Jordan is in charge, sir. He is checking and watching staff. So far no luck."

"Schultz had to be communicating with someone. Rotate the staff. Get new ones from another unit. Do something."

"Yes, sir. But the mole may not be in my unit."

"What do you mean?"

"The mole could be in another unit and the information is communicated to Schultz through intermediaries."

"Aha! Yes. That protects the mole from exposure. And that makes it harder to find him. Or her."

"Still, I'll continue to look for him. ... Anything else, sir?"

"Yes. You should also know that Schultz has agreed to a truce. I have arranged for him to go to the Health Unit. I don't want him to die. If he has to go to the hospital, make sure that everyone there knows that Schultz is a dangerous inmate on death row, and they should have very tight security. No one, except those on his approved visitors list, gets to see him."

"Right away sir."

"If the truce holds, we are all safe. But, that's a big if."

"I wonder why he agreed to the truce at this time? He didn't pay attention to it in the past."

"I, too, wondered. It could be because of the treatment he got. Anyway, when he comes back from the Health Unit or the hospital, whichever it might be, more of the same. We need to break his spirit, break to the point where he begs to die."

The message to Martinez clearly was, 'Use the truce to stop the attacks now, then remove that threat entirely by totally subduing the leader who had the power to renew the campaign.'

Karcher, satisfied with his accomplishments, immediately left for his home.

He saw Carolyn and Satya at the kitchen table, drinking coffee, and talking. He did not want to face them. What if they knew what had happened to Schultz? Carolyn, particularly, would be bitching. He could not take it, not at this time. He went straight to the bathroom and locked himself inside.

'I should have stayed in the office. That way I would not have to face these peace mongers,' he thought angrily.

Peace mongers! He remembered his row with Carolyn over his treatment of Schultz and also remembered Satya's talk with the police investigator which had been published in the news media.

Then it occurred to him that he was making the whole situation worse by overreacting to the peace postures of the two women. By his behavior, he might alert them that something was afoot and then they would really get on his case. Maybe not both, but certainly Carolyn. 'Change your attitude and behavior, play it cool, present to them the whole thing in a manner that they think of it as unfortunate,' he ordered himself.

He came out of the bathroom, went to the women directly, and said, "I don't know if you heard, Schultz has been misbehaving."

"How?" asked Carolyn.

"I don't know the details. He got in a fight with the staff, and now he is on his way to the Health Unit as we talk."

"That's sad," Satya said.

Carolyn looked at Karcher penetratingly and said in a pained voice, "It's getting worse, the war, I mean."

"I tried to end it. I went to him waving a white flag. I think it is working." He felt comfortable to be telling the truth for a change.

But, the truth had a darker side, 'What if the truce did not hold?'

Karcher's comfort was very short lived.

CHAPTER THIRTY-FIVE
THANK YOU, MY ENEMY

GEORGE SCHULTZ KNEW he would die without treatment. That did not particularly bother him. What bothered him was that he would die at the hands of his enemy, in bondage. That was humiliating. He had to escape, put his plan to work. Besides, he still had a lot of AV work to do, and it was too soon to die.

He remembered Karcher's visit asking for a truce. The terms of the truce were not acceptable to him, but he agreed to them. In retrospect, it seemed like a good thing. If he agreed to the truce, he would be able to go to the hospital; this would buy him time to assess losses, regroup, fortify his positions, increase his troop strength and fire power, and give him an opportunity to be free. He did not agree to a truce to surrender.

All that meant was that the truce was temporary, and the war would be renewed.

Ever since the Gopal murder, he was sure the offer for a truce would be coming, because the first time it had come was after the Robinson murder.

Schultz reasoned that Karcher would want the truce for his own agenda. The agenda did not include killing him. If he wanted to kill him, he would have done so already. He probably knew that killing him would not save him, it would only increase the resolve of the AVs to carry on the fight, and carry it on indefinitely. A truce, on the other hand, would save his skin. How dumb he was! Sure, a truce would work if all the parties kept their word. But who would? Not in a war, no one would. He was convinced that Karcher would honor the truce only as long as he was weak, vulnerable. Was he really so stupid that he could not see the reality?

He waited for the truce signal to arrive.

It did. But, before it came, there arrived Ibarra with his cattle prod. Schultz had not expected it, but when it came, he welcomed it. Only he knew that the torturous punishment he got was welcome, for it was likely to get him to the a hospital and to eventual freedom. Then came the truce, another welcome sign.

He had agreed to the truce but he had no intention of honoring any of the terms after he got what he wanted.

In less than an hour he was on his way to the Health Unit in a prison ambulance. He made sure he had his family photos with him.

A doctor was waiting to receive him. He examined him thoroughly, took X-rays, gave him some pain killers, and asked, "How did you get these injuries?"

Schultz did not want to answer. He adopted the posture of being too much in pain to answer. He was, in fact, in pain, so there was no drama involved. He could have pointed his finger at Ibarra, which would have triggered an investigation, and who knew what might have come out, some of which was likely to put him and his brother into jeopardy. Also, his 'Happy Birthday' message would have become exposed, compromising his escape plans. Better to keep silent about it. After all he did get what he wanted, no need to complicate matters.

About an hour later, he heard the doctor call Martinez and say in plain English, "Inmate Schultz has intestinal bleeding. It's going to require surgery. We are not equipped. He needs to go to a hospital."

A moment later he heard him say, "All right, I will give him something for the pain and transfer him to the county hospital. ... But, do you know how it happened? Is there an incident report or video record of the event I could see?"

Another pause and then the doctor said, "I see. Of course, I will say nothing."

Schultz guessed what had transpired, 'Martinez told the doctor that he would call the county hospital and make the necessary security arrangements, that there was no incident report or video recording for obvious reasons, and that the doctor should keep his mouth shut.' Or, something like that.

Schultz was happy. Although, before his abuse by the prison started, he was not sure if he would actually get to a hospital, but he did, and exactly the way he wanted. Now, all he needed was for his brother to show up.

For this happy outcome, he was particularly thankful to Ibarra, his enemy, for giving him the cattle prod treatment in his behind which tore his intestines apart. The injuries from other abuses were not so serious as to require going to a hospital or to be admitted to the Health Unit. He would have been treated either in his own cell or briefly in the Health Unit and immediately sent back to his solitary confinement. It was different now. Heaven had smiled upon him when he expected it least, and in the craziest way imaginable. Of course, he too had a hand in it, having created the conditions for the kind of attack he received. Maybe Heaven had nothing to do with it, and he should take all the credit.

It was late afternoon when Schultz was pulled out of the ambulance in the emergency section of the hospital. He saw four cops surround the vehicle immediately. While being transported to the secure section of the hospital with cops following him, Schultz watched the layout carefully. Once inside the ward he was faced with a swarm of nurses who got busy completing paper work for his admission. A half hour later, he found himself in a bed within a single room of a locked ward, manned around the clock by a security officer at the entrance.

A doctor attended to him within an hour of his admission. First, he took some urgent measures to stop the internal bleeding. Then, he studied X-rays and the narrative report prepared at the Health Unit of the prison. After that, he did his own examinations, took some more

X-rays, and asked Schultz the same question the doctor in the Health Unit had asked.

Schultz was not in much pain this time, thanks to the treatment received in the Health Unit. He still pretended to be too much in pain to talk for the same reason which prevented him from talking to the doctors in the prison.

The doctor said, "It's none of my business. It's between you and the prison. I am here to provide medical treatment."

Schultz thought, 'Smart doctor. Must have seen numerous cases like this pass under his nose and must have learned that there were secret codes and protocols under which the prison and the inmates operated. And, if he knew what was good for him, he would just keep his pretty little nose out of it.'

Schultz kept silent. The doctor then added, "I am scheduling you for surgery, first thing in the morning. The nurses will keep you comfortable during the night."

The doctor left. And the metal door was shut behind him, imprisoning Schultz in the tiny room.

All this was routine, boring, and inconsequential. However, something really important did take place a little later that night.

He had a visit from his brother, Albert.

CHAPTER THIRTY-SIX

THE FATE OF A WARRIOR

ALBERT WAS PUZZLED by the clandestine message from George. Why would George want to send him a 'Happy Birthday' greeting when it was not his birthday? What did the message mean?

Sitting on the open porch of his farmhouse, he pondered over it restlessly, sleeplessly. The night grew darker and the stars came out with a shimmering revue. But, he remained oblivious to it. In front of his closed eyes, he could see his brother's life projected on an invisible screen. Life from the time he was a baby to the time when he was locked up in the prison. Sometime in the middle of it, his wife shook him and said, "Aren't you coming to bed tonight?" The image of George disintegrated into thin air and the drama ended abruptly.

He got up reluctantly and followed his wife to bed.

"You worried about George, aren't you? Ever since that phone call you haven't been yourself."

Still he said nothing.

"Here, let me hold you. Maybe this will help." She pulled him toward her and let his head rest against her breasts.

A few minutes later, sleep overtook Albert. Even then, he could not get the thought of George out of his mind. He dreamed of his first visit with him in the prison: George had winked at him and said, "I think of your birthday whenever I am in serious trouble and need your help."

He woke up startled. The mystery was solved. From the open window he could see that the sky had turned a faded blue with a bright orange border on the horizon. Yet, there was darkness behind it. 'What adversity was George facing?' he asked himself. He must talk to him and find out what was going on. Then he would move to protect him.

He waited until the next day, Monday, when the prison authorities would be in their offices to hear his request for an emergency visit; a regular visit would have taken weeks to process.

He did what he always did in the past whenever there was a need to contact George. He dialed Robinson's number. Before the first ring was complete, he realized his mistake; she was gone and her replacement would not be familiar with her case load. He disconnected and dialed again, this time for Martinez.

When his call was answered he said, "This is Albert Schultz. I'd like to arrange a visit with my brother George Schultz."

"Sorry. All visits are suspended while inmate Schultz is in isolation," answered Martinez's secretary.

"Isn't there any way?"

"No. I am sorry."

What should he do next? Go to court? No court would grant his request, he had no justifiable reason for it. What else? He struggled with his problem, all day long.

All of a sudden it was not a problem any more. The next day he got a call from Goodwin, "We have information through our usual confidential sources that George is hurt. You may want to visit him."

Realizing that the prison could not refuse his request to visit George under the condition of a medical emergency, he decided to call Martinez again. Before he could do that he got a call from Warden Karcher. He could not believe that his visit with George had been approved, even before he had asked for it. All he could say was, "Thank you."

As suggested by Karcher, he called the Health Unit, "My name is Albert Schultz, I am George Schultz's brother. I am calling to find out when can I see him."

The Unit Secretary answered, "I am sorry, Mr. Schultz is in the examination room. Please call back in an hour or so."

Albert called back. This time he was told, "I am sorry. Mr. Schultz has been sent to the County Hospital."

So, Albert called the County Hospital. After a few switches, he was connected with the nurses' station of the secure unit reserved for prison or jail inmates. Albert repeated his request.

A nurse answered, "Mr. Schultz is with a doctor. Please call back in a few hours."

A few hours? Albert was getting nervous. It must be serious. But he had no choice. He waited.

It was late in the evening when he called again. This time he got a response he had been hoping for all day. "Mr. Schultz is scheduled for surgery in the morning. You could see him this evening. Or, if you prefer, you may come tomorrow, after the surgery. Call before coming though. We don't know how long after surgery Mr. Schultz will be in a position to receive visitors."

"I am coming now," said Albert.

He prepared to leave for the hospital immediately in his green 4-wheel drive van. It brought back the memory of the day when George had saved his life from a bear in the forest so many years ago while hunting for deer. They never went hunting together again, never caught that deer which was to provide venison for their father. They had been walking different paths. But they were one emotionally, one in heart, and would remain so forever.

Albert looked at his prosthetic leg and limped toward his vehicle. He would save his baby brother from whatever had befallen him.

He had to wait in the hospital lobby for several hours before he got to see George. It pained him to see his dear brother handcuffed to a metal bed which was nailed to the floor. But, at least he was alive.

"How you doing?" Albert asked the usual customary question, knowing full well that he wasn't doing well at all.

"Hanging in there. They gave me something to ease the pain and stop the bleeding. Surgery is tomorrow. After that I'll be as good as new."

"That's nice to know, but how did it come to this?"

"I believe you got my birthday message."

Birthday? Albert deduced, there had been trouble and George was hurt. Still, he wanted details. "Yes, I did. What about it?"

"The messenger." George pointed to his groin area.

Albert understood. He also understood that George did not want the police and prison authorities, who most certainly were audio-taping their conversation, to hear about the 'messenger' connection with Albert. Still, Albert did not understand the need for secrecy. So, he said, "I will get him. I will give the prison the tape of our conversation."

George pursed his lips in a gesture of 'no'.

Albert tried to figure out the reason for this. If the Albert-messenger conversation came to light, the messenger would get fired, which was really no punishment for what he did to George. Albert thought that George apparently had something else planned for the messenger, something more painful, a lot more painful than just losing his job, and for this to happen the whole messenger episode had to be kept secret until its time. Okay.

A quick review of their conversation, so far, told Albert that it was not likely to compromise George's plan for the messenger, whatever that might be, nor was it likely to raise any red flags. Still, the direction of the conversation was dangerous. Before anything went wrong he had to stop this talk.

So, he kept silent and waited for George to take a lead and keep full control over the contents of their verbal interaction.

George apparently got the hint, because he said, "There's something you would like to know. Something good."

"Good?" Albert asked incredulously.

"Yes. The war, you know. It's over, for the time being."

"How so?"

"I made an agreement with the Warden. So, tell Goodwin to stay put until further notice, tell him I said so. He will believe you."

There was nothing to hide here. It was all known to everyone, anyway.

"I will, after our visit. But..." Albert's face contorted like he was trying to hold back tears. In a choking voice he said, "I can't bear to see what they are doing to you."

"That's the fate of a warrior. You know that," George said gravely.

"I still can't take it. I am no warrior, I guess."

"Not everyone has to be in the battlefield to be a warrior. You are supporting our struggle in your own way. You are a warrior too."

"I don't want to be a warrior. I really don't. All I want is to have you back with me in one piece."

"You are forgetting, I have been sentenced to die."

"I can still wish. Can't I?"

"Of course. Now, let's change the subject. How's my nephew and his mom?"

"They're fine. They miss you, too. The boy, he was little when you left home, but he remembers you. You're his hero. He might end up following your steps. One part of me feels proud, another is scared. Can you believe that?"

"Yes, I can. I would want him to support our cause, too, when he grows up, but I wouldn't want him to end up where I am."

"Life's a series of conflicts, isn't it?"

"Yes, and we never know what the correct choice is. Sometimes we take a path that takes us to our destination safely, sometimes we fall off a precipice and disappear into nonentity."

"When did you become a philosopher?" Albert cracked a smile, for the first time during this visit.

"When you are in solitary, there's nothing else to do. You think and think and think until you become a philosopher. It is not by choice, it just happens."

"Anyway, let's just hope you get out of this ordeal safely. After this is over, we will worry about what to do next."

"Absolutely. Whatever the shit the world offers, we will handle it the best way we can. Giving up is never an option."

"Well said, brother. ... So, is there anything you need, anything I can do, in addition to talking to Goodwin?"

"There's a lot I need, but I don't want you involved in my business. I'll take care of it by myself."

"I know. But, there might be something you need that has nothing to do with your business."

"Indeed, like a house, a wife, a car, ... Never mind. that's a joke."

Albert noticed a twinkle in George's eye and a soft drag on the word car, and he knew. He knew that George wanted anyone hearing their conversation to think it was a joke, but it was a plea for a getaway car.

Albert carried the joke further for the benefit of the spies, but also to answer George, "You would, wouldn't you? A double story 5-bedroom house in the suburbs, a demure but sexy twenty something for a wife, and a silver blue Mustang with racing stripes for a car." Then he laughed out loud to complete the effect.

"Right. Of course, couldn't do anything about anything until after midnight, 'cause today is pretty much gone." George laughed too.

"Goes without saying."

The joke might have gone too far. Time to end it, particularly since the communication had already been made.

So, George changed the subject and said, "Kidding aside, there's one thing you can do."

"What?"

"Go get that deer. Take your son with you. I don't think I will ever be able to join you in the hunt, but I will be with you in spirit."

Albert knew this was designed to impress on anyone, who might have started to put the word puzzle together, that this indeed was a lighthearted conversation to dilute the emotional pain the brothers were experiencing, and nothing more.

To continue with the diversionary conversation for a little while longer, Albert said, "And I will take the same green 4-wheel drive, the one we took to go hunting that long time ago and the one in which I came to see you."

"You still have that clunker?"

"It runs. Occasionally it coughs and spits, but runs."

"Good old car. Fills me with nostalgia."

At that Albert thought of that day in the woods, the bear attack, George risking his life to save his. Now, he must save George's life, he must do what George wanted.

They talked some more. Trivialities. In the middle of it, the nurse came and announced that the visit was over. Albert got up to leave.

George said, "Say hi to everyone for me."

Albert noticed George's depressed tone. He felt his own heart heaving and throat choking, but managed to say, "I will."

Before he could do that he had to take care of an urgent business. He went to the hospital lobby and located a pay phone. He toyed with the idea of calling Goodwin but abandoned it. No need to complicate matters, considering that not only was Goodwin's phone bugged but Goodwin himself was under constant watch. So, Haney's wife, Emily, became his next choice. He hoped that her phone was not tapped, but not being sure of it, he played it safe and said, "Meet me at the Riverview Mall in the food court, right away."

He drove to the mall and waited for Emily. It was a short, very short meeting lasting only a couple of minutes. Albert spoke fast, "First, tell Goodwin that George wants all attacks on prison personnel stopped until further notice. It's part of a deal he has made with the Warden. Second, George needs a car. Have someone pick up that silver Mustang with racing stripes from the AV garage, bring it to the County Hospital by midnight, and wait for George in the parking lot until daybreak."

"Daybreak?" Emily asked.

"Yes, if George is not out by then, the car needs to go. No need to leave an AV car with phony plates for the police to find."

"But from midnight until daybreak, it would be more than five hours. Isn't it too much for someone to wait in the parking lot, and wouldn't it draw attention from other people there, one of whom might call the police to investigate?"

"Hopefully, the wait will be short. And, the driver might just leave the car and watch for George's arrival from some hidden and secure place. I am sure he will know what to do. They are professionals."

"I suppose it is not for me to worry about. I will take care of my assignment."

"Thank you. If George is successful in doing what I think he intends to do, there will be police at my door and yours too. It will be a happy visit."

"What will I tell them if they ask about your phone call to me? I am sure my phone is bugged, and they would know that you called."

"Just that I wanted to tell you about my visit with George."

"And what did you tell me?"

"That he is scheduled for surgery tomorrow."

They drove away in different directions.

CHAPTER THIRTY-SEVEN

BACK IN THE SADDLE

AFTER ALBERT LEFT, George Schultz lay in his bed thinking, planning. He mulled over the layout of his hospital ward reserved for violent criminals, often referred to as the maximum security ward. He had scanned it as he was brought in and processed. It was a small area containing four single bedrooms with baths, a staff lounge equipped with a bathroom and uniform changing area, a medicine room, laundry room, a janitor's closet, and a nurses' station. The nurses' station was manned by a nurse around the clock, who electronically operated the only bulletproof Plexiglas paneled door connecting the ward with the rest of the hospital. Only authorized personnel, patients, and approved visitors, could pass through that door. Beyond the door there was a long corridor, at the end of which there was another steel barred barrier, guarded by a uniformed and armed policeman. Both the nurse and the policeman were required to check picture IDs of the people entering and exiting their areas. They often let people pass through their gates without an identity check if they knew them.

Schultz noticed a lot of activity when he was admitted. He thought that the activities involving two doctors, four nurses, and a cleaning lady, were rather extravagant, considering the fact that he was the only patient in that area. Maybe this was unusual, and most other days there were more patients, still the patient to staff ratio seemed lopsided and very concerning to him. This many staff could prove to be a major hindrance to carrying out his plan. So, he was quite happy to notice that the number of staff and overall activity in the ward diminished considerably as darkness fell over the gloomy environment. By the time it was ten, there were only two nurses. One, most likely the head nurse, seemed glued to the nurses' station, and the other, probably an aide, ran around doing routine nursing tasks. He also noticed that several doctors would emerge and disappear as if by magic. Among the minimal staff, which seemed like a perfect setup, he saw the nurses to be a bigger hindrance than the police guard. If he could get past the nurses, it would be a breeze dealing with the bored and sleepy guard who would be able to provide only a cursory and quick identity check. He must make use of this opportunity. The next day, after surgery, he would be promptly whisked back to his prison cell and his freedom plan would be thwarted.

He reviewed his plan in his mind and realized that there were so many unknowns that there was no certainty of its success. That, however, would not deter him. The worst that could happen was that he would get caught. So? He did not care. Also, success depended upon being creative and spontaneous, upon changing strategy according to changed circumstances. He would do all that. He was willing to do anything for freedom, even die, if necessary. But, dying was not his goal.

His plan involved physical acts which, in his condition, would be torturous. Again, so? Again, he did not care. He knew he was strong and could withstand any pain or discomfort. Sure, it would make his physical condition worse. So? One more time, he did not care. Once free, he would get the needed medical care from his own AV physicians.

He did not sleep that night. When things really quieted down around midnight, he put his plan into action. First, deal with the nurses.

Schultz screamed at the top of his lungs which had the desired effect. A male nurse appeared at the door of his room and asked, "What's the matter?"

The sight of a male nurse did not surprise Schultz. He knew it was customary to employ strong male nurses in a secure area. It just made his job a little more difficult. He did not answer. Instead he contorted his face like he was in terrible pain.

"What's wrong?" asked the nurse again.

This time Schultz answered in a belabored voice, "Terrible pain. Think I am bleeding." He screamed again.

"Hold a minute," said the nurse and disappeared. Within a few seconds, he was back with the other nurse. A female. Of course, he knew that not all nurses in the secure area were male, but there was no surety that he would get a female. So, her sight was a welcome relief to him. He felt his job becoming easier.

The male nurse came beside Schultz's bed and uncovered him. "There is no blood," he said.

"It's probably oozing underneath, not pouring, you asshole," screamed Schultz, "call a doctor."

"I don't want to call the doctor unnecessarily. Let me see first." He tried to turn Schultz over but the chained hands and feet prevented the procedure. "Give me a hand," he asked the other nurse. "Release one of his hands, and one foot too, then help me roll him over."

The female nurse rushed back to the nurses' station, opened the key cabinet accessible only to authorized personnel for emergency use, took out the handcuff key, and came back to the patient room. She unlocked Schultz's right handcuff. Schultz let the hand drop limply. The nurse moved toward his feet and unlocked the cuff on his right leg. She put the key in her pocket. Schultz lay still.

Both nurses stood on his right side, the female near his thigh and the male near his torso. The male nurse said, "Now."

The nurses bent over Schultz and firmly held his body parts nearest them. They gently tried to roll him over. Just then, in a flash, Schultz sprung his free hand and leg. He caught the male nurse's windpipe in his fingers and squeezed hard, his muscles tightening. Simultaneously, he lifted his leg high and threw it over the female nurse's head catching her neck between his thighs like two grinding stones. The attack was so sudden that the victims could not even scream. Schultz increased his squeeze over the necks of both nurses. The male nurse let out a blast of air from his mouth, flayed his hands, made some unintelligible sound, and slumped, his eyes popping, tongue hanging, and facial muscles taut. The female nurse produced a muffled scream, tried unsuccessfully to free her hands caught between Schultz's thighs along with her neck, and went limp when Schultz increased his pressure. When Schultz was convinced that they were either unconscious or dead, he released his grip. No, he didn't know he had that much strength in him even when well. The abuse to his digestive and eliminatory systems had made him even weaker. Yet, one could run fast beyond belief when chased by a bear.

Strong or not, under the circumstances Schultz could do it and he did. The bodies of the nurses lay upon him like rag dolls.

He pushed the male nurse off of him, letting him fall to the floor, grabbed the collar of the lab coat of the female nurse and pulled her up toward him. Then he reached into her pocket, retrieved the handcuff key, and pushed her aside, too.

In a moment, his shackles gone, he was out of the bed. Throwing the handcuff key away, he rushed to the closet and retrieved his own jeans, denim shirt, and sneakers and put them on. While pulling his jeans up, he noticed blood upon his legs and on the floor. He must have undone the blood stopping treatment of a few hours ago in his attempt to subdue the nurses. He went to the bathroom and stuffed his anus with a lot of toilet paper. He had to go on, could not let something like bleeding get in the way of his freedom. After getting dressed he, while keeping an eye on the two bodies on the floor for any movement, unclipped the picture ID from the male nurse's lab coat. With his fingernails he gently propped up the lamination in one corner closest to the photo. A little more, he was able to reach the photo. Once more, he used his fingernails, putting them under the photo and pulling it out. He took his own photo from his pocket which he had brought with him along with the other family photos. Then he rushed to the nurse's station, found a pair of scissors in a drawer, and used them to crop his own photo to fit the ID tag. He slipped it into the nurse's ID card and pressed the laminated edges around it. Then, he placed the photo part of the ID against a light bulb allowing the heat from the bulb to seal the plastic covering, somewhat, if not perfectly. He now had the nurse's ID with his own photo on it. It was not a perfect job, and anyone checking it carefully would know that it was a forgery. He hoped no one would. After that, he removed the male nurse's lab coat from his body and put it on. He hung the fake ID over the chest pocket of the lab coat.

He was quite confident that security would treat him like any other nurse. Still, he would have to be careful, not to come face-to-face with another nurse or doctor, particularly those who constituted his treatment team and would have known who he was. He did not want to be caught but was not terribly concerned about it. If caught, he would get another two year sentence. What an idiocy! How would an additional two years or even two hundred years matter to someone who was going to be executed? Still, not getting caught was important for his freedom.

He looked around and found the electric switch which opened the gate. He pressed the button and hoped that there was no one conscious or alive to hear the buzzer and metallic clang of the door as it slid open. Before exiting, he checked the nurses' bodies one more time to make sure they were unresponsive to any stimuli and would remain so for a while anyway. Then he stealthily snaked out of the area. As he was walking in the corridor, he noticed that his denim shirt, jeans, and sneakers, the only clothes and shoes he had, were incongruous with a professional nurse's attire, but only for a second. Very quickly he realized that his shirt was completely hidden under the lab coat, and his jeans and sneakers were really not out of place, since a lot of nurses, and even some doctors, wore them for comfort.

As he approached the guarded door he was jumpy, excited, and anxious at the same time. His walk exhausting, he was feeling faint, and sweat was oozing out of every pore in his body. He began to feel stretch and pain in his groin area much more severely now than before. He gritted his teeth, took a few deep breaths, calmed down, and slowly walked towards the guard. He was determined not to falter, physically or emotionally. He ordered his pain to go away, walked erect with confidence, and came face-to-face with the guard. Schultz hoped that the guard would not recognize the real him. Actually, he was quite sure that the guard would not. He knew the guards changed shifts, and there were always new ones, so it was not possible for them to remember and recognize all the patients, doctors, nurses, other hospital employees, and visitors, who passed through their door. He also knew that they just looked at the clothing and the ID carelessly. At that moment another concern popped into his head. What if the guard asked him the reason for going out and questioned him about going out of the unit, leaving only one nurse inside with a dangerous patient? He canceled the possibility of such a question quickly. What did a guard care about the reason for going out, so long as he was convinced that the person exiting was an authorized person? Also what did a guard know about the hospital staffing patterns? He might not even know how many staff and what kind were there inside the secure unit. This did not sound very convincing. The guard had a log of all the people going in and out of the unit and would know that there were two nurses on duty. Anyone with any kind of brain would know that it was not prudent to leave the unit in charge of just one nurse.

So what would he say if the question was asked? To get some supplies. Totally absurd. Nurses didn't go to get the supplies, they ordered the supplies which were delivered. To get fresh air, smoke. Even more absurd. It was not allowed without a replacement. Then he hit upon a more convincing answer, an emergency summons from the surgical unit. What if the guard called to check?

George had come so far, freedom was very close, and he was not going to let a guard's challenge derail his plan. He would just challenge the guard, attack him, take his keys, and be gone long before an alarm was sounded. No matter what, he was going, going past those steel doors into the vast expanses of freedom.

Schultz removed his ID from his pocket, held it between his fingers, and showed it to the guard who looked at the picture, looked at Schultz's face and asked, "Leaving?"

"No," Schultz said bravely while clipping the ID back on his pocket, "going to the surgical ward. Emergency summons, you know."

He noticed with relief that the guard just leaned back in his chair without asking any further questions, pushed the sign-in-out log toward him and said, "Sign out please."

Schultz found in the log the name of the nurse whose identity he had assumed, copied the signature placed at the time of sign-in the best way he could, and stood beside the gate for it to open. It did within a few seconds.

Schultz walked past the guard and continued walking in an unhurried way until he was out of the building, wondering if his getaway car was waiting for him. If not, he would break the window of any car in the lot, hot-wire it, and take off in it. If he failed, so what? He would be caught. Big deal! He quickened his pace, jumped over some flower beds and road curbs, and entered the parking lot. There he saw the car, a silver Mustang with racing stripes. He moved toward it. As he got closer, he noticed that the car started and moved slowly and deliberately toward him, which assured him that it was there to whisk him away. Positioning himself so that he would be on the passenger side of the car, he took off his lab coat with the ID dangling by its pocket, and threw it on the ground. He had no use for it any more. The car stopped beside him. Then he noticed the italicized '88' displayed in the right lower corner in an artistic, decorative way to hide its real message, which confirmed to him beyond doubt that it was an AV car. He opened the passenger side door and got in. The two exchanged a quick '88' greeting.

In no time the car was out of the parking lot, heading towards... George knew not what? And, he did not care.

He was free. In his exhilaration he had lost all sense of pain. He did not even notice that he had begun to bleed from the intestinal area, not until he had been sitting for a while, five minutes at least. He wondered how long he had been bleeding and if he left a trail from the secure ward to the parking lot. What, if he did?

The driver kept silent. The code of the AV ethics required sharing of information strictly on an as needed basis only. The driver did not need to know anything George was doing. His task was to drive him to the destination given to him by his superiors. The same ethics required George to keep his mouth shut. Of course, he could talk about trivial matters, but trivial was trivial, for his taste. So, he chose to reflect instead.

Everything had happened exactly the way he had envisioned it. It was not a novel idea. An inmate who had worked as a janitor in the prison Health Unit had escaped that way. It occurred to him that escaping from the prison was not all that difficult. He recalled many other escapes using other methods. Except for a few daring ones, involving firearms and gun fights, all others were simple and easy. So, how come so many prisoners were still behind walls and razor wires? His theory was stunning even to him. The prison could not hold anyone inside, no matter what kind of security precautions they took and what kind of force they used, if the inmates simply refused to be locked up. Even if the inmates just started walking out without any weapons in their hands. What would happen? Some of them would get killed and all the others would be gone. A few hundred guards, even with weapons, could not control a few thousand inmates. No way. The system did not work. It appeared to work because the inmates just stayed locked up, they accepted their fate and did not choose to rebel. They were wimps without spines, self respect, and the desire to be free. In this respect, the life of a slave was actually easier than the life of a free person. In a society, that is designed for the purpose of control and enslavement of individuals through its laws and regulations, a person had to fight for his freedom. Almost everyone in the world feared freedom and agreed to be enslaved, not just the prisoners. Euphemistically, this agreement was called respect for authority and the laws of society. What a crock! He was one of the few who wasn't going to be herded like cattle. He was free and intended to remain free. He was going to fight for his freedom and that of the white people, until his last breath. The nonwhite people, by virtue of their skin color, had to be slaves, had to accept their inferior lot. It was simply ordained.

Then he remembered the wooded mountains, where he used to train his recruits to fight for the freedom and supremacy of the whites. There were secret places where they camped. One of them would be a great place for him to hide, until he was ready to assume his old leadership role again. From behind a curtain, figuratively speaking.

Most likely, there he would find some of his men carrying out the training and other organizational activities under someone else's direction during his absence. Also, they would surely find one of their physicians to treat him. What an exciting prospect!

He looked at his driver who seemed intent on driving. Wanting to know about their destination, he asked, "Where are we going?"

"To our main hide-out in the mountains."

"Do they know I am coming?"

"Yes, they do. Someone will be waiting for you at the trailhead."

After that they did not exchange a single word. Did not need to.

An hour later, the car left the city and the metallic pavement. It drove on the country roads. Schultz figured, it was not only because this was the way to his destination, but also because these roads were least likely to be patrolled by the police and would be the last, if at all, to be blocked. Surely, by this time an 'All Points Bulletin' would be out for his recapture.

Several hours later, when the sky in the East began to turn crimson, he found himself in his territory.

It was certainly wilderness, bereft of any comfort of any kind. So what? This was the best place for his safety. He could not go to any of his old friends and associates anyway. They would be the first to be contacted by the police, as soon as his escape was noticed. For that matter, it probably already had been noticed.

After another hour or so, the road ended. Schultz got out and stood on his wobbly feet. So did the driver, who gave him a Nazi salute and said, "Welcome back."

He had barely returned the salute when he saw two men in camouflage fatigues emerge from behind some bushes. He saw them stand at attention in front of him and give the Nazi salute. He knew they were there to receive him. He returned the salute although feeling faint. Presently, he knew the cause of it. His jeans were soaked with blood which had also accumulated in his sneakers. All of a sudden he crumbled. The two AV warriors and the driver grabbed him before he could hit the ground. One of them said, "We knew you were hurt, so we came prepared."

At this point the driver said, "I need to go, get this car out of sight."

Without waiting for an answer he got back in the car, turned around and disappeared behind a dust cloud.

Schultz felt secure as one of the two warriors supported him and kept him from falling, while the other went into the thickness of the forest, no more than 50 feet, came out with a two handled hammock style stretcher, and laid it down on the ground. He felt doubly secure as he was helped by them to lie down on the stretcher. He was filled with feelings of comfort and gratitude and said, "You intend to carry me to the cave?"

"Yes, sir," said the two.

Schultz watched with admiration, as the warriors positioned themselves at opposite ends of the stretcher, firmly lifted the stretcher by its handles, and placed it on their shoulders.

In the faint brightness of the dawn, Schultz, as he was being slowly carried on the trail leading to his final destination, saw several other trails snaking up the hills. He knew them all, which gave him a sense of being home.

He lay comfortably in his rocking bed, ignoring all pain and bleeding. After an hour or so, he felt his bed begin to wobble violently which told him that his carriers had left the trail, and had started climbing up the hill through the bushes, around the trees, and over the boulders. Two more hours, finally, he had reached his abode of freedom.

At the camp site he saw smoke. Not surprising. It was breakfast time.

As he felt being lowered to the ground, he saw several AV warriors, about 15, gather around him, some with their guns and rifles.

He could not allow himself to be seen as a broken down wimp. So, he slowly got up and gave the Nazi salute to his comrades.

The scene changed quickly.

All the AV warriors had just two questions for him, "How did you manage to get out?" and "How did you get hurt?"

Schultz only said, "Later, later," and collapsed on the floor against a massive rock.

A couple of warriors quickly placed themselves between him and the rock and saved his head from getting injured. With the help of several of them, Schultz was slowly lowered on the ground and allowed to rest against the rock.

One of the warriors came forward, stood in front of Schultz, and said, "I think you are too much in pain for social chit chat. I would like to move you to a comfortable sick bed in our underground cave. I'm sure you are familiar with it. ... By the way, I am the Camp Master."

"That would be nice," said Schultz and closed his eyes.

As if something just came to his mind, he opened his eyes and said feebly, "Send someone into town to bring one of our doctors. I need one badly."

The Camp Master answered, "Right away."

Then, he turned to one of his warriors and said, "You go into town and bring our doc."

The warrior who was picked for the job left immediately.

The protective hands were all around Schultz, and they made him feel loved and cared for.

As he was being lifted for placement on a regular four-handled stretcher to be carried to his sanctuary, he said, "One more thing. I need someone to carry a message to Goodwin, someone dressed like a United Parcel Service employee, so that it would look like normal delivery business."

The Camp Master answered, "I'll send one to you after you are in your bed."

Schultz had to wait only five minutes when an AV brother appeared before him and said, "I will take your message to Mr. Goodwin."

Schultz dictated the message, "No need for a truce any more. Also, add two more names to the list of enemies to be eliminated. One, Ruben Ibarra. He is a prison guard, and he is the reason I need a doctor. Good thing though, because it helped me escape. But the asshole acted like an enemy. He really enjoyed hurting me. Give him his just reward. Two, that Indian bitch who blew away two of our warriors. I understand she is a smart woman. I want someone smarter to go after her."

The messenger left. Soon after that, two warriors came and settled in wooden chairs next to Schultz's bed, apparently to keep watch over him while waiting for the medical help to arrive.

What with his assault on the nurses, walk out from the hospital, a long drive partly on bumpy dirt roads, and a demanding climb on a steep trail in a narrow stretcher while bleeding, Schultz had gone through a lot, but had almost forgotten his pain in the excitement of escape. Now, in a comfortable bed with the excitement gone, the pain returned. He would have to endure it, somehow, until the physician arrived.

For that purpose, he started replaying the entire escape drama in his mind. He did that two times. Then, he felt that it must be told to others who had already made a request for it. He would, when he was able to sit and talk in reasonable comfort. Yes, it was a story worthy of remembrance through generations to come.

Even though nobody told him, it was easy to notice that the AV communication system was working flawlessly. His orders, directives, and suggestions, both direct and indirect, through the AV mole in the prison and other informants, had been received by the AV principals and faithfully obeyed. He was aware of some of the outcomes already, others were beginning to come to his notice.

It was very satisfying to him to know that even when he was in prison, he was the leader. Now that he was back, he could reclaim control over all the AV operations within his region, all operations designed to take revenge against the prison and to extend the AV domination over it.

CHAPTER THIRTY-EIGHT

TOWARD THE PRECIPICE

Sheriff Belford was unhappy and upset. Not only because the shrill whine of the phone disturbed his peaceful sleep at about two in the morning; his job demanded his attention 24 hours a day, seven days a week. Not only because it meant bad news; his job was always about bad news. But, because it meant really bad news, so bad that the on-duty staff could not handle it. He picked up the receiver and growled into it, "Yeah."

"Sir, Schultz has escaped. We just got a call from the hospital."

"Damn, damn it. Where was the guard? ... Never mind. I will be over."

He had to move fast and take whatever steps he could to get Schultz back into prison to prevent public backlash and evaporation of his pension fortune.

The first thing he did after arriving at the police station was to issue an 'All Points Bulletin' and order the hospital security staff to secure the crime scene. Within an hour the police had set up strategic road blocks, sent helicopters to search off-road areas, displayed Schultz's photo on TV, exhorted everyone through the news media to watch for the escapee, warned the public to treat Schultz as armed and dangerous and not to take any action against him but to contact the police with the details of the sighting. While this was going on, Belford collected a team of detectives and went to the hospital to investigate the case and collect information which might assist him in catching the escapee.

He attacked the policeman on duty at the security ward entry gate, "How? How, did it happen?"

The guard meekly reported, "Sir, a nurse came out of the ward to go to the main building. He looked genuine, his face matched the photo on his ID. As the nurse exited the area, I noticed a trail of blood, or what looked like blood to me. I suspected a bleeding patient had escaped in the guise of a nurse."

"Why didn't you try to stop, stop, him?"

"I could not leave my post to go after the bleeding nurse, or patient."

"Even when a dangerous criminal might be escaping, escaping?"

"Sir, I did think it might be a ruse, the blood might not be real, and the whole drama was enacted by someone, a patient, or a staff in cahoots with a patient, to get me away from my post so that others from that ward could escape. ... Sir, I was going by the book."

"And, you did not recognize, recognize, Schultz?"

"I didn't know he was Schultz. He was dressed like a nurse and had a convincing ID. Actually, I had seen no patients that day. Didn't even know how many of them were there in the secure ward."

"Did you call the ward to find out if anyone was missing, missing?"

"Yes, sir. There was no answer. That's what got me really worried. There's always someone there."

"When did you find out that the escapee, escapee, was Schultz? Or, did you ever find that out?"

"When I got no answer from the ward, I checked the sign-in and out roster at my post. There were supposed to be two nurses and one patient, Schultz. I suspected the worst. So, I immediately radioed the station."

"All right. Effective immediately, you are off duty, duty, on administrative leave, pending the investigation. Go, now. Now."

The guard left. Belford replaced him with one of the policemen he had brought with him. Then, he went inside, following the trail of blood which was beginning to jell and change color.

What he found inside was what he had feared while hoping that he was wrong.

He found two dead nurses near Schultz's bed and a handcuff key lying on the floor. The ward was empty of any living beings; the patient was gone. The file in the nurse's station confirmed that the patient was Schultz. It detailed his problem and the prescribed treatment. It also documented that Schultz had a visitor late in the evening, his brother, Albert Schultz.

He figured Schultz killed the two nurses but could not figure out how. How did he manage to lure the nurses so close to him as to make it possible for him to kill them? Where did he find enough strength to kill two healthy nurses, considering his own terrible physical condition? And how how did he find the handcuff key and free himself?

Whatever the answers to those questions, one thing was certain. His whole Department was in a deep pile of shit. He better find Schultz. The 'hows' and 'whys' weren't important at that time.

Leaving the forensics team and other staff at the crime scene in the secure ward of the hospital for routine procedures, Belford went to his office and pondered over the situation. He reasoned that Schultz had help. From whom and what kind? His brother Albert, most likely. He came to visit him and could have done something to assist his escape. So, examine the tape recording of his conversation with Schultz for clues, give the tape to Karcher and ask him to do the same. Also talk to Albert, find out who he was in touch with him, face-to-face or by phone, a few hours before and after his visit with his brother in the hospital. He called the police surveillance department and found that Albert had indeed called Haney's wife Emily and had asked her to meet him at the Riverview mall. It was not known what they talked about. There was the AV connection. Put Emily on the list of people to talk to, find out what she knew, rape her with words if she proved to be difficult. Then, there was Goodwin. While there had not been anything to link him with the horrible things going on with the prison personnel, he had to be involved. Being an AV, how could he not be?

Interrogate him too, lean on him, crush him. He got the necessary court orders and then put his plan into action.

Belford assigned the task of interviewing the three chosen people to one of his trusted detectives who was a master of intimidation. "Get it done, done, in a day," he ordered.

He also ordered his communications staff to forward a copy of the tape-recording of the Schultz brothers' conversation to Karcher with a request to examine its contents for any clues to the escape mystery.

Belford waited for a breakthrough, any breakthrough. He got a report at the end of the day from his staff. It provided information which was anything but a breakthrough.

Albert admitted to having visited George in the hospital. What was so terrible about that? Yes, he had also talked with Emily about George and his condition. They were old friends and this was what friends did, shared their pain with each other. And doing this in person instead of on the phone was more intimate, more meaningful.

Emily just echoed Albert's story. When the police contacted him, Goodwin had a hangover, having had too much to drink in celebration of Schultz's escape. He told the police that he was happy that Schultz was out but had nothing to do with his escape. About his whereabouts during the night, he reported that he was playing cards with a friend in his house, the card game in which he lost money, which he called entertainment rather than gambling. In the middle of it, he heard about Schultz's escape. When the police asked him how he heard, he explained that he always kept the radio on for music, on which the regular programming was interrupted to announce Schultz's escape. So, he and his friend celebrated. Police asked who was the friend and Goodwin gave a name. When contacted, the friend confirmed Goodwin's story.

After the interviews, the police quickly obtained a court order to impound Albert's truck, the one he had driven to the hospital, and Emily's car, to check for fingerprints and other evidence which might give a lead to solving the case.

Albert's truck and Emily's car were checked thoroughly. Nothing incriminating was found in them.

That was that. No breakthroughs. Belford was disappointed. But, he was sure Schultz had help from some close family member or friend. He was now most likely holed up in his helper's place. However, it could not last long. He would certainly make contacts with his other close friends and family for money, clothes, food, and a place to live in secrecy for an extended period of time. And most critically, for medical care.

So, Belford placed round the clock watch on the movements of Albert, Emily, Goodwin, and the Commanders on the AV list. It was expensive, but then Schultz was dangerous.

Then he called Karcher. He filled him in on the details concerning Schultz's escape and police efforts to find him. In the end he asked, "Did you get the Schultz tape?"

"No, not yet. I will examine it as soon as it arrives and give you a call."

"I hope there's something in it which will give us a lead," he said.

For a few seconds there was total silence on the phone line which was broken by Belford rather dejectedly, "Looks like we are losing, losing, the battle. The person who started this war has slipped out of our control. This simply strengthens AVs hands and weakens ours. On top of that, we have nothing, nothing, on anyone, not even on Goodwin, who, I am sure, is behind all this. We don't even know where to look for Schultz. You got any ideas, ideas?"

"No," Karcher said in a sinking voice.

"There's only one small ray of sunshine."

"What?"

"Chris Huddy and Travis Torte. Our men are watching their homes, homes. I believe that sooner than later they will come home after they think it is safe, safe. When that happens, we will get them. We have plenty of evidence, evidence, against them. They will get a death sentence. Through them we might snare, snare, even others, even Schultz."

"In the mean time we wait and watch more mayhem?"

"Don't, don't think like that. We haven't totally lost the war. The tide must turn, turn in our favor."

That was the thing to say and, so, Belford said it even though he did not believe a word of it.

In the end, Belford was down, depressed, and angry. He was sure that Karcher was, too.

Belford felt like he, Karcher, and everyone else fighting the AVs, were headed toward a precipice and would soon go over it.

CHAPTER THIRTY-NINE

A CHICKEN OR A LION

KARCHER ENJOYED HIS adrenaline rush, which came after each attack on Schultz. He had neither planned nor executed the attacks, yet he got his high because he had ordered them. He was almost addicted to it. It was a high he never wanted to let go. But, like all highs, it had to crash. Two of his men had already been killed by the AVs and now Schultz had escaped. He heard about the escape from the news media. He was depressed and afraid at the same time. With this changed scenario, he did not have an enemy he could punish and abuse at will, and get his fix. It was like someone had stolen his stash of personal poison. Who was to blame for it? He, himself? Martinez? Jordan? Someone else? Blame aside, he was worried. Scared shitless was more like it. Schultz free, the AVs would be even bolder to carry out their mission, to move on the path to more conquests. Who would be the next victim? Martinez? He? Both together? At one time, these were theoretical possibilities, now they were real. Before this war started, he had thought of annihilating the enemy. Now, the reality was different and it was sobering. He had suffered major defeats, and he had to prevent any more. Most critically, prevent his own murder.

Then came a call from Belford with a positive spin on a hopeless situation. It did not help. He knew it was phony. Still, he was not ready to admit defeat. Did a drug addict ever give up hope of finding his fix, no matter what the odds?

There wasn't much he could do, however. It was a police matter now. Still, he could help. He would examine the tape Belford talked about and see what he could find in it.

The tape arrived a few hours later by a special courier. Karcher closed his office door, pushed the tape into a player, and listened to the Schultz brothers' conversation, intently, carefully. His eyes sparkled with excitement. He thought he had found something useful.

But before he could call Belford with his finding, he got a jolt. The Director of The Department of Corrections came to see him. Whenever the Director came to see anyone personally, it was bad news. He gave it to him right away, "The Governor is angry."

"I can imagine," said Karcher, shaking inside but trying to act calm outside.

"Really angry. Wants me to fire you, right now."

Karcher knew, being in an exempt position, he could be terminated without any notice, without any formalities. It was patently unfair. Schultz had escaped from the hospital, Belford's jurisdiction. Why should Karcher be punished for it? He knew the answer, the Governor had to find a scapegoat to appease the public, and Karcher, not Belford, was within his easy reach. He was tempted to put the blame on Belford but did not. For one thing, it would be futile, the Governor had already made his decision. Besides, Belford was an ally, an indispensable ally, who had the authority, power, and means to capture Schultz, something that had to be accomplished if Karcher was going to save his career. But there had to be a career to save. Karcher saw his world crumbling. After devoting all his life to the prison, this was how it was going to end? He didn't deserve this ignoble finale. But it was there, and there was nothing he could do about it. All because of Schultz. That damn fucking bastard had chalked up another victory over him. No, no, no. This was too much. He could not let it happen. It must be prevented. Even if he had to beg, lick the boots of higher ups, he just had to somehow keep his job and have another chance to bury his enemy, and bury him alive.

He said meekly, "I know it looks bad..."

"Still, don't sweat," the Director interrupted. "I hired you. Firing you would reflect upon me. So, I told the Governor that you weren't responsible for what happened. Schultz was out of your jurisdiction when he escaped. Still, the Governor had to do something. To maintain the public's trust, you know. We talked about it and then agreed to put you on administrative leave instead, while we investigate the escape."

Realizing that there was a chance that he could be back in his chair, Karcher felt his heartbeat becoming steady. He asked submissively, "When?"

"Now. Leave everything as is and go." He presented the letter which formally placed Karcher on administrative leave for an indefinite period. Then he asked, "By the way, is there someone you recommend to run the prison in your absence?"

Karcher saw this as an opportunity to keep effective control over the affairs of the prison, even when out of authority. All he had to do was find someone who would do his bidding, play his tune. He knew the right person. "Mr. Humberto Martinez ," he suggested.

"Who is he?"

"Deputy Warden of ASU. Very experienced and well qualified."

"ASU? Did you say ASU? Wasn't Schultz in ASU? Doesn't that make Martinez as much responsible for this debacle as you?"

"Yes. But, he is not being disciplined. So, I thought we could use him."

Karcher knew this was all for show. The Governor would look good in the eyes of the public, if he took action against someone, anyone. He would look even better, if he took to task the top figure. He, Karcher, was the top figure. Martinez, therefore, was safe.

He had figured right because the Director said, "That's right, of course. You talk to him before leaving. I will send a letter confirming this arrangement."

After the Director left, Karcher complied with the directive and called Martinez, "Come to my office. It's urgent." Before he disconnected, it occurred to him that if Martinez was going to take his place, someone else had to run the ASU and Jordan, being the next in command in the ASU, would be the logical person. So, he quickly added, "And bring Jordan with you."

Both Martinez and Jordan appeared before him within a few minutes of each other. Martinez looked worried and Jordan seemed droopy and depressed.

After Martinez and Jordan were seated in guest chairs, Karcher came to the point, "I have been placed on administrative leave effective immediately. Mr. Martinez, you are the Warden during my absence. I recommended you for the position and the Director has approved. Also, Mr. Jordan, you are to run the ASU now. Find someone to take over your duties during the period of this new assignment."

"I don't understand, sir..." Martinez wanted to play the role of a submissive servant who sympathized with the adversity of his boss.

"You understand very well," Karcher said curtly. He could afford to be curt with his subordinates. As he did it, he became aware that he was really angry and depressed at the same time. A combination of the two emotions made him feel belligerent, "But, mark my word. Schultz will be caught, Belford has promised, and I will be back." The words helped dissipate his depression, gave vent to his anger, and made him feel in control of the situation. But how? It was not clear to him.

Before anyone could say anything, he quickly added, "Although I am not your boss at this time, still keep me informed of everything that happens. We need to work together."

"We will," Martinez confirmed.

At this point, Karcher turned to Jordan, who had been ignored all this time by everyone, and said, "And Mr. Jordan, it won't be long before you will have Schultz back under your care. In the meantime, make sure ASU is run as efficiently under you as it did under Mr. Martinez."

Jordan answered, "Yes, sir. Mr. Martinez, when he comes back to ASU, will find it in as good a shape as now."

"All right then." Karcher got up from his chair, walked around the desk, and came face to face with Martinez. He pointed to the chair he had just vacated and said, "It's all yours."

Then he quickly walked out of the room.

But he had not vacated his position, not really. He went home and without responding to his wife's question, "You got home early, you okay?" he went to his den and called Belford. "Hector, Karcher here. Got a minute?"

"Sure, sure. For you, any time."

"I have been relieved of my duties. Don't worry. It's temporary."

"Because of this Schultz, Schultz, business?"

"Yes. And the only way I can regain my position and credibility is by bringing him back to the prison. So, I need help from you."

"Of course, of course, we are already on it."

"I am sure. But, here's something that might be of some help."

"What, what?"

"The tape you sent me. There is a mention of a car, a silver blue Mustang with racing stripes. It could have been a getaway car."

"Perhaps, perhaps." Belford agreed without quite agreeing.

"Maybe someone noticed a car like that in the parking lot on the night in question."

"Who, who, would? There's hardly any traffic at that time anywhere on the hospital property and virtually nil, nil, in the secure area."

"Still, I think we need to look for a car with this description. Might provide some lead."

"If it's a getaway, getaway, car, it's probably already hiding in the AV garage or trashed."

"I thought it might be worth considering."

"Yes, yes."

"And please, Schultz has to to be caught. Do anything you can. I am counting on you. My job, and even my life, depends on it." Karcher sounded panicky because he was.

"I will do everything I can to catch Schultz. I promise, promise."

When he turned around after replacing the receiver on its cradle, he saw Carolyn standing next to him with a curious glance. She asked, "What's going on? You got fired?"

"No, just put on administrative leave. But, I will get fired if we don't catch Schultz, and soon."

"And you still want this job? Isn't this the time to quit? ... We will get by with what we have saved. You could find something else to do. Also, we have two grown, well placed children who will help us out, if needed."

This sensible talk irritated Karcher who quipped, "Why do you keep haranguing me about my job? This is my life and I don't intend to throw it away."

He saw Carolyn throw a look of disgust at him, turn around, and walk away. He was sure that she found it hopeless to talk to such a hopeless creature. He didn't care. He knew what was important to him and would not let anyone derail his plans.

He threw himself in a chair and closed his eyes, letting his mind race. There was humiliation in front of the Director, resignation and bravado when talking with Martinez and Jordan, begging and pleading with Belford, and anger and frustration at the sight of Carolyn. But, most of all there was fear, fear for his life. He felt like a chicken who pretended to be a lion.

CHAPTER FORTY
THE DEVIL'S WRATH

Jeff Borchert was slower than Huddy and Searle in proceeding with his scheme. But he did not feel guilty; he had a more difficult target requiring more time-consuming planning than the others. At least, that was what he thought. Besides, he was delayed by Goodwin, who had called him at his work site, most likely to keep the conversation secure from the police, "Hold everything until further notice."

"Why?" he asked.

"Because there is a 24-hour guard duty in front of the Martinez residence. You will be bogged down fighting the guard and, before you can get to Martinez, the place would be swarming with security personnel."

"So, you abandoning the task?"

"No, of course not. We will arrange for the guard to be absent from duty at a certain time. I will let you know when, and then you can move in."

"How will you arrange that?"

"That's a secret and it does not concern you. Just wait for my call. While waiting, get ready for the job so that you can get on with it at a moment's notice."

Borchert recruited three associates who went by the names of Wyndell, Everett, and Glinel. They were low ranking members of the AV organization. Low rank was to make them invisible, but it was not the main selection criterion. They were chosen primarily for their ability to be brutal and for their inclination to see risk as a challenge. Borchert told them only, "We're going for the kill. Details later."

He got busy with the preparations. He chose a bulletproof, black Chevy Blazer, with dark tinted glass, from the AV warehouse. The four-wheel drive had phony Canadian plates. He filled it with several M-16s, a lot of ammunition, and four daggers.

Borchert knew where Martinez lived, everybody did; in the administrative staff housing complex just outside the prison boundary. First, he checked out the area by casually driving past the Martinez residence, slowly without stopping and raising no suspicion. After that, he drove past it at different times and learned that the house was, in fact, guarded round the clock. The area surrounding the house was also under watch by the tower guards and foot security patrol.

He waited for his signal to proceed.

A week later he got the word from Goodwin, "There will not be a guard in front of the Martinez residence tomorrow night during the 11 to 7 shift. This shift was chosen to make your task easier." It was four days from the day Schultz had escaped, and almost four weeks from the day Borchert was told to wait for the right time. Oh well!

Borchert knew the operation would be daring. Not stupid daring though. He decided to go after Martinez at about one in the morning. At that time there was less chance of any interference from the regular security staff who were scarce and sleepy. Also there would be almost no traffic at that time making it easy to escape after grabbing the target.

On the day of the attack, Borchert instructed Wyndell, "Drive within speed limits and observe all traffic laws. No need to jeopardize the mission before it gets started on account of a silly traffic violation."

As they drove, he directed the others, "The plan is to kidnap Martinez from his house, and then, in the safety of our own place, do the job on him. By the way, I know the layout of the house. Learned it from one of our brothers who was in the prison and worked in the Martinez house as a janitor. Wyndell, park in front and stay behind the wheel, motor running, ready to take off as soon as we are back with our victim. Everett and Glinel, grab your rifles and follow me. We will riddle the lock area of Martinez's entry door with lead and steel, and kick the door open. We will enter the house together but diverge right after that. I will go to the master bedroom. Glinel will take the first one in sight and Everett will take the next. Turn on whatever lights you can find to be able to see. Rush in and silence everyone, because by that time they will all be howling. Then come to assist me. ... Any questions?"

"Assist you, how?" asked Glinel.

Borchert got irritated with the question, even though he had encouraged it, "Just follow my lead and obey my orders. Improvise your actions as needed and make decisions at the spur of the moment for any unanticipated problems. Remember, this is a war and you need to be prepared for any eventuality."

After that, total silence.

Everything took place as planned.

Smashing through the entry door had awakened everyone.

Borchert, as he entered the master bedroom, could see the lights go on in the hall, hear girls' screams and the sound of shuffling feet coming from the room Glinel had entered. A few moments later, he heard the machine gun and the quiet.

He heard nothing from the room Everett had entered, for a few seconds anyway. Even before the sound of Glinel's machine gun had died down, he heard the sound of a scuffle coming from the room Everett had entered. This was followed by the sound of a thud and machine gun fire.

A painful cry of a dying boy mingled with the withering sobs of the girls.

While hearing what was going on in the other rooms, Borchert, in the light from the hall and the faint glow of the night light in the room, saw Martinez grab a pistol from the night stand and whisper to someone, most likely his wife, "Slip under the bed quietly," and actually heard the sound of a woman crying and saw a figure getting out of the bed.

Borchert could have shot Martinez dead but did not. The purpose was to kidnap him alive. So, he just shot Martinez's hand holding the gun, rendering it useless.

He heard Martinez scream with pain and yell in fragmented syllables, "Co-war-ds."

He also heard his wife praying to the saints under the bed, "St. Christopher, St. Catherine of Alexandria, St. Margaret, St. George of Erasmus." It was amusing because the woman was obviously calling on saints that came to her mind without any regard to their specific roles.

His smile faded when he saw Martinez jump out of the bed, his right hand bleeding and limp, and rush toward him. Not that he thought Martinez could do any real damage to him, still to be on the safe side, he shot at his knees making him fall. He quickly put his heavy boot on Martinez's throat and heard him gurgle.

By this time Borchert noticed that both Glinel and Everett were by his side. He ordered them, "Get that bitch under the bed."

He saw Everett bend down, peep under the bed, and pull the woman out by her hair. The woman began crying and pleading for her family's life in accented and broken English, "Please, no kill us, please."

Borchert was pleased with Everett's take-charge action, when he saw him put the end of his gun at the woman's temple and pull the trigger.

The job pretty much done, in that theater anyway, he said to Martinez, "You're coming with us." Then he addressed his associates, "Let's go."

While Glinel and Everett pulled Martinez up by his arms and dragged him outside the house, Borchert, following them, ordered Martinez, "Don't make a sound and don't resist, unless you want your brains splattered all over the walls and the floor right here."

Borchert heard not a peep. How interesting! All his family gone, what was the obedience for? He couldn't be so stupid as to think that he would be spared. Borchert guessed, 'It must be the instinct to fight for life till the end.'

They threw Martinez on the floor in the back cargo area of the vehicle. Borchert ordered, "Everett, you sit beside our prisoner and Glinel, you sit beside me."

It took only a few seconds to settle down, and the Blazer took off like a cheetah. The vehicle had only moved a little, when Borchert turned his head back toward Everett and said, "Tie his hands and feet, and shut his mouth with duct tape." Everett complied.

During the operation, Borchert saw no activity anywhere around the Martinez residence. But, as the Blazer pulled away and he looked toward the tower, he noticed the guard talking on his radio. He mused, 'The guard has heard the gunfire and is calling the authorities. What a stupid bunch these are! By the time they get their asses here, we will be gone to where no one can find us.'

The Blazer was taken to a predetermined place in a canyon, only about four miles from the prison, hidden behind a huge rock cropping and overhanging trees. That was where the punishment was carried out. Borchert directed the action.

Martinez was hoisted from the vehicle floor, Borchert and Everett holding his arms and Wyndell and Glinel holding his legs. He was swung in the air a couple of times and thrown on the dry, rocky canyon floor. He fell on his back.

Borchert ordered, "Get your daggers and follow me."

The four operatives picked up their daggers and put them in sheaths, which they hung by their waists. They walked over to where Martinez lay.

Borchert then directed, "Wyndell, free Martinez's legs from restraints, spread them apart as far as possible, and hold them down. Everett, pull Martinez's pajama bottoms down to his knees. Glinel, you slice off Martinez's testicles."

The orders were carried out swiftly and efficiently.

Blood flowed from between Martinez's legs and began to stain the ground below. Martinez thrashed in pain. Borchert put his palms over

Martinez's forehead, pushed the head down, and kept it immobile and said, "Everett, remove the duct tape, and Glinel, you feed his mouth." Everett yanked the tape off from Martinez's mouth. Martinez screamed but only briefly. Glinel quickly stuffed the severed testicles into Martinez's mouth and kept them inside with a firm pressure of his hands, choking him until the gurgling stopped and the body went limp.

Everyone released their grip on Martinez. Then Borchert stabbed Martinez in the chest completing the task.

Borchert and company became aware of the risks inherent in their bold operation only when they saw a helicopter floodlight. Borchert exclaimed, "Fuck! They got going sooner than I thought they would."

He knew the Blazer would be soon spotted and easily tracked. He cast a last glance at dead Martinez and ordered his party, "Let's scram. Take your weapons, emergency food and water, and follow me. Don't forget the first aid."

They abandoned their vehicle and scurried off into the recesses of boulders and scraggy ridges to evade their capture. Borchert knew the area well, every nook and cranny.

CHAPTER FORTY-ONE

OPERATION KICK ASS

Russell Lohman got the job by default. He was a senior police officer who happened to be on duty on that fateful night when Martinez was abducted.

He got a call from the prison shift commander, "Our Warden, Mr. Martinez, has been abducted, his family slaughtered. We need help."

Lohman had a lot of questions, which must wait. The request was so urgent that it must be attended to immediately. He gave charge of the police station to his immediate assistant and, with a small army of detectives, reached the crime scene as fast as he could. What he saw made him sick and angry at the same time, in spite of his training to remain objective and emotionless. Sick with the scene where four innocent lives were lost in extreme violence, anger at the culprits who committed such a heinous act. His professional status, however, demanded that he remain emotionless and carry out his duty like a robot.

He asked the Shift Commander to fill him in on the details, so that he could decide in a more informed way about what action to take. He got a summary.

"A little after 11 last night the officer on guard duty at the Martinez residence radioed me that his relief had not arrived and wanted to know what he should do. I told him to stay put while I checked what was going on. I called Mr. Jordan, appraised him of the situation, and asked for instructions. He told me that he was on his way and asked me if I had anyone to relieve the guard. I told him, no. You see, the officers in the units could not be removed, and in the yard office, I was managing with just one person besides myself. Mr. Jordan, at that, instructed me to ask the tired guard to remain on duty until relieved by him within the next hour or less. I did as I was told. About five minutes later, I got another call from Mr. Jordan. This time he told me to let the guard go home and have the tower guard watch the Martinez residence instead. He even explained that overtaxing the guard did not seem necessary, in view of the fact that the arrangement was for only a few minutes, and the task could be adequately accomplished by the tower guard. Again, I followed the instructions. While waiting for Mr. Jordan to arrive, I got a buzz on my radio. It was the tower guard watching the Warden's residence. He frantically reported that a black Blazer had driven up to the Warden's house. Three men had jumped out of it and had blasted their way into Mr. Martinez's house, while one had stayed behind the wheel. I immediately rushed to the scene and found all members of the Martinez family slaughtered and Martinez missing. The Blazer, along with the attackers and presumably Martinez with them, had already gone. I, at this time, called you. I also talked with the neighbors who admitted hearing machine gun noise, but were too afraid to do anything, even to pick up the phone and call the police."

Lohman listened patiently to this long narration, then asked a pointed question, "Why didn't the tower guard try to stop the Blazer and the intruders?"

"They are there to prevent escape. In a situation like this, he could not fire a gun without permission from higher ups."

He understood the bureaucratic process. He, himself, was bound by the rules, such as the one that required him to call Belford for permission to launch a search operation.

Just then there came a car making a screeching halt in front of them. A man emerged, who screamed authoritatively, "What's going on?"

The Shift Commander came up to him and said, "Mr. Jordan, the unthinkable has happened, while you were on your way. I had to call the police. This is Mr. Lohman." He pointed to the policeman he was conversing with.

Lohman extended his hand toward Jordan and said, "I am detective Lohman. Who do I have the pleasure to talk to?"

Jordan returned the courtesy, barely, by just touching the fingers of Lohman and said, "I am Tommy Jordan, Deputy Warden, in charge of Mr. Martinez's security." Then, he turned to the Shift Commander and asked, "What happened?"

The Shift Commander repeated what the tower guard had told him and what he had seen when he got to the crime scene.

Jordan spewed, "How come there was no guard? I told you to keep him until I got here."

"But sir, you called me back a few minutes later to let the guard go and have the tower guard take over."

"I did? I did no such thing. ..."

"But sir ..."

"You sure it was me?"

"Yes sir, it sounded like you."

"There's something fishy here. I'm gonna get to the bottom of it. And that officer who was supposed to be on guard duty tonight, he is gonna get it."

Lohman politely intervened, "This is not the time to play the blame game. We need to find the killers."

He left Jordan and the Shift Commander to do whatever they needed to do and moved on to do his duty. He called Belford at his home, briefed him on the situation, and requested, "We need road blocks in all directions from the prison, search and attack helicopters, at least three with six armed personnel each, plus a search and rescue team."

Of course, he got the permission, and also an assurance, "I'll take care of the road, road, blocks. You should get the helicopters with needed personnel, personnel, in about an hour. After that it is your, your, show. Get those, those, sons-of-bitches. What with the Schultz escape, escape, our reputation is in the dirt already. We don't want to make it worse, worse."

Once the police helicopters arrived in about an hour, Lohman asked the Shift Commander, "In which direction did the Blazer go?"

He did not know, so he asked the tower guard on the radio, then answered, "Due west."

Lohman sent one helicopter in a Northwesterly and the other in a Southwesterly direction, with the instructions, "We are looking for a black Chevy Blazer with Mr. Martinez and four men in it. Stop it without killing anyone, if possible." He, himself, rode in one, which was the largest. It had room for six armed policemen, a search and rescue team of four, and with Lohman, it still had an extra seat.

Lohman directed his helicopter to go straight west, searchlights on.

A few miles of zigzagging brought him to a canyon with rock walls on both sides. He scanned the canyon floor. All of a sudden, the searchlight bounced off a metallic object. Alerted, Lohman ordered them to look for the reflector. Within a minute, he spotted a van-type vehicle and a bloody body nearby. He ordered the helicopter pilot to land as close to them as possible and instructed the other men to be ready with their weapons, just in case.

The vehicle was a black Blazer like the one described by the Shift Commander. This meant that the dead man next to it was Martinez.

This time he did better than he had done in the Martinez residence. He looked at the body as dispassionately as he could. He treated it as an object of attention and suppressed any feelings and emotions aroused by it. Of course, he was trained to be that way, to treat each case as a job and to remain detached from the people involved. Toward those alive, he was expected to express compassion, care, sorrow, and sadness; only to express, not to feel. Even expression was not needed in the case of Martinez. He knew that it meant nothing to a dead person.

Then he became curious. There was something weird about the body. Not just that it had been stabbed, was covered with blood and was motionless, but there was something unusual, not normally seen in corpses. Within a moment, he noticed the face. Sure, it was contorted with pain and fear, which was to be expected. It was the mouth which was giving the face a strange look. The cheeks were stretched outwards. Surely something was stuffed in the mouth. He bent down and impulsively put his fingers inside the mouth and extracted the object within. Even before the object was out, he realized that what he had done was against the rules, but assured himself that it was excusable under the circumstances. For a moment, he was not sure what the object was, but only for a moment. As soon as he realized what it was, he dropped it on the ground with disgust. Yes, he could be disgusted, that was allowed. He automatically turned his eyes toward the crotch area of the dead body and noticed blood there too, for the first time, probably because until now his eyes had been focused on the face and the chest areas. The missing part below the penis confirmed that he did indeed see what he thought he had seen. He had nothing to wipe his hands on so he scooped some dirt from the canyon floor and rubbed his hands clean, as clean as was possible.

He took a few steps away from the body, put his disgust aside, and became all business again. The prospect of doing his job actually made him feel good. Yes, that was okay. The Department actually encouraged it. But he felt more than good, he felt elated. What a turn around. The task in front of him offered an opportunity for career advancement.

Now he looked at the crime scene with the keen eye of a detective. The freshness of the blood was enough for him to conclude that the killers could have not gone very far and had to be hiding in the canyon walls. He radioed other search units to converge on the spot immediately. Once the entire force had gathered, he picked twelve men for what he called "Operation Kick Ass", and asked the others to guard the Blazer and the body until further notice.

He divided the men in the Operation into four equal groups, appointed one person in each group as the leader, pretty much at random since he did not know the special qualifications of the men assigned to him, and gave each group an identification number from one to four.

Then he ordered, "One and two, hit the East wall, and three and four, cover the West. Keep an eye on the floor too. Remain in touch with me by radio. ... Go."

And they went.

The night had given way to faint streaks of faded, rose-colored light in the East. The visibility had improved.

Lohman knew that his enemy was like a wild, hunted animal, which would watch him and his men from its hiding place and would not risk exposure by an attack, unless it felt threatened. There was not much comfort in this knowledge, because his job was to apprehend the culprits, which was sure to bring a violent response. But, realizing that the response, if it came, would be aimed at the forward units, he felt secure for himself. Selfishness? The thought crossed his mind and he rejected it. No, just carefulness. The Head of the Army had to stay alive for the troops to fight on. Rationalization? Maybe. So what?

With his binoculars, he watched the movement of his men. He saw them take slow steps with their backs to solid rocks. He was sure that they were ever vigilant for any sight, sound, smell, and movement, not naturally belonging to the environment, and would react swiftly if any of them were sensed. That was part of their training.

The sunlight matured into a burnt orange hue, and the shadows shrunk. Almost five hours of operation, and nothing seemed to have been accomplished. His men must already be tired, maybe exhausted, but the Operation must go on.

The sky slowly turned into liquid silver, eliminating almost all shadows. The caves, fissures, the rock curves, and the sunken floors, all lost their mystery.

Suddenly there was a glint between the boulders on the Western canyon wall, about 400 feet above the canyon floor. The bright momentary shine indicated light reflecting off some moving metal. There had to be people. Check it out. Lohman noted that the search group number four was in close proximity to the source of the glint. This time he decided to join the group and not worry about saving himself. Such opportunities to fight and show bravery were few and far between. He could not miss it, particularly when it held promise of a hefty promotion. That he, himself, could get killed or be injured, ending his rosy future, did not enter his mind at that time. He rushed ahead and assumed the leadership role of the group.

He looked through his binoculars in the direction of the short lived glint. A cave opening, about 30 feet wide and 15 feet high with a lot of flat footing all around it, came into view. Looked like campers' paradise, could easily double for the criminals' hide-out.

"That's our target, the cave. Let's disperse and move stealthily from different directions toward it," Lohman directed.

The men followed the order. Loose rocks, snappy bushes, scary birds, and rodents, all rendered stealth worthless. Still, the men climbed as quietly as possible to within 100 feet of the cave. And then it happened.

Several shots rang out. One officer was hit, whose body rolled down the canyon wall. Lohman and the other officers immediately took shelter behind boulders. Lohman knew he had found his enemy, but at what cost? He was angry, scared, and sad at the same time. Also confused. Why would the enemy shoot, giving away his location? Unless he was threatened with the approaching police and had no escape route through the cave. So, now the fight was on.

He figured, 'It would be bloody. The four AVs together, having a sense of strength in a group, were likely to fight. They might separate to have a better chance at escape, only if they thought the battle was lost. But, why would they think so, particularly when the odds were in their favor? They were at a higher level and in a cave, possibly with a good view of a wide swath of the canyon and the movement of the officers.'

'So it would be bloody,' Lohman resolved and geared for the assault. First, he instructed his officers, "I'm calling for reinforcement. Until it arrives, watch the cave, shoot if anyone tries to leave, keep the enemy pinned down."

Then he called the Headquarters on his radio, "Need officers with mountaineering, tracking, and combat experience. Immediately. At least six. If that's not possible, send all you can. Ask them to position themselves at the top of the Western canyon wall. They will be at the right place when they can see the police chopper in the canyon. Make sure they have all the equipment necessary to fight a battle in the mountains. Ask them to wait for my instructions on the radio. Ten-four."

In about half an hour, Lohman saw six officers in combat ready outfit, exactly where he had asked them to be. He adjusted the frequency on his radio and directed the attack party, "Move slowly, quietly. Get the enemy dead or alive. There are four men, hiding in a cave, directly below you. And we are just below the cave. I don't think the enemy has an escape route, he is pinned in. He knows we are on his tail and would be expecting an attack from us, from below, but not from you, doesn't even know you are there. That's your advantage. And, even if he did expect you guys, you still have the edge being above him. Ten-four."

Within minutes, Lohman saw the attack force descend from the top of the canyon wall and surround the cave. Then he heard the crackle of his radio. The leader of the attack party was on the other end, "We don't see or hear anything, anyone. We don't know what kind of cave it is, a simple deep hole, curved, zigzagged, or crisscrossed with passages going in different directions. So, I think we should throw a few canisters of tear gas, fire a few bullets inside, and wait for a response. If there is a response, any kind of response, we will engage the enemy. If there isn't any, we will assume the cave to be complex, and the enemy to be safely entrenched. We can't go into the cave looking for the enemy. Too risky and dangerous even with night vision goggles. What do you want us to do? Ten-four."

"Check for the enemy response first. Then, blow up the cave. The enemy will either surface and be killed by you or die within. Ten-four." He also wanted to add, 'And, even if the enemy is safely out through another opening, it will a good public relations move. We will claim to have destroyed the enemy and declare victory.' But, did not, wisely, not on the radio for the message to be picked up by anyone with any kind of savvy with radio signals.

"You and your men will have to move away to a safer area, before we start our operation. Ten-four."

Lohman immediately left the area with his men. Once on the canyon floor, he withdrew all the search groups, abandoned the command post, moved everyone at least a mile away from the cave, and informed the attack party about it.

After that he watched the operation with his binoculars. He saw tear gas smoke and also heard the sound of the bullets and their echoes. After that, he saw the attack party place dynamite strategically around the cave, move away to a safe distance, and charge the explosive.

It was like a small earthquake. The blast echoed all around, the canyon walls and bottom shook, rocks slid down with a rumble, and dust enveloped the whole area.

After everything quieted down, Lohman joined the attack team. Together they examined the rubble outside the cave and found nothing. They could not go inside the cave since it was now blocked by the blast-induced falling rocks and debris.

Lohman had the Blazer towed to the police vehicle compound for examination, and had the bodies of the dead officer and Martinez sent to the coroner's office for autopsies. Forensic evidence collection was routine and did not interest him, particularly when there was no one to charge with any crime. Besides, he knew what had happened. Nothing. He also knew what would happen. Nothing. The whole operation started out with a promise of brilliant fireworks and ended with a fizzle.

For public consumption, however, he issued a press release which briefly narrated the events surrounding the Martinez murder and ended with the words, "... the four criminals perished inside the cave."

For his own consumption and that of the Department, 'That was the end of it all. 'Operation Kick Ass' was successful. And, if it was not, and the enemy resurfaced later, well, it would be dealt with then.'

In the meantime, he was drooling over a possible promotion or a merit pay increase.

CHAPTER FORTY-TWO

AN AMATEUR DETECTIVE

AFTER BEING IN a daze for a long time, Phil Bottillo gathered himself, went out of the house where only death lived, informed the police officer about what had happened, and said, "I'm gonna stay until morning when I can reach a funeral home and make final arrangements for the three bodies. If you need to go, go, I'll take a cab."

"I'll check with Mr. Hefferly."

Bottillo waited while the officer talked on his radio for no more than a minute.

After he put the radio away, the officer said, "Mr. Hefferly wants me to stay with you as long as necessary."

It was not until ten in the morning, when Bottillo was able to contact a funeral home. He felt that it was his right and responsibility to bid farewell to Robinson, her son, and her mother, realizing that there was no one else to do so.

Once the body of Robinson's mother was given to the funeral home, Bottillo took a ride with the police officer back to Robinson's trailer court. He looked for Hefferly to thank him for the help and to say goodbye, but found only two policemen guarding the crime scene. They told him that Hefferly, along with the crowd that had descended upon the Robinson trailer the previous evening, had gone. So, Bottillo just got in his car and went home, exhausted, drained.

Still, he cleaned himself and lay down on the couch to take a nap. His rest was disturbed by the ringing of his phone. Before picking up the receiver, he automatically looked at the clock displaying one-thirteen in the afternoon. Hefferly was on the line wanting to see him the same day. He readily agreed. In the midst of his sadness, he felt a bit of satisfaction in being able to help the police and also find a way to avenge Robinson's death.

A few days later, Robinson's mother were buried. But Robinson's and her son's bodies were held by the police for many more days for autopsies, before they could be released for burial. A memorial service was held. Many prison staff showed up. There were a lot of speeches, eulogizing Robinson in glowing terms. Bottillo saw them for what they were, superficial and even phony. Everyone knew her as a coworker, a woman with a title. They certainly didn't know her as a person, a person with a past, a personality, a bundle of crushed hopes and wishes, and a flower bed where new dreams were sprouting. No one really knew her. But, he still appreciated the gesture.

Afterwards he went to her grave for a visit, alone, the first of many which would follow. But, this was a special visit which would not be repeated again, for it could happen only once. It was a visit of blending of hearts and promises, past understandings, and future hopes. It was a visit in which he spoke and Robinson listened; he knew she listened, "I know our togetherness was short, but in the end, you got to know you were loved, maybe for the first time. I am sorry I could not save you and your son, but I promise your death will be avenged."

Tenderly, he let his right index finger pass over the inscriptions on her headstone, which had been chosen by him; her name, year of her birth and death, and just one word, "WILTED". After that he wiped his damp eyelashes and walked away without saying a goodbye.

As he drove home, he kept thinking about his promise to Robinson. It was easy to make but not so easy to carry out. How was he going to take revenge? And against who? All AVs? Or, against just the two remaining Robinson murderers? Or, against Schultz, the instigator of this insanity? All by himself? Was he kidding? The AVs were too many, and most of them unknown. He knew, from what Hefferly had told him about the AV officers' address file obtained from the Goodwin home computer and the results of his investigation, that the Robinson murderers were in hiding, no one knew where. Schultz was not housed in his unit and so, for all practical purposes, was out of his reach. He toyed with the idea of using a staff in Schultz's unit, but he did not know anyone who would be willing to carry out his revenge wish.

All that became academic, when he first learned about the Gopal murder and then about Schultz's escape. He felt really sad for Satya. He could feel her pain having suffered the same himself. He wished he could console her in some way, but did not know how. He did not even know her, had never met her. But, he hoped and prayed that she would survive the ordeal and eventually, maybe, go on with her life, as he himself would, mercifully. The transition would be easier, if the AVs could be subdued. But was that possible? They seemed to be too much for anyone. Looked like they were unstoppable. Yes, they lost a couple of their people, but that was nothing compared to the gains they had made. The most ironic thing of all was that everyone knew that they were behind all these murders, and not even one of them had been arrested. How could you contain a force that had a power of its own, a force which kept generating and regenerating with each act of violence?

The matter assumed urgency. Something had to be done. The only something he could think of was catching the Robinson killers. They had to be found and, once found, the tide might turn. He knew them, he had seen them, and it was his help in drawing their portraits which had helped the police locate their residences. Why could he not do more? There would not be any satisfaction for him until the Robinson killers were caught. He thought and thought, and then came up with an idea which had potential for success. At that moment, he took upon himself a task which rightfully belonged to the police.

He decided to find Huddy, who would be a lead to Torte. His logic was simple. Huddy had a wife, so there was a good possibility that a contact between them would be made, somehow, sometime, for communication and for supply of essential items to the fugitive. All he had to do was keep a tab on Huddy's wife, who would inadvertently lead him to her husband. No such thing was possible with Torte, who had no wife or anyone else close enough to want to risk communicating with him.

He, of course, knew the pitfalls. His presence in the neighborhood, day after day, at different times, some at odd hours, and often for considerable periods of time, was likely to arouse suspicion about him among residents who might report him to the police. So, he decided to do this with police knowledge. Before starting his surveillance, he called Hefferly and informed him about what he was going to do and why. Hefferly answered, "No problem. I understand your need to do this and I will support it, so long as no laws are broken. Go ahead, but only collect information. Don't talk to anyone, and certainly don't take any action of any kind. Leave that to us. Call me when you find something. If anyone calls us about you, we will tell them not to worry cause we know you and you're okay."

Bottillo staked out Huddy's home, which was being watched by the police also. Only he was watching Huddy's wife, Sally, while the police were waiting for Huddy himself to show up. Of course, he could not watch her 24 hours a day; after all he had to work and sleep and eat. There was nothing he could do about his work hours, which were dictated to him by the prison, but he could use his non-work hours in a way that provided him with an opportunity for the most effective surveillance. Sometimes, he even took a day or a few hours off work on weekdays for the same purpose. He decided to watch Sally's comings and going randomly. While watching her, he could carry out many other activities such as eating, reading, and would do without such activities as sleeping and going to the bathroom, which were incompatible with his task at hand.

He made progress. In the beginning, he thought it was a wild goose chase, because he found that Sally, most of the time, moved in predictable ways, and her movements did not involve meeting her husband. Then, something about her caught his attention, something out of her pattern, something that did not look quite normal for her.

A couple of times he saw her meet a man in a cheap restaurant during lunch. The man was neither Huddy nor Torte. Bottillo knew what these men looked like because he had been face-to-face with them not too long ago.

Bottillo also noticed that Sally did not eat anything in the restaurant, sometimes she had a coke.

Did she have a lover? The two looked friendly enough. They laughed easily, touched each other on the hand or on the back. They even hugged sometimes. They did not appear overtly romantic, but then who would in public, considering that one of them, for sure, was married? Bottillo thought that he might get a better feel for what was going on, if he could hear some of their conversation. So, one day he decided to seat himself next to them in the restaurant and overhear their talk.

From his car in the parking lot he saw Sally enter the restaurant, occupy a booth, order something, and sit, waiting. He got out of the car and went inside the restaurant casually, exchanged a few pleasantries with the help behind the counter, then moved on to an empty booth next to Sally. He ordered a coffee. Sally's man arrived about five minutes later. Bottillo' eyes and ears were alerted.

"Hi there," said the man and took a seat facing Sally across the dining table.

"Hi, nice weather today," Sally chortled.

"Sure is. If I didn't have to work, I would go fishing."

"I don't have to work. I am going sunbathing in my back yard."

"Providing a view to the neighbors?"

"My neighbors aren't nosy, and I have a five-foot fence."

Just then a waitress came with a bottle of coke and a glass filled with ice, put it in front of Sally, and asked her male companion, "What can I get you?"

"A coffee."

After the waitress left, the man explained, "I had my ham sandwich. I'm not hungry."

Sally clearly ignored the explanation and started with the purpose of the meeting, "Thanks for coming to see me. I know it takes time away from your lunch, and it's a hassle."

"Don't worry about it. I ate while driving. I still have about 20 minutes. No one is going to worry, if I'm a few minutes late. They never know where anyone is at any time. That's the good thing about working for the parks department; you could be anywhere within the park spread over several acres."

"You got a good job. I need to be looking for a job, too. The money Chris left is all used up. I don't know when he's coming back. The police want him badly. I'm sure they are following me too. Often I see a car tailing me. I wish there was some way to meet Chris." She had lowered her voice, like she was afraid someone might hear her, even though, having chosen this place for meeting, she must have been confident of engaging in confidential conversation without fear that someone else could hear it. Interesting, how her fears overpowered her convictions, although not surprising, considering the fact that everyone else also behaved in the same fashion.

"Maybe when this investigation is over." The man tried to console her.

"You know, they suspect Chris is involved somehow. Chris doesn't tell me everything, so I don't really know what's going on. If he had nothing to do with these murders, and the police find their man, sure, he will return, and we'll go back to living normal lives. But, if he is in the middle of this shit pile, we may never see each other."

"In that case you could move some place else, settle even in Mexico."

"Mexico man. I'll die if I have to go there."

"Just a thought. It may not come to that. There are a lot of other places, too."

"I don't want to think about that."

"I don't blame you. Now, anything you want me to tell Chris?"

Bottillo's ears pricked up.

"Just that I love him," Sally answered. "Tell him to take care of himself and come back home soon."

"That's what you tell me every time. Anything new?"

"I don't know if he wants to know this. He might already know it. The police have his artist's sketch everywhere. That's how they reached me. Somebody in the neighborhood must have recognized the face and called the cops."

"I'll tell him. Who knows, it might be useful information."

"When are you going to see him?"

"Soon, I hope. They must be short on supplies."

"Last time you visited him, did he say anything about me?"

"Of course, he loves you. Sorry, he got in this mess."

"So, how is he doing? I cry over him every night. Good thing I don't have any children; I don't have to deal with them missing their papa. Then also, it may not be such a good thing either. With children, I could occupy myself and not miss Chris so much."

"He's all right, health wise. Of course, he misses you too, wants to know that you are okay. That's why he asked me to see you every now and then and take care of anything you need. That's all he can do at this time. You know yourself, with the police on his tail, what can he do?"

"I know. So, I guess... I mean when will I see you again?"

"It will have to be a few days, maybe a week. I have to do shopping and then make the delivery. That will eat up several days."

"All right. Let's make it a week. Same time, same place."

"Yup. Same time, same place."

So, that's what it was, Bottillo mused. She didn't have a lover, she had a family friend who was looking after her on the behest of her husband and who was also an AV providing supplies to Huddy and other AVs in their hide-out. The man had to be a trusted AV, quite low in the hierarchy, certainly low enough to be saddled with a menial delivery job.

While he was musing, Sally and her contact got up and went to the cashier together. Bottillo watched. The man paid for their orders. The two went out.

Bottillo also got up quickly, paid for his coffee, and rushed out of the restaurant. He saw Sally and the man hug each other, separate, wave at each other, get into their respective cars, and drive away in different directions. Bottillo, too, hurriedly got into his car and began tailing the man. He followed him to a city park and took note of his car registration.

The way Sally's contact had talked about his lunch break gave Bottillo the impression that he had a day job. This meant that he would be working until evening. After that, who knew what he would do? Go home, go shopping for supplies, go to a bar, hang out with friends, whatever? Bottillo figured, if he was going to use this contact to find Huddy's hide-out, he would have to keep an eye on him pretty much 24-hours a day for several days, maybe even a week. He could not do that all alone. That was when he decided to go to the police with his information.

He found a pay phone and called the Sheriff's office, "My name is Phil Bottillo. I work at the state prison. I have some information that Mr. Hefferly would appreciate."

Bottillo felt that the secretary knew him and his role, because she said, "Okay, just a minute."

A few seconds later, he heard Hefferly's voice, "Yes, Mr. Bottillo, nice to hear from you again. Our secretary says that you have something for me."

Bottillo explained the situation and said, "We need to watch this man continuously and follow him to Huddy's hide-out when he goes there to make the delivery. I figure a week, since the delivery is expected to be made within that period. I can't do that, but I hope your Department can. By the way, I got his car registration number. I thought it might be of some use to you."

The response was not what he had expected, "Yeah, I can use it to find out where he lives. But, we need to know where he goes. ... You know, instead of watching his movements, why don't we just grab the son-of-a-bitch and make him talk?"

"Well, he may not talk, or give us wrong information, or stall until Huddy gets wise and moves on to another location. Also, if we find out Huddy's hiding place without the AV knowing about it, it will allow us a surprise raid on the place. Who knows, we might find other AVs hiding there too, like Torte."

"You may be right. Okay, I'll talk with Mr. Belford. Thanks for the info."

"I don't want thanks. I want Chris Huddy."

"We will get him. Now, could you stay in the park's North end parking lot and wait for me? I want to see Huddy's contact. I can get his photo from the motor vehicle department, but it would be better to see him in person."

"Sure."

Bottillo waited for Hefferly at the suggested spot. About half an hour later, a car pulled into the parking lot and Hefferly, wearing street clothes, carrying an expensive camera, snaked out. Bottillo approached him and shook hands.

Hefferly said, "Let's take a walk in the park, pretending to be enjoying the outdoors, and you can point out the Huddy contact. At this time, all I want to know is what the man looks like."

Bottillo did as suggested. They found the man working a flower bed. Hefferly pulled out a camera equipped with a zoom lens and took a photo of the man from a distance, acting as if he was a nature photographer. After that he said, "You may leave now if you wish. I take over from here."

"Could you keep me informed of the developments? You know, it matters to me a lot that the Robinson murderers are caught."

"Absolutely."

Bottillo walked towards his car, satisfied with what he had accomplished.

CHAPTER FORTY-THREE

THE MOTORCYCLE GANG

In the midst of the chase for Huddy, Hefferly saw promotion. After rushing back to his desk at the police station, he got busy. First, he gave the film to the photo lab and requested that a dozen copies of the photo be delivered to his office as soon as they were ready. Then he did some thinking and planning. He decided to employ motorcycle policemen since some of the tailing might be off road. Then, he called Belford, explained what Bottillo had found, and requested 10 officers on motorcycles to tail the Huddy contact round the clock until he made his delivery to Huddy, which was expected to be within a week.

Belford asked, "Why ten, ten?"

"Actually I need only six, but I want the other four to be kept in reserve to provide coverage for someone who might be absent due to some emergency."

His request was granted, but he was entrusted with the responsibility of finding the officers who were willing to participate in the task.

He checked the officer assignments and was able to find only eight, who were not occupied with any major project and were available immediately. 'This will still do,' he told himself. He asked them to come for a meeting an hour later in the station conference room.

This task was barely finished when the photos of the Huddy contact were delivered to him.

During the meeting, he briefed the officers, "We have found a man who meets Chris Huddy in his hide-out and delivers his supplies to him. You know Chris Huddy, one of the Robinson killers? We want him. You have been selected to follow this Huddy contact continuously until he leads us to our target. This man is expected to make the next delivery to Huddy within a week. So, it is not a very long term project. And we start right away."

"Who is this man? And why today?" asked one of the officers.

"We don't know his name at this time, and it's not important. But, I have his photo taken only a few hours ago. Here it is. Take a good look at it." Hefferly distributed the copies of the man's photo and said, "You keep it for positive identification of the man. He works in the city park." After a moment's pause he added, "As for as 'why today', the man might visit Huddy today, who knows."

"So how's this gonna work?" asked another officer.

"This is how," Hefferly answered. "I am going to divide you into three groups of twos. That will leave two extra officers, who will replace others as needed. The three groups will cover three shifts. Let's do this now." Hefferly randomly assigned the staff to three different groups, and designated one person in each group as its leader. The groups were given identification numbers from 1 to 3. Then he instructed, "Each shift will be eight-hour long, starting at five today. I know this is not your typical shift start time, but that's when our man is expected to leave work, and I want to start tailing him right away. Group one will take the first shift followed by group two and three, then back to one, and so on. If there is an emergency, and someone can't keep his assignment, call me immediately. I'll arrange a replacement. The surveillance will end as soon as we find Huddy's hide-out."

Hefferly paused to let the information sink in, then he continued, "Yours will be a motorcycle team. It's easier to follow someone on motorcycles, they can travel on most any kind of terrain. You never know where this man might go. Now remember, you will neither dress like motorcycle cops nor behave like them. You will be dressed like bikers with no apparent gang affiliation. You will be like ordinary men trying to play bikers behaving badly. That will look cute. So, if our man sees any of you, he won't suspect a thing. Do whatever else you have to do, but don't alarm the man in any way."

"Any actors among us?" Hefferly heard an officer ask jokingly.

Hefferly, however, retained the serious tone of the briefing and answered, "You all can act, I'm sure. … Now remember, even though you will present yourself as ordinary bikers you will still carry your badge, the Department issued pistol hidden in your clothing, binoculars, handcuffs, and other stuff that you, as a police officer, must carry. Other emergency items should be in the bike box. You know all that, I don't have to spell it out, do I?"

"No," several officers said simultaneously.

Hefferly continued, "While shadowing the man you will stay out of his sight as much as possible and, when in his sight, act like you have no interest in him. Keep a simple record of what this man does, where, and for how long. Turn that information over to me at the end of your shift. Any questions?"

"Yes, sir," one officer said, "What if something goes wrong, and one of us is caught by the AV?"

"That's when you become the police officer. Show your badge. Don't explain anything about why you were tailing him. If he won't let you go, then you become a hostage with no rights and privileges of the Department. You know the policy. Still, we will do everything we can to free you. Of course, in that case, the whole operation will be called off and new strategies will be explored. Anything else?"

No one said a thing. Hefferly concluded, "Let's go to the city park; all of us together, but on bikes, to get to know the man we will be tailing. But first, go to the locker room and change into civilian clothing. Quick. We don't have much time."

The stage was set.

It was about four when Hefferly pulled into the parking lot along with eight officers on bikes. After parking, all the men started strolling, Hefferly acted like the leader of a hiking group. Within minutes, he spotted the target who was trimming some bushes. Pointing to the man, he said, "That's our man."

After that, the group strolled for about 10 more minutes, creating the illusion of hiking for anyone who might be watching. During the stroll, Hefferly said, "It's very close to five, so Group One will have to stay behind for its shift. I know this is in addition to hours you already put in, but you will get comp time. Just so your families are not worried, call them right away and explain the situation. Others can go to their work stations."

The Group One leader said, "In that case we can leave you guys. We will find a pay phone and call our homes. After that we will start our shift. By the way, what about our meals?"

"We will deliver your meals. I'll take care of that. Just let us know where you are at the time," answered Hefferly.

That settled, Hefferly watched his men. The two men of Group One separated and headed toward the park administration building to find a phone. The other six men returned to the parking lot and took off on their bikes.

Back in his office, Hefferly got on the phone with the state police headquarters in the State Capital and the Attorney General's office. He knew the surveillance of the Huddy contact was likely to take his men out of their jurisdiction, and he wanted to make sure that there would not be any administrative hiccups. Not only that, he might even need the cooperation and participation of state troopers to launch an assault on Huddy's hide-out, once it was found, and make arrests. He had no difficulty in obtaining the necessary cooperation and commitment.

Two days passed. He got regular reports from his motorcycle gang, which revealed nothing about Huddy's hide-out. The Huddy contact had not been seen doing anything but the routine, like moving between home and work. He had not been seen purchasing and carrying any stuff which could be appropriate for delivery to people in hiding. He began to wonder if Bottillo had made a mistake and he had the wrong guy. But then he told himself not to be impatient; there were several more days to go.

Next morning, after cleaning up, dressing, and pouring himself a cup of coffee, he turned on the TV. It was his weekday routine to watch the early news while getting his caffeine fix for a few minutes before leaving for work. It was breaking news about the Martinez murder during the night. There was continuous coverage of the police action against the murderers, occasionally interjecting news about Martinez, his family, and their murder, with speculation about AV involvement in all this.

Any other day it would have been a murder like any other murder, and ignored. But, today it had a special significance. If he and his team had been able to find Huddy and make him talk, this murder could have been avoided, and he would have been looking at professional advancement. But now this represented another setback for the whole Department. Forget about promotions, some heads were likely to roll. Could Belford's head be among them for failing to solve the murders of three prison staff? Could it be his own for failing to solve the Robinson murder?

Still he consoled himself. Everything was not lost. The Huddy hide-out might still be found and he might yet become the savior of the Department, not to mention his own ass.

CHAPTER FORTY-FOUR
BITE ME

Sanderson was not a happy man. He had a case which, due to its nature, had become high profile. The brutal murder of a psychiatrist and then the killing of the murderers themselves by the psychiatrist's wife did not fall into the category of routine crimes. It was an imposing, hair-raising, eye-popping crime drama, attracting public attention with an embarrassing lack of answers to a perplexing question, 'A second prison staff had been murdered, presumably by the AVs, and what the fuck were the police doing?'

A follow up question was even worse, 'Would there be more killings of similar nature?'

The second question was answered in the affirmative, when a few days later he learned about the gruesome murder of Martinez and his family.

Even though these murders were of prison personnel, he was sure that the public perception they created was that of police incompetence to stop any murders. Of course, he knew he was not in charge of the Department and he had no responsibility to shore up its image, he was also aware that someone would be sacrificed to appease the public, and the sacrificial lamb was always chosen from the lower rungs of the hierarchal ladder. That simply meant officers like himself.

A little more reflection on the murders of the three prison staff made him realize that not all officers like him were in trouble. The Department as a whole, and Hefferly and Lohman in particular, were quite safe. Hefferly was following a very strong lead to capture the Robinson murderers, Huddy, Torte, and possibly other associates, and Lohman had blown away four Martinez murderers in a cave. Both these officers had saved the Department's reputation to a certain extent and had secured promotion for themselves. Because of them, the Department did not look all that bad. But, what had he done with his case, the Gopal murder? Actually nothing.

At the face of it, the case was closed; the criminals were dead. But, the crime had not been solved. In the eyes of the Department and the public, the case was not solved until someone was caught, killed, or prosecuted. It didn't really matter who. It could be someone in the AV organization who had planned and ordered the killings, or someone who was remotely associated with the murderers, or even some totally innocent person.

Sanderson's eyes lit up. Now he knew exactly what he was going to do. He would arrest Christi again for the Gopal murder, this time he would cook up some strong evidence against her, and get her convicted. He had no qualms about fabricating the case, and felt totally justified in doing so, primarily because he was convinced that Christi had something to do with the Gopal murder, and also because the Department did this kind of thing all the time.

He reviewed his plan in his mind:

'Step one. Check the guys in detention and pick a sap, arrested for drug dealing, possession, and use. Offer him a deal; If he testified in court that he was asked by Christi to kill Gopal, the Department will charge him with possession of drugs only and he might get away with just probation. His testimony would include a few critical items to make it convincing to the court: He had entered Christi's home to burglarize it, but Christi had surprised him with a gun to his head. Then, she had offered to spare his life if he agreed to her demand. He was too scared to refuse the job. But, he knew he could not kill anyone. So, when he was let go by Christi he turned the business over to one of his AV friends who was also a drug dealer, knowing that he would be only too happy to get rid of a colored foreigner, and he did it with the help of another friend. Since both of them got killed, there was no one to refute his story.

'Step two. Arrest Christi for her complicity in the Gopal murder.

'Step three. Convince the prosecutor of the legitimacy and strength of the case. For this, offer the testimony of the drug dealer. In addition, explain that Christi wanted Gopal killed because she hated him for divorcing her and marrying another woman. Also, point out a need for asking the court to give Christi a long sentence, because she was jealous of Gopal's wife Satya, therefore, a serious threat to her life.'

The plan seemed workable. It also explained why Christi did not know the killers, had not made any incriminating phone calls, and had not paid any money to anyone for the job.

The only problem that he could foresee was a shrewd defense attorney who would shred the drug dealer testimony to pieces. All he had to do was prove that the burglary in Christi's home never took place and that the guy providing testimony was a criminal himself and could not be trusted and considered reliable.

Still, Sanderson was not worried because he knew that shrewd defense attorneys were expensive and Christi's finances could not afford them. Besides, he had used such methods in the past successfully.

Happy with his plan, Sanderson went to work.

He went to the records office and pulled out the files of every person in detention.

It was easy to find a person arrested for a drug offense; every day there were several, sometimes more than the detention facility could hold. He chose one who was facing the most serious charge, giving a fatal dose of meth-amphetamine to a minor. Such a person was most likely to listen to a deal.

Sanderson went to the cell of this criminal and said, "You know you are facing a murder rap?"

"It's all a mistake. I didn't do nothing." The guy, a black man in his mid twenties, with a shaved head and a goatee, showed his disgust at the system and arrogance toward authority by just sitting on the floor of his cell without even raising his head.

"Whatever you say, but you are looking at a very long sentence."

"So?" The man said without lifting his head and making eye contact with Sanderson.

"I have a deal if you are willing to listen."

"The only deal I am interested in is the one that lets me out of this joint."

"It does, eventually."

"What does that mean?"

"That means you cooperate with me, you get a lesser charge, and you get out sooner. I can fix the whole thing now. No formal charges have been filed yet, you know."

"Fuck you."

"But you haven't listened to what I am offering."

"What are you offering?"

Sanderson told him the deal.

He got the answer very quickly, "Fuck you."

He tried to enlist the help of another guy charged with selling coke to an undercover cop. Once more he got nowhere.

His ego deflated, he did not want to try any more.

Sanderson knew at that point that it was useless to go any further. He also knew that he had been fooling himself, thinking that the deal could be worked out so easily. For these guys, prison was just a holiday. What did they care for the length of the sentence?

Rationalizing his failure did not solve the problem. How was he going to take the second step when he was floundering on the first?

Happiness of only a few minutes ago was turning into a major depression. He sat at his desk and pondered the next move. A few minutes later he had a decision: Arrest Christi anyway and charge her for hiring someone to murder Gopal. Tell her that even though her hired hand did not do the killing, she still broke the law. Tell her also that the person she had hired to kill Gopal was in police custody and was ready to testify against her in court. Just lie. What was wrong in lying so long as it brought about the truth? And the truth was that she was guilty. Knowing that someone pretending to be a hired hand was about to implicate her in the Gopal murder, she herself would crack and admit to her crime. He didn't really need someone to testify against Christi; the matter didn't even have to go to court.

He went to see Christi.

When he told her why he was there, he saw emotions change on her face, from shock to fear, to disbelief, to anger, all of which resulted in a response he was beginning to get used to, "Fuck you. I'm calling my attorney."

There wasn't much he could do, certainly not arrest her since he had no arrest warrant. Actually, he did not need it since his plan was to frighten her into admitting to a crime. Besides, he could not get a warrant anyway, he had no evidentiary material against her. Lack of such material also prevented him from arresting her on suspicion of her involvement in a crime.

Still, to keep his dignity and to keep Christi on edge, he made an empty threat, "I will be back with an arrest warrant."

With the crumbling of step two there was nowhere to go. The anticipated excitement of the achievement of step three had turned into an impossible dream.

He must work on a different plan. This Christi woman had to be behind bars.

He never got a chance to put her there. Instead, he got summoned by Belford, a few days later.

He, not knowing what it was about, therefore, fearful and trepidacious, had barely taken his seat in front of his boss, when he got hit, "What, what is it I'm hearing about?"

"What sir?" He really didn't know what Belford was referring to.

"I have a complaint, complaint, filed against you by the attorney of Christi Gopal. You been harassing her?"

"No, sir." Reality sunk in. He had no choice but to deny it.

"What were you doing, doing, at her place?"

"Investigating her involvement in the Gopal murder. That's a case assigned to me."

"Investigation had already been completed. Did you have anything new, new?"

"No, sir. I just wanted to ask her a few questions."

"That's not what the complaint says. Besides you have no business talking to her unless you have some evidence, evidence, of a crime. Do you understand me?"

"Yes, sir."

"This time I am letting you off with a warning, warning. Next time it happens, you will be disciplined."

Sanderson never thought that his simple desire for a promotion was going to bite him. Of course, he never looked at the fact that what got him in trouble was not his desire but his actions.

When he left Belford's office he was dejected but also full of anger and hate toward Christi, 'the bitch' in his opinion.

He resolved to get her.

CHAPTER FORTY-FIVE

WALK WITH ME

During her stay at the Karchers, Satya had time to think about what had happened, what was likely to happen, and what she needed to do.

She was grateful to the Karchers. She found them to be kind, welcoming, sympathetic, understanding, and emotionally supportive. But she saw the two to be very different in some of their reactions to her.

She found Karcher to be courteous, polite, a bit aloof, but very admiring of her intelligence, flying and shooting skills, especially her courage and strength in dealing with the trauma of her husband's murder. She felt awkward when addressed by him formally as Mrs. Gopal, deferred to in conversation, respectfully offered a chair at the dining table. But she was very touched, also, when asked if there was anything she needed that he could provide, and when told that she could stay in his home as long as she wished. Yet, she sensed an air around him which communicated to her that she did not belong there. To her, he came across as a conflicted personality who saw great qualities in her but had difficulty recognizing them in a colored woman of foreign origin. Satya was not offended by this at all. She had encountered this kind of reaction before, many times before, from many people in her adopted country, and had become used to it.

Carolyn, on the other hand, came across as a friend, mother, and sister, all rolled in one. After Satya had been picked up at the hospital, as promised, she was touched by Carolyn's reactions: she had wiped her tears, held her in her arms, and told her not to despair because she was there for her as long as she was alive. At home, Satya saw her anticipate her needs, physical and emotional, and try to meet them in whatever way she could. Like, trying to provide her with vegetarian meals, not exactly knowing how to do it, or clumsily asking her if she would like to go to church with her to ease her heartache, not sure if that was the right thing to suggest to a person who was not a Christian.

Satya appreciated everything the Karchers did for her, but she did not want to be a burden. So, she tried to take care of her needs herself and tried to participate in daily household chores like cleaning the house, doing laundry, and cooking. She often sat with Carolyn sipping coffee at the kitchen table or on the patio and talked about life, the frustrations and rewards of it, invariably ending with a cry over her losses and disappointments. She would find comfort when Carolyn would hold her in her arms and console her, "Everything will be all right."

In one emotionally touching moment, while having coffee at the kitchen table, she heard Carolyn say, "I understand your pain because I can feel it every time I think of the day when what happened to you will happen to me."

"It shouldn't happen to anyone, not even to my enemies. Why do you think so?"

The question just popped out of her mouth. She knew the answer. She knew about the conflict between the AVs and the prison, which got her husband killed. Still, politeness required that she should wait for the answer and she did.

Carolyn answered, "Bernard is also on the hit list. It's a matter of time."

"Why don't you just leave? We were going to but were hit before we could."

"I would like to, but Bernard doesn't want to."

"Why so?"

"He sees it as accepting defeat. He sees himself as a warrior, and warriors don't run away."

"Many of them die in the battlefield."

"I know, but I don't think he does. I think he believes that he is invincible, that the enemy will be vanquished, and he will win the war."

"Maybe he will. But history seems to suggest that winning a war doesn't really solve anything. Victories are temporary. For that matter, defeats are temporary too, except for the men who die. But the suffering is endless."

"That's right. I wish Bernard could see it."

"I think he can. I don't see him as a hateful, cruel person. I have always found him to be considerate, kind, and caring."

"That's because he is all that, but only with people who are not his adversary. You see?"

"Can one person carry such opposites?"

"Obviously can. Bernard is the perfect example. ... Anyway, I think he is in denial, he does not think that he could be defeated or killed. But I think that's a good possibility. I may be wrong but I think it is coming. I don't know what I will do when it comes. You are strong, you bounced back so quickly."

"I have help actually. At least I don't have to struggle financially. My husband had the foresight to get life and mortgage insurances."

"Talk about that, I am not so lucky. I will get Bernard's pension. There is a small life insurance policy. That's all. I will have to find a place to live, too. Couldn't live in the state-provided home anymore. Calling my sons crossed my mind. Maybe they will take me in. But I dropped the idea. I don't want to be a burden."

"You don't need to be so gloomy. I hope nothing happens to Mr. Karcher, but if it were to, you come to me. Move in with me. It's a big house, and it's free. And we would help each other."

"That would be imposing."

"No, it would not. I see you as my lifelong sister."

Satya saw Carolyn jerk in surprise and ask, "You are planning to stay in America? I had thought that you, after settling your affairs here, would go back to your roots, to your family in India."

"Yes. I will stay here. In India I would be living either in my parent's or in my in-law's home. That's the custom. I would be secure and comfortable, but I would not have my own life. My life would be dictated by my elders. Here I will be able to live my life my way. Sure, it will be difficult but rewarding. Besides, here I have my own home, where I would feel my husband's spirit. I would feel I am with him and get his guidance when needed."

"Wouldn't that remind you of the tragedy?"

"That tragedy would be with me wherever I go. It would be easier to deal with it in a place where I could feel his presence. ... Also, I will be near you."

While the two women were absorbing the essence of their talk, Karcher came home looking angry and worried. This was the way he seemed to be all the time lately. Satya noticed that he barely acknowledged them and rushed to the bathroom. It appeared something had happened, something destabilizing, something not quite routine. In a few minutes she saw Karcher come out of the bathroom, artificially composed, telling them that Schultz was misbehaving again and exchanging a few sentences with Carolyn. It was quite clear that he was not telling the whole story which most likely was rather unpleasant.

No one said anything after that.

During the coming days, Satya learned about two major and very frightening events: Schultz had escaped and Martinez and his family had been butchered.

Satya saw a film of fear and anxiety enveloping the Karcher family and felt she was in the way. She thought that maybe they could better deal with their situation, plan a workable course of action, talk and fight with each other privately, and reach some resolution, if she were not there.

So she decided to leave. The decision was made easier by a call from the medical examiner's office telling her that Dr. Gopal's body was ready for release. She called a mortuary and ordered cremation, then decided to go and see Gopal.

She was grateful for the emotional support offered by Carolyn, "I will go with you, drive you there."

But Satya felt this was something she had to do alone, so she said, "No. Let me have my one last private moment with him. Just call me a taxi."

In the morgue, Satya was taken to where Gopal's body lay. She told the attendant, "Please tell whoever needs to know that funeral arrangements have been made and someone from the mortuary will soon be here to take the body." Then hesitatingly she asked, "May I stay with him for a few minutes?"

"Sure, as long as you wish," answered the attendant.

Satya sat in a resin chair beside the body. She looked at Gopal's impassive face for several minutes. It was distorted and showed unmistakable signs of trauma, pain, and humiliation. Tears started to flow down Satya's cheeks. She did not bother to wipe them. After a few minutes, she said, "You will be with me forever."

It was a goodbye which was not a goodbye.

Satya walked out of the building, into her waiting taxi, and asked the driver to take her home, her home, the home she had built with Gopal.

She stood frozen at the gate. Many times she had walked into this house by herself but had never felt alone. Today, the walk would be truly lonely. Her body began to tremble and sag, her facial muscles began to quiver, her throat tightened, and her hands reached for the bars of the gate to keep her from falling. At that moment she heard a voice, 'We walk together.'

It sounded like Gopal. She felt him beside her. Still shaky, but filled with a feeling of strength, she opened the gate and looked inside.

It was a mess. The front garden had been totally destroyed by all those police and press vehicles which had now disappeared, chasing some other crime, some other tragedy, some other news.

Satya walked inside the house.

The living room smelled stale, filled with the odor of, ... what? Blood, sweat, bodily secretions? The carpet was marked up, torn up, and stained. The furniture was in disarray, upholstery torn. The curtains seemed to have been pulled down, hanging unbalanced. The whole house seemed to have been disturbed, things strewn all over the place. Were there burglars? Nothing seemed to have been taken, even expensive items, guns, and jewelry were there, just not in their usual places. The police, it had to be the police, had been looking for something to connect Gopal with the men who killed him, trying to find some clue to the crime, some explanation of what happened.

What was she going to do?

In the bedroom, she threw herself on the bed, depressed and dejected. Then she saw Gopal's photo on the dresser. At that moment, she knew exactly what she was going to do. She was going to rebuild the house, and she was going to rebuild her life.

Satya walked throughout the house, opening all the windows to let the air in.

CHAPTER FORTY-SIX

THE BLOODIED CHAIR

Jordan left Lohman and his men to do their job, went into his own office, and checked the Martinez security duty roster. Officer Sandoval had been assigned to cover the night shift. He decided to summon the guilty officer immediately, and berate and punish him for dereliction of duty. He picked up the phone and dialed his number.

Upon hearing a groggy, "Hello", he yelled, "I want to see you in my office, right this very moment."

Instead of "Yes, sir" he heard, "But, sir..."

He knew the rest of the sentence, '... this is the middle of the night', and was not interested in it. He yelled, "Right here, this minute, or you're fired. Also you are looking at criminal charges of a very serious nature."

That had the expected effect. He heard, "Yes, sir, I am on my way."

He sat in his chair, and waited. About half an hour later, Sandoval appeared, looking very worried.

"How come you were not on your guard duty last night? Mr. Martinez and his family got killed because of it. Do you understand how serious it is?"

"Mr. Martinez's family? No sir, I did not know. How did it happen? Yes sir, it's serious. I am sorry, but I received no duty schedule."

"I put one in your mail box myself. Everyone else got his."

"I didn't get any, sir. I am not lying. I am very reliable. You can check my work record."

"Why didn't you check with me when you did not get your schedule?"

"I don't mean to be argumentative, but I thought I was not assigned any guard duty. There was no need to check."

"What do you think happened to it, the schedule?"

"I don't know, sir. Maybe it fell out of my box. I don't know."

"Let's go look. ... And if I find that you misplaced or lost the schedule, or did something else to avoid the duty, you are in a heap of trouble. Might even face a murder rap."

"No, sir, I did nothing."

Jordan got up and Sandoval followed. They stopped in front of the mail boxes, which were empty. Everyone obviously had picked up their mail. Jordan started looking at the area around the mail boxes, which had a few folding chairs, a small square card table used for sorting mail, and a huge garbage can to accommodate all the discarded pieces of communication. He moved everything.

He found it. The schedule was partly hidden by the garbage can. Actually, it was so well hidden that no one could have seen it. He was sure that if someone had spotted it on the floor, he would have put it back in Sandoval's box. He pulled it out, looked at it, and said, "Here it is, your schedule. Your name is written on top of it. And see here, you were on duty last night."

He showed it to Sandoval.

But Sandoval was not budging, "It was not in my box yesterday, I swear. I checked my box, and there was nothing."

"All right. I will assume, for now, that it somehow got out of your box, fell behind the garbage can, and then got covered by the can when someone accidentally moved it. But, only for now. I am investigating it. It is a serious matter."

"Yes, sir."

Jordan dismissed Sandoval who, he was sure, must have gone home, partly relieved, partly worried. He came back to his office with the Sandoval schedule. He had promised an investigation, but did not really know what to do. So, he put it aside and started thinking about what he would do when the ax started to come down upon him. Whether or not he did anything wrong, he would be blamed and questioned, simply because he was in charge of Martinez's security.

After a little pondering over the situation, it occurred to him that all he needed to do was just tell the truth. He directed himself, 'Tell the authorities investigating the matter that Sandoval's guard duty schedule was lost, that it was an accident. Sure, the consequences were severe, but no one was to blame. It was just an accident.'

Prepared to deal with the questioning, he went on to check on Lohman's progress. All he found was that Lohman had cordoned off Martinez's home, had posted policemen to prevent any unauthorized people from entering it, and gone off with his crew in helicopters and ground vehicles, looking for the offending Blazer and its occupants. He was one of the unauthorized persons in his own territory, so he went home. There was really nothing else to do at that time, not for him. All he could do was wait for news from the police, and wait for the questioning from someone higher up in the prison hierarchy. From the Director perhaps?

The news of the police operation against the Martinez killers came in bits and pieces the next morning on TV. As he sat watching it, while sipping bitter black coffee in his kitchen, his mind was worried about his fate. The questioning came that afternoon as he sat in his office, his mind still worried about his fate. It came in the form of a call from the Director, Department of Corrections, "How did it happen?"

To his surprise the tone in which the question was posed was quite professional, and very controlled. He knew exactly what was being asked, but he felt a need to clarify the background, in case the Director was not aware of it. So he said, "The AVs are killing off Schultz's program review staff, one at a time." His tone was also emotionless, well modulated, and low key, as if they were discussing an undercooked hot dog at a barbecue.

"Everybody knows that. What I want to know is what security arrangements were made, and how come they did not work?" There was irritation in the Director's voice now.

'Still keep your cool. Don't fuck up now. Handle it calmly,' he implored himself. Then he spoke, "We did have a 24-hour watch of Mr. Martinez's residence by an armed guard. The night when Mr. Martinez was attacked, officer Sandoval, who was supposed to be on duty, did not show up."

"Just like that?"

"No, sir. I talked with him, and he says he never got the assignment."

"What do you mean, 'never got the assignment'?"

Jordan briefly described the whole situation, and added, "A minor mistake with heavy consequences. I admit, it's my fault. I should have put some kind of weight on the schedules. I didn't think it was needed, at the time. We never put a weight on papers in the past and never lost anything either." He played smart. By taking the blame for some minor inconsequential event, he hoped to diffuse the major problem. It worked. In a way.

The Director appeared pacified, although not fully relieved, "Okay. But, how come the guard on duty left his post without the arrival of his relief?"

Once more Jordan narrated what had happened and, in the end, emphasized, "Sir, I never made that second call to the Shift Commander. I didn't need to, because I was going to relieve the guard myself."

"Looks like the whole thing was planned very carefully. First, someone, on purpose, removed the schedule from Sandoval's box, so he would not show up. Then that same someone impersonated you to make sure that the Martinez residence remained unguarded for a while anyway. ... Looks like that someone is one of your staff."

"No, sir, not likely. Mr. Martinez had no enemies. I can't think of anyone who might have done this. Mr. Martinez was well liked by the staff. He was my boss for many years, and I can attest that he was the best boss I ever had. I feel terrible about what happened."

"But he did have enemies. The AVs. They killed him and his whole family."

"Yes, sir. But, among the staff…?"

"You think there are no AVs among the staff?"

That reminded Jordan of the mole he was ordered to find by the Warden. "Yes, sir, that is possible. Mr. Karcher also thought there was an AV mole somewhere. Unfortunately, we have yet to find him or her."

"I think he is in ASU, in your unit."

"In my unit? How? I would think he could be anywhere in the prison."

"No. From outside, the mole would have to depend upon others for information about the events in your unit. He could not do that without exposing himself. To be effective, he should not be known to anyone, not even to his own people."

"I see your point, sir. … Is our mole male?"

"I just used 'he', it doesn't necessarily mean male. Still, most likely he is male. The AVs don't use women for this kind of work. But, I could be wrong. Anyway, I think it would be a good idea to find this mole. The sooner the better. One thing that would help is a voice analysis of the call to the Shift Commander from the person who impersonated you."

"But sir, we have no tape of that conversation. We don't record staff conversations. We record only conversations in which one of the parties is an inmate or someone we don't know."

"In that case we are going to need a new policy which will require recordings of all conversations concerning prison security, no matter who is talking. One other thing, we are going to need a caller ID. The police have it, why can't we? But, none of that helps us at this time. Anyway, we must find this mole. Do whatever you have to do, find this mole. Give it top priority."

"I will."

"Now, there is something else I need to discuss with you."

"Yes, sir."

"You know Mr. Karcher is on Administrative leave. With Mr. Martinez gone, the top seat is empty. There are many senior staff who could be promoted, but I am inclined towards you. You are already a Deputy Warden of a unit which is the cause of all this turmoil, so you understand the situation better than anyone. I would like to appoint you acting Warden temporarily. Would you accept the position? We need someone there immediately."

"What about my current position? That needs to be filled, too."

"Of course. Why don't you recommend someone, someone who could do both jobs, his and yours. We will compensate him for extra work. It's just temporary, so it would not be a major hardship."

"Offhand I can't think of anyone. But, since the arrangement is temporary, I will oversee the ASU also. So, you do expect Mr. Karcher to be back soon?"

"I don't know if I expect but I certainly hope. So far the investigation has not found him guilty of anything."

Jordan was a bit disappointed. It would have been better for him if Karcher never came back, and he could be Warden permanently. For appearances' sake, however, he said, "That's good news. Of course, I will be happy to accept the appointment. Thank you. I hope not to disappoint you."

"I am sure you won't. I will formalize the appointment by this evening and circulate the news, so everyone will know. ... Also, if you wish, you may move into Mr. Martinez's residence."

"Is it livable?"

"It will be in a month's time. Mr. Martinez's brothers called after getting the news of the tragedy. I gave them a month within which to vacate the premises. They will start removing the things in the house as soon as the police release them."

"What about the bodies, sir?"

"All the bodies found in the house are in the morgue for mandatory autopsies. Mr. Martinez's body too. You know it has been found?"

"Yes, sir. It was on the TV this morning."

"Right. So, you must have also heard that all the bodies will be given to Mr. Martinez's brothers for last rites. ... Once the house is completely empty, we will have it thoroughly cleaned and painted. There will be new carpet, fixtures, and appliances. You could pick out the color of the walls and the carpet."

This was so sudden and so ghastly. Jordan said, "Thank you. Could I have a little time to think?"

"Sure. I know it could be uncomfortable to think about moving into a residence which had been a scene of multiple murders. Sure, think about it. But let me know about your decision as soon as possible."

"I will."

At the end of the conversation, Jordan leaned back in his chair with a sigh of satisfaction. He always had his eye on the Warden's chair but had not expected it to fall into his lap so soon. Actually, his rise from Shift Commander to Warden had come about in a matter of weeks.

By the evening that same day, Jordan got the news about the successful ending of the Lohman operation from the radio in his office. This news was totally eclipsed by a memo he received by fax from the Director, Department of Corrections:

Effective immediately Mr. Tommy Jordan is appointed Acting Warden. Please welcome him and offer him your full support.

The memo had also been distributed throughout the prison.

Jordan was happy. The anxiety he experienced in the morning had evaporated.

Once more he leaned back in his chair, the fingers of his hands intertwined behind the back of his head.

All of a sudden, he saw Martinez's house all covered in blood. He was horrified to look at it. How could he ever live in it?

Then the Warden's office came into his view with Warden Karcher sitting in his chair, bloodied and dead. He was aghast. Within a moment, he saw the body melt and morph into goo and slime which spread, covering everything, furniture, walls, ceiling, and floor. His head started to spin. He wanted to shriek, but no sound came out of his throat. His heart began to pound furiously and his legs became weak.

Was it prophetic, his wishful thinking, or something else? He did not know.

CHAPTER FORTY-SEVEN

INCHING ALONG

Goodwin got a call from Emily, "Could you come to my home for a short visit? It's important." He knew important between two AVs always meant affairs of the organization. He immediately drove over to her place. So what if the police were watching, so long as they did not know what they talked about?

When he got to her house, Emily let him in but did not even offer a seat. She quickly told him about her visit with Albert and dismissed him, saying, "You don't have much time."

Sure enough, he did not have much time, but still enough to send a volunteer to their main mountain hide-out with a message to expect Schultz in the morning, and to find a volunteer driver, chosen for his reliability and driving skill, who was given the keys to the Mustang, instructed about when and where to pick up Schultz, and where to take him after that. Once the car was dispatched, he thought about the other item, the truce. How was he going to cancel that? He would have to contact Borchert and Daboob not to carry out their assignments. He decided to do that the next day. There was no hurry about that.

In the morning, he got the confirmation from the newspaper that George Schultz had escaped. Then he received a messenger, dressed in the uniform of a United Parcel Service. He drove a big brown van with the company name and logo on it, which had been stolen a few months ago for just such purposes. The messenger had only a verbal message for him, although he did give him an empty box, most likely to complete the subterfuge.

So, while the old attack plans remained intact, Goodwin had two new targets, Ibarra and Satya. Although he was not happy about the additional responsibility, he was still excited at the prospect of having the opportunity to create more mayhem in the enemy camp. Hell, in his position he had learned to live with contradictions. The new assignments did not sound too urgent, so he decided to take his time planning for their execution.

In the meantime, he celebrated Schultz's escape by drinking and gambling with friends.

Except for the police interviewing him in the wake of the Schultz escape, nothing exciting happened for four days. Then, he got another piece of welcome news.

He was sipping his morning coffee and reading about the Martinez drama in the newspaper. There was action, fierce action, and tragedy, a steel melting tragedy, all enacted only a few hours ago. From the time he had given the assignment, this was the first time he had any news of Borchert and his deeds. Too bad he had to read about it in the newspaper. It would have been better to receive the news from the leader of the attack force himself. But he probably perished along with his assistants, if the police claims were to be believed. Still, he hoped that his warriors had somehow survived, and he would hear from them soon.

And he did. At his work site, the next day.

Around lunch time the secretary from the onsite construction office came to him and said, "Someone looking for you."

"Who?"

"Daniel's the name."

"I don't know any Daniel."

"So, you want me to send him away?"

Anxious but also curious, he said, "No. I'll come, see who he is."

He, carrying his partly eaten ham sandwich in his hands, followed the secretary to the office.

As soon as he entered the office, he noticed a man in a designer casual shirt and pants come toward him, "Mr. Goodwin, I presume. I am Daniel. Do you have a few minutes?"

"I am on lunch break. Yes. But, what's it about?"

"A job. Could we take a walk?"

'What kind of job?' Goodwin wondered. A carpentry job needn't be secret. He didn't like the idea of talking privately to strangers who knew him. Sounded like bad news. Could he be lured into some trap, led into some dangerous territory? To play it safe he said, "Can't go far. Got only a half hour for lunch. We can walk around the construction site."

"That's fine."

They started strolling around the dugout foundations. Daniel looked around to make sure no one was listening and said, "Borchert sent me."

Goodwin's anxiety evaporated. Now he knew the purpose of the visit and the need for privacy. "Is he okay?" he asked excitedly, even though it was clear that he must be okay to send him an emissary.

"Yes. He didn't come because he is exhausted, and also because he did not want to be seen with you. You know how it is. Police following you. Seeing him with you, they might begin following him too. Before you know it, they would be searching his home and comparing his fingerprints with the ones found in the Blazer. Me? They can follow me all they want. I am clean. If the police question me, I can claim that I came to visit you about some carpentry work in my house."

The lengthy explanation wasn't necessary, but Goodwin figured that Daniel wanted to be convincing, wanted to make him feel secure that it was not an undercover cop operation to trick him. "I understand," he answered.

"Well, you know the news, what he and his men did. It's everywhere. But, no one knows the whole story. I am here to give you the rest of it."

Goodwin stopped in his tracks, turned to look at the messenger, "Okay. What is it? Good, I hope."

"Very briefly, Borchert and his men were already in another cave a couple of miles away, when the police blasted their entrance. They stayed put for several hours. Later, hiding their rifles, ammunition, and daggers behind rocks and dirt, they came out of another cave opening. Sometime in the future, Borchert plans to go back and retrieve all that stuff. They brought out with them only their backpacks containing food, water, and first aid kits. When they got out, they were surprised to find that it was the middle of the night. They separated and walked in different directions toward their homes. That way no one would associate them with the events of yesterday and the night before. Police or anyone else would be looking for a group of four."

Through smacking his lips, Goodwin said, "Good job. Now you tell them to go about their usual everyday business. Just make sure, none of them talks about it with anyone, not even with family members. They won't be bothered because the police have no clue about them, won't be looking for them, believing that they all died in the cave."

"Still, the police do suspect the AV involvement."

"Yeah, but they don't know who specifically. Yes, Borchert's name is on the list of the AV officers they have, but in order for them to connect Borchert with Martinez's murder, they would have to take fingerprints of all the AV members and compare them with the ones found in the Blazer. This would be an impossible task. Their work would have been easy, if Borchert had a police record, but he doesn't. I am sure they would be comparing the prints lifted from the Blazer with the ones they have in their records and would come up with nothing." He moistened his lips with his tongue; he was badly in need of a drink.

"What if? We may not know all the tricks the police have in their bag."

"Then just like Huddy before him, he would have to go into hiding until the whole thing blows over."

"Okay. I will tell him."

Daniel left, and Goodwin rushed to the office area to get a soda before starting work.

As he worked, he could not suppress a smug smile and a spiteful thought: Send an anonymous message to the press and the police telling them that the four Martinez killers were alive and well. That would put a pin in their balloon.

He discarded the idea immediately. It would embarrass and irritate the police certainly, but it would also give them a reason to start investigating him, all his movements and those of other AVs. They might even start fingerprinting all AVs, a task which he had thought impossible. No need to invite trouble. Later, after all the commotion had died down and final victory had been achieved, he would claim his bragging rights.

He could still celebrate the intermediate victories, including Schultz's escape, which were paving the way for that ultimate goal: the elimination of three adversaries; an old one, Karcher, and two new ones, Ibarra and Satya.

The elimination of Karcher was most critical, although not urgent, for still another victory: gaining control of the prison by installing a Warden sympathetic to their movement. It would be consistent with the overall justification for this war. He knew Karcher was on administrative leave, but that was temporary, and a permanent solution was needed.

Since he was working, he put all these thoughts aside to be picked up later at home after his shower and dinner.

The Karcher case had already been assigned. So, he directed his attention toward Ibarra and Satya.

First, Ibarra. How to kill him without any AV casualties? Of course, not sustaining any losses while attacking the enemy was always an implicit goal, but not always achievable. He thought of the Gopal case. This time he should do better. He thought and thought. A couple of hours later, he came up with a plan which seemed flawless. It was also straightforward and brilliant. He would let the Hispanic prisoners carry it out. All he had to do was let them believe that Ibarra had been bought by the AVs and was working for them.

Again he needed insider assistance, and the name of his old reliable standby brother popped up in his head, Samuel Haney.

He could not talk to Haney because he was not on his visitors' list, but Haney's wife could. He called her. Knowing that his phone was tapped and probably Emily's also, he decided to make the conversation sound casual, "How's Sam doing? Haven't heard about him in a long time. When is he getting out?"

"Not sure. Soon, he told me last time I talked with him. He has asked for his recent comp time and waiting for it."

"Comp time?"

"Yeah. Time computation, which changes periodically depending upon a lot of factors, including how is he behaving."

"I do hope it is soon. Next time he calls you, give him my regards."

As soon as he said that he had an insight. Haney is smart. He could take care of Satya right after his release from the prison. He was so excited about that idea that he barely heard when Emily said, "I will do that. And how are you doing, and your family?"

"Fine, except for the police harassment."

"Oh that! Sam is concerned about that too. Thinks that they would keep tab on him for a long time, even after he is out of prison."

"They probably will, but he shouldn't worry. Tell him so. Tell him also, the police are stupid. They have been watching me and other AVs all this time, and guess what? They haven't been able to find anything incriminating against us."

"I will tell him that, too. Maybe that will ease his mind. Maybe not. Who knows? He seems to be a worry wart."

"What do you mean?"

"He is worried about a job, employment, you know, after he gets out. He was fired from the university because of his felony conviction. You know that. Now, he thinks he will starve, because he has no skills to do anything else."

"There's a lot he can do. Write, for one thing."

"I didn't think of that. But, I did tell him that I work, and we could live on my income. Frugally, but we could live."

"Besides, he has friends."

"Yes, indeed. But, he has this big ego. Does not want to depend on anyone."

"Maybe not, but he is smart, the smartest among us. He will find something, I am sure. Tell him that too. Tell him that I am waiting for him to come out. We will get together and talk about his future. Come to think of it, I haven't seen you in a long time either, and that short visit of a few days ago doesn't count. How about dinner tomorrow night at my place? My wife and kids would love to see you, too."

It was an invitation to seek Emily's help on the Ibarra project. Goodwin was pleased when he heard, "What time?"

"Six. Is that okay?"

"Six it is."

At dinner time Goodwin slipped a note to Emily, in case his house was bugged, too. It said, "Next time Sam calls you, tell him that a prison guard Ruben Ibarra is an AV plant, and what he did to Schultz was a front. Let the prison communication system hear you."

Emily wrote back, "A Hispanic?"

"Yes. He has been bought. Once the word gets out, other Hispanics will destroy him." Goodwin answered in writing.

Emily said nothing. She just tore up the paper on which they had communicated and gave it back to Goodwin.

Goodwin took the note, went to the sink, put a match to it, and watched it turn into ashes. As he was watching, he thought of asking Emily to let Haney know that a new assignment, Satya, was waiting for him after his release, but decided against it. He would get together with Haney after his release and discuss the assignment along with the method to carry it out. Safer that way. And, they would discuss other things as well, like Haney 's new career as a writer.

CHAPTER FORTY-EIGHT
THE SHRINE

Karcher lay awake in bed beside Carolyn, who was sleeping. He had noticed that his wife had been sleeping better since he was put on administrative leave. In contrast, this leave probably was, in part if not fully, responsible for his sleepless nights.

He reflected over the events which had taken so many lives and which were now threatening his own. The events were so brutal that they not only killed the intended victims but subjected them to torture. In the case of Martinez, the entire family had been wiped out. The one exception, however, was Satya. Sure, she lost her husband. Yet, not only did she save herself, but actually shot dead her husband's assailants. Karcher liked her, even admired her, for the sheer audacity she showed in eliminating her enemies. But the spunk might make her vulnerable and a new AV target for revenge. He felt a sort of obligation to warn her.

Somehow that did not seem enough. Satya had lived in his home for a while, and he had been aloof although sympathetic to her. Now that she had gone back to her home, living alone in a place where her hopes of building a long life with her husband had been shattered, she needed his sympathy even more. She had been married only a few months, and being a young widow was not an enviable state to be in. Plus, she was in a foreign country. She did not know anyone here, not in any real sense. She was probably having a hard time trying to learn the ways of an alien culture and trying to adjust with unfamiliar mores and customs. Perhaps, she needed to go back to India where she would be at ease and would be safe. Perhaps, she should go back to India where she belonged. Karcher had not talked with Carolyn about Satya and did not know about the conversation the two women had concerning just this matter. He felt he needed to give Satya not only comfort but also advice.

He shook Carolyn who asked startlingly, "What, what?"

"We need to go see Mrs. Gopal. See how she is doing."

"This came to you in the middle of the night?"

"I could not sleep. I was thinking about her plight."

"Okay. Let's go this week, any day that works for her."

Carolyn went back to sleep. Surprisingly, Karcher too.

In the morning, he took it upon himself to call Satya. He heard, "Hello."

"Mrs. Gopal?" Karcher inquired.

"Yes."

"This is Warden Karcher at the state prison. How are you doing? Haven't heard from you since you left."

"I'm so sorry. How ungrateful of me not to acknowledge your hospitality! Please excuse me."

"No need to apologize. We were just concerned."

"Thank you for your kindness. I did think of calling you a few times, but I did not want to be a bother. I guess I should have anyway."

"No, no bother. ... Would it be too much trouble if Carolyn and I came to visit you?"

"No, not at all. I will be honored with your presence. When should I expect you?"

"Will tomorrow be okay, about seven in the evening?"

"That will be fine. Could I interest you and Carolyn in dinner?"

"No, no, that will not be necessary. We will have eaten by that time. You know that."

Karcher told Carolyn his arrangement for their visit with Satya and suggested, "We will get something to eat at a steakhouse before going to her place."

Although going to visit Satya had a serious purpose, Karcher also saw it as a night out. They would have dinner, visit Satya, and then take in a movie. For safety's sake, he put a loaded pistol in the glove compartment of his car and packed his radio with a 50-mile range.

When Karcher pushed the intercom button at the left post of the electronic gate in front of the Gopal residence, the wrought iron filigreed panels parted immediately. As they walked toward the entrance to the house, he noticed that the front lawn was totally in shambles. When they reached the house entrance, he found the door open with Satya standing in the middle of the doorway to greet them.

Karcher looked at the young woman who seemed like a somewhat wilted rose, still exuding brilliant color and captivating fragrance. He was stunned at her calm and poise. For a moment he did not know how to proceed, then he said, "Hello, I hope we are not too early?" The question was irrelevant, since he was a very punctual person and had made sure to be exactly on time.

"Not at all, please come in," Satya said and led them inside.

Karcher followed Carolyn into the formal entry. He was impressed with the marble flooring and immediately was struck by its contrast with the bare concrete floor in the living room beyond. Satya took short steps into it and, while pointing to a couch, requested, "Please."

Karcher sat on the couch hesitatingly. He felt chilled sitting in a room which, very recently, had been the scene of three murders, gruesome murders. That was when he understood, the concrete floor was bare because the bloodied carpet had been removed. He felt strange thinking that his feet might be placed at the same spot where blood was spilled and three dead bodies lay. Strange? Rather dispirited, and disturbed, he thought, 'How could this woman live here alone?'

He looked at Carolyn who had apparently decided to stand beside Satya. Not wanting to betray his discomfort, he smiled effortfully and addressed Satya, "We came to see how you are doing?"

"Okay, under the circumstances. ... Would you like some coffee or perhaps fruit juice, or…"

Karcher interrupted, "Nothing. Please sit."

"You're my guest. I will feel honored if you will accept something."

Carolyn chimed in, "Yeah. Let's make some coffee." She walked toward the kitchen which was visible from the living room. Satya followed.

Karcher was thankful to Carolyn who had obviously sensed that he was floundering, had come to his rescue, and had taken charge of the situation. Besides, she probably wanted to be with Satya in the spirit of bonding.

As he sat, Karcher became aware of the mess the police had made of the magnificent house, not to mention the destruction that was caused by the killers of Satya's husband. The couch they sat on had rich silk fabric but was torn. There was a desk, a straight back chair, and a coffee table; all badly scratched and obviously mishandled. It appeared that there used to be other furniture which most likely had been removed, either to be thrown away or restored. The floor and walls had been washed, and they were all streaked. There was just one photograph of Satya and her husband together on the fireplace mantle and no other adornments. The drapes were stained and off their hooks in many places.

He was wondering what shape the rest of the house was in, when the women came back with Carolyn carrying a tray loaded with freshly brewed coffee, sugar, and cream. She put it on the coffee table and addressed Karcher, "Have a cup."

Satya poured coffee in cups. Karcher leaned forward from the couch, picked up a cup, leaned back again, and started to sip coffee, black. Carolyn picked a cup too, added some cream, and sat beside Karcher.

Satya picked up the last cup, added cream and sugar, sat in the only chair in the room after pulling it in front of the Karchers, and apologized, "Please excuse the condition of my home. I have had it cleaned to make it livable. It needs a lot of work, and it will take time,"

"Yes, of course," said Karcher. After pausing for a second like changing gears, he added, "We're so sorry for your loss, Mrs. Gopal."

This sounded corny, they had gone over this formality before. The women seemed to ignore it, though. But Karcher realized that he was clumsy and did not know how to engage in talk with a grieving widow. Still, he tried to be make a gesture appropriate to the occasion, "Dr. Gopal was a brilliant psychiatrist, a good employee, and a kind and compassionate man. We will miss him very much."

It didn't work. As soon as he said it, he felt like a hypocrite, because he did not believe in any of that. In reality, he always thought psychiatrists were stupid people who saw criminals as victims of circumstance rather than the scum of society who needed to be punished. Also, he did not know Gopal as an employee or as a human being, simply because of never having him directly under his supervision.

Karcher was relieved when Carolyn took over, obviously sensing his ineptitude at social correctness, "We feel your loss, Satya. How do you manage, totally alone?"

"I manage. I have never lived alone, but I manage." She began to sob and dab her eyes with the end of her saree.

Carolyn put her cup on the coffee table, got up, went to where Satya was sitting, stood on her right side, put her left arm behind her neck gently, and said, "I'm sorry."

Satya leaned toward her and buried her face in Carolyn's breasts. Carolyn then lowered her left hand, patted Satya's back, and said, "Come, sit with me."

Satya got up and moved toward the sofa with Carolyn.

Sensing that the couch now belonged to the women, Karcher got up and sat in the chair Satya had occupied. "I promise we'll bring the culprits, the AVs who are behind the crime, to justice," Karcher opened his mouth again. He thought he was consoling. But, even to him the words sounded hollow, and the promise false.

"Please, I don't want any revenge."

"But we can't let these criminals go unpunished."

"Punishment doesn't solve anything. It just breeds hate and more violence."

"But you punished those criminals, you shot them dead?"

"I am sorry, that was evil. It just happened. My instinct overcame my reason. I will suffer the guilt, I will repent for what I did the rest of my life. I hope never to do it again."

"Not even in self defense?"

"No. I can't justify taking another life to save mine."

At this point Carolyn changed the subject by going back to her earlier question, "How do you manage living here alone? Don't you feel lonely?"

'On purpose?' Karcher wondered. He felt snubbed but also relieved at Carolyn taking control of the conversation which was beginning to take on unpleasant tones.

"Not really. I have a lot to do. Get this house fixed. Get my commercial pilot's and civil engineering licenses, and then get a job. I don't need one to make a living. There's the insurance settlement. But I would like to be productive. Also, I go to 'Widows of Violence' meetings, once a week."

Satya's answer meant she was going to stay in America and that disturbed Karcher. To him, she belonged in India. He had sympathy for her loss and admiration for how she wielded a gun against the AVs, was even in awe of her qualifications as a pilot and civil engineer, but still, he felt that she was a colored foreigner who did not belong in 'his' country. Although he was happy when Carolyn had taken over the conversation, this was a subject matter which could not keep him silent.

"Aren't you going back home?" he asked.

"This is my home. My husband and I built it together," Satya answered firmly like she did not want this line of talk to continue.

Carolyn addressed Karcher, "She has a lot of reasons why she would not want to go back to India. She told me. If you would like to know…"

Karcher interrupted, "No. I was only thinking about her safety. The AVs might hurt her, you know."

He was pleased with himself for making the point that Satya needed to leave this country without making it sound like it was his desire. After all, this was a sympathy call, and he did not want to be seen as hostile to her.

Even though Karcher had addressed his remarks to Carolyn, Satya chose to answer, "Yes, I could be killed, but I can't leave my home for fear of death."

"Don't you want to avoid death?"

"I will not invite it, but when it comes, I will not run away from it."

Karcher wanted to say, 'Isn't staying here really inviting death?' but prudently kept his mouth shut. It would have been argumentative, and Carolyn would not have liked it.

Carolyn once more changed the direction of the conversation and said to Satya, "You said you go to 'Widows of Violence'. What is that?"

Satya seemed to relax talking with Carolyn. She answered in a subdued voice, with a hint of sadness, "It's a support group facilitated by a psychologist. Helps to deal with our losses."

"Interesting. How did you find it?"

"There was a flyer in the library. That's another thing I do, go to the library."

"Who knows, I might need it myself, this 'Widows' thing."

"What do you mean?" Karcher countered. He did not like the implication of what Carolyn said.

"You know what I mean. You are talking about Satya's life being in danger. What about yours? I wish they would fire you, not take you back."

Karcher seethed inside but kept silent. Of course, everyone knew that he was on administrative leave, this was in the newspaper, on the radio, and on the TV. Still, it was humiliating to talk about it. However, He did not want to get into an argument with his wife, not in front of someone who was not a member of his family.

It was clear to him that the visit was not going well, and he wanted it to end. But he did not want to be the one to end it, did not want to be the bad guy. So, he waited to see what the women were going to do and felt relieved when they ignored him.

It looked like Carolyn had made her point and did not want to dwell on it, or perhaps she wanted to dwell on another point more important to her, a topic which had intrigued her tremendously. She turned to Satya and asked, "How does it help, this group you go to?"

"Women tell their stories, tell how they cope with the tragedies in their lives. They give us ideas about what we can do. You get a new perspective on life, a renewed strength to go on, and sometimes guidance and direction. Somehow life doesn't seem meaningless and hopeless."

"You get all that?"

"Yes."

"From the group?"

"Yes. And also from my husband? When I flounder, I seek his advice."

Karcher was startled. "What?" he asked. 'How did one seek advice from a dead man?' he wondered.

"I talk to him. He is with me always, spiritually. For physical comfort, I hold the urn which contains his ashes."

"The urn gives you a sense of physical closeness with your husband?"

"Yes."

Karcher noticed incredulously that sadness had drained off from Satya's face, her body had become energized like someone had filled a balloon doll with air, someone had cranked a mechanical toy which had regained life and started to move.

"So, you have this urn in the house?" This time Carolyn asked the question, looking as bewildered as Karcher.

"Yes. I keep it in my bedroom. I have built a shrine for him."

"A shrine?" Karcher asked. The whole thing was beyond comprehension.

"Yes. I will show you if you like."

"I would, sure." Carolyn sounded excited.

Karcher capitulated, "Yes, of course."

Satya got up. Karcher and Carolyn followed her to her bedroom. This room seemed to be in a fairly good shape, although there was some damage to the walls, the bed and the dresser appeared scratched up, and there were some stains on the carpet and drapes. It gave the appearance of a room that was lived in, but roughly. There, in a corner, a chair had been turned into a throne with a red cloth, embroidered in gold, draped over it. A square cushioned pillow, encased in red velvet fabric and trimmed in gold, was placed in the middle of the chair. On that sat a brass urn. A garland of jasmine flowers hung around its neck. Several incense sticks were protruding out of a brass incense holder. Satya sat on the floor in front of it, brought her palms together, and bowed her head.

After a few seconds, she got up. Karcher saw that her face radiated peace and confidence.

Carolyn asked, "Did you say something to your husband while you were…"

"Just returned the love and respect he always showed me."

Karcher was confused. Obviously, to him, Satya was devoted to her dead husband. How in the world was she going to build a life for herself? Wouldn't she need to free herself from his memory? Shouldn't she seek a new and vibrant life with someone else? He could not contain himself and asked, "You wouldn't remarry, ever?"

"I could, but the man would have to be above jealousy."

"You couldn't be emotionally tied to two people simultaneously?"

"Perhaps not. I haven't given much thought to that possibility."

Karcher had difficulty understanding Satya's thinking and felt that she must have a perspective on life which was beyond him. He decided that there was no sense belaboring the point and chose to shut up, this time from his own side.

Carolyn took over, "Tell me something. I noticed that you did not refer to your husband even once by his name. Any particular reason?"

Satya smiled, "That's out of respect for those who are higher than me in age or status or both."

"Higher? Isn't marriage an equal proposition?"

"It is. That's why he never called me by my name either."

Once more Karcher was confused. 'How could two people be higher than each other simultaneously? They could be equal but not higher,' he thought.

However, he had a faint glimpse into Satya's logic when he heard Carolyn's reaction, "I see. Marriage can be equal based on respect for each other and giving each other a higher position, instead of fighting to secure it for oneself."

"I suppose," Satya said in a subdued voice.

"I am glad to know you. You are so strong yet humble," said Carolyn.

"You are very kind. No, I have no illusions about my strength or humility. I am weak like anyone else and have that evil streak we are all saddled with. ... I am also happy to know you. I do need a friend."

"You got one. For life," Carolyn assured.

Karcher now had an entirely new vision of Satya. He had always thought of Asian women, especially Indian, to be subservient to men. Satya appeared to be anything but that. She loved and respected her husband, even humbled herself before his memory, yet was strong, determined, powerful in her own right. She could fly a plane, build skyscrapers, wield a gun, stand on her own two feet, and make a place for herself in a hostile world, without raising a sword to claim her rights. She was like an ultimate feminist who forgot to demonize men.

He felt like saying something, something complementary to Satya, but felt at a loss for words. Then he realized, she didn't need any compliments, she was quite self assured.

Karcher felt that they had been in Satya's bedroom for quite a while, and it was time to get out of her private area. He made a slow move toward the door, which must have given a direction to the women because they followed.

Once more they settled in the living room, Karcher in the chair and the women on the couch. Mercifully for everyone, the talk turned to weather and gardening.

When the time came for the Karchers to leave, Carolyn hugged Satya, and Karcher clumsily shook hands with her.

Before getting into the car, Karcher looked back and saw Satya silhouetted against the bright picture window. That image made him feel the truth behind the cliché 'love conquers all'. Suddenly, he felt all his disappointment, anger, and frustration at Carolyn's criticisms of his behavior melting away. He saw Carolyn in a new light, one who loved him enough to try to save his life and save him from evil. He knew at that moment that he loved her in spite of who she was, and he loved her more than his own life.

He turned toward her and kissed her on the left cheek. The start of a new relationship.

CHAPTER FORTY-NINE

WIDOWS OF VIOLENCE

Christi picked out a psychologist randomly from the Yellow Pages for psychotherapy, a few days after it was recommended by her psychiatrist. During the first session, she didn't know what to expect, so she simply sat in the chair and answered questions obediently.

Within two weeks she made some changes in her life.

Dropping Gopal from her name and going back to her maiden name 'Comora' was the first. It gave her a sense of personal pride and identity.

Selling her big house, and using the equity to buy a smaller and cheaper house was the second. To execute a quick sale, she sold it at below market value. She was very happy about it because it lowered her property taxes and maintenance costs, and provided her with a positive bank balance.

Going back to her old nursing profession was the third. Not only did this keep her depression at bay, it also brought in money sorely needed for daily living expenses and psychotherapy.

None of these changes were characteristic of her. Even she was surprised at them. They were not consistent with the way she used to be: an old conniving, selfish, greedy, spendthrift, jealous, controlling, money-hungry, hateful, angry, vindictive woman with a very low self-concept and an inclination toward violence. She had certainly never seen herself with all these negative traits, not in the past when they defined her personality. Now, thanks to her psychotherapy, she could see them, and also see a movement away from them, a progression toward a new Christi. Maybe all the changes were temporary, and she would go back to being the old Christi. Maybe she wouldn't.

Where did this critical self-evaluation come from? Could it be that psychotherapy was working?

She did not remember everything that transpired in the sessions, but as she tried to recall what the topics of discussion were, one thing that the psychologist had said popped up in her head, "You have to take charge of your own life, be your own person." Huh! That explained some of the changes in her life style.

Recall of this suggestion brought in another, "You need to learn acceptance, tolerance, and forgiveness." She did not know what those terms meant, and how those behaviors could be learned, but she did know that recently she had not thought of Gopal and his new wife in nasty terms.

Then there was the recall of still another recommendation, "Join a support group, where you can learn a lot from those who share your experiences. 'Widows of Violence' is a good one for you."

That had been totally confusing. "What?" she had asked. "I never heard of it."

"Now you have," the psychologist had answered. "You are not technically a widow of violence, but in your mind you are. You see, even after your divorce, you never really let go of Dr. Gopal. Emotionally, he continued to be your husband. So, when you saw him with another woman, you hated him and were jealous of his new wife. It also brought about so many other pathological thoughts about him. You were consumed with anger and the need for revenge. Even after his death, you have not really released him. You are obsessed with him. You have to learn that you don't own people."

"Huh! I never saw it that way."

"Well, I hope you do now. ... So, in this support group, you will learn from other widows of violence how they cope. I will give you the phone number of the psychologist who leads it. Call her and become a member. Right away."

"Her?"

"Yes. There are women psychologists. Besides, who would be better qualified to lead a group of widows but a woman?"

Her question, which in retrospect seemed stupid, and the psychologist's response made her realize that her low self-concept, not completely gone, enveloped all women. How absurd! She certainly needed a new beginning. And 'Widows of Violence' might be just that.

She picked up the phone, called the number, and became a member. She also got the address of the group's meeting place, an office building, The Centurion, and the schedule, Thursdays at 7:00 pm.

Ambivalent still, partly reluctant, partly enthused, Comora resolved to attend a few meetings and then decide if she should continue. She showed up for the next meeting.

There were six women of varied ages and build. Her heart skipped a beat when she saw Satya among them, sitting and talking to someone next to her, rather casually. Having seen her in Macy's some time ago, it was easy for Comora to recognize Satya. Interesting, she had not known her name until it was splashed in the news media after Gopal's murder. All her resolve of acceptance and tolerance dissolved like a sugar cube in a hot cup of tea. She was tempted to run, but did not. She was here for therapy, to learn to deal with just such disturbing, destabilizing situations. She stayed. What made it easier was that Satya did not seem to recognize her. Maybe Gopal never shared her picture with Satya. Still, it was hard for her to face her rival, so she fixed her eyes on the psychologist.

The psychologist looked around and said, "I see a new face today. Would the new member please introduce yourself? ... Just give us your name, any name, so that we may be able to address you. After that, it's up to you what you want us to know."

Comora saw the psychologist turn toward her as if saying, 'Your turn.'

"My name is Cora." She decided right on the spot that she was not going to give her real name, which had been in the media recently, connected with some very unsavory activities. She certainly did not want Satya to know who she was. She was glad that her picture had not been in circulation, so no one could know her real identity. But why all this secrecy? Why was she so fearful of recognition? Despite all the changes she had made in her lifestyle and behavior, she still could not allow public scrutiny of her past or, for that matter, present. Obviously, she had a long way to go in her therapy. It seemed to her that if the women in the group knew who she was they might not like her, and Satya might treat her like the proverbial 'other woman', all of which was unflattering to her. Besides, she was there for therapy not self disclosure. Really? Self-disclosure was what these support groups were all about. Of course. But, these groups also protected the member's identity. She would disclose what was necessary and still remain anonymous. The decision made her feel relaxed.

All this reflection only took a few seconds. She noticed that the group silently sat during this time, clearly waiting for her to tell more about herself. No, she could not, not at this time. The expectant eyes of the group felt like stings. She felt relieved when the psychologist took over, most likely realizing that she had nothing else to add, "How about all others introducing themselves to the newcomer?"

They did. Some only mentioned their names as Comora had, while others presented their life history.

That done, the psychologist moved on with the meeting, "So, what do we want to talk about today?"

Someone said, "I don't know if the group wants to dwell on this point, but I am confused about something that came up in the last meeting."

"What's that?" asked the psychologist.

"Someone had said that violence was normal, it was instinctual. Does that mean we are doomed?"

"What does the group think? Anyone?" the psychologist urged.

Many statements, questions, and answers, from different members flew around, and Comora just listened. Some of them made sense, others seemed totally absurd. But, all of them had a message.

"Violence is natural, yes, and also pervasive. It's everywhere and has been around for as long as mankind has inhabited the earth. We use it to control others, others whom we don't like or hate. But nonviolence can be learned. Isn't that why we are here?"

"True. But we are here also to learn how to cope with violence when it visits us."

"Often we deal with it by violent means. We execute murderers, don't we?"

"That only perpetuates violence. That's not dealing with it."

"What is it then?"

"It is learning to solve our problems by nonviolent means."

"But that's impossible."

"No, it's not. There are examples; Martin Luther King, Gandhi, others."

"And they got killed."

"Yes, but more people get killed by violence than by nonviolence. Don't you see? When you don't answer violence by violence you have fewer enemies, which in itself makes you safer."

"What? I don't get it."

At this point the psychologist intervened, "Does anyone have an example of pathological effects of violence, and nonviolent means of dealing with violence?"

One woman raised her hand, "Yes, I do. This actually happened to me. … Once my husband and I were driving at night, and our car broke down on a country road. A half hour or so later, this truck pulled up with three teenagers. We thought we would get help. Instead the kids decided to rape me. My husband intervened, so they shot and killed him, then raped me. They left me for dead, only I survived. The kids were eventually caught, and I wanted them hanged. I mean gassed, electrocuted, shot, whatever. I was in a rage all the time, full of hate. This continued even after the kids were sentenced to life in prison…"

"I thought you were giving an example of nonviolence."

"Later. In the beginning, however, what I was doing and feeling was violence, not physical violence toward the kids, but violence nonetheless. And quite pathological. My health, both physical and mental, was ruined. You won't believe the physical ailments I had; headaches, upset stomach, high blood pressure, weight loss. On the mental side, I had anger, depression, paranoia, anxiety, you name it. I was a basket case."

Comora saw herself in this description and became curious about what happened to this woman. Still, she kept silent while someone else asked, "So what did you do? You seem pretty healthy to me."

"I am reasonably healthy, yes. So, what did I do? I learned nonviolence and forgiveness, right here in this group. Now, I am at peace and going on with the task of living and doing a hell of a job of it too. And, you know, I also learned to protect myself without violence. I watch what I do, where I go. I avoid places where I could be assaulted. I don't go to bars alone, don't walk or drive on dark streets. Don't give me the bullshit about having a right to be where I want to be, and the punks need to be controlled and changed. You catch a few, others emerge. No one is changed. They go to prison, then get out, and do the same shit all over again. No, you don't change the world, just save your own ass..."

"Wouldn't it be better if you carried a gun?"

"No. Guns kill. As someone said earlier, violence perpetuates violence. So, instead of using a gun, I might try to run away, hide, talk the attacker out of it, something like that, but I would not kill him. I might still get killed, happens sometimes, but this is less likely than if I reacted violently."

"I don't think I could do that. If someone is going to die, it would be my attacker, not me. Criminals don't deserve to live."

"That's what the criminals think, we don't deserve to live. This is the kind of thinking which keeps violence going. We are both wrong."

"I am all for not killing anyone from my own side, but when it comes to saving my own life, I will kill if I have to."

At that point a woman, who had been totally silent all this time, spoke in a subdued, gentle voice, "May I say something?"

Comora looked at the speaker curiously, and saw a young, slim, and attractive woman shift in her seat. She had bright, intelligent eyes, a sad face, slumped posture, discount store clothing, and a bedraggled look, as if life had not been kind to her during her few years on earth.

She heard the psychologist encourage the woman, "Certainly,"

The woman said, "First, I want to apologize for not giving my real name to the group. I didn't want to be identified, didn't want to be judged harshly. Now that I have attended the group a few times I don't feel that way. Anyway, I am Susan Madrill."

The name sounded familiar to Comora. Where had she heard it? The answer was provided by Susan as she continued, "My husband, Sonny, committed suicide."

Someone in the group asked, "I remember reading about him. But, didn't he live with his sister? That's what the papers said."

"Yes. He lived with me."

Sudden comprehension of what it meant unsettled Comora, but only for a moment. She looked around for the group's reaction and didn't notice any ripples, let alone any tumult. Looking within herself, she found admiration and respect for Susan, for her bravery. Could she, herself, ever be so brave? At this juncture she had no answer.

"So what was it you wanted to tell us?" the Psychologist asked. To Comora it looked like she was trying to prevent the talk from falling into trivialities and issues which were rather tangential to the discussion on hand. Smart woman.

Susan said, "What I wanted to tell was that violence visited me also, but in a very different way. I was a victim of violence without an enemy. I mean, no one attacked me. ... You see, after Sonny killed himself, I also died, sort of, had no desire to live. Then, I saw an announcement for this group in the paper, and I decided to come here. In the beginning, I didn't know what to expect, but I felt there must be something to it, or else the group would not exist. Anyway, I was looking for an answer to my problem, looking for a way to cope with my situation."

Comora thought, 'Good point.' She and Susan were similar in that respect. So, what to do?

The psychologist asked, "Anyone has any ideas?"

Someone said, "Susan, what about you? Have you found a way to cope with your trauma, your loss?"

"I am not sure, but maybe. Since coming to this group, I have learned to let go of the person whose loss has been so devastating. Not forget, but just let go. I love Sonny, I always did, I always will. But, now I can release him and not be so emotionally dependent upon him, go on with my life. Sure, I still cry sometimes, I probably will until my death, but I don't find life so hopeless any more. Anyway, I have learned a lot and I hope to learn a lot more in the future. Thanks to you all."

The psychologist commented, "I guess there's a lesson in this. Violence can visit us in many ways and from many different sources, requiring many different approaches to deal with it. I don't think we can resolve the issue of violence and ways of curbing it in this one meeting. It is an emotional issue which revolves around the question of survival, who deserves to live and who deserves to die. It is also a philosophical, moral, and ethical question. We will have to continue talking about it. I don't think we will ever find an answer that will be acceptable to everyone. We all have to find our own answers. Our discussions here help us find those answers. So, keep thinking, keep talking, keep helping."

As she headed home, Comora was struck with the fact that half the group had suffered because of the prison and the conflict caused by the AVs. Half! Would there be more from the same source joining this group? She hoped not. For once in her life, violence was not so attractive, so enticing. She thought of the time when she had ended up being a psychiatric case. She had not committed physical violence toward anyone, but she had been violent in thought, both towards others and herself. Only after attempting to put those thoughts aside had she begun to gain a certain measure of sanity. Forgiveness and nonviolence still seemed difficult, almost impossible, to accomplish. Letting go of Gopal also did not seem to be an easy task. Maybe there would be some other ways, equally difficult to follow. Whatever, she would have to learn and practice many of these ways, because she could not see any other way out, that's if she wanted to live and die in peace. Good thing her psychologist suggested this group, good thing she came.

CHAPTER FIFTY

THE STONE WOMB

It happened exactly one week after the motorcycle gang was formed. The sun was making its laborious climb over the Eastern ridges of the mountains, when Hefferly got an excited call from one of his field officer, "I think we got it. We tailed the Huddy contact from his home to the hide-out entrance. At least, that's what it looks like with the Huddy contact talking with an armed guard in a World War II Nazi uniform."

"Good job. Are you guys okay, haven't been spotted?"

"I don't think so. But, it wasn't easy. The first part was easy enough when the guy drove his car, full of stuff, to the end of a dirt road, some couple of hundred miles away. Then, it got hairy, as he started with a backpack full of supplies on an unmarked trail of sorts. A couple or so miles later, he left the trail and started bushwhacking. At that point it became really difficult to keep him in sight without exposing ourselves. Now he is talking to a guard."

"So he left some supplies in the car to be picked up later."

"Yes, a lot. Pretty soon there will be people coming down the trail to pick up stuff from the car, I'm sure. Maybe not all together to avoid being noticed, but they will. I don't know how they will do the hauling. Backpacking will require too many people and too many trips, not efficient. Who knows, maybe they have mountain bikes, or even mules."

"That's not our problem. Now, the question is how to mobilize a force quickly to capture Huddy and company? ... Anyway, give me the details of the area."

After getting the relevant details of the area, Hefferly once more thanked the officer for the superb job he and his companion had done and instructed, "Leave the area quietly and come back. I might need you as a guide."

Then he chewed on the information he had received and examined the topographical map of the area. All that area was rugged, hard to reach, and, most likely, rarely visited by anyone. It was also public land, and whoever was living there was doing so illegally, unless they were just backpackers camping for a few days. The illegal occupation of public land itself justified action against the intruders.

Now the question was, how to capture the enemy? He decided on a surprise attack. The next question was, what would be the size of the attack force and equipment? Not knowing how many people were there in the hide-out and the type and number of weapons among them, he did not know the answer to the question. All he could do was guess. He figured that being a hide-out it could not contain a very large force. Therefore, he guessed, maybe a couple of attack helicopters, which could carry out rescue, transportation, and surveillance functions also, and a ground attack force of maybe a dozen people. He knew it was a very dumb way to plan a combat operation, but under the circumstances, this was the best he could do. If it turned out that he was wrong, and the size of the enemy force proved to be larger than he had guessed, he would just beat a hasty retreat. For the time being anyway.

Finding men did not seem to be a major problem, he could coax the officers under his supervision. For helicopters, he called the Transportation Department, "I need two helicopters immediately with pilots expert at camouflage flying in the mountainous area."

The answer was not what he had expected, "We are not a military, you know. We have a fleet of just three helicopters, and they are already on assignment. Besides, do you have an authorization from the boss?"

"Forget it," said Hefferly with irritation. If there were no helicopters, what's the purpose in talking to the boss about it?

He couldn't understand why he was having such difficulty getting help. Lohman had no problem when he went on an attack mission following the Martinez murder. Of course, he knew why. Lohman had several dead bodies which made the case urgent. Still, he liked to suffer from a 'poor me' syndrome. Somehow it made him feel better.

He sat for several minutes thinking about what to do now, how to proceed? Then, a plan emerged.

He should seek help from the State police. Get them to provide helicopters and also a ground force of state troopers. That was when he realized that the area of operation was out of his jurisdiction, and he would have to get cooperation of the state authorities anyway.

With this decision he went to Belford for the approval of his plan. Belford simply said, "Go, go. I will get you a written authorization, authorization, within an hour. I'll call the sate, state, and ask their cooperation. We haven't had anything, anything, but bad news lately. We need something. If it works, works, the public might stop looking at us as incompetents."

With the blessing of his boss, he went to work. It took him a week, but finally he got a force of 14 armed men, sufficient ammunition to last for at least six hours of continuous use, and two unmarked helicopters, one of which was combat ready, and four jeeps. Then he ran into another problem. The state wanted to run the show. A few more days were wasted in convincing them that he knew the case and the criminals better than they did and, therefore, was in a better position to lead the assault.

Then came the day of the attack. Hefferly took the officer who had tracked the Huddy contact to the guard post of the hide-out as the co-leader, and got the force together at the police headquarters before day break.

First, he made sure that all radios were set to secure frequencies. Then, he sent the helicopters ahead of the ground force which rode in Jeeps. They all assembled in a meadow about two miles from the suspected hide-out. Hefferly ordered the road vehicles to be hidden in the woods. He instructed one unarmed helicopter to stay on the ground in 'wait' position for rescue and transport after the battle, the other, attack helicopter, to scan the hide-out area and radio back whatever it saw. The attack helicopter was also asked to provide cover for the ground force, when it started moving toward the area of the potential operation.

A few minutes later, he heard the crackling of the radio and listened to the message, "There is a clearing on top of a hill looking directly East at 12 o'clock. There's activity, but no concern, no panic evident. Could be some campers preparing breakfast, could be the AVs, I don't know. They seem to be oblivious of us, maybe because we are flying pretty high and quite a ways south of their location. Ten-four."

"Good. Now tell me what the mountain top looks like, the physical features. I need to know the best route for an assault."

"It would be from the Southwest. North and East sides have sheer cliffs and require a technical climb of many hours. Clearly not practical. In a way, good for us. It would not offer any escape route for the enemy either. They, too, will need ropes to rappel and would not have enough time for that. Ten-four."

"Thanks. Now, stay away from the area and cause no suspicion, but keep watch and wait for my instructions."

Hefferly felt it was the right moment to make a move. His own heart was racing at the prospect of a gun battle, partly out of fear and partly out of excitement. What about the troops? Their hearts were probably racing like his, he imagined.

He moved his force to southwest of the hill and led it very slowly and very quietly toward the top. A couple hours later, he could see and smell smoke. Time to interrupt breakfast. Make a surprise attack, not 'firing the guns' attack, but 'descending upon the enemy' attack. Sure, respond in kind only if fired upon. If the people turned out to be innocent campers, he would just apologize and back off. If they turned out to be the AVs, as suspected, he would make arrests with or without violence, depending upon how the enemy reacted.

Another 10 minutes, and Hefferly spotted human movement. "Stop," he whispered and everyone froze and lay low in the bushes.

He, with his binoculars, looked at the moving figure and knew him to be a guard by the way he was dressed and armed. Also, by the way he moved.

Hefferly now had no doubt that it was an AV camp. He radioed the attack helicopter, "Go over the target area and drop tear gas. We are moving to charge."

In less than a minute, Hefferly saw the helicopter flying low over the mountain top. A second later, he saw tear gas smoke spreading. He ordered his ground troops to move swiftly with the purpose to overwhelm the enemy. He believed that the tear gas and sudden ground attack would render the enemy almost paralyzed, no matter how many they were.

He gave his men an order and a firm warning, "Charge, but don't fire unless fired upon."

All of a sudden it was a battlefield, a small battlefield but battlefield nonetheless. Gun fire was exchanged for about five minutes, then it died down.

Hefferly ordered the combat helicopter hovering in the air, "Situation appears under control. But, check also from above. If safe, land for evacuation and support. Call back before landing. Ten-four."

"Looks like there are some casualties. But, I think it's safe enough to land. However, we will be ready to respond if attacked. Ten-four."

Hefferly saw the helicopter descend. He, himself, climbed to the top of the hill.

That the enemy fought back was surprising but not totally unexpected. Four men, including the guard and a trooper, were lying on the ground covered in blood, six stood with their arms behind their heads in a gesture of surrender around the campfire on which coffee was brewing and beef steaks were roasting.

Hefferly checked the fallen men. One, the guard, was badly injured but alive, and the other three dead. He ordered his men to take all the living bodies into custody, handcuff them, and tie chains around their legs. Then, he called the helicopter 'in wait' at the base of the mountain, "Come up here. We're going to need you. Ten-four."

After that he looked at his enemies, dead and alive, carefully. Huddy was not among them.

"Where's Chris Huddy and Travis Torte?" Hefferly yelled at the prisoners. "We know they are here."

The captives said nothing.

Hefferly ordered his troops, "Four of you stand guard at the prisoners. Others come with me. We're going to find Huddy and Torte. They have to be here. Couldn't have escaped our noose, it was too tight."

They looked around, guns drawn. There wasn't much to search. The mountain top was almost bare, except for four tents which had backpacks, sleeping bags, clothes, boots, rifles, ammunition, and grenades. Still, they searched and searched. An hour passed. Hefferly began to wonder if the entire operation was for nothing. A failure of this magnitude would surely sink his career. He could not let that happen. A success of this magnitude, on the other hand, would elevate him to a very high position. He must search some more, go even beyond the mountain top.

Another hour, and he noticed crumpled vegetation leading toward a boulder. It was not a game path. If it were, it would be clearer, more defined. Curiously, he looked around and found more crumpled vegetation leading to a small gap about three feet wide under the boulder. Some vegetation was crushed and completely destroyed suggesting the spot had been used often. There was also some vegetation around there which was barely crumpled indicating it had been walked on within minutes. And, there were also drops of blood. Human blood? Couldn't be from the brief skirmish of a few minutes ago, because it took place over 50 feet away.

Hefferly examined the gap beneath the boulder more carefully, suspecting there might be a passage of some kind. There seemed to be a rocky slope behind it going underground. Was it possible for a human to crawl into it? He asked one of his men, "Try to go in, legs first."

The trooper slid into the gap. He felt he could go farther if he entered sideways to who knew where. He said, "My feet are dangling, so there's an opening."

Hefferly ordered, "Don't go any further. Come out." He did not want his man to lose his leg if someone inside were to attack him.

After the trooper extricated himself, Hefferly put his mouth to the opening and yelled, "I know you are there. Come out empty handed, you won't be hurt. I'll count to ten. If you don't come out before the count is over, we're coming in. You won't like that."

He started counting.

When he reached nine he heard some stirring, so he moved away. Soon a head emerged, then shoulders, then a body, sideways. When the man was outside, Hefferly recognized him immediately and said sarcastically, "Chris Huddy, finally. You're under arrest for the murder of Stella Robinson." Then he read him his rights. A trooper handcuffed him.

Hefferly noticed that there was blood on Huddy's clothes, pretty much all over, and rather fresh. He came close and asked, "Are you injured? Were you in the fight and ran underground to elude capture?"

Huddy did not answer. He just looked at Hefferly contemptuously.

Hefferly examined his body under his clothes. There were some scratches but no sign of any injury sufficient to produce blood spots all over his clothing. He also smelled something medicinal, like the kind noticed in the surgical ward of a hospital. His mind went into an 'aha' mode.

"Someone else is under there, and he is injured. You have been moving him. Right? You decided to come out to get us off the track of this person? Loyalty? Who is he?"

Huddy said nothing. Hefferly ordered, "Get him out of here." Two troopers led Huddy to the other captives.

Hefferly went back to the boulder and shouted again into the opening, "If you can, come out. If not, say 'help'. I'll send someone down to assist you."

He did not get a response. This was a sign that the person inside was either dead or preparing to fight. So, he ordered one of the troopers, "Put on your gas mask, helmet, and headlight. You have your bullet proof vest on? Good. I'm gonna throw a tear gas can inside. After I do that, you enter the opening and subdue whoever is there. I would prefer to get him alive, but protect yourself, and if that means killing the bastard, do it."

After the trooper was ready, Hefferly threw the tear gas can into the cavity and waited for a minute for its effect. Nothing happened. At that, he motioned the trooper to go in.

As soon as the trooper's head disappeared underground, Hefferly heard a gun shot, some shuffling, some thumping. Then he heard the trooper's echoing, reverberating voice, "The guy here is unconscious. Send one more person to hoist him up. I can't do it alone."

"Right away," said Hefferly. Then he ordered another trooper, "Put on your gas mask and go in."

About five minutes later a head emerged and then shoulders. Two troopers grabbed the shoulders, put their hands under the armpits of the man, and pulled out the rest of his body.

The unconscious man was bloodied but only in the lower part of his body. Hefferly looked at him and exclaimed, "My, oh my. I came for a little fish, and see what we got? A barracuda."

The troopers looked at him quizzically. Hefferly said, "Don't you know who he is? This is George Schultz. Looks like he had his intestinal surgery done here. Hadn't the time to heal before we came. Apparently, Huddy was with him in the cave, probably trying to hide him behind something, and got bloodied himself. ... Carry him to the chopper and secure him."

One trooper tied Schultz with ropes, four together lifted him over their shoulders, carried him to the humming, whirring chopper, and loaded him into it.

Hefferly looked at the stone womb as the two troopers came out of it. He asked the trooper who had gone in first, "What's in there? What happened?"

"I couldn't see very clearly because of the tear gas. It was reflecting the light from my headlight back at me. ... It seemed like a small cave. Schultz was lying on the floor next to his sick bed, rubbing his eyes, wheezing and coughing. He was probably being moved before I got there. He had a small pistol in his hand ready to fire. I tried to take the gun away from him. He fired but missed. I guess he couldn't see clearly in the haze of tear gas. That's when I thumped him. I must have used more force than I intended to. He went limp. And I called for help."

"Thank you. You did well. Let's get back to the prisoners."

Once more he looked at the dead bodies and felt sad. Not so much for the two enemies but for the trooper. Was it worth his sacrifice? So, Schultz and Huddy had been captured, would that make the world any safer? He had no answers, only doubts. In a battlefield, doubts could be deadly. He put them aside and ordered his men, "Put the dead on the floor of the transport helicopter and the living in the seats. Fly them to the city. Two troopers go with them."

Suddenly, he felt his job was not quite done. The place, except for the small cave where Schultz and Huddy were hiding, did not seem much like a hide-out. There had to be some other place where the AVs kept their supplies and arms. He asked the remaining troopers, "Look around. Look for storage and living places. They have to be nearby."

The search started and continued for a couple of hours. Hefferly's instincts were right. About a quarter mile away in the midst of the pines and alders, there was a trap door which opened into an underground bunker. The troopers, their headlights fastened, dropped in carefully, ready with their pistols. Hefferly went with them. They found nine frightened men crouched behind some sacks and boxes in a corner. They were ordered to get up with hands in the air. They did and were handcuffed.

Hefferly's face lit up, "Here's Torte, too."

Then he decided to check the place out. It was filled with food, medical supplies, many kinds of uniforms including Nazi regalia, arms, and ammunition. It was also equipped with communications equipment, sleeping bunks for 10, two water containers, and an electric generator.

The new prisoners were brought out.

Back in the open area, Hefferly called the state police headquarters. He told the authorities about his catch, and requested, "Send some men to take possession of all the stuff as evidence. Needs to be done right away. I don't want the AVs to have any chance of removing anything. I will leave four troopers here to guard the place until your men arrive."

He got the assurance he needed, "We will send four men and a couple of transport vehicles. Should be there in a few hours."

The job almost over, Hefferly gave one last order, "Two troopers go with the new prisoners in the combat helicopter. The rest must walk down with me to the jeeps and drive back to the state police headquarters."

In a couple of hours, a caravan of Jeeps was moving toward the city with some very tired and sad people. Hefferly watched, plaintively in his mind's eye, the dead men lying on the floor of the helicopter.

In spite of the promise of hefty rewards at having won the battle against the AVs and having caught big prizes, he was not celebrating.

CHAPTER FIFTY-ONE

A THORN

Things were not going well for Tommy Jordan. At least, that's what it seemed to him.

He had been in the Warden's chair only a little over a week, and he started to have problems. And when he tried to do something about them, all he got was more problems.

It started with a call from the prison phone monitor, "I picked up a conversation which is disconcerting. I don't know what it really means, so I thought I would let you examine it."

"What is it?" asked Jordan.

The phone monitor summarized a specific part of the conversation between Samuel Haney and his wife, "The wife says, 'I heard something strange.' He asks, 'What?' She answers, 'An officer Ibarra, a Hispanic, helping us.' He says, 'I don't know any Ibarra.' Sounded like he did not want his wife to talk about this Ibarra person. I disconnected the line immediately, went over to Haney and asked him, 'What was that talk about Ibarra?' He pleaded ignorance, 'I don't even know who he is.' That would be logical since Ibarra and Haney are in different units. Still, I wonder why his wife would mention Ibarra. Could he have some connection with the AVs? Ibarra worked for you, sir, when you ran ASU. I thought you should know."

"A Hispanic working for the AVs? Sounds unlikely. Yet, how would Haney's wife know about him? Thanks for alerting me. Get me a copy of that conversation. I'll check it out."

He got the copy of the conversation in a few minutes, which did not tell him anything new, but confirmed what the phone monitor had told him. He decided to confront Ibarra with this information. Finding that it was Friday and rather late in the day, he waited until Monday to call him to his office.

Ibarra appeared before Jordan looking meek and apprehensive. Most likely because it was one thing to deal with Jordan, the Shift Commander, it was a totally different matter to deal with Jordan, the Warden. He took a side chair, squirming, as if expecting some kind of sword to fall on him.

Jordan came to the point right away, "What is it I am hearing, you working for the AVs?"

"AVs? No, sir. I just work for the prison?"

"I mean do you know them? Have special relationship with them?"

"No. Yes, I know many AVs here, but they are all prisoners, and I treat them like I treat any prisoner."

"Do you know Samuel Haney?"

"I have heard the name."

"His wife has heard that you are working for the AVs."

"I don't know where she got it. Sir, I assure you, I have nothing to do with the AVs."

"Maybe not. But if people think you are connected with them in any way, you know what it means?"

"Yes, sir. The Hispanics might think I am a traitor, and they might harm me."

"Precisely. So, all I can say is watch out. And, if I have evidence that you are, in fact, working for the AVs and lied to me about it, you are in serious trouble."

"I understand, sir."

Jordan dismissed Ibarra.

Right after that he called his Chief of Security, who also took the same chair Ibarra had occupied only a few minutes ago. Without preliminaries, he dictated, "I want an officer Ibarra watched continuously. It has come to my attention that he might be an AV plant. I want firm proof of that. Any behavior, any talk, any writing, anything which might give the proof, bring to me. Use your staff throughout the prison, if you have to. I want this problem taken care of before it becomes a big one."

"Yes, sir."

A few days later Jordan became aware of his mistake. By trying to make the staff watch Ibarra, he had virtually informed everyone about his suspicion. He found out that his suspicion was being taken by others as fact, and that put Ibarra's life in jeopardy. If anything happened to Ibarra, he might be blamed for it.

Still, he figured he was doing his job, and Ibarra would have to take care of himself. But he had not expected the way Ibarra seemed to be taking care of himself, or he was being taken care of. He found out about it in a horrible way, compounding his problem.

About ten days later, there was a near riot in the prison. Strangely, it was between two Hispanic gangs, Huracan and Cuervo. They faced off each other in the exercise yard of a minimum custody unit. He used the standard procedure; ordered the armed guard to perch on the catwalk and asked the yard office to yell at the gangs on the PA system to freeze in their places or they would be shot. The prisoners did stop, were taken into custody, and the cell blocks were locked down. It prevented bloodshed. He felt good about this accomplishment but also foolish after finding out the cause of it. When the dust settled, he called the Shift Commander of the unit where the inmates had rioted and asked, "What was that about? You know?"

"I talked with the two gang leaders. Huracans want to eliminate Ibarra for working for the AVs. Cuervos want to protect Ibarra because they feel he is one of them. I don't know what the truth is."

"But Ibarra works in ASU. Why would these gangs fight over him in the minimum unit?"

"Location means nothing, sir. If they want to hurt or protect Ibarra, they can do so anywhere, even in his home, or on the street."

"True. Their reach is long. ... Now, have you talked with Ibarra? Maybe he can clear the mystery."

"No, sir. He is not in my unit."

"Oh, that's right. Okay, I'll talk to him."

Once more he called Ibarra to his office. "What is it I am hearing?" he asked.

"What, sir?" Ibarra asked in response.

"That you're a Cuervo."

"No, sir. I am not a member of anything, no gang for me. But I do believe that the Cuervos have adopted me."

"Adopted?"

"To protect me. You had told me, sir, that some people think that I'm working for the AVs. Now the rumor is all over the place. I already told you, it's a lie, sir, totally false."

"But, why you? Why would anyone want to do this to you?"

"I don't know, sir."

"I'll investigate. If you are lying, you know, it's not going to be good for you. Remember."

He saw Ibarra's dejected face become more dejected, drawn out, like it was going to melt and flow down over his shoulders any minute.

Jordan did not really want to do any investigation. He wanted Ibarra, who had become a thorn in his side, gone, gone out of the prison, gone like dead. Only he did not want to be responsible for it.

Then he got a call from the Director a few days later, "Is it true that you have an employee, Rubin Ibarra, who is an AV mole? And you had a riot because of him?"

"The riot, sir, was put down. Nothing happened. You know, sir."

"Yes. But you haven't answered my question."

"Well, sir, we don't know the truth. There is no firm evidence to prove that Ibarra is an AV mole. Some people even think he is a Cuervo. I am investigating."

"Then do some fast investigating. I don't want any staff working with any gangs. And, why don't you suspend him or put him on paid leave, or something, while you are investigating him?"

Jordan knew, of course, the staff were not allowed to have any gang ties. "Yes, sir, I will do something," he assured.

Once more he wished Ibarra dead. But if Ibarra, indeed, had Cuervo protection, he was not going to die, not an unnatural death. Or, maybe he would die an unnatural death. Let Huracan get him for being an AV, or let the AVs get him for being a Cuervo. Whatever, the whole thing was totally distressing.

As if this was not enough, he got more bad news.

Two days later he learned, like everyone else, that Schultz had been caught. What should have been good news proved to be bad for him.

He got another call from the Director a couple of days later on a Monday morning, "You will be happy to know that Mr. Karcher has been found totally blameless for Schultz's escape, because it took place outside his jurisdiction. Another bit of happy news, which you probably already know, Schultz has been captured. This changes the whole scenario. Now, punishing someone for Schultz's escape is rather pointless. Anyway, Mr. Karcher will be coming back as the Warden tomorrow, and you may go back to your post. … And, I thank you for the splendid job you did running the prison during Mr. Karcher's absence. I will remember this when the time comes for the next promotion."

The Director's promise did not mean a thing to Jordan. He was demoted and, therefore, distraught. He had his dream job, and all of a sudden it was gone. He wanted to cry like a child whose favorite toy had slipped out of his hand and fallen into a fast flowing river. All he could do was see it drift away until it was no more.

No, he did not cry. 'There would be better opportunities in the future,' he consoled himself.

Now the top priority for him was to get rid of Ibarra, the thorn. The easiest thing would be to transfer him to another unit, preferably minimum. That way, not only Ibarra would be out of his sight, he would also be dead. In ASU, there was maximum protection for the staff because of minimal physical contact between them and the inmates. In a minimum unit, there were no such restraints. Surely, either the AV or the Huracan, or maybe both, would get him. There was a possibility of Cuervo protection, if Ibarra indeed was their member. So, there would be riots, some killings, maybe Ibarra's. No problem for him since all that would be someone else's headache.

But he couldn't transfer Ibarra himself. It would have to be agreed upon by the receiving unit and would have to be approved by the Warden.

So, he decided to plead with the Warden the next day, making it part of his phony ceremonial welcome. He called Karcher late in the morning, allowing him to at least settle back in his old chair, and, therefore, be more receptive to his request. "Welcome back, sir," he said. "I hope you are well."

"Thank you. ... I'm fine. And, thank you also for calling. I meant to call you myself to extend my appreciation for the great job you did during my absence. But, what is this mess with Ibarra? Everyone is talking about him. How did he become so important, so suddenly?"

"I can fill you in on the facts. I don't know what they mean."

"Sure. Why don't you come on over and tell me all about it. I am just settling in. So, stop by next week on Monday, say around two."

"I'll be there, sir." He had several days till his meeting during which he worked up a rationale, a very convincing argument, in his opinion, for his request to transfer Ibarra.

Jordan had garnered some measure of satisfaction. He was sure that he would bring about his thorn's destruction.

CHAPTER FIFTY-TWO

THE FISHING TRIP THAT WASN'T

GOODWIN, TOO, CAME to know of the plans for Ibarra's transfer, from his trusted mole. His plan was working. All he had to do was wait, and, once Ibarra was in a minimum custody unit, either the AVs or the Huracan would take care of the problem, in due course. He had more urgent things to attend to, like how to eliminate Satya and Karcher.

And what about Bottillo? He had almost forgotten about him, being busy with the relentless war. Yes, but wasn't Bottillo part of this very war? Suddenly it occurred to him that Bottillo may have had something to do with the recent AV setback, the capture of Schultz along with Huddy and Torte. He wasn't sure, however, what Bottillo might have done.

It didn't matter if Bottillo did anything or not, he was associated with the enemy camp, therefore, was an enemy, and must be eliminated. He had already lived long enough due to the AVs fault. Not any more. Originally, he had thought of employing some AV inmates, but he did not want to give this job to just any AV. He needed someone reliable and trustworthy, also someone with brains to be able to execute the job prudently so as not to attract attention to himself and to the organization. At that he remembered Haney, who was due out soon. He would talk to him about this project.

After some contemplation, he decided to hold off the attack on Karcher, 'Let things cool off. Let Karcher think he is not a target. Let him become careless. Wait a few weeks, a few months, as long as needed. In the meantime, teach that bitch, Satya, a lesson.' All his losses were at her hands only. She needed to know that no one messed with the AVs.

Once more Haney's name popped up in his head. Haney was relatively young, soon to be free, and very smart. The last quality made him a prime candidate for the job. Someone had to match wits with Satya.

If he was going to ask Haney for a favor, he had to show he cared, cared enough to go and receive him at the prison upon his release. He called Emily to find out the date when Haney would be getting out.

She said, "Don't know, not the exact date. No one does. It's supposed to be any time now."

Goodwin called her daily. He did not have to hide these calls; they did not involve any intrigue. Thirteen days later, they were not necessary. Emily told him, "I got the word from Sam today. He will be released this week, Friday, in the morning at eleven."

On the day of Haney's release, Goodwin went to see Emily in the morning at about eight. Without preliminaries he asked, "Could I ride with you to receive Sam?"

"Sure. He would be happy. Only you would have to wait outside, not being on his visitation list."

"I know that."

He waited at the prison gate. About two hours later, he saw Emily come out, hanging on Haney's left arm.

He shook hands with Haney, gave him a warm hug, and said, "You look good."

"Thank you. I stay out of trouble. It can be done in the prison, but you have to use your brains."

"And most inmates have gray matter missing." Goodwin laughed at his joke and Haney just smiled.

Back at the Haney residence, Goodwin did not go inside. He said, "I'll leave you lovebirds alone. You have a lot of catching up to do. Give me a call sometime. I need your advice on a couple of things."

"I will. Tomorrow, okay?"

"Okay."

Tomorrow could not come soon enough for Goodwin. He kept running to the phone every time it rang. Finally, after maybe a dozen calls, there was the promised call from Haney, "Well, you make me feel important. What is it?"

"Nothing. Just wanted to invite you to go fishing, for old times' sake. Can you get here this Sunday? I'll be ready."

Goodwin was sure that Haney would know that this was an invitation, not for fishing, but for some secret talks.

"Sure can."

In order to throw anyone tailing them off the track, Goodwin carried with him all the fishing equipment, and made it look like he was really serious about catching fish. After picking up Haney, he drove to a nearby manmade city lake. He picked a lonely and wide open spot where they could talk without being overheard by anyone. The spot also made it possible for them to see if someone was approaching them.

After the two had cast their lines and sat comfortably in their canvas chairs drinking beer, Goodwin came to the point, "I have a couple of big jobs for you. I know, I know, you just got out of the prison and may not be interested in any new job so soon. But, you are the only one who can do it."

"Well, what is it?" Haney asked.

"You know Satya, Dr, Gopal's wife, and a CPO, Phil Bottillo?"

"Yes. Man, know both of them, at least by name."

"Let's talk about Satya first."

"Does she have guts? Snuffed two of our guys."

"That's a major blow to our pride. We have to reestablish our superiority. Let everyone know that we are supreme, no one crosses us."

"What are you suggesting?"

"Kill her. She's smart, very smart. You are the only one who is her match. You see, I don't want to send any half-ass zealots on this assignment who are going to be blown away."

Haney said with alarm, "That's really a tough assignment. I haven't really done anything like that, ever."

"You don't have to have a track record to be capable. There's always a first time for everything."

"I know. But killing?"

"Yeah. But, what are your concerns?"

"Many. First, Satya is known to be a skilled shooter, and I had only a bare acquaintance with firearms, having done some target practice at the AV firing range. I might get killed. Second, it is an understatement that Satya is smart. I have read stories about her. She is an engineer, man, and a flier. Third, I can't kill a woman and sneakily. It is cowardly."

"I can't believe that you would be intimidated by a woman. Besides, see her as an enemy. You are not killing a woman, you are getting rid of an enemy. You can do it. I know, you can do it."

"I guess I could do it," Haney said in a blunt tone, like he knew he had to do it but was not relishing the idea.

"I knew you would not let us down." Goodwin thumped him on the back in a gesture of intimate approval.

Ignoring Goodwin's reaction, Haney asked, "Do you want to tell me how to do it or want to leave it entirely up to me?"

Goodwin gave a lengthy and indirect reply, "Well, I toyed with the idea of following Searle's lead, going to Satya's home to kill her, but discarded it as soon as it came to my mind. Follow a disaster? It isn't that I am superstitious, that I believe that you would be wiped out just because Searle and Ellsworth had been…"

"Actually, it's a good possibility," Haney interrupted.

Goodwin nodded his head in agreement and said, "Yeah, it gave me an uncomfortable, an uneasy feeling. … What then? You could kidnap her to some place where you have total control over the situation. We have plenty of such places all over the state, many homes and apartments, where the membership meets secretly. Even our warehouses and garages would work perfectly. You would have to make sure that you were not being followed by police or someone else, that's all. Yet, that's the biggest problem. You could not be sure of that. Police have been on our tail for some time now. ... So, in fact, I have nothing."

"Meaning I can do whatever I want, so long the subject is eliminated without implicating us?"

"You said it."

"But it's too soon."

"I wasn't thinking of going after Satya right away. I just wanted to talk to you about it. Get the plan finalized. You take your time. Besides, it's not safe to do it immediately. The cops are shadowing all our brothers they know of, that means all the top brass. I am sure they are watching you, too, you being a known sympathizer of the AV, and here going fishing with me. Take a few weeks, if you want. Don't wait too long though, otherwise the impact we want to create will be lost."

"So, it's not just about killing, it's also about creating an impact, letting everyone know what we can do if you cross us. It's about ego, about superiority, ... about being delusional." Haney said.

"Delusional?"

"Delusions of grandeur, you know."

"What's the matter with you? Are you slipping?"

"No, no, no, not slipping. Just thinking out loud. ... So, what about Bottillo? How does he get in the picture?"

"Oh, he had slipped out of my mind. You had been in the prison so you probably don't know that the police claim to have someone who saw our men after the Robinson job. I think it is Bottillo. I think he might have helped the police track down Huddy and Torte and indirectly made it possible for them to catch Schultz also. A major defeat for us. So, Bottillo should be punished."

"And, you want me to punish him?"

"Yes."

"Based on a lot of suppositions?"

"Suppositions, yes, but they are quite logical. If we relied on facts only, we wouldn't get anything done."

"What if he is innocent?"

"A few innocents always get killed in a war."

"So, as soon as I get out of the prison I get two jobs, both involve killing. Just my luck. ... By the way, is this an order?"

"Take it anyway you want."

"And I assume you want me to handle this also my way."

"Yes. Telling you how to do it would only restrict you. That could not be good."

"Is there a time limit?"

"No. Neither job is urgent, but both are important enough to be carried out as soon as possible."

Haney hung his head like he was thinking. After a minute or so he asked, "Do we have to kill everyone we don't like?"

"It has nothing to do with like or not like. These people are a threat to our organization."

"How? Satya killed those two men in self-defense, and Bottillo has not committed any violence of any kind. I don't understand the logic."

"Both of them have acted like our enemies. They must be punished. That's the logic. Now, if you don't want to do it..."

"That's not it. I am an AV. I will do it because our code demands it. I will just have to find a convincing argument for it."

"You better find it soon. You don't go into a battlefield dragging your feet."

Haney said nothing.

It was clear to Goodwin that Haney was wavering in his self-confidence and had questions about the AV motives but was reluctant to be vocal about it. Well, he did express his feelings but in a conversational rather than in an argumentative way. Probably did not want to sound like he was opposed to the AV ideology.

Goodwin did toy with the idea of withdrawing the assignment but decided against it. He was sure Haney would overcome his self-doubts and questions about the AVs, because an AV was always an AV.

So, he assumed that the assignments had been understood and accepted, and said, "Good. Now remember, we need to continue meeting impromptu to communicate with each other. For safety's sake, during other fishing trips, in different places, at different times. We, ourselves, will not know when and where until a few hours prior to our meeting."

"Okay." Haney agreed. He sounded like a robot.

Goodwin ignored it and enjoyed the remainder of his day getting drunk.

No one caught any fish.

CHAPTER FIFTY-THREE

A CIRCUS

Some people have all the bad luck. Sanderson thought he was one of them. Lohman got a big drama in a canyon, blew away a few bad guys, got a letter of commendation in his personnel file, and was assured of a big promotion. Hefferly caught the big fish, Schultz, along with a number of small ones, and became the talk of the town with prospects of a photo-op with the Governor and move-up to some cushy job. In contrast, what did he get? A reprimand and a warning. This had to change. Christi Comora still seemed like the key to this change. All that was needed was for him to catch her in something illegal. This would require watching her, something he could not do in an official capacity. He remembered Belford's words, '... you have no business talking to her unless you have some evidence, evidence, of crime.' Well, he would watch Comora privately, on his own time, and once he had collected evidence of crime, he would get her in an official capacity.

So, when he was not on duty, Sanderson would drive around Comora's house in his own car, wearing street clothes. If he spotted her, he would watch and follow her. He kept a mini tape recorder in his shirt pocket to record Comora's statements, which would surely betray her criminal agenda, that was if he got a chance to talk to her. He also carried a gun, hidden in his pants, just in case.

Much of the time, he found her doing the same boring things which most law abiding people did; working, shopping, staying home. If she was doing anything illegal in the privacy of her home, he had no clue. Then he noticed something unusual one day, which sent blood rushing to his temple; Comora going to a building 'Centurion' on Thursday, at seven, in the evening. What could she be doing there? He saw a few other women go in there too. One of them was Satya. What brought Comora and Satya together?

After the women had disappeared behind the doors, Sanderson walked into the building himself. He saw no one in the lobby but noticed a board on the wall which listed the day's activities. Now, he knew, a meeting of 'Widows of Violence' was taking place from seven to eight.

That day he went home wondering what Comora was up to? The question prompted him to berate himself for leaving the Centurion building. He should have stayed until the end of the meeting and found out what Comora did. He ordered himself to go and watch her next week and hoped it was not already too late.

Next Thursday, he drove his car to a secluded spot, not far from the Centurion gate, and parked in a place which appeared hidden from the building. He sat waiting and thinking about the incongruity of two rival women in the same support group. All of a sudden his heart, lungs, spleen, liver, and all other internal body parts together, started to jump out of his skin. He knew what this was all about: 'Comora, having gotten rid of Gopal, was there now to get Satya. Everyone knew Satya, who had been prominently displayed in the media after her husband's death, but Comora was known only to the police. Satya would not even know that she had an enemy in the room with her, an enemy who was there to kill her.'

This was his chance. He could even arrest Comora for stalking Satya, and what she was doing was clearly stalking. He was sure that Comora would not be foolish enough to do anything to Satya in the meeting and in the presence of other women, but afterwards it was a different story.

It proved to be the longest one hour he had ever spent. Finally, he saw the Centurion door open and two women come out, then another, then Satya, then still a couple more, then in the end Comora. Aha! She chose to stay back. To watch Satya? To follow her in her car? To push her off the road in some secluded area and then attack her?

He did wonder if his imagination was running wild. Then, maybe it wasn't. Even if he was all wrong in his speculation, the setting gave him every reason to arrest Comora, make a case against her, and reverse the direction of his fate. There was only one problem. He was not on duty and could not arrest anyone in an official capacity. So, he decided to confront Comora, get something incriminating out of her, then go back and arrest her the next day. Once an arrest had been made, and a charge, which was likely to stick, had been leveled, no one would bother about how the evidence had been collected. He turned on his tape recorder and drove toward the area of the parking lot where the women had their cars. A couple had already taken off. Satya was talking to one woman and did not seem to be in any hurry to go anywhere. Comora was doing the same with another woman, perhaps waiting for Satya to move first.

Sanderson parked next to Comora, got out, stood in front of her and asked, "What are you doing here?"

"You again? This time I will have your ass in a sling, you know," Comora said in anger.

The other woman asked, "What's this about? Is this man bothering you?"

"Harassing is more like it. For a long time," Comora answered.

"I will go call the police," offered the woman.

"I am the police," Sanderson said without thinking.

"Where's your badge?" asked the woman.

"I am off duty." He had to admit.

"Then you have no business here. Get away."

Sanderson wasn't going to be dissuaded by a woman's order. Besides he was there to prevent a crime. He said sternly, "You do not know this woman, Miss. She is here to kill that Indian woman. You see her standing there?"

The woman looked at Comora, then at Satya, then back at Comora and asked, "Is it true?"

Comora sharply moved her right leg, kicked Sanderson in his balls, and said, "The lying bastard."

Sanderson bent over covering his crotch area. He wanted to scream but didn't; men, in his book, took women's assaults like men. But, he did not believe in letting assaults go unpunished, men's or women's. He let his left hand hold his fiercely pulsating testicles, brought his right hand to his right pant pocket, and retrieved his gun. In a fraction of a second, he stood erect, gun pointed at Comora, and said, "You're coming with me. This is a citizen's arrest."

"The fuck it is," Comora retorted. Once more she swung her right leg toward Sanderson.

Sanderson, having anticipated something like this, moved swiftly aside letting Comora swipe the air, become unbalanced, and fall on the ground. That's when he shot her. The bullet hit her in the stomach.

He saw blood ooze out of Comora's clothes. Simultaneously, he noticed that Satya and the woman she was conversing with come running toward him and the scene of commotion he had created with his shooting. With his eyes going bleary, Sanderson didn't know what to do. He didn't have any incriminating statement from Comora on his tape recorder, so, in effect, had no case against her. To make matters worse, now he, himself, was in the frightful situation of being a criminal. Would he be charged with attempted murder? Or, even murder, if Comora were to die?

His instincts just forced him to run. He forgot his pain, got in his car, and shot out of the parking lot like someone from a cannon in a circus.

This was a circus? Right? A circus where somebody got hit in the groin and someone else got shot?

Sanderson didn't really think so. Nor did anyone else present there, he was sure.

CHAPTER FIFTY-FOUR

A FORGOTTEN DANCE

Karcher had two reasons to be happy; Schultz had been captured, and he had his job back. There was one more reason, although a bit tentative; the mole had been identified and measures had been taken to neutralize him. Still, there was some uneasiness. So, what was eating him?

He didn't know for sure, but it probably had something to do with that visit with Satya, because his mind kept going back to it. He knew that his perspective on life and feelings toward his wife had changed since visiting Satya in her home. Interesting. Satya had spent some time in his place and had made no impact on him, maybe because there she had not had any opportunity to express her views. Whatever, something new was stirring in him, and his life was beginning to destabilize, destabilize in the sense that it was not the kind of life he had ever known. A little reflection and finally he knew what was eating him. He wanted the changes that were taking place, but his personality, which he had nurtured all his life, was rebelling against them.

Nonetheless, he liked the changes, particularly the change in his perception of Carolyn. Oh, he always loved her, sure, but he never cared about her pacifist views and had been irritated at her constant bitching about how he did his job or how he handled his opponents, firmly and brutally. Not any more. Now, he found himself actually agreeing with his wife's views, to a certain extent, anyway.

He recalled the image of Satya in the picture window and the tender face of his wife as he had kissed her in the car. These two women had suffered a lot because of his ego. If he had not gone to war against the AVs, Gopal might still be alive, and Carolyn would be happy. A lot of other people would also be spared the tragedies and the resulting pain. Yes, the world probably would have still continued on its path of self destruction, but, at least, he would have not been a contributory factor. Good that he finally realized his folly. It was time to call it quits. Time to take Carolyn's advice and take to heart Satya's philosophy, and just withdraw. Leave the job, call a unilateral truce with the AVs, lay down his arms, and retire in some peaceful place with his wife.

All those lofty ideas made sense, yet he had a hard time really implementing them. It required humility, and he had little of it. So, what was he going to do?

After a little more reflection over the situation a sort of direction emerged, involving a number of things which needed to be done. He made a list.

On the top of the list: Take an early retirement. This would allow him a steady pension for the rest of his life. He wouldn't have to depend upon his children or anyone else financially, and would be able to spend his last days with Carolyn, doing mundane things and finding joy in them.

Next item: Go, visit Schultz. Tell him that he would get all the needed medical attention without any strings attached to it. Tell him also that there would not be any attacks on him from his side any more.

Another thing: Thank Belford for all that he had done so far; recaptured Schultz, caught the Robinson killers, eliminated the Martinez killers, and brought about AV's almost total defeat. Yes, the

AVs had some successes, too, but they had been neutralized by their losses. Now, they had only two more targets, Karcher, himself, and Satya. By withdrawing himself from the conflict, he might be able to bring an end to the whole insanity and save himself. And Satya? He now saw her in a new light, as a good woman who did not deserve to be devoured by a monster he had created. So what if she was a colored Asian? He needed to rise above these petty considerations and appreciate people for what they were. Along with thanking him, he must also request Belford to provide protection for Satya.

And after that: Neutralize the mole.

Finally: Tell Carolyn all about it.

The resolutions made him feel like he had been rescued from under the debris of an earthquake. He got moving.

Getting in touch with the Department of Corrections administration was a snap. He found out that he would qualify for an early retirement in just three years. He also got all the information about what he needed to do for it.

Then he took a slow walk toward Schultz's cell in ASU.

When he reached there he found that Schultz was being attended by a doctor and two nurses, and guarded by two armed officers. Of course, that was to be expected. He had, himself, ordered that Schultz, for security reasons, must be treated in his cell, and should be considered for a move to a hospital only if it was a life and death situation which could not be handled locally.

Karcher asked the doctor, "How is he doing?"

The doctor answered, "Whoever did the surgery on him while he was gone did a good job. There is still some bleeding which is a result of the trauma to the area that had been operated upon."

"Trauma?"

"Yeah. Caused most likely by his effort to hide, by being hit during his capture, and by being handled rough during transportation to the jail afterwards. He should be okay soon."

Karcher watched him dress Schultz's bleeding wounds, give him antibiotics, some pain killers, and leave along with his nurses. He also watched the guard come out of the cell and lock it. After that he dismissed the guards, "I need to talk to Mr. Schultz alone."

The guards left. Karcher came close to the cell, looked through the bars, and said, "I'm sorry all this had to happen, Mr. Schultz."

"Get the fuck away from me," retorted Schultz, as he turned on his mattress to face his uninvited visitor.

Karcher mustered enough self-control necessary for the mission and said, "I will, Mr. Schultz. But, first I need to tell you something, and I hope you will listen to it."

"Why should I? I know you want to torture-kill me before my execution. So, whatever you have to say means shit to me." Schultz contorted his face in disgust.

Karcher actually wanted to go into the cell and hit this impudent man. But that would defeat his purpose of coming here. He tightened his stomach muscles and said, "You are wrong, Mr. Schultz. I have come to tell you that no one will mistreat you ever, as long as you and I are here. I am sorry for what happened in the past. I hold no animosity toward you and the AVs any more. I will simply do my job, which includes taking care of your health needs and assuring your well being. So far as I am concerned, the war is over. You do whatever you feel like. That's all I have to say."

"I don't believe a word of it. ... You must think I am a fool."

"No, not at all. I think you are right not to believe me. But you will believe me when you see that I mean what I say." Karcher was surprised at the conciliatory tone which was not characteristic of him.

"Just go. Leave me alone and let me contemplate my next escape plan."

"You are already facing one escape charge, you want more?"

"Does it matter? Two more years tacked to my death sentence. ... Man, you must be stupid. Can't you see I have nothing to lose? If I fail again, you can tack more time, and more time, all of which is meaningless to a death row inmate. And, if I succeed? Aha! ... Man, why am I talking to jerks like you anyway?"

Yes, Karcher was offended, but he did not let it show. "You are right, you have nothing to lose. But it is my job to prevent escape. However, like I already told you, it is also my job to make sure that you are treated humanely. Time will tell that what I am saying is the truth. So, goodbye for now."

He left abruptly, did not wish to prolong this unpleasant conversation. Still, he was proud of himself for not becoming provoked by Schultz's words, and for being able to communicate to him what he needed to. Actually, it was not quite true. He was certainly provoked, but he was able to control himself from reacting violently. And, he was sure, Schultz did not get his message, not at this time anyway. But soon he would. He would.

Back in his office, Karcher picked up the phone and dialed the number for Jordan. He could not wait for his Monday meeting with him. This was urgent. When the phone was answered he gave a brief order, "Starting immediately, Schultz must be treated like any other inmate. No special treatment. You know what I mean. ... I will see you Monday."

Right after that he called Belford. He took a little time to tell him how grateful he was for all his help and how good it felt to know that his side was winning the war with the AVs. When he was done, he did not get the expected 'thank you.' What he got actually deflated his enthusiasm, "No need to get excited. Sure, sure, we got Schultz back. So, that's our gain, but not their loss. How could you lose something which you didn't have? Yeah, yeah, we got the Robinson murderers and they lost two, two, warriors. Everyone knows, in a war there are casualties. But, it doesn't mean the war is lost. In fact, the AVs are winning. They accomplished most everything, everything they set out to accomplish."

"Not really. I am still alive."

"So, they are not done yet. They might just be waiting, waiting for a right moment."

"Maybe. But, I am not worried about myself any more. I have decided to take an early retirement and get out of this madness. Once I am out of sight, they will forget about me."

"Maybe, maybe not. Still, a good idea."

"But there is someone else who needs to be protected, and I need your help."

"Who, who?"

"Satya. You know Satya?"

"Who doesn't?"

"Well, she blew away two of their warriors. A nasty blow to their pride. I think they will take revenge."

"It has been some time, and they haven't done anything."

"They have been busy killing others. Now, all that is left is me. So they can add one more target to their list."

"What do you want, want me to do?"

"Just keep an eye on her and catch the attacker. That's all."

"You know what you're asking? A round-the-clock protection for a private citizen. Against, against the state laws. She should hire her own bodyguard."

"But, she is not asking for protection, I am. If you watch her, who knows, you might catch another fish, a big one. Look at it as containing the AVs or as a continuation of war against the bastards."

"You really want it, don't you?"

"Yes."

"All right, all right. I will do it as a favor. But, for how long? It can't be forever."

"As long as you can, or until you catch someone in the process, and Satya appears safe."

"I think this is a losing proposition. They will get her if they want to get her. And they can wait, wait for a long time, too."

"Just because it looks hopeless doesn't mean it should not be done. We should do it, because this is a right thing to do."

"No convincing needed. I already agreed. Okay, okay?"

He had to wait until Monday to work on the mole problem. Jordan came on the appointed time.

Once the courtesies and preliminaries were complete, Jordan summarized all the happenings involving Ibarra.

Karcher said, "None of this makes any sense. If Ibarra is working for the AVs, why would Haney's wife mention his name so casually for the prison monitor to hear? Don't the AVs protect their men? Then, if he is working for the AVs, how could Cuervos accept him in their ranks?"

"I don't know either, sir. But, one thing I'm sure of. Rumors may not be entirely correct, but there is always a germ of truth in them."

"True. But we have rumors which contradict each other."

"At the face only. I have a feeling, sir, that Ibarra does have some connection with the AVs and has somehow fooled the Cuervos into believing that he is a double agent and committed to the Hispanic, not the white cause."

"Supposing he is working for the AV, why would he then punish Schultz the way he did?"

"Just to throw off any suspicion from him."

"Then he could have faked it. He didn't have to hurt him as seriously as he did."

"Of course, part of their plan, as I see it. In order for Ibarra to be convincing to us, he had to do a good job. Schultz must have known it and endured. We know he never filed any complaints. I think it was part of Schultz's escape plan. His injuries had to be substantial, but not life threatening, to justify going to the hospital from where his escape was relatively easy."

"My God! Ibarra could be the AV mole we have been looking for. Who would have thought? Do you think he had a hand in the Martinez murder?"

"It's possible. He might have removed Sandoval's schedule to guard Mr. Martinez's house from his mail box and informed the AVs about it. After that the AVs must have impersonated me and made sure that Mr. Martinez's residence remained unguarded long enough for them to do their job."

"Okay. Then how do you explain Emily's behavior?"

"She may just have made a silly mistake in mentioning Ibarra to her husband, for which she might have to pay a dear price. Seems like neither Haneys really knows Ibarra, because Emily referred to him as 'an officer Ibarra' as if not certain as to who he was, and Haney said that he did not know any such person. It further goes to show that Ibarra's identity as a mole has been well guarded by the AVs."

"What if we are wrong in our speculation and take unwarranted action against a faithful employee?"

"It doesn't hurt to take safety precautions. We can't punish Ibarra without evidence, but we can surely neutralize him."

"How?"

"Move him out of ASU. ... Sir, there is an additional reason Ibarra should be moved. He was responsible for Schultz's escape. Now that Schultz is back in ASU, and faces additional escape charges, Ibarra needs to be kept away from him, to avoid any other debacle."

Karcher okayed Ibarra's transfer to the minimum custody unit.

For once, Karcher felt relaxed and peaceful.

Immediately after that, he called Carolyn on the phone and intimated to her all that he had done and why. It was important to him that Carolyn should feel relaxed and peaceful too.

He heard Carolyn sob in the phone and say, "Thank you. ... I love you."

He got up from his chair, took a couple of steps forward, then one to a side, the other following it, then another step forward. Was he dancing? When was the last time he had danced? A long, very long time ago.

This weekend he would go dancing. With his wife.

CHAPTER FIFTY-FIVE

THE OTHER WOMAN

THE QUIET OF the night was disturbed by the gun shot, and so were the hearts of three women in the Centurion parking lot. Satya felt her heart pounding furiously. She turned toward the source of the disturbance and noticed a man driving away from there and Comora on the ground. She rushed toward Comora abandoning her conversation, followed by the woman she was talking with.

Things happened quickly. Satya bent down, held Comora's head and said, "She is breathing, thank God. But she is unconscious, I think."

At that point, Satya saw the woman Comora was talking with, run into the building. To dial 911? Looking around, she found the woman she had been chatting with standing beside her, sobbing with tears running down her cheeks. What a horrible ending to a peaceful evening!

Satya saw the woman who had run into the building came back in less than a couple of minutes and heard her say, "The ambulance and the police are on their way."

Satya and the other two women followed the ambulance to the hospital, where they were allowed to sit in the lobby and wait for any announcement or news from the hospital staff about the unconscious and injured woman. While waiting, Satya turned to the woman who had been with Comora and asked, "You know what happened?"

She narrated what she had seen and heard, and then asked, "Why would the policeman think that Cora was there to kill you?"

"I don't know. I don't know Cora. She has been coming to our group for what, two weeks, three?"

"This was her third week, as I recall."

"She has been quiet and shown no hostility toward anyone. I can't imagine her trying to harm me."

"I can't either. But, there's some secret Cora is carrying we don't know anything about."

"We are not supposed to know. This is a therapy group."

"I understand, but she is one of us. What affects her affects us. Right?"

"True. That's why we are here, to wish her well, and do whatever we can to help her."

They received no request for any help from anyone. Hours passed, midnight came and went. Satya and her companions looked weary, with droopy eyes and slumped posture. Finally, a man in a long white coat, apparently a physician, emerged from behind closed double doors, came straight to the waiting women, and asked, "Did you ladies come with Ms. Comora?"

The women looked at each other confused and with inquiring glances. The physician also appeared perplexed and said, "The receptionist told me that you came with the ambulance and have been waiting for news."

Satya spoke, "Yes. But we don't know any Comora."

"Why don't you come with me. Let's see if we are talking about the same person."

As all three women got up to follow him, he said, "No. Just one of you. As it is, I am bending the rule. No one other than the immediate family is allowed with the patient, not at this time."

Satya, having spoken with the physician first, automatically became the leader of the group and followed the physician, while the other two women retreated back to their chairs.

As they went past the double doors, the physician said, "I am Dr. Harris, on duty in emergency."

Satya, feeling she had to say something in response, said, "I'm Satya."

"Nice to meet you."

They walked in silence for a minute or so and entered an intensive care room. There, in a bed, lay a still body hooked to all kinds of life support devices. The doctor pointed to the body and asked, "Do you recognize her? Is that the woman you followed?"

"Yes," Satya said, "She is a member of our 'Widows of Violence' therapy group. We didn't know her last name."

"Of course, that explains the confusion. ... Ironic, isn't it, that she should meet with violence herself? ... Anyway, the ID on her person says she is Comora, Christi Comora."

"Christi? We know her as Cora. I guess she did not want us to know her real name. You know, in our group we respect individual privacy."

"All right, then we are talking about the same person. You may go and tell your friends that Ms. Comora is out of danger. She had a bullet lodged in her intestines. We were able to get it out. She is still under sedation. You may be able to visit and talk with her after 12 to 15 hours. Better call before you come. It's hard to predict the rate of progress."

"I understand." Satya went back to her companions and gave them the happy news.

Although pleased to hear that Comora was out of danger, the woman who had called 911 appeared dissatisfied with Satya's explanation of why Comora did not tell the group her real first name and said, "There's more to it than meets the eye. We all protect our identities. That's why we use our first names only. She didn't have to make one up. Then you see a man claiming to be a policeman accuse her of trying to kill you, you Satya, and she attacks him, and he shoots her. I bet there's some mystery there."

"I don't want to speculate anything. Let's go home, get some rest. Tomorrow, maybe we can visit her."

At that the other companion said, "And find out what the truth is?"

"I don't think so. You do what you think is right, but I won't ask her to reveal her secrets. We have to respect individual privacy."

This could have been the topic of a lengthy argument, but the women were tired. They left the hospital carrying their thoughts with them.

Even though, in front of the other two women, she had adopted an air of indifference toward Comora's attempt at hiding her identity, Satya was also uncomfortable with it. As she lay in bed, sleep eluded her and she wondered if Comora, in fact, was there to kill her. She kept asking herself that question, and the answer kept coming without hesitation, "No."

Satya knew why she was getting this answer. Comora had been coming to the group for three weeks, and if she really wanted to kill her there was plenty of opportunity for it. But, if there was nothing to it, why would the policeman accuse her of this horrible crime and then get into a fight with her jeopardizing his career?

Although Satya was not worried by the thought of death, she had no death wish either. So, she determined to find the truth, rejecting all the claims about not asking Comora to reveal her secrets and respecting individual privacy. With this determination she was able to sleep.

The next day Satya was able to visit Comora, not in intensive care as she had expected, but in a semiprivate patient room. She was happy for her visit but also concerned about what she might find out.

Comora looked pale and drained of spirit but was able to sport a faint smile and welcome Satya with a simple, "Hi."

"How you doing?" Satya asked ritualistically. She wanted to ask all kinds of questions but refrained from it, not knowing where and how to start.

Comora made an opening, "Okay. ... You wondering what happened?"

"Yes."

"Well, Sanderson..."

"Sanderson?" Satya interrupted. She recalled him as the policeman who was investigating her husband's murder.

"Yeah. You know him?"

"He came to talk to me after my husband was killed."

"I see." Comora was silent for a while, maybe gathering her energy, maybe figuring out what to say next. In the end, she said in a gravelly voice, "No matter what Sanderson says, I don't want to kill you. I came to the group because my psychologist asked me to."

"Why did you hide your name, why did he shoot you?" The gate was opened by Comora, Satya just walked in.

"Name? ... It would have been uncomfortable for both you and me."

"How? I don't know you."

"I thought you knew my name, if not my face."

"No I don't. Should I?"

"Perhaps. I was married to, you know..."

The revelation sunk her into the ground. It was one thing not to know anything about the other woman, it was something totally different to be face-to-face with her. As she was sinking deeper into the imaginary ground, it occurred to her that Comora really was not the proverbial 'other woman'. She was her husband's ex-wife. So what, she seemed like the other woman. Satya never knew that she had jealousy in her. She was so confused that she just hung her head.

"Sorry. Didn't mean to shock you."

Okay, so the news only stunned her. Now, she could deal with more shocking news. "And the shooting?" Satya asked boldly.

"Sanderson thinks I was a party to the Gopal murder, and now I'm plotting to kill you. Angry at his lie, I kicked him and he shot me."

"But shooting? So drastic."

"Only he knows why he did it. He is in jail now."

"How do you know?"

"The police came to talk to me on account of the shooting. I told them who he was. They said they were going to arrest him. I guess they are also investigating me."

"Why?"

"Because of his allegation that I planned to hurt you. I'm sure they will be talking to all the girls who were present when I was shot."

The answers were so straightforward that Satya believed Comora. The mystery was solved, if there ever was a mystery. But the heartache would not go away. She had been in the same room with 'the other woman' week after week. She sat silent, wondering, wondering.

Comora spoke again, "The group has helped me a lot. I have released Gopal from my life. But, if it will help you, I will stop coming to the group. Maybe find another."

Satya felt guilty. Why should Comora have to give up her source of self-improvement because of Satya's own insecurity? Besides, Satya was creating insecurity out of nothing. Comora was not stealing anything from her. Gopal was gone, and with him were gone all his past associations. She needed to let go of Gopal and go on with her life. "No," she said, "No one needs to leave the group on account of me. I am not the group. I don't own it. I am there to help myself, too. We are together in it. We will have to find ways to help each other."

Where did these words come from? Satya did not know. But they made her feel calm. Once more, Comora was what she originally was, a member of 'Widows of Violence'. Nothing else.

Her reverie was broken by Comora, "I know. I need it. You see, I have not been able to embrace nonviolence. Not yet. I did hit Sanderson and sent him to jail. Maybe one day I will get over my vindictiveness also. I have a long way to go."

At this point Satya wanted to touch Comora. They both had lost something and they were both learning to let it go. For different reasons though. Comora suddenly changed from 'the other woman' to 'a sister'. Satya felt better, a lot better, in her mind and in her heart. But she still could not touch Comora. Maybe one day not only would she be able to touch her but also to embrace her.

As she drove home with the radio on to an easy listening station, she felt very comfortable. The heaviness of the heart and the strain on the body were gone. Comora would get well and come back to the group. She would be able to accept her as a fellow member and not as an adversary. Sanderson would learn that it was not a good thing to shoot someone. She wished there were some other way of teaching him this lesson rather than punishment.

Her mind was distracted when the music changed to the five-minute news, which came on with regularity, every hour. Actually, it was a specific item which attracted her attention to it, "A high ranking police officer, Troy Sanderson, shot himself in the head when the police went to his residence to arrest him for shooting a woman, Christi Comora, last night in the Centurion parking lot. Mr. Sanderson was pronounced dead on the scene. Ms. Comora, when interviewed by the police earlier today, had told the police that Mr. Sanderson had falsely accused her of planning to kill Mrs. Satya Gopal and had harassed her for quite some time. She had kicked him in anger, and he had responded by shooting her. The police examined the scene of the crime, searched Ms. Comora's personal belongings and her home, and found nothing to support Mr. Sanderson's allegations. However, the police still plan to interview three other women who were present at the crime scene."

A sad ending to a sad story. Satya turned off the radio and drove like a robot.

All of a sudden, it occurred to her that someone was following her in a metallic blue Chevrolet Monte Carlo. She had seen this car before, weaving in and out of traffic, for miles on end. It was the same pattern again. Whoever was following her did not seem to be experienced in this task, otherwise she would have not been able to spot the tail. Experienced or not, a tail could not be welcome. Her heart started to flutter like a Mexican jumping bean. Once she became aware of this tail, she began watching her rearview and side-view mirrors more often and realized that there was another car, a white nondescript sedan, behind her, only it appeared to be more careful.

'Would there ever be an end to this tragic drama?' she wondered.

CHAPTER FIFTY-SIX

INSANITY OF SANITY

Haney had been procrastinating. Maybe he did not want to do his job. After all he had no experience in killing anyone. But, he had accepted the assignment and he had to do it. Maybe he needed some prodding.

He got it during one of his fishing trips with Goodwin. These trips had proven to be the best way to plan their war maneuvers secretly.

Goodwin started, "How long are you going to wait?"

Haney hedged, "I don't know how to do it safely. I mean without bringing the AV into focus."

"You're the brains. Come up with something."

"I'll try."

The prod worked. Haney got busy.

To start with, he decided to go after one target at a time, first the high profile Satya, then the no profile Bottillo.

He started with some Satya watching to get a feel of her movements so that he could pick the best opportunity. Not wanting to be picked out easily as a recently released AV, he decided to change his appearance and behavior. So, now he wore closely cropped hair, a bushy mustache, and a one-inch beard. He darkened his face and hands with tanning material, and wore an expression which was devoid of any human emotion. For clothing, he chose light blue Levi's, a checkered flannel shirt, and Adidas walking shoes.

Clumsily, he started following Satya in a metallic blue Chevrolet, Monte Carlo, borrowed from the AV garage. Most of Satya's outings turned out to be random, grocery shopping, pumping gas in the car, going to different malls, visiting the library, meandering on the university campus from the student union to the planetarium to something else. Hard to use them for planning. After three weeks of watching, he found that there was one thing, however, which she did consistently: going to a building 'Centurion' once a week, every Thursday night from seven to eight. She came out of the building usually with a few other women, six mostly, sometimes four or five, other times even seven. Each would drive off in a different direction. Always someone was last to leave, sometimes it was Satya.

Haney did not know what Satya did in the Centurion, and he had no interest in finding out. That knowledge was totally useless for his goal. Besides, to get that information he would have to go inside the building. That meant running into someone, maybe even Satya herself, and exposing himself which would be tantamount to leaving a clue, virtually inviting his arrest. He had no intention of doing something that foolish. He wanted Satya alone with no place to hide and no place to run to.

He thought of getting into her car while she was in the building, hiding in the back seat, and surprising her from behind after she had driven away and was on a lonely stretch of road. The only problem was that her car seemed to be alarmed. He would have to wait until she had opened the car door. Then he would point his gun at her, make her move over to the passenger seat, get in the driver's seat himself, and take control of the steering wheel. After that he would go to one of the AV secret places and do his thing. This amounted to kidnapping, which had already been discarded by Goodwin as being too risky.

What now? The only thing he could think of was getting Satya alone in some secluded spot and quickly killing her. For this, he needed to wait for her in the Centurion parking lot and follow her until she was out of town cruising through the dead spaces so far as humans were concerned. But why? A bright man like him doing a stupid thing like waiting for his victim in a place where people breathed. Maybe when you did something out of character, your mind refused to cooperate. Still, he was able to see his folly and decided to modify the plan.

Instead of going to the Centurion parking lot this one Thursday, he drove within two miles of Satya's home, hid his car behind some trees beside the road, and sat in it waiting. He did not expect anyone on that road who might wonder about him, sitting alone in a car for a long time, doing nothing. He felt safe and secure.

Only after a little over half an hour he saw Satya's car approaching. Rather slow for a performance car. Maybe because of the dirt road. This gave Haney a better opportunity to intercept her. When she was only about fifty feet away from him, he started his engine, pulled out of his hiding place, tires squealing, and slammed his brakes right in front of her. He heard Satya's brakes screeching and saw her car stopping just inches away from his.

Haney quickly got out of his car, approached Satya, pointed his gun at her head, and ordered, "Out."

Satya came out. She looked surprised, a little scared, but outwardly calm. "What it's about?" she asked. "You want money? I will give you all I have."

"I don't want your money. I want you for killing my colleagues."

"You want to kill me?" A little tremor in her voice.

"Yes."

What he saw in response surprised him. Satya sat down cross legged on the dirt road, put her forearms in her lap, closed her eyes, and assumed a posture which pronounced, 'Do it.'

"What is this? I came to kill an enemy." Haney was bewildered.

"I am not your enemy." Satya opened her eyes, fixed them on Haney's face, and said, "I'm sorry I killed your friends. To prevent something like that from happening again, I don't carry a gun or even keep one in the house."

Haney felt like something exploded in his head. He dropped his gun, plopped down beside Satya, held his head in his hands, and mumbled, "I can't do this."

Just then he saw a nondescript white sedan appear and stop in front of him and Satya. Two men in business suits jumped out, guns drawn, ordering him, "Police. Lie face down, hands stretched away from the body."

It was anticlimactic after that. Haney put up no resistance and even extended his hands to be cuffed.

One policeman asked Satya, "You okay ma'm?"

Satya said in a shaky voice, "Yes." After a moment's hesitation, she asked, "Have you been following me?"

"Protecting you. The Department felt you might be harmed. We were right."

As he was led to the police car, Haney turned his head toward Satya and Said, "I probably will be executed for this by the AVs, if not by the state. But somehow I feel I will die peacefully."

He got no response. But, he overheard one of the police officers asking Satya, "You need some help? Need to go to the hospital?"

"No. I'm okay. Thank you."

"We will escort you to your home then."

Haney watched Satya get in her car and drive toward her home slowly. 'What is she thinking?' he wondered.

At the police station, Haney gave his statement, told all that he knew, told all that he did.

The policeman taking notes said, "You mean you went to all this trouble to kill the woman and then could not? I don't believe you. The AVs don't have that kind of conscience. There must be another reason. Also, it does not make any sense that Satya didn't resist and just waited to be executed. I'm gonna check all that out. ... And, what's this about your assignment to kill Bottillo? You certainly won't be able to do that."

"I don't want to. Someone else, most likely, will be given the task. Now that you know the threat to his life, perhaps you can do something about it."

"This is speculative. Besides, we are not personal body guards. The most we can do is inform Bottillo what you told us."

"Even that will be helpful." Still, he was not sure the police would do what they said they would. And, even if they did, he was not sure it would have the impact that was needed. He must find some other way, a more effective way, to warn Bottillo about what the AVs had in store for him.

He was resigned to staying in jail for a while, going to trial, confessing his guilt, going to prison, and getting killed by someone. With this kind of future promised for him, he felt no need to act like an AV any more.

After a day and a half in jail, Haney was visited by the same policeman who had arrested him. The policeman said, "We talked with Mrs. Gopal. She corroborated your story, the later part she was witness to. I'll be damned. Such things don't happen in real life."

Haney said nothing.

In the coming days he had access to the newspapers and could see from the reports that the press, just like the police, had a hard time swallowing the story of the two actors in this weird drama. They practiced their skill at sarcasm, when they wrote, "And, of course, Satya was willing to die calmly, and Haney was not willing to kill. Can you believe this? Can anyone? Why don't the police try to get the truth?"

Haney, in spite of his predicament, had to chuckle at the statement of one editor, "Both are nuts."

CHAPTER FIFTY-SEVEN

NOW IT'S PERSONAL

IBARRA KNEW HE was a doomed man. He blamed Schultz for it. Sure, Schultz started it all, but he, Ibarra, wasn't entirely blameless. After all, he allowed the AVs to snare him in their web. While he was punishing Schultz, he felt in control of the situation, even filled with arrogant ecstasy of having an upper hand in his fight with the mighty AVs. His mood began to change after Martinez and his family were killed. He felt depressed at the loss of his mentor. Then, after Schultz escaped, he began to feel afraid of the enemy and its power. Still, he thought he would just put all the past conflicts behind him and go on with his life, like a sail boat on a placid lake. That was not to happen. When he was accused, or at least suspected, of being an AV mole, and when two hispanic gangs almost came to blows on account of him, the world around him began to collapse. He got the jolt of a high magnitude earthquake, when he learned from the grapevine that he would be transferred to a minimum custody unit, away from the relative safety of ASU, where he would be killed by the AVs who considered him their enemy for his treatment of Schultz, or by Huracans who considered him to be a traitor.

He did toy with the idea of resigning and running away to a place where no one knew him, but discarded it quickly. Both the AV and Huracan gangs had long reaches, and he could not consider himself safe anywhere.

So, he must face the inevitable death. Too bad it would arrive so soon, even before he had a chance to get married and have a family. Well, he would accept the reality, but not on someone else's terms. The gangs could decide that he must die, but they could not dictate how. The 'how' was in his hands. At this juncture, he began planning what he would do. He was sure he had a few weeks, which was what normally took to effect a transfer in the prison bureaucracy. Irrespective of the amount of time he had, he must accomplish his task soon, so that it was surely done before he was moved out of ASU. Once it was done, the Huracans would never doubt his loyalty to his race. And, everyone would know that he was no AV plant. He would give Schultz his best medicine. It was personal now.

It was hard for him to work on his plan while attending to his duties in the prison. He needed to dissociate himself from the place, particularly from Schultz to be able to think clearly about what to do. Finally, he decided to take his two-week vacation for this purpose, the vacation which he would not be able to enjoy after he was killed.

During his time off, he was able to finalize his plan after discarding many scenarios. Actually, he got it done the first week and savored the imaginary fruits of anticipated accomplishment in the second week. What he decided was more like a crash operation, a bravado spectacular, a devil-may-care gesture. He chose a Sunday after his vacation for the implementation of his plan, when there would be fewer staff to interfere.

That day, he picked up his keys from the key room, a routine. After that he was expected to go to the briefing room, something required of every guard before going on the yard. Instead, he went straight to the area in which Schultz was housed, taking slow, calculated steps.

He opened Schultz's cell door quietly. It must have not been quiet enough, because Schultz stirred in his mattress and looked toward the entrance.

Ibarra pounced on him. He didn't care that the video cameras were recording every move he made. In the past, these cameras were turned off, and although the staff knew what was going on they had no evidence on which to base any allegations which they might have wished to make. This day Ibarra wanted them to have evidence, so that everyone would know what he did. Facing certain death, he had nothing to lose, but a lot of accolades to gain from a lot of people, including prison administration.

Schultz moved his arms to fend off the attack and yelled, "He lied to me. He said no one will hurt me."

Ibarra kicked him in the face hard with his steel-toe boot and said, "Who said that?"

"The fucking Warden. Who else?" A gash under his right eye had begun to bleed.

Ibarra was in a trancelike state, focused on doing his job well and quickly before other staff came and intervened. Without saying anything, he connected his boot with the spot in the stomach which had recently been operated upon and had not fully healed. Schultz screamed, put his hands on his stomach to protect it, and tried to sit up.

This time Ibarra kicked him in the chest, and Schultz fell backward and off the mattress on the concrete floor. Ibarra watched Schultz's dissolution with relish. Schultz's ribs broke, one sticking out of his chest cavity. His intestines tore apart and hung out. He defecated and urinated involuntarily. Blood poured out of his intestinal area like rain water through spouts. Ibarra then stomped first on Schultz's right elbow, then on his left, and rendered both hands useless. Schultz lifted his legs to kick, which only made Ibarra direct his attention to the lower part of his body. He destroyed Schultz's leg movements by breaking his tibias, one at a time, by pressing down hard on the thigh by his foot and lifting up the leg so far back as to effect a crack.

All this happened in less than a minute, and Ibarra could hear commotion and footsteps in the corridors. The video monitoring staff must have seen what he was doing and alerted security. But, security, both incoming and outgoing, must have been in the briefing room, and slow to respond. Nonetheless, it was necessary for Ibarra to speed up.

He sat on Schultz's chest, grabbed his ears, pulled his head up, and then smashed it down with great force on the hard surface, cracking his skull like a squashed watermelon. Schultz's eyes popped out, and blood started to ooze out of his head, mouth, and nose. Ibarra repeated this action once more, widening the fissure in the head and exposing the brain.

Schultz's mouth gaped open with the tongue hanging out of one side. His eyes stopped blinking and his chest stopped heaving.

Ibarra believed that Schultz was dead. He stood back and viewed his art work. It looked beautiful to him. Then his knees gave out. He buckled under them and fell on the floor made slippery with Schultz's blood.

Just then several guards barged into the cell and grabbed Ibarra.

"What are you doing?" asked one guard.

Ibarra said nothing. His eyes were glazed and fixed on the front wall.

Another guard shook him and got no physical or verbal response. So, he gave an order to no one in particular, "Go, call the Health Unit. Ask for an ambulance. And someone, secure Ibarra."

One guard ran to a nearby phone and one other guard put handcuffs on Ibarra's limp wrists.

About five minutes later, an ambulance took Schultz to the Health unit, and a prison inmate transportation vehicle took Ibarra to the police station.

Ibarra sat motionless, as the police proceeded to interview him after taking the statement of the prison guard. The interview didn't go anywhere, it didn't even start, because Ibarra would not respond to any questions. He sat in a rickety resin chair, blankly looking at the wall. After about five minutes of futile attempt at eliciting any response from their prisoner, one of the officers said, "He is in shock."

Another officer asked incredulously, "Shock? He almost killed the prisoner."

"Shock, yes. In combat soldiers often go into shock after killing enemies. I have seen it in Vietnam."

"Let's leave him alone for a day or so and then see if we can get him to talk."

Ibarra heard the words but did not understand what they meant.

The police officers lifted him by his arms and led him to a detention cell. Ibarra walked like a robot. He had no clue as to where he was and what he was doing.

CHAPTER FIFTY-EIGHT

GOOD NEWS, BAD NEWS, AND SHIT

To Karcher it was the often repeated, ironic 'good news, bad news' situation, but with a twist.

The good news was that Schultz was badly hurt and might die.

And, the bad news was that Schultz was badly hurt and he might die.

It was good for what happened to Schultz, and the whole thing would be blamed on a wayward staff. He remembered that at one time he had declared, 'Worse fate than death awaits him', but he had no idea what it would be like. Now he knew. He was aghast at what Ibarra had done and a bit in awe of him for his bravery and resoluteness. He was also pleased with him. Surely the leader would be gone or at least disabled. It was a good thing. During his stint in Vietnam, he had learned a basic principle of military psychology; eliminate the commander, and the troops will be demoralized and easily defeated. Of course, this was not always the case. Sometimes, there was the martyr syndrome; the fallen commander would become a big inspiration for his troops to fight on. So, the AVs might fight on, but they would not have the same fire they did before. Maybe their desire to do him in would also fade. Why didn't he think of it earlier when he wanted Schultz to suffer and not die? He knew the answer. At that time he was being vindictive and had not realized that it would start a war. If he had eliminated Schultz or waited for him to be executed, he would have avoided all the mayhem that ensued. Well, it was too late to worry about that. And it was never too late to get his shit together. As these thoughts passed through his mind, he remembered what he had decided only a few weeks ago, and what he had decided was in total contradiction to what he was thinking now. What happened to his resolve of not getting into conflicts any more, letting Schultz be, and retreating to a safe, peaceful place with his wife as soon as possible? No, it was still there, only he could not suppress the elation that bubbled over at the news of his enemy's predicament. Whatever, Ibarra deserved a Medal of Honor. But why did Ibarra do what he did? Why did he put his life on line? Could it be that Ibarra hated the AVs as much as he did? Wrong question. Karcher did not hate the AVs. He agreed with their philosophy, just found them in an adversarial position. Ibarra probably did hate them. Now, there was no doubt in his mind that Ibarra was not the AV mole he had been suspected of being. Then who was the mole and where was he? This was not the time to worry about that. This was the time for celebration of a major victory.

It was bad for what happened to Schultz because it might anger the AV top brass, bringing about more severe retaliation, maybe against him. They would not know that he had decided to become non-punitive toward Schultz. Not only decided, but actually told Schultz about it and instructed Jordan to implement his decision. This meant that nothing had changed really, that he still was a target and might get hit before he could retire.

Before he was through analyzing his 'good news, bad news', more news came in. A doctor from the Health Unit called him on the phone, "Schultz needs to go to the hospital. We are not equipped to treat severe brain injuries, the cracked rib cage, broken arms and legs, not to mention damaged intestines."

"But, what's his prognosis? In your opinion."

"Not good. If he doesn't die during treatment, he will be in a coma for the rest of his life. I think."

"In that case he would never be executed." 'In that case he would forever remain a threat to my life,' Karcher thought simultaneously.

"Most likely," answered the doctor.

"All right. Send him to the hospital."

As soon as he put down the phone, it rang again. This time it was Belford on the other end, "Your staff is in our custody. Do you know, know what it means?"

"Yeah. It means, he will get convicted, end up in the prison, and the inmates will eat him up, simply because he was a guard."

"And, and the AVs?"

"They, too, will quarter him for what he did to their leader."

"You, you like that?"

"No, of course not. He is our hero. But, what can I do? He committed a crime. And it's on tape."

"Well, I, I have an idea."

"I am all ears."

"He is in shock, shock. How about we send him to a psychiatric ward. A judge, judge, would have to approve that. But I don't think that would be a problem considering the condition he is in. He would be safe there. In due course he might, might get well. By that time the commotion would die down, and he might just get away with a slap, slap on the wrist."

"Sounds like a good plan."

"Just wanted to talk, talk it over with you before doing anything about it."

"Thank you."

Right after that his secretary walked in and whispered, "Albert Schultz, you know Schultz's brother, he is on line one. Sounds very agitated and insists on talking with you."

"Put him through. I don't want to look like an uncaring bureaucrat. It would be a disaster if he went public."

"All right, sir." The secretary left.

Within a couple seconds he saw the light on line one flashing and picked up the phone, "Mr. Schultz, thank you for calling. I was going to contact you myself. I am sorry, very sorry, about your brother."

"You fucking bastard. You killed my brother."

Why did he expect cordiality from an aggrieved brother? Still, he told himself, 'Handle it nicely, don't turn it into a public relations nightmare.'

So he said politely, "Mr. Schultz, I know how you feel. But it was one of our staff who had gone mad. He is in police custody. I am sure you know that. Justice will be done, I assure you. And your brother will get the best treatment available."

"The fuck he will."

Karcher heard the receiver being slammed down hard making his ear drum and the tiny bones inside vibrate furiously. 'What will Albert Schultz do?' he wondered.

He got a hint of it. There was furious rumbling in the air, 'vroom, vroom' sound of numerous motorcycles on the street just outside his office. What was going on? He parted the curtains of his window facing the public street at a distance and saw many bikers, maybe hundreds, driving past the prison gate at a slow speed, while revving up their engines. The riders balanced their vehicles by one hand and raised the other in a fist, their leather jackets emblazoned with bold bright silver letters 'ARYAN VISION'. It was clearly an act of defiance against the prison authority and, at the same time, an act of solidarity with their mutilated leader. Clearly, ominous dark clouds were on the horizon.

Karcher closed the window and threw himself in his chair. He took deep breaths and tried to calm his furiously beating heart.

He had barely composed himself when he got a call from his Chief of Security, "Sir, the AVs are stirring. All over the prison, I'm told. I expect a major riot. What do you suggest we do?"

Karcher barked an order, "Lock down the whole prison, station armed guards on the catwalk, and alert all tower guards to look out for any disturbance. Shoot to kill if any inmate gets out of line."

"Yes, sir."

'What is happening to me?' asked Karcher. 'I wanted to get away from it all, and here I am embroiled in the shit up to my eyeballs. God, what's wrong with me?' It was like he was propelled by a mysterious and evil force, which was hidden and over which he had no control.

Karcher went limp in his chair, with his elbows on the desk, hands holding his head.

After that meeting with Satya, he had wanted to be a loving and kind man, just wanted to spend his last years in peace and quiet with his wife. Instead, he was sabotaging everything that could have made that possible. All the sunshine that he had been dreaming of had been replaced by the thundering clouds threatening to drown his existence. Yes, and this had been brought about by what? By the things he had done, he himself: Feeling giddy at Schultz's suffering, protecting Ibarra, lying to Albert Schultz, and lining up his troops to battle the AV inmates. Was he just destined to die an ignoble death and drag his wife down with him? Was he an evil wolf fooling himself into thinking that he could be a sheep?

Why was everything crumbling down around him all of a sudden? All of a sudden? It had been crumbling down for a long time.

CHAPTER FIFTY-NINE

DREAMING OF DREAMS

Haney sat in jail sleepless through the night, thinking about his life and what he had done with it; subjecting it to an ideal which had robbed him of his profession, his dignity, his wife's embrace, and almost his life. He also thought about what lay ahead, the trial. It would be a formality. He would plead guilty and get a long sentence for attempted murder, what with it being his second conviction within a very short time after his release. That was all right with him. What was not all right was the certainty of the AV wrath. He did not know the nature of it, but was sure it would be cruel and brutal. He had betrayed his organization. It was treason, and it would have to be paid for with his blood drawn laboriously. Haney did not want that. He was not going to allow that to happen. Believing that he was smarter than anyone in the entire organization, he was sure to find a way to survive and leave this whole bullshit behind. And he did come up with an idea. It required the help of his wife and his lawyer. He anxiously waited for the streaks of light to penetrate the darkness of his cell. Sometime before the light faded, his wife would come to visit him and he would be able to discuss his plan with her.

In the afternoon his wish was fulfilled. The guard came to fetch him to meet his visitor, Emily, his wife.

This meeting was not private.

The visitation area had a string of 12 booths, each divided in the middle by plexiglas. Each side of the plexiglas had a small shelf wide enough to rest a hand or an elbow, a phone hanging on the side partition, and a chair. The arrangement prevented any physical contact between the inmate and his visitor, but allowed them to see each other, put their hands and their lips on the plexiglas, and pretend they were touching and kissing each other. It also allowed them to talk using the phone.

Visitation was limited to 15 minutes.

Emily was teary eyed, and Haney was somber.

"We had so little time together," moaned Emily.

"I know, but this is the last time," Haney answered in a consoling way.

"How?" Emily questioned.

"You see, I am an intelligent man, but I have been acting like a fool. It is one thing to believe in white supremacy, it is another to try to kill everyone who is not white or whom you don't like for whatever stupid reason. You can't do it, not possible, not even sensible."

"You sound bitter."

"You bet I am. Let me tell you something. That day when I saw that woman sitting on the ground awaiting execution, calmly, something stirred in me. It seemed like she was living while facing death, and I was like a breathing corpse. She was living by her convictions, and I was following someone else's ideology. You know what I am saying."

"Yeah. So, you leaving the organization?"

"I don't have to. They will kill me."

"This is the end? Is this what you are saying?"

"No. I'll go away, with you, to some faraway place where no one knows us. We will change our names and appearances, and live out our lives in peace."

"Aren't you dreaming dreams? You think you will get out, alive? Or, even I? Being your wife they see me as an enemy, too, I am sure."

"Yes, I will get out, and with the help of the court. And my lawyer. Call him and ask him to come and see me tonight, if possible, or certainly by tomorrow. And, you should divorce me to let the AVs think that you don't want to have anything to do with someone who let the organization down. Then, sell the house and move away to set up a new dig for ourselves. Sell the house to a real estate company so the AVs would not know that I am escaping. Sell it below market value, if needed. That's the price you will have to pay for getting away from this place quickly and secretly."

"Aren't you worried that the AVs will get wind of your plan?"

"No. The guards here listen to everything, but react to security threats only. They couldn't care less about inmates' personal problems."

"But, there could be AVs among the guards."

"Well, nothing is foolproof. Still, I think my plan will work even with the AVs knowing about it, because I plan to act before they can react. You will see."

"All right, I trust you. I will do what you want me to do while you do your bit."

At that Haney became emotional. In a choking voice he said, "I love you. You are so supportive."

"I love you, too. We will weather this storm together. ... Anything else you want me to do?"

"Yeah. Find some way to warn Bottillo about the AV threat. Even though I told the police about it, I am not sure they will treat it with the urgency it deserves. And, even if they do, it doesn't hurt to be extra cautious."

"And?" Emily felt there was something more.

"And tell him also that I am going to write a book about this war between the prison and the AV, and would like to send the manuscript to him, when complete, in the hope that he will get it published."

"A book?"

"Sure. It's my way of atonement."

"Wouldn't that expose us? Didn't we agree to disappear?"

"No. First, I will use a pen name. Second, We will use a confidential mail service. Bottillo could rent a mail box from one of those private mail box facilities which will keep his name and address confidential. We will deliver the manuscript to it when ready. For this to work, he will need to find one right away and tell you about it. If he moves, he could arrange to have his packages forwarded to a new company in his new city. There will be no need for him to contact us."

When the couple hung up their phones, Haney noticed that Emily was more composed and her tears had dried. His heartbeat slowed down.

The next day, in the morning, Haney got a summon by the guard, this time to visit with his counselor.

They met in a small room, about 6' X 6', reserved for inmate-lawyer consultation. It was private in the sense that the conversation within could not be heard by anyone, although it was constantly under the electronic eye, monitored by a guard in a visual surveillance room, which was a part of the jail administration area. The room itself had only two folding chairs and a small folding table.

After formal greetings, Haney said, "Look, I am going to make it easy for you. I will plead guilty and accept whatever sentence they give me."

"Why?" asked the lawyer incredulously. "We should at least try to get you off."

"Another day, another time, maybe. ... You see, I will be killed for betrayal. To save myself I need to go where no one knows me, away from this AV region." Haney's tone was a combination of worry and hope. He shuffled his feet and rubbed his hands.

"How would you do that?" The lawyer's tone was, 'You're kidding me, right?'

Haney stopped fidgeting, sat straight, and spoke confidently, like he was giving a lecture to his college students, "With your help. Please, talk to the prosecutor. Tell him that my life is threatened here. Ask him for a quick trial, within days, and request that I be sent to another state, as far away from here as possible, secretly under interstate compact, to serve my sentence. I'm not asking for any leniency. How's that?"

"That shouldn't be difficult. The prosecutors love guilty pleas, which save them time and work."

"Please do it before I am killed."

"I'll talk to the prosecutor today. Okay?"

After that there was nothing more to talk about.

Haney got his wish within a week. He also got a five-year sentence for attempted murder.

He was pleased.

As the plane flew toward his new home, Haney was not thinking of the prison. Instead the images that formed in his mind were those of a home he and Emily would build in a sparsely inhabited, hard to reach mountainous area, where they would grow fruit trees.

And, while waiting in prison for that day to come, he would write a war story.

CHAPTER SIXTY

A BEGGING BOWL

THE BRUTAL BEATING of Schultz by a correctional officer made front-page story in newspapers, prime time item on TV, and talk of the day on all radio stations. Everyone blamed the prison administration, and the reason why Schultz was on death row was mentioned only as a passing remark.

Satya knew what it meant. Karcher, already a marked man, would be executed now more quickly. What after that? Killings and more killings. She was disturbed at the prospect of widespread bloodshed, and especially frightened at the prospect of Carolyn becoming a new member of the 'Widows of Violence'.

What was she to do? She felt emotionally bonded to Carolyn, had been so ever since Gopal's death and Carolyn's friendly overture toward her. Not only that, ever since Karcher's visit, she had even come to like Karcher himself. No, she could not condone what he had done, but he came across as a man who sincerely loved his wife. From her window, she had seen him kissing Carolyn as they were leaving after visiting with her not so long ago. 'He must live so that Carolyn can have a life,' she thought and asked herself, 'What can I do?' Finding no answer, she decided to talk to Carolyn. Who knew, she might have some suggestion?

She hurriedly drove over to Carolyn's.

They sat in the living room on a couch, side by side, but facing each other. Both had gloom written all over their faces, and both were teary-eyed.

"What's gonna happen, I don't know?" Carolyn said dejectedly.

"There must be a way to stop it. He doesn't deserve it, you don't deserve it," Satya said emphatically.

"No, he doesn't. Maybe in the past he did. But ever since our visit to your place, he has been a changed man. He told me what he had resolved to do, and then he did what he resolved."

"Resolved?" Satya did not know what was meant.

Carolyn summarized everything Karcher had resolved, and then said, "He really did lay down his arms unilaterally. He sincerely wanted to make a life with me, a life of love and peace. We even went dancing that weekend. Can you believe that?"

"Yes, I do. I am sure he had no hand in that inmate's abuse. But, it looks bad. Doesn't it?"

"Yes. If there were only some way to get the truth out to those people who matter?"

"Meaning the AVs?"

"Yes."

All of a sudden Satya felt she had an answer to the question which had brought her to see Carolyn. Her eyes brightened up, and the haze of depression evaporated from her face. She said, "I know what we could do."

"What?" asked Carolyn curiously. She even changed her slumped posture to an upright position.

"Go to Schultz, tell him the truth."

Carolyn slumped. "He won't believe us. Besides, he may not even understand us. He is brain damaged, you know. Also, I don't think security would let anyone get near him, certainly not you, thinking that you might want to exact revenge from his organization for trying to kill you."

"You are probably right. But I would like to try. Who knows, AVs might see it as waving a white flag and the end of the conflict."

Carolyn still had her doubts which she expressed. Satya did not press the matter. In her mind she decided to do it by herself; go to her enemy with a begging bowl. It needed to be done, irrespective of whether she succeeded or failed. No need to convince Carolyn about its necessity. No need to even tell her about it to avoid any possibility of Carolyn dissuading her from following her plan. So, she changed the subject and said, "Why don't you guys just leave the area now and go into hiding until the whole thing blows over, or take your chances, quit the job and forgo the retirement. You won't have to worry about money, I have plenty of it for all of us."

"We couldn't depend upon you for money. Besides, that's the least of our problems. We have two grown children, well placed. They would help us, I am sure. And hiding. Where can we hide? You are not hiding even after they tried to kill you."

"My life doesn't matter. No one will be really affected after I am gone. I have no family here."

"Don't say that. We are your family. We will be affected."

"You are very kind. But the reality says that if something happened to Mr. Karcher, it would happen to you in equal measure. It is not the same with me."

"I think it is. I wish there was some way to neutralize the threat against you, too. They did not succeed last time, they might try again."

"It does not matter. I didn't thwart their plan last time. I was willing to go. So would I be in the future. Whatever they do, it is a total failure since my death does not punish me, it only frees me from the bondage of life."

The words seemed to pain Carolyn who started to cry softly and said, "Don't say that."

Once more Satya chose not to press the matter. She was not here to win an argument. She was not here to argue about anything. Need to change the subject again. So she said, "Why don't we just sleep on it? If you get any ideas, give me a call, and if I do I will call you."

They agreed. With that the two women spent the rest of their time drinking coffee and talking about how they were occupying themselves. The uneasy visit ended with Carolyn looking worried and agitated, possibly about the future of her life, and Satya concerned about how she was to proceed with her plan and what she would do if it failed.

Satya did not lose any time. She thought and thought and decided on the steps she was going to take and improvise her actions as she encountered the unknowns.

The next day in the morning, she walked into the Sheriff's office and requested to see Mr. Belford. The receptionist asked, "What's your name ma'm and what's this about?"

She answered, "Satya Gopal, and it's about George Schultz, an inmate who..."

"Yes, I know," the receptionist cut in and said, "just a minute please."

Satya waited while the receptionist made a call and talked, supposedly with Belford. Then she said, "Please wait in the lobby. An officer will escort you to Mr. Belford's office."

Even though it was only after about five minutes that an officer appeared before Satya, it seemed like an eternity to her. When shown into Belford's office, she was nervous, never having had any experience of talking with a top police officer. She stood at the door hoping for someone to tell her what to do. Belford must have recognized Satya's quandary, because he got up and said, "Mrs., Mrs. Gopal, please take a seat." He pointed to a guest chair facing him.

After Satya was seated, Belford said, "I am sorry about your loss. We, we all are."

"Thank you. But, that's in the past," Satya answered in a faltering tone.

"Yes, yes. of course. But, Schultz is still a problem. Our receptionist told me that you wanted to talk, talk to me about him?"

"Yes sir." Satya, feeling encouraged by Belford's sympathetic tone, found her tongue, finally, "Actually it concerns Mr. Karcher. His life is threatened."

"Yes, yes. I know."

"I want to beg Mr. Schultz to spare his life."

"What, what?" Belford sounded incredulous.

"I want to request that you allow me to see Mr. Schultz. As I understand, he is in your custody in the hospital. I want to beg him to withdraw his order to kill Mr. Karcher."

"Why are you so, so interested in Mr. Karcher's life, and what makes you think that Schultz, Schultz would respond to your appeal?"

"We are close, very close, Mr. Karcher, his wife, and I. ... I don't know if Mr. Schultz will respond but I want to try anyway."

"You know, of course, that Schultz is totally, totally unresponsive because of his injuries. I don't think he has any awareness of any kind."

"Yes, I have read about his condition in the papers. It is possible that he understands but is not able to react."

"I doubt, doubt it."

"Just in case, sir. Please, let me plead."

"Assuming he hears you, what makes you think that he will grant, grant your request?"

"He may not, but it does not hurt to try."

"True, true. Assuming again that he grants your request, how will he communicate it to those who matter?"

"I don't know, sir. But, if he accepted my plea, I am sure he will find some way to let his men know."

"Ma'm, you are expecting, expecting miracles."

"I don't know what I am expecting, sir. I just want to talk to him, beg him to stop the killings, that's all. Begging is all I can do. The result is not in my hand."

"All right, all right. None of this makes any sense, but, since you insist, and I don't see any harm, harm in it, I will allow you to see Schultz. But, it will not be a private visit. An officer will go with you, and stay, stay with you throughout the period of your visit, visit. And, the most I will allow is five, five minutes."

"Thank you. I will be forever grateful to you for your generosity."

"Okay, okay. ... I suppose you want it done immediately?"

"As soon as possible, sir."

"All right. Come back this afternoon at three, three. Report at the front desk."

"Thank you. I will, sir. Thank you."

Satya kept her appointment. The receptionist called the officer assigned to escort duty who showed up in a few minutes.

Satya looked at him anxiously, expectantly.

He only said, "This way ma'm."

He walked ahead and Satya followed. They walked out of the building and into the official vehicle parking area. Stopping in front of a police car with mounted emergency lights, he opened the passenger door and said, "Please."

Satya got in. The officer took the driver's seat, pulled out of the parking lot and into the busy traffic. Throughout the drive no one uttered a word. The officer cruised at a pretty scary speed, using his siren and flashing lights every time he wanted to cross an intersection or pass other motorists, illegally. They reached their destination in less than fifteen minutes.

At the entrance to the secure ward where Schultz lay, Satya had to walk through a metal detector, then had to be embarrassingly frisked by a female security officer. After that her photo ID was checked and a 'VISITOR' display card was issued which she had to wear around her neck. Because of the prior clearance from the Sheriff's office and escort by a police officer, no tiring interview was conducted.

After obtaining her security clearance, she was led by her escort into the ward in which Schultz was kept. She had to wear a mask before being allowed to enter Schultz's room, which was guarded by a police officer around the clock. She and her escort entered the room without any hindrance by the guard.

As she stood beside Schultz's bed, her escort said, "Ma'm you have five minutes."

Satya nodded her head in a gesture of understanding of the limitation on her time. She looked at the mutilated body on the bed which was almost completely wrapped in bandages from head to toe. The skull seemed to have been held together with something that looked like a clamp. Below it, the face had visible cuts and bruises. There were splints attached to elbows and knees, and the hands and feet were in slings supported by weird looking metal contraptions. Many different tubes were protruding out of his nose, mouth, and veins in the hand, and were connected to various medicine and nutrition dispensing devices. There were also many different kinds of instruments which were recording vital functions through wires reaching into his chest and head. Satya had no knowledge of the function of any of the instruments, tools, tubes, and wires, nor was she interested in knowing about them. To her, Schultz looked like a bizarre creature from outer space, being studied by humans. She felt pity for the once powerful Schultz, reduced to an immobile mass of tissue and bones. But, in the physical sense only. Psychologically, he still wielded power over a large number of people. If he didn't, she would not be here begging for his mercy.

Since she had come here to talk to, or, at least, say something to Schultz, she focused her eyes on his face which was like a stone devoid of any sensation or reaction. She spoke in a monotonous and subdued but respectful tone, "Mr. Schultz, I hope you can hear me." She paused to see any sign of reaction on Schultz's face. Finding none she continued, "My name is Satya Gopal. I am sorry for what happened to you. But Mr. Karcher had nothing to do with it. Mr. Ibarra acted on his own. Mr. Karcher has already, on his own, withdrawn from this conflict. Now, it is in your hands. You have the power to end this war, to prevent suffering of others. Please, recall your warriors. Let Mr. Karcher live. I have come to beg you to spare his life. Please. Take mine instead. Please, please."

By the end of her monologue, Satya was shaking like a reed in a breeze. Her face was contorted with pain, and her eyes were wet. She waited, hoping for some answer. There was none, not even any sign of recognition on Schultz's face. Still, Satya said, laboriously this time, "If you have heard me, I hope, you will grant my request. ... I wish you a speedy recovery. Goodbye."

She turned and walked out of the room, unsteadily, followed by her escort.

It had turned out to be a futile effort and Satya was depressed. It seemed that Belford, after all, was right about it. More than that, she was also depressed at the sight of Schultz, a powerful man broken down into a rotting vegetable state, all because of his delusional arrogance of being a superior being. Her depression increased many folds at the realization of the fact that a lot of people in the world shared Schultz's philosophy and consequent fate.

What next? Would she just sit there and wait for the day when Karcher would be killed? In spite of her depressed mood, she could not entertain that possibility. So, what was she going to do, if anything?

All of a sudden it occurred to her that it was not Schultz, the person, but the AV, the organization, which was responsible for the mayhem. If Schultz could not respond to her request, maybe Goodwin, the de facto Regional Commander of the AV, could. She should talk to him.

Having been in the news, Goodwin's address and phone number were easily available. Satya did not bother calling him and making an appointment to see him, afraid that her request to see him might be denied. And, she did not want to present her request on the phone, believing that a face-to-face pleading was likely to be more effective.

Satya drove over to see Goodwin in the evening when he was likely to be at home. All through her drive, she was filled with hope, optimism, and even excitement. But, once at the door of the Goodwin residence, she became nervous, not knowing how she would be received and even how to make her request. However, she had come with a purpose and decided that she might as well go through with the task. Her finger shook as she pressed the door bell.

"Who is it?" She heard a male voice call from inside the house and, before she could answer, the door opened. There stood a burly, well built man in a t-shirt and jeans. Satya saw him scan her from head to foot and exclaim, "I know who you are. What do you want?"

Satya read contempt in his voice. Ignoring that, she said politely and directly, "Sir, I have come to beg you to spare Mr. Karcher's life."

"What are you talking about?"

"Sir, the AVs want to kill Mr. Karcher and, as the head of the organization, you could ask them not to. Take my life instead. Please."

"Lady, you are out of your mind. Also stupid. Accusing a fine humanitarian organization of murderous activities. I could sue you for that. Now, get the hell away from here before I call the cops."

The reception she got was unimaginable to her. She had considered the possibility that her request might not be granted, but it never occurred to her that Goodwin would deny the AVs involvement in the war in which its members were openly fighting, killing, and dying.

The vehemence of Goodwin's response destabilized Satya, and she withdrew from the doorsteps, quickly making it to her car, and driving away, filled with a sense of defeat and shame at being treated so insultingly. Filled also with self-recrimination for being so stupid as not to recognize that criminals hardly ever admit their crimes.

Whatever, she had accomplished nothing, and her begging bowl was empty.

CHAPTER SIXTY-ONE
FLOWERS BLOOM ONLY TO DIE

Bottillo got a call from Emily Haney, in his office. He was not sure if he should accept it, it being from the wife of an inmate who was serving time in a faraway state under interstate compact. Curiosity made him respond, however, "Yes, Mrs. Haney, what can I do for you?"

"I need to talk to you, privately."

"I can't. It's against the prison policy."

"But, it isn't against the prison policy to see you in your office concerning my husband."

"True. But, I am not his CPO, and don't know anything about him."

"Sir, I don't need to know anything about him. I need to give you a message from my husband."

"Oh! Why don't you give it to me now, on the phone?"

"It's not that kind of message."

"What kind is it?"

Emily sounded frustrated as she said, "Okay, if you insist. It's concerning the AVs. You will want that message. The prison will too. If you wish, you can share it with your supervisors."

A message about the AVs from the mouth of an AV! No wonder it needed to be communicated in person. Also, she did say that he would want it, and he could share it with his superiors. So, there was nothing fishy about it. But why would he want it? Why would the prison? And why would Emily and her husband betray their own organization by talking to him about it? Why indeed? All the more intriguing, all the more tempting to find out what it was all about.

Still, he could not fully trust an AV and decided to play it safe, "Meet me in visitation then. This afternoon at one. Will that work for you?" He chose visitation because it was very public and secure, constantly under the watchful eyes of the guards, but it also allowed private conversation.

Emily confirmed, "Thank you. I'll be there."

Once they were face-to-face and courtesies had been exchanged, Emily said in a matter of fact way, "I had a talk with my husband before he was shipped to another state. He wanted me to talk to you, to tell you that the AVs have decided to kill you. Actually, he told the police about it but was not sure if they would warn you. Did they?"

"No. But, how does he know?"

"He knows because he was asked to kill you along with Mrs. Gopal. Now that he has failed and is in prison, someone else will be assigned this task."

"Why are you telling me this?"

"I am telling you all this because we are not sympathetic to the AV cause any more."

"You're not? How come?"

"Let's just say, we have developed a conscience."

"Conscience, huh! But, why would the AV want to kill me? I have not harmed them in any way, I am not in conflict with them."

"They know, or at least strongly suspect, that your are the eyewitness that the police are talking about. You saw the Robinson murderers, right? They also suspect your hand in the capture of Huddy, Torte, and Schultz."

So, the AVs knew. Now, Bottillo was scared. It showed in the worry lines on his forehead and in his nervous stomach. He felt his heartbeat go up, and his breathing become uneven. He was confused about why Emily, an AV, or even an AV with a new found conscience, would take a risk of meeting with him. So, he asked, "Don't you think it is dangerous for you to be talking to me like this?"

"It is. The AVs are already after my husband for betraying them, and probably looking at me with suspicion, too. Logical. Husband and wife, might think alike. Actually, we do think alike. If they see me with you, an enemy in their eyes, it will only reinforce their suspicion of me. But, I still decided to see you. We felt you needed to be warned so that you could take safety precautions."

"Is that the whole purpose of this meeting?"

"No. There is one more thing." She told him about the book Haney was planning to write under a pen name and his desire for Bottillo to find a publisher for it.

"Why me? I have no publishing experience. What can I do?" Bottillo asked, totally bewildered.

"You can do the same as any novice would do, even Haney himself. Just show it around and hope someone picks it up. ... And, he chose you because, I think, he admires you for suffering a loss and not resorting to evil in its response."

Bottillo did not believe it to be true, yet he did not see any sense in arguing with Emily about it. So, he ignored the compliment and asked, "Why not he himself, or you? after all..."

"Because...," And she told Bottillo her plans made with her husband to go into hiding, become unknowns; the divorce, finding a place safe from the AVs, waiting for Haney to join her after his release.

"So, he wants to remain anonymous, just wants to get his message out."

"Yes. And, that's the reason he will be using a pen name."

"I see. What name will that be?"

"You will know when you get the manuscript. I don't think he has yet picked one out."

"Supposing I am unsuccessful in finding a publisher, can I give it to someone else better equipped for the task?"

"Yes, by all means."

"What about the royalties? Assuming, of course, that the book gets published and earns money."

"We didn't talk about it. But, you could keep it, I suppose."

"How, in good conscience, could I do that?"

"What I mean is you could do anything you want with the proceeds, if any. Give it to charity, to other victims of violence. Anything. You could not give it to us, because we would hopefully be unreachable by anyone we know at present."

"Then how will I be able to communicate with you guys? How will Mr. Haney be able to deliver the manuscript to me?"

Emily told him about the private mail box service Haney had suggested and the need to find one right away.

The initial shock of finding out that he was an AV target had subsided somewhat, primarily because of the talk. So, he said calmly, "What it boils down to is that I should run and hide for my safety?"

"Essentially."

"Thank you. I will seriously consider your advice. And, mail box. I'll rent one today. If you call me tomorrow, I will give you the name of the company."

"Here?"

"No. Call me at home." By this time he was so comfortable with Emily that he had no hesitation sharing his unlisted phone number with her. Besides, he was not sure he would be in his office tomorrow, or day after tomorrow, or even after that.

As he got up to say goodbye and stretched his hand toward Emily, she said, "There is something else I want to tell you. Please sit. Just a couple more minutes."

Bottillo sat down and looked at Emily expectantly.

Emily spoke, "Since we want to protect you, there is something else you should know. It is an AV secret. I know this secret because I work in their office."

"No, I didn't know that you worked in their office."

"Well, anyway. Don't go to work this Sunday. There will be trouble started by the AVs. I don't know many details, like how it will be started, how it will be directed, what actually will be done, who will be the target, etcetera. But I know it's coming."

"I don't work on Sundays, so it does not affect me. But others will be hurt. I could tell the prison about it, and the whole operation would be thwarted."

"You can, if you want to. But it's not going to make any difference. No amount of preparation by the prison will be able to stop this. That's how well planned it is."

"Really?"

"Oh, they might be able to hinder it a little, make it bumpy, but can't stop it."

"But how, how would the AVs be able to foment this trouble, communicate with the white inmates? Or, are the staff involved too?" Bottillo could not believe what he was hearing.

"Yes, the staff are also involved. The AV orders have already been communicated to select inmates and employees. Once the operation gets going, they hope other white inmates, who have no AV ties, will also be roped in automatically. The whole thing will be handled in a way that will tip the scale in favor of the whites."

"I have worked in the prison for so many years and I still do not know much about the AV operations here. All I know is that they are a white supremacist gang."

"Well, they are that, and more. And, they are good, very good, at what they do. How else do you think Schultz always knew about what the prison was up to, concerning him and the AVs? How do you think the AVs knew that there would not be a guard at the Martinez home the night his home was invaded?"

"Now I remember Mr. Karcher worrying about an AV mole in the prison. He had all his staff look for it with no success."

"There you go."

"Who is this mole?"

"That I don't know, but I know there is one."

Bottillo couldn't care less about the mole. He had already decided to leave the prison to protect himself. Yet, he was curious about this upcoming trouble on Sunday.

So, he asked, "What's the purpose of all this?"

"I guess you really do not know much about the AVs. Briefly, it's like this. The AVs have always aimed at taking over the prison, actually the world, but one piece at a time. The trouble this coming Sunday is designed for that purpose. It will oust Mr. Karcher as an incompetent administrator, and an AV will become the Warden. He will carry out the AV agenda without anybody ever knowing that he is an AV."

"This could have been done long ago without plotting all this conflict between the AVs and the prison. There was no need to pick certain staff for killing."

"True. But the goals evolve and plans change accordingly. You see, at the time when Schultz had behaved abusively toward the program committee members, the goal was his escape. The killings were planned to intimidate staff, to vent hate and anger, and to show their superiority. Later, the scenario changed, particularly by Schultz's capture and his mangling by Ibarra. A new goal emerged; discredit Karcher then kill him, put an AV in the Warden's chair, take control of the prison, and facilitate Schultz's escape while discouraging Belford to do anything about it. The coming trouble on Sunday that I told you about is a means to that end."

This long discourse totally confused Bottillo. So, he asked, "You mean that this Sunday the AVs will win, and the war will be over?"

"No, not really. Look at it this way. Life is like a continuous stream with no beginning and no end. What the AVs are doing has been around forever under different names in different places, and it will continue to be so forever. The goals and plans you see are just bubbles in a boiling pot of water, having little significance in themselves. They appear to have a beginning and an end. You set a goal, you start working toward it and end it when it is achieved. But this is delusion. Actually, this is simply a part of the bigger whole which is infinite."

Now Bottillo was even more confused. So, he said, "This is too much for me to grasp. I am not that bright. You seem to be so smart. So, how come you are working for the AVs as a secretary?"

"For the same reason that my husband has worked for them as a bomb maker and a potential killer. You probably know, he is a brilliant scientist, and yet... you see, the AVs have no use for our intelligence, our ideas."

"I still don't understand why?"

"Because of the ideology. We believed in their ideology and did whatever was needed to support it. We sacrificed our individuality, our talent, our life's goals and ambitions."

"How come smart people like you bought the AV ideology?"

"You don't buy ideology. It just grows on you. We are all ideologues, it's instinctual."

"I don't understand." Bottillo was getting more and more confused. Still, the conversation was so fascinating to him that he wanted it to continue.

"All right. You know we all want to be better than others, better educated, better dressed, richer, stronger, more beautiful, smarter, whatever. It is instinctual. We have not learned it. We are born with it. The AVs want to be superior, think they are superior, due to their skin color. We thought so too."

"So what made you and your husband change?"

"The growth of our ideals."

"You mean there is a difference between ideology and ideals?"

"Yes. Ideology is instinctual, ideals are rational. We examined this concept and came to the realization that all ideologies are evil. Now, we want to be rational, have sane ideals which can be defended logically."

"What are your ideals?"

"At this time just one, not to hurt anyone. ... And yes, there is another. We don't want to feel superior to others, either. We just want to live in peace and let others live in peace, too."

"You keep saying 'we'. Are you including your husband in it, too?"

"Yes."

"Then this growth of your ideals must be very recent. Wasn't Haney just a few days ago on a mission to kill that Indian lady and, according to you, me, too?"

"Yes. Now, you see why he couldn't kill her or you."

"True. But, what I meant was, when did you two get a chance to discuss and adopt these ideals?"

"We never discussed them. Not even during my meeting with him in the jail. But, I could sense their growth in him. Why else do you think he aborted his mission and sacrificed everything he had? ... I just adopted his ideals because they were his, for sure, but primarily because they made logical sense to me."

Bottillo, by this time, had lost his suspicion of Emily and was talking with her in a friendly tone, shedding his formal stance. "All this is way too heavy for me. I am not sure I understand it all. But it sounds good."

"I hope it will do some good, too."

"You are very optimistic."

"I don't know if it is optimism or wishful thinking. But I do know one thing: The flowers bloom only to die; but they do bloom."

Bottillo was neither a philosopher nor a poet, but he was touched by Emily's expressions. They made him feel sad, yet strangely, not dispirited.

After the meeting Bottillo sat in his office and brooded, his mind not on his work. He brooded, not about Haney's book, but about ideology and ideal, Emily's big words. He was convinced that he had been snared into ideology when he had determined that the AVs needed to be caught and punished for killing Robinson. Logically, what was the difference, the AVs sending their agents to kill Robinson and he using the police as his agents to kill the AVs? Both were instinctually guided by revenge.

That made him brood over something else Emily had said, something about him, or more accurately, what Emily had thought Haney believed about him. He asked himself, 'What made Haney think that he, Bottillo, had not resorted to violence in the face of his violent loss?'

True, he had not committed any violence himself, but he had assisted the police in tracking down AVs resulting in many casualties. And he never felt apologetic about it. It was violence by proxy. In contrast, Haney had risked his and his wife's life for nonviolence. He was going to prison for not wanting to kill someone. How absurd that he was being punished for desisting from violence.

All of a sudden, Bottillo had a new respect for this past AV member. All of a sudden, it also occurred to him that Haney was not alone. There were some others who had escaped death by the AV violence and had not retaliated. Satya Gopal was willing to die without resorting to violence to defend herself. And even after being targeted for execution, she had not taken any action against anyone in any way. Then, there was Susan Madrill. Her brother had committed suicide because of the AV web around him, and she had done nothing to avenge his death, never made a venomous expression of any kind toward anyone. There was one other person affected by the AVs, although indirectly, Christi Comora. Ever since joining 'Widows of Violence' she had become a subdued and mellow person, and was not talking about revenge any more.

These persons needed to be recognized, not he. Obviously Haney did not know him well, and only saw his surface behavior which did not betray his inner aggression.

Bottillo felt ashamed.

At that moment he made a decision; he would resign his position and go away from this culture of hate and violence. Maybe that would be his ideal. Like Haney and Emily he would look for a spot where he would not have to live under the AV shadow.

He was sure that sooner or later the prison, once in AV control, would find out about the project he had accepted, and he would not only be fired but also prosecuted. He needed to be proactive, needed to get out before that happened. If he left his job, he would be a free man and the prison could not sanction him. And the AVs might leave him alone seeing that he was not in the enemy camp any more. Besides, if he stayed at the prison and the AVs took over, they would expect him to promote their ideology. Would he be able to do it? No, he could not, not morally. Not legally either. Well, the laws could be circumvented and often were. Forget about laws, he just could not do it, would not do it.

With that decision he composed his letter of resignation from his job and took it over to his Deputy Warden.

It was unusual for a prison employee to just walk into the office of his superior for a meeting without prior appointment, but then Bottillo was not dealing with the usual state of affairs. So, when the secretary told him, "He is busy. Would you like an appointment?", he retorted, "No. I must see him now. I have to tell him something very critical, very urgent." At this time he was not thinking about his resignation but about the upcoming Sunday disturbance.

He heard and watched the secretary communicate his statement to the Deputy Warden on the phone, listen to him for a moment, put the phone down, and then tell him, "You may go in."

Sitting in front of his boss, Bottillo spoke calmly and firmly, like a man who had shed all his indecision and was poised to embark on a chosen journey, totally oblivious of the inherent dangers, "Sir, I am here to submit my resignation. I have my private reasons why I must leave right away. I am sorry I can't give a two-week notice."

"But, you could have left the letter with my secretary."

"Yes, sir. But, there is something else which can be told in person only."

"And, that is?"

Bottillo told him about his meeting with Emily and about the upcoming Sunday upheaval.

"I appreciate the info. I will pass it on to the Warden. ... I am sorry you are leaving. Good luck. "

"Thank you, sir," Bottillo said and left.

After that he collected his things and left the prison.

In his apartment he checked the Yellow Pages, picked a private mail box company at random, drove there, and rented a mail box. This was easy. Now when Emily would call him the next day, he would be able to tell her where Haney could send his manuscript.

Now, all he needed to do was decide where to go, and decide it soon. This place where he had lived, worked, and loved, not only was filled with bad memories, it had become very thorny. He needed to go where he could live in peace without fearing the AVs.

But, he could not leave without saying a very important goodbye.

He drove over to a flower shop, bought a bunch of white irises, and then went to the cemetery where Robinson lay along with her son and mother .

He placed the irises on the ground in front of the simple headstone and whispered, "Emily is right. Flowers do bloom."

CHAPTER SIXTY-TWO

ROME IS BURNING

It was Sunday. A peaceful and calm Sunday.

Yes, Karcher had been informed by the Deputy Warden of Bottillo's unit about a disturbance planned by the AVs for the coming Sunday. But, he was not terribly worried. He got dozens of such warnings every year, and eight out of ten turned out to be false alarms. Besides, disturbances and riots were common in the prison, at least one major and five or six minor ones every year. Still, in the light of recent AV activities, this information was somewhat destabilizing, and he could not ignore it. He ordered the Chief of Security to post extra armed guards at catwalks, in the exercise and recreation yards, and even within the less secure minimum and medium custody units, and to contact him immediately on the radio if anything did happen. Lacking specifics about the location, time, and nature of the disturbance, he could take only general precautions.

The sunshine slowly made its way through the steel and concrete fortress housing thousands of society's discards. Most inmates stirred lazily in their beds or on the floor mattresses. They thought of a special weekend meal; their place in heaven through prayers and reverential listening to the exhortations of their chaplains, rabbis, priests, whatever; exercises and workouts; warm showers; sports like, football, basketball, horsing around; phone calls; visits by family and friends; watching porn on TV or in magazines; or just lying around.

It was almost the same in ASU, except that, being a small 50-cell high-security unit, there were fewer activities and staff, and the inmates had little freedom of movement, and no opportunity for sports or access to porn.

Contrasted with the bloody Sunday of two weeks ago when Schultz was butchered, this morning started normally, like most other Sunday mornings.

It started with just skeleton security and essential services staff; four guards, two cooks, one video monitor, one chaplain, one key officer, one Shift Commander, one gate operator, and one gate keeper. It started also with expectation of minimal activity; no therapy sessions, program reviews, classifications, or disciplinary courts. The unit had never had any educational, vocational, or occupational activities. Later in the day, a nurse was expected to come and dispense medication, and some lucky inmates expected visits from their families or attorneys.

Yes, the morning did appear to be peaceful and calm to the 12 staff and 42 inmates in the unit on that day. But only on the surface. Underneath, it was uneasy, for some inmates.

ASU was a closed rectangular box. Entry to it was through an electronically operated metal gate. Next to the gate was a holding area beside which was a plexiglas enclosed cubicle manned 24-hours a day by a gate operator. Two other small cubicles, a video monitor room and a key room, were adjacent to the gate operator's area, which were also manned around the clock. The administrative section of the unit had two six-foot-square rooms for visitation between the inmates and their family and lawyers; offices for Deputy Warden, Shift Commander, and CPOs and a yard office; a gun room; a record room; a small room used by a visiting nurse, teacher, psychologist, psychiatrist, chaplain, or any other program staff as a landing spot; a large multipurpose room used for shift change briefings, conferences, staff training, lounging, or any other activity one could think of; and a bathroom for staff and visitors only. The essential services section of the unit had a kitchen, a huge pantry, and a janitor's closet. The center of the unit contained 50 individual inmate cells, 8' X 6', with concrete walls on three sides and steel bars on the side facing a hallway. Each cell was furnished with a recessed steel toilet, a water faucet, and a mattress made of so-called indestructible and fire retardant material. Light was provided by electric bulbs fixed in the hall ceilings and focused into the cells. On one side of the unit, there were four shower stalls for inmates. There was also an outside exercise area which had a latticed steel roof, and was divided into four individual pens, separated by a three-foot space between them.

The Schultz incident had made the social climate thick with hatred and apprehension. Both staff and inmates were on edge. The attack on a white inmate by a colored staff stirred suppressed staff-inmate and white-colored animosities simultaneously. As a result, inmate leaders emerged spontaneously to avenge injustice.

Sunday, with low staff numbers and absence of the top administrative officers, was the ideal day for the uprising. The seven o'clock shift change had already taken place, and the staff were on their assigned posts and duties. Some inmates, the ones who did not have death sentences and were on trustee status because of their good conduct, were allowed to work as janitors and cooks, free from the usual handcuffs and leg and belly chains. Breakfast had been served. The inmates on kitchen duty were back in their cells, but the work of the janitors had just started.

The hell broke loose soon after that.

Two trustee inmates, both white, assigned to janitorial duties, were in the hallway. They, while moving their mops on the floor, would confer with each other as they crossed paths. Among them they decided a plan of action against the staff and the colored inmates. Following their plan, one of them passed by each cell addressing white inmates only in a whisper, "Revenge Day." He *de facto* became the leader.

Having assumed the lead position, the inmate walked over to the key room and said to the officer inside, "May I come in to pick up the garbage and mop the floor?"

"Sure," said the officer and opened the door from inside to let the janitor-inmate come in. He stood at the door, a safety precaution taught to all staff during orientation, and watched the inmate empty out the trash can into a huge plastic bag.

After putting the bag near the door, the inmate took his mop out of a plastic bucket and, instead of mopping the floor, stabbed the officer in the stomach with its hard end. The officer let out a blast of air and collapsed. There was no camera in the key room, and no one saw the incident.

The inmate picked up the master key to the cells, keys to the exit, video monitoring area, yard office, kitchen, and gun room, and put them into his pant pocket. Then, in a nonchalant way he wheeled his mop bucket out, pushing the key officer aside.

Once outside, he quickly connected with the other janitor-inmate and said, "Got the keys. Come get the guns."

The two made their way to the gun room. They opened the door, grabbed the only two rifles available, the other two having already been issued to two tower guards. They also took some ammunition, pepper spray cans, and handcuffs. They looked for a cattle prod superficially and gave up quickly when it was not found, simply because there was not enough time to do a thorough search. Of course, it was there, everyone knew it, and everyone also knew that it had been used on Schultz. But, it must have been so well hidden that even the inspectors, in charge of assuring that the prison followed all laws and regulations, wouldn't be able to find it.

Being sure that their actions must have been noticed by the video monitor, who must have alerted the security officers both inside and outside the unit, they quickly loaded their guns and came out ready for a shootout. Their supposition was correct, because they, upon coming out of the yard office, saw three officers rushing toward the gate to get away from the armed inmates. The gate operator must have opened the gate for them. The inmates shot at the back of the fleeing staff. Two fell and one got away.

The lead inmate ordered the other armed inmate, "Secure the gate and do not let any one else out, or let anyone in, and shoot to kill if necessary."

Then he looked at the fallen staff and immediately recognized them to be the gate operator and video monitor. He examined their pulses and, upon finding them alive, handcuffed and left them where they had fallen. That done, he quickly made his way to the key room and handcuffed the unconscious key officer. The staff who got away must have been the gate keeper.

Although the unit was in his control now, he knew that soon there would be a siege and assault on it. That created the need for fast action. Quickly, at gun point, he rounded up the remaining staff in the unit, the Shift Commander, the cooks, the chaplain, and four guards, took them to an empty cell, and locked them in. The sobs and pleadings from the staff who surrendered did not mean a thing, those who resisted with their meager means of batons and pepper spray got clobbered with rifle butts.

After this, the leader rushed to open the cells of the white inmates, 33 of them, who having seen the uprising by this time, obviously were clamoring to get out themselves and take part in the brutalities.

They did not get their wish, not quite, although they were displaying their shanks and other weapon-quality objects secured earlier from the offices and the kitchen. After getting the white inmates out, the lead inmate ordered them, "Take your revenge. Trash this place. Leave the TV and telephone alone, though. We may need them for communication and information. ... I will take care of the coloreds."

He went to those cells in which Hispanic and black inmates were locked up and shot them through the openings of the bars. The other white inmates, in the meantime, started breaking furniture and equipment, tearing down everything that was hanging, and setting fire to everything that would burn, including the indestructible and fire retardant mattresses and blankets.

Within minutes, the unit was filled with cries, moans and groans of the dying and the injured colored inmates, shouts of insults and degradation from the white inmates, and crackling of the weapons. The entire unit reeked of blood, flesh, vomit, and expelled feces and urine. It was made many times more noxious and poisonous with the spilling, mixing, and burning of numerous medicines, cleaning agents, cooking grease, meat, vegetables, other food, assorted chemicals, furniture, paper, plastic, wood, and cloth.

In the midst of all this, the lead inmate remembered the three injured and unconscious staff, two at the gate and one in the key room. With the help of two other inmates, he dragged them into the cell where other staff were imprisoned, removed their handcuffs, and left them locked inside to gain their consciousness by themselves, if they did not die.

Looking at the staff stuffed in the small cell like sardines, one inmate chuckled, then said, "What about the black employees? Aren't they part of the revenge?"

There were two colored employees, a Hispanic cook and a black guard.

"Oh, them? We need to finish them, too," said the lead inmate. He went and separated the two dark skin staff from the rest, took them into another empty cell, locked them in, then shot them like caged animals.

Revenge had been taken, now what? Sing ballads of white glory, tell each other tales of revenge taken successfully, and then die of starvation and disease? Hell no. There was another purpose for all this mayhem, communicated to him by the AV mole: freedom. So he called out to everyone and announced, "We did what we set out to do. Now we go for our freedom. We negotiate our way out."

One rioting inmate, who was not privy to AV communication, did not like the answer and shouted, "Negotiate my ass. We want freedom now," and headed toward the door, followed by several others.

The lead inmate screamed at them, "Idiots! Go out and you're dead meat. I tell you, they are waiting for you outside."

"So what the fuck is this all about?" asked an insolent inmate.

"We will get our freedom. Like I said, we negotiate."

"Negotiate, man? You crazy? Why would they negotiate when they got the big guns, lots of them."

"We got their men. Don't you see? Also, I am sure that our actions, by now, will be known to everyone, not only all the inmates and staff in other units, but the public as well. Thanks to the staff who escaped. I am hoping our brothers in other units will rise also, and start a huge bonfire. ... I'll call the Warden."

He dialed the number and everyone waited anxiously. There was no answer. He tried all the other numbers of top administrators of the prison found in the rolodex. No answer anywhere. "We will wait," said the lead inmate, "They are bound to contact us."

The inmates settled in for a long haul. They scattered throughout the unit sitting, lying, pacing, and even crying, with a few, selected by the leader, guarding all the captured staff.

The air inside the unit, by this time, was heavy with the putrid smell of blood and tissue, involuntarily expelled urine and feces, vomit, and a suffocating haze of smoke. Everyone was getting sluggish.

About an hour later, all the inmates were startled by the shrill ringing of the telephone in the yard office.

"Looks like they want to talk," said the leader and went to pick up the receiver.

He heard, "This is Warden Jordan. Lay down your arms, come out with your hands above your heads, and no one will be molested. We know you have control of the unit, the escaped guard told us that much, but for how long?"

"Just like that?" said the leader sarcastically.

"Yeah! Otherwise, I have the order to cut off the electricity and water, and your food won't last very long. It will get pretty hot pretty soon, and you will all die of hunger and thirst, and maybe of disease, since I know the place will be filthy. I tell you, it is a very painful death."

"Don't forget we got 11 of your men. They will die the same death we will."

"Let them go, surrender, and we can end this whole thing peacefully."

"That's no deal."

"I am not negotiating. I am telling you what I have been told to do."

"Told by who? Karcher?"

"No, the Director. We can't find Mr. Karcher, we tried everywhere we could think of. Maybe his radio is out of reach. I don't know. I have been appointed Warden now, and I take my orders from the Director."

"Now you are going to take orders from me. Listen and listen carefully. We got nothing against you. Karcher is a different matter. We would wring his neck if we could find him. Since you are the big cheese now, I will tell you what we want. We want safe passage to wherever we want to go, all 33 of us, the white guys."

"You serious?"

"Yes. That or we start killing your men, one at a time, on the hour, every hour."

"You don't seem to understand, I'm on your side, but we have to do this methodically. You surrender, and I promise no one will be punished, that is, if everyone keeps their mouth shut. You got your revenge, in due course, you might even get freedom. Got it? Know what I'm saying?"

"Not really, but I will think about it." He hung up.

The original message, that the lead inmate had received from the AV mole a few days ago, was to riot for the purpose of taking revenge against the colored by killing them, then going free. Looked like the circumstances had changed, and now surrender was being suggested. He didn't really want to think about it. What he wanted was to buy time, see what happened next, and then do it only when he was absolutely sure that this was what the AV authorities dictated.

In the meantime, he needed to do some public relations.

Leisurely, he went to the multipurpose room and dialed the number of a TV station. Wanted the world to know about his and his comrades' triumph, and also to advertise their demands.

When the call was answered, he spoke, "Here is a news item for you..."

"Who are you?" He was interrupted.

"My name is not important. I am calling from ASU..."

"ASU?"

"Yeah, Administrative Segregation Unit in the state prison..."

He was interrupted again, "Oh that! I'll let you talk to a reporter."

A few seconds later, he heard a male voice, "May I have your name please?"

"My name is not important, the news I have is."

"We don't broadcast news from anonymous sources."

"That's your problem. If you don't want the news, I will go to another station."

"All right, let's hear. What do you have?"

"What do we have? We have a riot. It's a reaction to the almost fatal attack on Schultz, you know Schultz? He was attacked last week here in this unit by a Mexican staff. You remember that?"

"Yeah. What else?"

"Warden Karcher has run away." That was not what he was told but that was what he chose to understand. "And we have taken over the unit. All colored inmates are dead. You can send someone here to see that I am telling the truth. We will let a reporter in. We demand freedom and safe passage from here. If our demands are not met, we kill the staff also. I have told this to the Acting Warden, Tommy Jordan, who used to be our Deputy Warden. He called, you know, asked us to surrender. Ha, ha!"

"We can't send anyone to ASU. No one is allowed in or out of the prison. Didn't you know that?"

"No. The prison, did you say? The entire prison?"

"Yes. Turn on the TV and you will see. We already have our reporters on the scene, a sky cam, and we are broadcasting live. How? A concerned citizen happened to see smoke rising from one of the units in the state prison and we got there pronto. ... Now listen. We will broadcast the news you gave us and your demands, but you have to give us your name for our records. We just won't publish it."

The lead inmate gave his name and hung up the receiver and got depressed. Here, his own show had been hijacked. How did it happen?

He turned on the TV. Actually, all local channels were broadcasting the news of the prison riot.

The prison riot, not just the taking over of ASU. The lead inmate called the other guys, "Come and listen to this. I didn't know that we started something big."

All the prisoners, except the one guarding the gate, gathered around the TV and listened to the newscast, "... smoke is rising from every building. Seems like even the women's unit is on fire. As you can see, inmates are fighting in the open common areas of the low and medium custody units. In other units, whatever is going on, fighting, burning, is all inside. We can't see. But our sky cam can see the fighting in the yards of the low and medium security units. Fighting? It's more like a war. Hand to hand. We know there are bunch of gangs in the prison, perhaps they are in the thick of it, too. There are the Aryan Vision people representing the whites, and there are the Cuervos and Huracans representing Hispanics, and I can't remember the names, but there are a couple of black and Asian gangs also. This might be an opportunity for all of them to carry out their vendettas against their opposition. I don't know where these knives, shanks as they call them, come from. Some inmates even have small hand guns, so it seems. What are the guards doing? I see them on the catwalk. But, what are they doing? Just standing with their rifles. I heard a little while ago an announcement on the PA for the inmates to stop fighting, otherwise they would be shot. But, no shots have been fired. The order apparently had no effect. I guess the authorities don't want to kill a lot of inmates. But, a lot of inmates will be killed anyway. Now let's go to our station. I got word that they have breaking news."

The News Director at the studio related what he had learned from the lead inmate in ASU. In the end, he speculated, "I think Warden Karcher has run away, and the administration has lost control of the prison. Also, I have a feeling, a lot of staff are hurt, killed, or taken hostage, particularly the staff of color. But I don't know for sure. The prison officials won't talk. When I called the Warden's office, no one answered. You believe this? Rome is burning and Nero, in this case, is not fiddling, but has fled. So it seems."

The News Director paused, consulted something with someone then came back on, "Anyway, from what an inmate in ASU told us on the phone, it is clear that the rioting started in ASU and spread to other units. An officer from there had escaped. He must have told others and others told others and before you know it, it is everywhere. Soon the inmates are talking about it, and within minutes whites are attacking coloreds. That's what I think happened. ... Now, there is other breaking news from our reporter in the chopper above the prison. ... Okay, what do we have?"

The reporter seemed very tired and spoke in an excited but hoarse voice, "Oh, there, there is some shooting by the officers. You can see it, it is on the screen. Dozens of officers are shooting simultaneously and the inmates are falling like flies. ... But, this is weird. How come all the officers appear white and most of the inmates falling are colureds? Its quite clear from our sky cam pictures. It couldn't be random. If it were indiscriminate, more whites would be killed simply because they are more in numbers. Now don't get me wrong. I am not suggesting that the officers are deliberately killing the coloreds. But this is certainly weird. Man, all this bloodshed, all these dead bodies, all this..."

The TV went dead. Actually, everything that ran on electricity went dead. All inmates looked at each other. Now what? No coolers any more, no air. They couldn't cook anything, because the kitchen was all electric. They couldn't clearly see much of anything either, it was dark inside with very little light filtering in from just a couple of windows in the administration area. The only thing they could do was shit and piss and there was a lot of that already all around. The jubilation of taking over the unit was suddenly muted.

"What do we do now?" asked an inmate.

"I don't know. This was not supposed to happen. Yes, for appearances sake, we were to be threatened but the threats were not supposed to be carried out. I guess our leader has to do all this to keep the appearance of neutrality," answered the lead inmate.

"We got to do something. Pretty soon the dead bodies will begin to decompose and smell."

"Let's burn them. We don't want to be killed by the dead."

"Good idea," everyone agreed.

No leader was needed for this. They sprinkled some cooking grease found in the kitchen and set fire to the bodies. The bodies burned but not fully. There was a lot of charred flesh, smoldering bones, coagulated blood, severed limbs, and exploding gases. Burst heads and intestines were creating gruesome abstract art on the wall and floor surfaces. The anticipation was that the burning would end the smell of decay, and everything would be cleansed. Instead, there was this horrible sight no one could tolerate to see and this terrible stench which no one could stand. In a closed unit with no air circulation and ventilation, the inmates had created a hell for themselves. The only escape was to go out or go into the exercise pens. The inmates, not part of the AV plan, felt both options unsafe, open to attack by the officers. They had just seen on TV how the bodies were falling like chopped tree limbs in other units, once the armed guards started shooting.

Several inmates suddenly started vomiting. They rushed to the shower stalls to wash and found to their chagrin, that there was no water.

It was serious now. What was the choice? Die outside by a bullet or die inside of poisoned air, sickness, and dehydration?

One inmate suggested, "We didn't start this to die. Let's just surrender."

"Surrender?" growled another.

"Yeah, surrender. We got our revenge. Now we save our asses," reasoned the inmate who had made the suggestion.

"You kidding? We will be charged with manslaughter. That's not saving our asses," countered another inmate.

"It is, if you look at it in a different way. Most of us are on death row, many others have life sentences. What do we have to lose? A few others might have something to lose but not much." After making the suggestion to surrender the inmate had to defend his position.

"Not much? What do you mean, not much?"

The question meant that the defending inmate still had a lot to defend. So he answered, "Well, each of us can always claim he had nothing to do with it, and there is no proof we did. Sure, someone or several of us did, but who specifically? They wouldn't know so long as everyone keeps his mouth shut. They would have to charge the whole group, which means they would have to prove a conspiracy. You know how difficult it would be to prove a conspiracy in a court. Man, just sit tight, say nothing. All that would happen is we would all get charged with rioting, we would all get a few more years tacked to our sentences. That would be nothing for most of us since most of us have nothing to lose."

"Are you a lawyer?" asked an inmate jokingly, or perhaps sarcastically.

"No. Paralegal."

"Same thing."

The lead inmate took over, "Makes sense to me. We got what we wanted, revenge. Freedom was an afterthought anyway. Besides, we were fooling ourselves. Even if the staff agreed to let us go, once outside, they would chase us down, capture or kill us. They wouldn't keep their word. We know we could not trust the government, it always lies. We wouldn't be able to get away very far. ... So, it is better to surrender and truly save our asses. ... I'll call the Warden."

He picked up the phone. No answer again. Worry lines formed on his forehead. He mumbled, "How do I negotiate when the bastard won't answer?"

A couple non AV inmates started throwing suppositions around.

"He might call back himself. He might want to free his hostages."

"Or he might just storm us, not caring for who lived or died."

"We can avoid that by surrendering, by walking out with our hands above our heads, like the Warden demanded."

"Yeah, we could do that. We can't sit in this hell hole much longer."

The message was communicated to all inmates. Some agreed to the proposal, some agreed reluctantly, and some opposed the proposal. Some of those who opposed agreed after being reasoned, the others were made to agree by a gun pointed to their foreheads.

The inmates left the staff locked and walked out, hands in the air.

The putsch was over. Something that had started with the anticipation of jubilation had ended with a sense of defeat.

For some of them anyway.

CHAPTER SIXTY-THREE

ENCOUNTER WITH DESTINY

KARCHER WAS NEITHER lost nor had he run away.

On this particular Sunday, when the prison exploded, Karcher and his wife were following their routine in violation of the safety rules that had been adopted by all the Schultz's program committee members. They took a slim breakfast of just coffee and toast to leave room for a big lunch later, and left their state-provided home in their private Taurus for an eight o'clock assembly in their Evangelical church in a small town near the prison. Karcher had to abandon his safety precautions if he did not want to give up his church, and he did not want to. Partly because of that and partly, also, because Karcher had become a bit complacent. Nothing threatening had happened to him in a while, and he felt nothing would, and if anything did come his way, he would be able to handle it. All he needed to do was remain vigilant and carry his trusted gun and radio. The crazy thing was that he knew he was rationalizing, and ignoring the rationalization by telling himself that he was not rationalizing.

Once on the church grounds, Karcher turned off his prison radio. Quiet in the church was more important than any communication from the prison. What could possibly happen requiring his immediate attention during the two hours that he would spend in the service of God? The riot planned by the AVs? It might not happen. Besides, he had already put in place a contingency plan in case it did happen. His staff should be able to contain any uprising and get in touch with him for instructions and direction. Furthermore, he felt ready to rush back to the prison, take charge of the situation, and get it under control, once he knew about it. No need to fret about something which might not even take place.

That day the minister talked about judgment and quoted from Matthew, Chapter 7, "Judge not, that ye be not judged. For with what judgment ye judge, ye shall be judged; and with what measure ye mete, it shall be measured to you again."

Karcher was not listening. He didn't go to church to listen. He went there to mark his presence, his Christian duty. After the service was over, he donated some money to the church and socialized with other church members, talking about their happy families and their charities to the poor. Then, he was off to his favorite steak house, 'The Buffalo Herd', in a larger city about 25 miles away.

The road passed through a hilly Indian reservation for about 9 miles, making radio reception from the prison almost impossible. Karcher decided to leave his radio with the direct link to the prison off, useless as it was in that stretch, and turned on a commercial station on his car radio for entertainment. Instead of music, there was a special bulletin, "... the entire prison is burning. We have no communication with the administration, so we have no official version of what's going on at this time. Stay tuned for more on the prison riot..."

Karcher turned the radio off and said to his wife, "We've got to go back."

He threw a quick glance at her and saw her pursed lips unable to utter a sound, worry lines on her forehead, and visibly shaking upper body.

"Calm down," Karcher added, "I'll have the situation under control in no time."

He drove on straight ahead looking for a spot to make a safe U-turn on that narrow two lane road without a shoulder. About half a mile ahead he found a small clearing on the side of the road. But it was occupied by a beat up green pickup truck, parked parallel to the road, facing the direction in which he was going. It was something common, something insignificant.

Karcher carefully pulled behind the truck, blew his horn to alert its occupant, if any, about his maneuver, and after getting no response, slowly made a U-turn. He had barely accelerated when he saw, in his rearview mirror, a man emerge from the green truck with a rifle aimed at him. The man looked vaguely familiar. Clearly, the man had been hiding in the truck, waiting for him to pass through that point, the first and only point from Karcher's church town, where someone could wait for the traffic to pass or turn around, if need be. Obviously the spot was carefully chosen. Karcher thought he could run away from the man and reach his church town in no time. He floored the accelerator.

He could have not gone more than a few feet when he heard gun fire disturbing the peace of the tranquil area and making Carolyn scream. He also felt his Taurus drag. Clearly, one of his back tires was hit and intentionally. Sensing immediate danger he continued to drive. Another shot rang out, and he felt the other back tire also go flat. He looked in his rear view mirror and saw the man standing in his driving lane with the rifle aimed at his car. Apparently, he had crossed the road so that he could take a good aim at the other back tire. The Taurus' drag increased. Karcher revved up the engine which failed to pick up speed, although it did increase the distance between the Taurus and the attacker.

Carolyn screamed again, hysterically this time, "What's going on?"

"I think it's an AV trying to stop us. Pull out the gun from the glove compartment and, while I drive, you shoot to kill the creep, if he follows us."

Karcher knew Carolyn had no expertise in handling a gun, and aiming at the man on the highway from a moving vehicle required a high level of shooting skill. However, since he could not shoot a gun and also drive, he had no choice but to ask his wife to handle this task. While he saw Carolyn take out the loaded pistol from the glove compartment, he heard another crack of a bullet and the Taurus' back window was shattered. Karcher continued to drive and observed with surprise that Carolyn changed from a frightened deer to a raging lioness. She turned around in her seat, balanced the revolver on the head rest, looked through the gaping hole in the back window, but did not shoot. Most likely because the man, by this time, was so far away from her that it was impossible to hit him with her small caliber gun. Presently, in his rear view mirror, Karcher saw the attacker run across the road, get in his truck, turn it around, and get behind him at a very fast speed. When it came to within ten feet, it veered off to the left swiftly, lurched forward, came parallel to the Karchers, and slammed itself against Taurus on the driver side, by swerving sharply to the right.

Karcher noticed that even now Carolyn was at a disadvantage, because he himself was between her and the truck driver. He also felt that he was losing control of the car, and as he tried to keep it on the pavement, he succeeded only in going off it and hitting a tree perched precariously at the edge of the road, tottering above a 200-foot drop.

He saw the truck driver stop his vehicle and jump out of it with his rifle. He was almost paralyzed when he saw the man point his rifle at him from the side window of the Taurus and order Carolyn, "Throw that gun out the window or I'll blow his head off." Now, even the voice sounded familiar.

Karcher turned his head toward Carolyn and with a sense of impotence, instructed, "Do as he says." He had never felt so vulnerable in his life. He saw Carolyn roll down her window and drop the gun, which tumbled down the hillside.

Then came a series of orders from the man with the rifle.

"Get out, you both."

The reality of the situation made the Karchers compliant. They got out.

"Raise your hands above your shoulders and turn around facing away from me."

The Karchers obeyed.

"Now, move and climb into the back of my truck."

The Karchers did so after opening the tail gate of the truck, the engine of which was still running.

The man with the gun climbed behind them displaying a characteristic limp.

At that point Karcher knew who the man was, he had seen him in the prison during visitation a couple of times and had even talked with him on the phone.

He mustered enough courage to ask, "What do you want?"

"You will know, you will know," was all the man said. He went to a corner of the truck bed, where lay some rope and duct tape brought purposely, so it seemed. He kicked some of it, toward Karcher and ordered, "Tie her hands and legs with it, and tape her mouth." He stood menacingly pointing his gun at Karcher, making sure his commands were obeyed.

That done, the gunman ordered Karcher, "Now, lie on your stomach with your arms stretched above your head." Once more Karcher obeyed.

The Gunman slung his rifle on his shoulder and quickly tied Karcher's hands and legs. Then, turning him over, he taped shut his mouth.

He carefully climbed down from the bed of the truck, closed the tail gate, got in the driver's seat, turned the truck around, and started speeding on the highway. Karcher wondered what the man would have done if someone happened to come upon them while this was going on? Probably shoot to silence the accidental intruder.

A few minutes later, Karcher saw and felt the truck leave the highway and enter a trackless area, bouncing on rough terrain.

Karcher, scared shitless, did not even stir. He had guessed what it was all about, wishing he was wrong, that it was all a mistake and would correct itself soon. He wished in vain.

The truck stopped after about an hour's drive. There was nothing in sight except assorted wild trees and brush.

Karcher heard the opening of the truck door, shuffle of the body emerging from it, and steps crunching the gravel coming towards him. Then, he saw the gunman open the tail gate and get into the cargo area. After that, he felt a quick kick of a boot to his side. He tumbled.

Another shove, and he rolled out of the platform and down on the rocky ground. Dust in his eyes prevented him from seeing much of anything, but he heard the gunman climb down and stand over him.

The irritated eyes began to water, and some of his sight was cleared. He saw the gunman gaze at him with fiery eyes, go to the driver compartment of the truck, and come back with a 12-inch hunting knife and a baseball bat.

Karcher was panicky. He wanted to beg, 'What do you want? Tell me, I will give it to you. Just let us go. I won't tell anyone about it.' But he could not. His voice smothered in his mouth, and his heart jumped to his throat. This was not the way he had imagined himself exiting the world.

Helplessly, he saw the gunman roughly cut off his Sunday best, leaving his shoes and socks in place. Skin bare but feet covered, he felt like a dark comedy sketch. Then, he felt the gunman first pulling his hands down to his chest and leaving them there, after which bending his knees and bringing his legs up as far as they would go, and finally, tying both the hands and legs together. Hog tied, Karcher felt very uncomfortable, all his hand, leg, and chest muscles stretching and aching. As if that was not enough, he was rolled over so that his face was facing the ground. He frantically tried to change his position, but was kicked in the face. He lay motionless with his butt sticking up. Feeling humiliated, he tried to turn over but was ordered, "Don't move." Once more he obeyed and became still.

A few seconds later, he heard the gunman mumble to himself, "This won't go in, I don't think."

Within a second, he heard the bat being dropped on the ground, and felt a sharp pain in his anus. Even in the midst of an excruciating burning and stinging sensation, he knew that the hunting knife had been thrust into him and was twisted around, like coring an apple, to make the hole larger. He could see the earth below him staining with his blood and let out a piercing scream, which only produced a whistling, unintelligible sound.

He heard Carolyn's shriek escape like a shrill whistle, too, but stop in the middle. She must have fainted. "Kill me. Why don't you just kill me?" he made a muffled plea, which was not answered, most likely, because it could not be heard.

Then he felt the knife pulled out, which only increased his pain. He writhed and cried. Suddenly, he felt something big and hard, the bigger end of the baseball bat, being thrust into him in a quick motion. He felt the flesh tearing, flow of blood increasing, pelvis bone cracking, spine breaking, bladder and bowels expelling, and his life force ebbing. His face contorted and he howled, but the sound reverberated within his chest. He fainted.

As his consciousness was evaporating, he heard the gunman say, "This is no good, no fucking good."

A few minutes later, his awareness began to return. He noticed water mingling with his other body excretions. The gunman must have revived him by splashing his face with water, brought with him for the purpose.

In his semiconscious state he heard the gunman say to Carolyn, "Miss, I have nothing against you. Just be quiet. I will take you back to the prison after I am done with this asshole. Then you can call the police or do whatever else you want to do. I don't care. I am sure you know who I am."

Then he heard the gunman address him, "Now, get this, you turd."

He felt himself being rolled over, the bat in his anus propping his body up at a grotesque angle. Then he saw the gunman come over to him.

As he saw the man, it crossed his mind that soon Schultz would know about the drama played out in this desolate place, would take a sigh of relief, and would feel avenged, if he ever came out of his coma.

Somehow, at this point, Karcher had no loathing for, fear of, or anger toward the man who was brutalizing him. He only hoped for mercy and an end to his suffering.

And it came to him quickly.

He saw the gunman stand over his body, felt the muzzle of the gun touching his forehead. Within a moment he felt a burst of light in his head, as if the universe had exploded.

EPILOGUE

ONLY THE DREAMS ENDURE

Wizard wondered if Bed Six really smiled mischievously. If he did, it meant that the AVs had found him.

He had been able to evade them for almost three years. Then came a new inmate to occupy bed number six, next to his. Right from the very beginning, Wizard found Bed Six to be very friendly, very helpful, very respectful, and very curious. One night he told Bed Six an otherworldly story. Since then he found Bed Six anxiously waiting to hear other stories from him at bedtime. The routine had continued for several months. Now, he had told his last story about the God of Evil. The time for his release had come, a little early due to his good conduct. Within a few hours, he would be on his way to realize his dream with his wife, only if Bed Six was not an AV looking for him, and if he was an AV, he was dumb enough not to have understood his expositions made inadvertently.

It was a big 'if', but possible. In the semidarkness of the dorm he might have misinterpreted Bed Six's facial expressions. Maybe there was no smile at all, and he was totally mistaken about it. He hoped.

But that was hoping too much.

The God of Evil, with his invisible hands, was creating shadow dancers on the brightly lit curtain of the world stage, where the music was thunderous, the actions were murderous, and the story was self-effacing.

And his hunger for the suffering and death of humans, actually that of all living beings, was insatiable. He had already claimed many human sacrifices at his altar; Stella Robinson along with her son and mother, Gopal, along with Wade Searle and Arthur Ellsworth, Humberto Martinez together with his wife and three children, Sonny Madrill, several policemen and AV warriors, and finally Bernard Karcher. There were other mutilated bodies and tortured souls also; Phil Bottillo, Satya Gopal, Susan Madrill, Rubin Ibarra, Carolyn Karcher, even George Schultz and Albert Schultz, and, in a way, Christi Comora and Stewart Goodwin. Not to be forgotten, also, Wizard himself and his wife Emily. They were also part of the sacrifice, although the sacrificial fire had burned them only partially. But the God of Evil was still hungry, would remain hungry as long as there was life to feed upon.

Was it his turn now? To die along with his dream?

The dream!

To live out his last days as a nonentity with a changed name, free from the clutches of evil. To build a log house in some unclaimed wilderness, walk the forests and mountains, wade the streams, grow some fruits and vegetables, do some fishing and hunting, occasionally go into a nearby town and buy some essentials which he, himself, could not produce, like packaged food, clothes, cooking utensils, a bike. To live with his wife frugally on the equity realized from the sale of their house, and some income from the sale of his produce. And to write books.

He should not be so discouraged, be so despondent. Maybe his dream would be realized. Part of it had already been. His wife had been able to find a place similar to what he wanted. Other parts of the dream could also materialize. The thought brought the images of some characters in this crazy drama, still alive, trying to rebuild their shattered lives with the left over debris. Some had gained a small measure of success, while others had found their lives to be like crumbled pieces of dry bread, worthless, discarded. All this he had learned from his wife during family visitations.

Schultz was out of coma but still a vegetable. Did he know what had become of his life and his ideologies? His date of execution had come and gone. Obviously, the State wanted to kill a healthy person, not one on a life support system.

Albert, after being forgiven by Carolyn, was taking care of his family and visiting and crying over his debilitated brother. Was he burdened with guilt and self-deprecation for what he had done to Karcher, and had he ever thought of turning himself in? Or did he still believe that he had exacted justice that society was unable to provide?

Goodwin had inherited Schultz's shoes. Was his chest puffed up with a sense of pride, importance, accomplishment? Was he planning more conquests? Or, did he think that Schultz's fate was waiting for him? He had dropped Satya from his list of people to be eliminated, thinking it to be stupid to spend time and resources and even jeopardize the AV lives to try to kill someone who had no regard for her own life. Did he regret his decision and want to reverse it?

Satya had become a civil engineer while continuing to be active, very active, in 'Widows of Violence'. Would she find someone to provide solace to her haunted soul? Did she know that the AV threat against her was no more, or would that matter?

Bottillo, who had quit his prison job, was now running a curio shop near a national park. He had received Wizard's manuscript and was looking for a publisher. Would he ever find someone as precious as Stella Robinson, or would he just carry her memory to his grave?

Carolyn was now living with Satya and working as a secretary for the psychologist who conducted the 'Widows of Violence' therapy group. Had she totally forgiven her husband's killer? She never identified him even though, after being left in front of the prison, she had called the police and told them about her ordeal. Karcher's body was picked up and buried in a private ceremony. Would she seek out someone more compatible to her values, or go it alone?

Susan was continuing to work as a secretary and attending the meetings of 'Widows of Violence'. Was she still grieving the loss of her forbidden love? Would she ever find anyone as close to her heart as her brother?

Christi, finally free from police harassment, was nursing, going to 'Widows of Violence' regularly, and, for a change, pursuing a modest existence. Would she consider sharing her life with someone, sharing, really?

Belford was waiting for his retirement. Having lost some of his men and seeing the prison fall in the hands of the AVs, had he given up hope of ever wining a war, any war? Or, did he finally realize that the AVs and others like them would always be there, no matter what he or anybody else did? And, did he finally understand that in a war everyone lost, or did he still believe that going after the enemy with brute force was the only way to solve mankind's ills?

Jordan had become the prison Warden. Did he believe that he had won a major victory for the AV and fantasize about others in the future? Or, did he realize that earthquakes were sure to come every now and then, bringing down all lofty edifices including his own?

Ibarra was breathing in a state psychiatric hospital. Did he even know his name?

Huddy and Torte were on death row having been convicted of first degree murder. Were they planning escape? Or had they accepted their fate and were waiting to be murdered by the state?

Borchert, Wendell, Everett, and Glinel had left their homes and settled in a South American country. Did they think that they had really fooled the police into believing that they had perished in a cave?

Daboob continued to hold his position in the AV hierarchy. Was he feeling sorry that Albert Schultz had robbed him of his glory of executing Karcher? Or, was he feeling relieved that he did not have to carry out his dangerous assignment?

Wizard lay motionless, eyes closed, but ears perked up to detect any sound indicative of any movement against his existence. Yes, if he had been found, the AVs would use him as a sacrificial lamb. Or, a goat. Or, a turd. Did it matter?

One part of his mind implored him to be ready for a joint defensive and offensive action.

The other part made him feel cringed, afraid, anxious. The anticipation of a sneak charge upon him made his nerves frayed, his heartbeat erratic. He could not sleep. He wanted the night to pass and the morning to bring the promise of his freedom. Once he was gone, no one would be able to find him, touch him, he believed. Just a few hours. He wished them to pass without incident.

Then, it occurred to him that these feelings were not helping him, they were making matters worse. They were just feelings and may not represent the reality. He would discard them and, instead, dream his dreams. Even if he were to become a victim of the AV, a sacrificial something for the God of Evil, his dream would endure.

Because only the dreams endured.

He became calm. His sense of vigilance eased. His muscles relaxed. He lay in his cot like a rag doll waiting for the early light of the sun to penetrate the dark inner sanctum of the prison, surrounded by thick concrete walls.

Sometime, in the midst of his waiting, he dozed off.

A succession of images crossed his mind; a dark shadow descending upon him, a string of diamond beads scratching his neck, an army of ants crawling upon his skin, the edge of an air knife slicing through his muscles like the sharp edge of horizon cutting into the expansive sky.

Startled, he opened his eyes. And, in a flash, the images evaporated but their impact lingered.

He saw a man hovering over him, covering his face with his shadow created by a faint light coming from a barred window behind him. He felt a long piece of thread, most likely dental floss, stretched firmly over his neck, just below his chin. In his mind's eye, he could see the ends of the floss wrapped around the index fingers of two hands, steadied above his shoulders, attached to the shadow man. The slight rubbing movement of the floss on his neck was stirring the nerve endings and propping up tiny hair from the follicles.

Wizard tilted his head slightly just to confirm his suspicion. He was right. It was Bed Six.

He wanted to jump up, strike back, grab the dental floss from his attacker and use it on him in retaliation. His instincts were subdued, however, by his reason. He saw the futility of it all. It would be a war all over. A mini war, but a war nonetheless. Somewhere a buffer had to be created to contain the spread of fire. For the time being, at least.

He lay still. He knew what it meant. Silently, efficiently, the floss would penetrate the skin and then cut the trachea. The blood would ooze slowly and the life would ebb. He even felt the floss press deeper. Or, maybe he was wrong. The man would suddenly be filled with compunction and would remove the floss from his neck. Wizard even felt the slackening of the sharp thread.

Whatever, he would accept either possibility. If he lived, the music of his life would reach a crescendo, if he died the melody of death would swell into an everlasting pitch.

He should let happen whatever must happen.

He closed his eyes.

Made in the USA